SHIPPED

Until You, Book One

Karrie Roman

A NineStar Press Publication

Published by NineStar Press
P.O. Box 91792,
Albuquerque, New Mexico, 87199 USA.
www.ninestarpress.com

Shipped

Printed in the USA
First Edition
June, 2018

Print ISBN: 978-1-948608-95-4

Also available in eBook, ISBN: 978-1-948608-85-5

Warning: This book contains sexually explicit content, which may only be suitable for mature readers.

Prologue

Unknown Aussie could be our new Sam

OUT OF THE half-dozen people in the room, he was the only one who was standing. It didn't matter to him; he needed to stand; it was the only way he knew how to do this and he had to do it well. This was his big chance; he felt it. Actually, it was the first real chance he'd had in months. He called on all of his training—which wasn't much—focused as he'd been taught, and gave it his best shot.

"I didn't do it for me, and I didn't do it for her." He bent down to look into the greenest eyes he'd ever seen. They were so bright—almost electric—and especially in this town, he couldn't even be sure they were real, but they were certainly breathtaking. "I did it for you—always for you," he finished on little more than a whisper.

The amazing green eyes flared with anger, darkening them. Their owner slammed his palm on the table in front of him. "I never asked you to. I never wanted you to—"

"Then what do you want from me?" He raised his voice in anger too.

"I don't want anything from you right now. I gave you a chance, Sam. I begged you and you chose to walk away. I don't know what else there is to talk about."

"Dominic, please. I made a mistake. I never should have listened to Trina, never should have gone with her. I believed it was the right thing to do. I thought it would help. Please...come back. It's dangerous for you out here, alone." He let fear bleed into his plea, hoping he was pulling this off. He kept his gaze on those green eyes, doing his best to block out every other person in the room. He knew any chemistry between them would sell it, and chemistry started with eye contact.

"Is that actual concern for me, Sam, or do you and the rest of the team only need me for my talents?"

"Of course, I'm concerned for you, Dom. I never once said I didn't care."

"And cut." A deep voice broke into the scene, and Ryan immediately relaxed. Acting never came easy to him, though it was this challenge and the rush of performing that attracted him to it. "Good job, both of you. Ryan, as you know, we've already cast Lucas as Dominic and you played off really well against him today as Sam. We'll take a look at your test on the screen to make sure the magic here in the room translates onto film. We should have an answer for you in a few days." Mike Faraday, one of the hottest producers in television these days, was far less intimidating than Ryan had expected. He was a big man, but his face was the complete opposite of a resting bitch face—he seemed to wear a perpetual smile.

"Thank you, Mr. Faraday, for this opportunity." Ryan then turned to Lucas Evers, who still sat at the table from where he'd read his lines. "Thank you, Lucas. I really enjoyed doing the scenes with you." This had been the last of three scenes he'd done with Lucas as part of the final audition, and he'd loved every second of it.

"Likewise, Ryan. Good job." Lucas finally stood and reached to shake Ryan's hand. Ryan had watched Lucas in his old role on *Tides* for many years, but the man was far better-looking in person and had a presence that, even being new to the industry, Ryan had no doubt was required for mega-stardom. Lucas Evers would one day be a Hollywood idol.

"Oh, Ryan, sorry, but just to make sure"—Ryan turned toward the casting agent with the delightful name of Molly Anne Moskin—"we want to double-check you understand the character of Sam Dawson is gay. Meaning you would be required, at some point, to do romantic scenes with men. We want to be sure it's not a problem for you."

The saying *beggars can't be choosers* flitted across Ryan's mind, but the simple fact was he didn't care. He had no experience with men, but he'd never ruled them out either. He'd found more than a few attractive from time to time. The truth was, though, he'd been far too busy working to support his acting classes and running around to auditions to care too much about a personal life. So, no, some gay scenes didn't bother him at all.

"Of course, Molly. It's no problem at all." He hastened to reassure her because he'd hate to lose this role over something he thought of as a non-issue.

"Excellent. Well, your look is spot-on: tall, dark, and handsome. And those dark-brown eyes are screaming to be on the screen, and don't get me started on that jawline. *Rawrr*. So I guess, well...we'll be in contact." Molly Anne reached out and shook his hand.

Ryan made his way around the room, thanking the others present before saying goodbye. He walked out the door and through the maze-like corridors of the enormous studio offices and couldn't help wondering if his life was about to change in extraordinary ways he'd hardly dared to imagine even in his wildest dreams.

Chapter One

Samdom is happening, y'all.

RYAN

The light cracked and flared too brightly even behind his closed lids. The sound of the clicks and the noise of the crowd thundered in his ears, and the stench coming from the masses of the overheated, overstimulated crowd assaulted his nose. Hundreds of people were crowded into this one giant room and every one of them seemed to be having the time of their lives—except for him.

"Ryan! Lucas! This way."

"Lucas! Over here."

"Eloise! Eloise!"

"James! Oh my god, James, marry me."

"Ryan! Ryan! *Samdom! Samdom!* We love you!"

Ryan had no idea which way to turn, who to look at, how to open his fucking eyes without being blinded by the flashes. Jesus fucking Christ, he never thought it'd be like this. He'd lost track of how long he'd been standing stationary, paralyzed by the overstimulation to his senses. He didn't even know if he could fucking breathe. He thought he'd made it maybe halfway to where his seat was on the stage, but he had no clue how he was going to make it the rest of the way. His body was trembling so bad his teeth were snapping together.

Just as he felt as though he was losing himself to the panic, a warm hand slipped into his and a soft, throaty voice whispered in his ear, "I've got you, Ryan." Then he felt his arm being raised in the air and shaken a little. Ryan tentatively opened his eyes; he'd known by the citrusy scent that it was Lucas who'd grabbed his hand—who'd freed him from his panic. He watched Lucas as he smiled and waved at the crowd, his other hand still linked with Ryan's above their heads as though they were doing some sort of victory salute. Lucas glanced briefly at him and gave a little nod. Ryan knew it was a question—*are you okay now?*

Ryan Lowe was far from fucking okay, but Lucas had him now and maybe he'd be able to get through this first Comic-Con panel. Lucas led them, still hand in hand, to their seats, and Ryan settled into his, calming as the crowd seemed to settle and take their own seats. Suddenly, the room didn't seem so daunting, so stripped of air. As Lucas took his seat next to Ryan, he gave his shoulder a little squeeze, so he was able to relax even more. Once the cast from *The Witches' Hammer* were seated, no time was wasted before the questions began.

"*Samdom* is now the most popular ship worldwide. What can you tell us regarding their story this season?"

Ryan glanced sideways at his costar, Lucas Evers. Surely the audience would understand they couldn't say much about what would be happening in the new season.

"Well, we can't give away too much, but I can say *Samdom* shippers will be happy—" A roar went up from the crowd who'd come to watch *The Witches' Hammer* cast panel. "—and sad," Lucas continued, laughing even as those in the crowd gasped and moaned. Ryan couldn't help but admire Lucas's poise and self-assurance in this situation, while Ryan himself was struggling to form a complete sentence.

"And can you tell us if you're nervous about kissing another man?"

Ryan had expected this question. His costar was a happily married man, and though there had been speculation in regards to his own sexuality, Ryan had never felt the need to confirm or deny any rumors. Truth be told, he wasn't keen on labels and had never applied one to himself.

Ryan's mind momentarily wandered to where it usually did these days—to thoughts of how the hell he'd gotten here. It was only when he felt a slight nudge to his arm that he came back to the enormous room and the crowd of fans, now with all eyes pinned to him.

"Sorry?" He winced, knowing he probably sounded completely daft.

"I was just wondering how difficult it was taking on this role so late in the show and knowing how much the fans had loved that Ray Starkey was originally going to play Sam."

Ryan took a breath, collecting himself as he struggled to give a coherent answer. "It was definitely intimidating. I knew going into the auditions fans loved the choice of Ray for Sam and how devastated they were when Ray had to pull out. I'll admit once I got the part I did check out the blogs, and I can't tell you how relieved I was that people were mostly happy I'd been given the role. I had to play catch-up with training and these guys had already shot the first two episodes when I joined, so it was hard, but everyone on set was a great help." *The Witches' Hammer* was a weekly series based on the wildly popular book series of the same name. Fans of the books were self-admitted fanatics and had scrupulously monitored the process of casting the roles for the show. They'd argued choices back and forth and discussed the pros and cons of each cast member in forums. And when Ryan had replaced Ray Starkey, he'd been terrified of their reaction.

"And this is your first television role?"

"Yes, before this I'd only done ads and bit parts. This is definitely my biggest role, and it was pretty terrifying knowing the rest of the cast were all well-known actors who'd each had success in previous roles, but they've been terribly welcoming and helpful. I've learned so much from each of them."

"What about you and Lucas? I mean the chemistry we've seen so far on screen has been off the charts, and we haven't even seen the kiss yet. How do you get along offscreen?"

"We're definitely friends. Lucas is a great guy. We've been working together for a few weeks now, but it doesn't feel like work at all. We have so much fun on set and we genuinely like each other, so I think that comes through in the show." Ryan turned to Lucas, hoping he'd got his answer right, and from Lucas's smile, it seemed he had.

"We're only up to episode four. Can you tell us in which episode we will get to see the *Samdom* kiss?"

They hadn't shot that scene yet, though Ryan knew it wasn't far off, and from the screams of the crowd when the kiss was mentioned, he knew it couldn't be soon enough for them. Ryan let their director, Lon, answer that question, and he sank back into his seat, hoping his turn to answer questions was over.

An hour later, Ryan was sitting at a table signing autographs for fans who had lined up and paid money for the privilege of meeting him; some had even paid a ridiculous extra amount for a photo. Mercifully, security ensured he was approached by only small groups at a time, and Ryan was able to breathe easily for the duration of his stint.

Though he looked for him, Ryan was unable to find Lucas to thank him for earlier when he'd nearly lost his shit. He was embarrassed by what had happened, but he wasn't going to let that stop him from letting Lucas know how much he appreciated what he'd done. All in all, it had been several hours of hell for Ryan, and by the time he made it home, he'd never been so glad to see the inside of his tiny little flat.

THROUGH THE CLOSED bathroom door, Ryan could hear the buzz of his intercom. It was probably his driver and that meant he had definitely stayed in the shower far too long. Now he'd miss breakfast and have to turn up to work on an empty stomach. Might be for the best, given the butterflies flittering inside there. He walked toward the intercom, rubbing his hair with the towel at the same time in an attempt to dry it a little.

"Hello." He spoke into the intercom.

"Hey, Ryan. You ready?" came a somewhat garbled voice.

"Lucas?" Ryan had expected his driver, not his costar.

"Yeah, it's me. Thought we could ride in together."

"Sure. Give me five and I'll be down."

"'Kay."

Ryan threw the damp towel onto the floor somewhere; he didn't much care at this point. He grabbed some fresh boxers, jeans and a T-shirt and threw them on. His apartment was tiny, but there was only him, and it was clean and affordable. He'd consider upgrading once the next season of his show was confirmed and he could feel more secure in his job.

He slipped his cheap Vans knockoffs on, grabbed his wallet, keys, and bag and headed out the door. It wasn't until he was in the elevator that he realized he hadn't even combed his hair down. He'd just started running his fingers through it when the elevator door opened, and Lucas Evers stood before him in all of his devastating sexiness.

"I could have waited if you weren't ready, man," Lucas said as he glanced up at Ryan's head.

"Hey, give me a break. I'm not a morning person." Ryan grinned. He followed Lucas toward a black town car, with a driver standing at the open back door.

"Ryan, this is my driver, Chris."

"Mr. Lowe," Chris addressed him.

Ryan stuck out his hand to shake and Chris took it, giving him a quick, business-like shake. "Please call me Ryan, Chris," he offered.

"Mr. Evers, Mr. Lowe, ready to go?" Chris asked and Ryan realized it was more of the fame...the divide between celebrity and reality. There would be no more simply Ryan; he'd be Mr. Lowe now, and he hated it already.

He bundled into the back of the car with Lucas, wondering for the millionth time how he'd ended up here and when the hell somebody would call him out for the fake he was.

What he'd seen of celebrity so far seemed like a strange beast to him. And he was sure it would only get stranger.

Only a week after he'd been cast, he'd been recognized for the first time when a couple of teenage girls had approached him at the bus stop, of all places, and asked if he was "the Aussie guy who'd be playing Sam?" They'd waited with him for his bus while giving him insights as to how he should play Sam, what his motivations were, and finished by cautioning him not to fuck up the romantic relationship with Dominic.

Many of Ryan's scenes were played out with Lucas Evers. Physically, Lucas was gorgeous. At just on six feet tall, he stood a couple of inches below Ryan's six-foot-two height, but his body was perfect. Ripped abs and toned everything, but his most compelling feature was his green eyes. Ryan remembered being transfixed by them during his audition. They were a glowing light green, the whites so clear and bright, and framed by thick, dark lashes. The contrast with Lucas's dark skin was striking. His shaggy black hair was incredibly sexy, and Ryan couldn't help thinking it would be perfect for running his fingers through or grabbing hold of the soft strands.

Physical beauty did not always guarantee beauty within, but Lucas had been nothing but welcoming and friendly toward Ryan, despite being an established star and Ryan being a complete unknown.

Of course, Ryan knew Sam and Dominic would become lovers at some point during the first season, and he was both terrified and excited about those particular scenes. He was thrilled to be a part of the growing number of TV shows with LGBTQ characters. And while the truth was that he'd never kissed a man before, he was definitely attracted to Lucas, so he wasn't worried about having to fake an interest.

"Are you okay? I mean after yesterday?" Lucas broke into his thoughts.

Ryan knew Lucas had to be concerned about his near panic attack at Comic-Con yesterday, and though appreciative of his concern, he couldn't help being a little ashamed of how he'd reacted. "Yeah. I'm sorry about that. It was just...so much more than I was expecting. Thanks for...well, for what you did."

"Of course, if you didn't get at least a little nervous the first time you encounter something like that, then I'd be worried. You're gonna be great though, Ryan."

"Thanks. I hope so. I don't wanna fuck this up."

"Don't worry. You answered the questions well. I know you can act, and god, you're so fucking hot, the fans are drinking you up."

Ryan coughed a little to try to cover his shock at being called hot so casually by Lucas. He knew nothing was meant by it; Lucas was married and this was Hollywood, where compliments were thrown around like confetti, but it still shocked him how open and over-the-top people were in this town. It wasn't the first time a man had called him hot here, and it was a far cry from what he was used to.

Showing an interest in another man in his hometown might have got him a fist to the face, or cold-shouldered at the very least. Ryan had hated it back there: the labels, the intolerance, the hatred. He'd gotten out as soon as he could, and there wasn't a single person he missed from that place.

"Yeah, maybe if they can see past you and the rest of the cast long enough to notice me." He congratulated himself for his own flattering reply—maybe he could make it in this town.

When he looked up, he found Lucas's gaze boring into him, his green eyes questioning, as though he was trying to figure him out. "I can't decide if you are truly that self-deprecating or you think it's the polite thing to say. Most people in this industry have an ego the size of Texas, but you don't seem to."

"Just the small-town boy in me, I guess."

"Where is it you're from again? The place with the great name."

Ryan never enjoyed opening this can of worms. He'd managed to avoid any deep and meaningful conversations for the last few weeks, usually because when he spent time with the cast or crew, they were too busy for personal questions. Riding into work with Lucas now with nothing else to do but talk nudged open that door into his private life. Did he want to let Lucas through? Maybe he did want that, just a little. He'd skim the surface of his past though; no point diving straight into the muck. "Toukley. It's a tiny little town on the Central Coast, a little north of Sydney. Nothing of note there."

"That's right. You never told me about your family, though. Are they still there?"

"Mum died when I was little, Dad's a...oh I guess you'd say he's a...a no-hoper, a drunk, a bastard. No brothers, no sisters. No friends." Ryan could feel Lucas's stare piercing him again. When he looked at those green eyes he couldn't read the expression he caught in them, but Lucas was definitely looking at him as though he was the most interesting person in the world. He guessed that was what real charisma looked like: making the other person believe there was nothing more important than them—and Lucas had charisma in spades.

"No one you regret leaving behind?"

"Nope. I was this *pretty* boy who wanted to act, never had a girlfriend, wasn't interested in having one either. People came to their own conclusions, and I wasn't very...well liked."

"Do you keep in contact with your dad?"

"No way. When I left, I left for good. He didn't want a bar of me, so I returned the favor. I don't think he even knows I'm here in the States." Ryan needed to change the subject. He didn't want to delve any deeper into his grotty past. He'd placed it firmly in his rearview mirror and that was where it would stay. "How about you? Where's your family?"

Lucas laughed and it was a sweet sound, honest and pure. Ryan could tell just from the laugh that Lucas loved his family. "Oh, they're around. They all came with me from Tacoma...and I mean they all came with me. Mom, Dad, two brothers and one sister. We're um...close in our way, I guess. My wife, Anna, grew up across the road from me. I'm pretty sure her folks would have come, too, but they were...they didn't...they weren't too happy with our marriage."

"Oh I'm sorry. Did they not like you? I mean... Sorry." He winced.

"No, it's okay. They're the kind of people who don't take to anyone. They didn't agree with the getting married part, among other things... They believed we were too young."

"You're never too young, if it's love, right?"

For the first time, Lucas turned his gaze from Ryan and stared out the window. Ryan barely caught his mumbled reply. "Sure."

Lucas kept his gaze fixed out the window and silence fell. Ryan wondered what he'd said wrong. He didn't think he'd insulted Lucas at all. Maybe it still hurt that his in-laws didn't approve of his marriage. Ryan wracked his brain for something to say, anything to break the quiet that was beginning to stifle the earlier ease of being around Lucas.

"So, umm...if our show was real life, would you rather be one of the witches or one of the hunters?" God, could he have come up with anything lamer?

Lucas turned to him, a grin on his full lips and his eyes sparkling. "Are you kidding? Definitely a witch. How much fun could you have with all of that magic? And let's face it, as good as the hunters are, a little bit of magic should be able to stop them, even if it doesn't on the show. What about you?"

"Well, I'm gonna say a hunter because they get to use all of those awesome weapons. And they're the good guys, fighting off the evil witches. Everyone wants to be the hero."

"Ah, but not all of the witches are evil. I'd be a good witch, but with a hint of a mischievous streak." Lucas completed his statement with an impish smirk that had Ryan's stomach flipping—just a little. Christ, Lucas was fucking hot.

By the time they arrived at the studio, they were in fits of laughter over the antics each of them had decided they'd get up to if they were the real-life embodiment of characters from the show. Ryan's remaining nerves had been left behind somewhere on Franklin Avenue. He couldn't help hoping a shared ride to the studio would become a daily thing. He liked Lucas, enjoyed his company, and in his up-till-now friendless life that was as new to him as this whole Hollywood stardom business.

Chapter Two

Samdom *deserves more screen time.*

LUCAS

Lucas wasn't quite sure when it had become routine that he picked Ryan up on the way to the set, but he was glad it had. Ryan's company was fun, but most importantly it was real. Ryan hadn't yet been tainted by the craziness of their industry, and he hoped he never would be, but everything was changing for Ryan, and based on his reaction at Comic-Con a few weeks ago, it wasn't all good. Lucas had already tasted fame, so he'd had an inkling of what to expect.

Chris had the door open and waiting, so Lucas was able to sit back and watch as Ryan strode toward the car. It was a far more confident stride than the first day he'd picked Ryan up. The man himself was even more stunning with the swagger he now had to his walk. It wasn't an arrogant, cocky swagger, though. Ryan walked as though he was sex on legs and Lucas was ninety-nine percent sure he had no idea he was doing it.

Of course, Ryan oozed sex appeal when he was sitting around in his jeans and tee waiting to get in the makeup chair. His tall, strong body, cupid's bow lips, and wild, just-out-of-bed hair screamed sex appeal. The producers had seen it, the casting agents had touted it, and Lucas had felt it in his bones at their first meeting.

His physical attraction to Ryan at his audition all those weeks ago had been instantaneous. From the second he'd walked into the audition, Lucas knew Ryan Lowe would take his breath away every time he looked at him.

Regardless of how close they would become as friends, he knew he would always have a physical reaction to him. He'd always be pulled in by the raw masculinity of Ryan's body, the deep tenor of his voice with his adorable Aussie accent, and that fucking gorgeous scent that wafted all around him. Ryan Lowe was his cream; every single thing about him attracted Lucas. The urge to reach out and touch would simmer just below the surface whenever Ryan was near.

Fortunately, or maybe unfortunately, he was allowed to touch as part of his role as Dominic, and Lucas had decided at some point early on that Dominic was an incredibly touchy-feely kind of person, at least with Ryan's character of Sam Dawson. It wasn't even a conscious decision; he simply couldn't keep his fucking hands to himself when it came to Ryan.

From the moment their characters had met, Lucas had let his touch linger on Ryan just a little too long; he'd stood a little too close and let his gaze stay on Ryan seconds longer than a passing glance. Thank Christ, his character was meant to be attracted to Ryan's or Lucas knew he'd be in a world of trouble. It was an exquisite sort of torture to be able to touch and stare, all while knowing the response he got from Ryan was only a performance. That it wasn't a real thing.

"Morning, Luke. Last shoot for the week?" Ryan asked as he entered the car. "Thanks, Chris." He called to the driver as he closed the door.

"Anytime, Mr. Lowe," Chris called back, laughing quietly at the ongoing joke between him and Ryan.

"I told you, it's Ryan." As usual, he received no reply from Chris so turned back to Lucas.

Lucas chuckled at Ryan's persistence in trying to keep some normalcy to his life. "It's not gonna happen, Ryan. You are Mr. Lowe now." He clapped his hands together. "Yeah, it's my last shoot for the week today. How 'bout you?"

"Yep. Should be done by midafternoon and then I'm done for the weekend." Ryan squirmed around, settling his big body into the seat before Chris drove off.

"Any plans?"

"Nah. Sleeping, I think."

"Well, the big social media campaign starts on Monday, so I'm guessing this will be your last relatively normal weekend for a while. How about you and I do something?" Where the hell had that idea come from? Ever since he'd seen Ryan, eyes closed, pale, sweaty and shaking on the stage at Comic-Con, Lucas had been worried for his costar. Ryan's panic had pinched at Lucas's heart. He really liked Ryan, and it hurt to see his pain. There was a sweetness to him, not naivety exactly, but more of an unwillingness to let the bad of the world in, and Lucas knew Ryan was probably ill-equipped to deal with the fame that had landed in his lap. He hoped he might be able to help him; it was just a bonus he also really enjoyed his company.

"Like what?" Ryan asked.

"Dunno, but I'll pick you up on my way home from the studio. Plenty of room at my place; we'll have a few drinks tonight and work out something to do tomorrow."

Ryan watched him for a few minutes. Maybe he was trying to figure out why Lucas had extended the invitation. If Ryan did work out what the hell Lucas was doing, he hoped Ryan would let him know, because Lucas sure didn't.

Whatever Ryan had been thinking, he seemed to come to a decision. He smiled broadly at Lucas and nodded. "Yeah. Yeah, that'd be great thanks. You know," he said, digging his elbow into Lucas's side, "I've never been to a sleepover before." Ryan chuckled and Lucas couldn't help joining in. Ryan's joy at something so simple—so normal—was contagious.

Lucas knew Ryan had been pretty much friendless growing up, though he couldn't imagine why. The people in that bum-fuck little town in Australia were all idiots as far as Lucas was concerned. Ryan Lowe was a sweetheart and a shit ton of fun to be around. Not to mention drop-dead gorgeous. Oh well, their loss was the rest of the world's gain.

The trip to the studio was no more than twenty minutes at this hour of the morning. As soon as they pulled in, Ryan and Lucas disgorged from their town car and headed off in different directions. Unusually, they were not shooting together today, and Lucas knew he'd miss Ryan. He enjoyed working with him. It was easy, almost effortless to act alongside Ryan. He also knew from Mike Faraday's gleeful reactions every time he viewed the rushes the chemistry between them was sizzling on screen.

Lucas pulled out his phone and almost made the mistake of calling Anna, before he realized how early it still was. He set an alarm instead, to remind himself to call his wife and let her know about their guest. Anna had liked Ryan after their brief meeting a couple of weeks ago, so he didn't foresee any problems; the polite thing to do was to okay it with her, though.

The makeup crew was ready to go by the time he made it to the trailer. James and Eloise were already seated and being made-up when he walked in. He was shooting most of his scenes with them today. Eloise Marshall had the face of an angel and the body of a warrior; she was whip-smart and dripping with sass. James Boyd was the image of a young Sean Connery and had the charm to match. James and Eloise got along like brother and sister, and Lucas wondered if that would be problematic, given they were an important romantic couple in the show.

"Morning all." He called out a group good morning, rather than individually addressing everyone in the room.

He got a couple of good mornings back—all from the makeup crew. James and Eloise offered only a simple head nod. *Well, this was new.* The cast had been getting along well, Hollywood egos considered. Lucas couldn't work out what might have happened to cause the cold shoulder he was clearly sensing coming his way. He'd find out soon enough, though, since Eloise and James weren't shy little wallflowers. They'd let him know what their problem was when they were ready, but he knew he'd done nothing wrong, so he didn't think too much of it. He'd encountered enough bruised egos in his time to recognize one or two.

With his character being a little more...flamboyant than the rest of the cast, Lucas usually spent a while longer in makeup and wardrobe than the others. Eloise and James left half an hour or so after he arrived, taking the frosty chill with them. Lucas could relax into his chair with their departure and think of ways to spend the weekend with Ryan.

First thing was to call Anna. She'd be up by now for her workout with Ed. She answered on the fifth ring. "Hey, everything okay, Lucas?"

"Yeah, babe. Listen, I invited Ryan over tonight for the weekend. He's a bit nervous because of the live streaming we'll be doing during and after Monday night's episode so we might do something to take his mind off it. What'd you say?"

"Sure, sounds great. What if I call the Curzon's, see if they're taking their boat out?"

Lucas may have been the bigger star in the family, but Anna definitely had the contacts. The Curzons were two sisters who ran one of the biggest production companies in Hollywood. Somehow Anna had become pretty tight with younger sister, Maria, and they all spent a fair bit of time together, especially on the boat. It was quiet and relaxing, and unless the paparazzi were willing to hire a helicopter, it was incredibly private.

"That'd be perfect, Anna. Thanks. We should be home earlyish tonight. Nothing fancy, okay? Ryan is a very laid-back guy."

Anna gave him a little uh-huh and rang off. No doubt he'd find a tub of chilled beers beside the big screen TV when they got home tonight.

Almost nine hours later what should have been an easy day of shooting had turned into an absolute nightmare. Eloise and James were definitely off. But they were off in such a way that somehow he came out looking bad. They missed their marks and improvised lines. Normally, the improvisation would have been fine, but they did it in such a way that it made it difficult for Lucas to react. He couldn't say his scripted lines as they didn't work, but he had trouble coming up with anything to keep his part of the story on track.

It made for an awfully tense set, and Lucas could tell their director, Lon, was none too pleased about it. What the fuck was wrong with these two?

It was after six by the time Lon finally called it for the day, much later than Lucas had hoped for. It was only the thought of a pleasant weekend with Ryan that had kept the lid on Lucas's temper.

In record time, Lucas removed his makeup and changed into his own clothes, Dominic's wardrobe was...uncomfortable, to say the least, too tight and far too gaudy for Lucas's taste. Jeans and a button-down were more his style. Chris was waiting with the town car and Lucas found himself standing in Ryan's lobby by seven thirty.

As always, Ryan looked fucking edible in his jeans and just-a-little-too-tight tee. As they settled into the back seat of the car, Lucas couldn't quite help shuffling a little closer to Ryan than strictly necessary. The heat coming from Ryan was soothing, and Jesus, he smelled good—woodsy and...mint—maybe from freshly brushed teeth. Everything about Ryan screamed comfort, closely followed by sex. How could one man inspire in him both the drowsy feeling of comfort and the restless flame of desire?

"How was your shoot?"

"Awful. What is up with Eloise and James? They fucked me around all day." Lucas didn't usually go in for gossip, but he was angry and just plain confused by their behavior.

"I was gonna ask. All I got was an icy nod when I saw James today."

So it hadn't only been Lucas on the receiving end of whatever had upset their costars. Damned if he could work out what the hell was wrong with them. What's more, he didn't want it to ruin his weekend. Monday would come soon enough, and he could worry about whatever the fuck was going on then.

Mike Faraday was huge on social media, his overused quote of "If it's good enough to help get that douche elected POTUS, then it's good enough for us to use to promote the show" was heard at least once a day around the studio. As a result, the cast would be live-streaming a cast reaction immediately after the airing of the next episode on Monday night, as well as tweeting during the screening. Lucas hoped like hell Eloise and James were over their…whatever it was, by then. It wouldn't exactly be great if fans picked up on discord on the set so early on. He'd seen behind-the-scenes fiascos overshadow productions before and had no desire to be involved in that again.

This was Ryan's first big role, and Lucas didn't want him to freak out over the kind of bullshit he knew happened on some sets. "They're probably just nervous about Monday. I'm not worried too much. Besides, it's the weekend, and hopefully, we'll be spending tomorrow aboard a luxury sixty-foot yacht, working on our tans and eating, drinking, and generally being merry."

Lucas watched as Ryan's eyes widened, and his face transformed into a younger, almost childlike version of himself. "Holy shit. Is it yours?"

"I'm not that wealthy—yet. Nah, Anna is good friends with the Curzon sisters. She's gonna see if they're taking their boat out. They usually do most weekends, so we'll just hitch a ride." Lucas didn't believe he was at the arrogant, boastful level of stardom yet, but he couldn't help a tinge of pride seeping into his tone.

"The Curzon sisters. Fuck. I mean, wow, that'd be awesome."

"They're surprisingly nice, down-to-earth people, considering their level of power and success in the industry. And so you know, they hate it when, and I quote, 'people try to crawl up our asses to get on our good side.' So just be yourself." Lucas wondered if Ryan had it in him to be other than himself.

Chris pulled the car into the temporary parking area of Lucas's building. Neither he nor Anna had been interested in a yard, so they'd gone for a luxury apartment in downtown LA. It had top security and most of the other residents were in the industry, so they didn't have to worry about stargazing neighbors. He'd bought apartments for his family in the building as well, though Anna hadn't been too keen on that idea. He'd done it because his mother had been distressed when he'd first moved to LA after the success of his role on *Tides*.

Five years on a top-rated show plus advertising jobs had left him with more money than he'd ever thought he'd have in his life, so he had no problem supporting his family, moving them to be closer to him. His parents had effectively retired when they'd moved and his siblings were doing their best to land their big breaks also. He could afford to look after them until they made it.

"Hey, this place looks great," Ryan commented as they moved through the lobby toward the elevator.

"The building's only a few years old. High security. Close to everything. My family lives here too."

"With you and Anna?"

"God, no. No way. I bought them each an apartment in the building."

"Really? That's...generous." Ryan appeared a little confounded at Lucas's revelation. Ryan had no family, well, none he was willing to acknowledge, so maybe he couldn't understand wanting to do something similar to what Lucas had done for his.

They entered the elevator and Lucas found himself standing close to Ryan despite the spaciousness of the elevator car. It was as though his body subconsciously sought out the warmth of Ryan's—wanting to be in his orbit. He pressed the button for the nineteenth floor and did his best to try not to be too obvious as he allowed himself to enjoy Ryan's tempting scent.

As he'd expected, Anna greeted them warmly at the door, took Ryan's overnight bag to the guest room, and rejoined them in the living room. She grabbed herself a beer from the ice bucket and sank down into one of the armchairs.

"Good to see you again, Ryan. How's the show going?"

"You too, Anna. It's going great, I hope. I'm having a blast, honestly. I get to use all these weapons, beat the shit out of people, and get all dirty and gross. It's a boy's dream."

Anna sparkled in company, the consummate people person. "Lucas showed me some of those moves for the knife fighting. It should look awesome on-screen."

"Those Filipino martial arts people are hard-core. The knife fighting is amazing and it does look awesome, well, what I've seen of it anyway." Ryan was again almost giddy, like a schoolboy, when he talked to Anna about the FMA fighting they'd learned. Lucas loved how excited Ryan got over certain things, the expressions on his face mesmerizing. If Ryan got enthusiastic about cut grass, Lucas was pretty sure it'd become the most fascinating thing ever for him too.

Anna stayed for two beers and then excused herself for the evening. She'd organized the trip on the Curzon's yacht tomorrow, but they'd need to leave early. Anna wasn't normally a morning person so she would need an early night tonight.

"She's great," Ryan said as soon as Anna had left the room.

"She is. She's my best friend, an absolute sweetheart." He adored Anna, always would. He wished they could love each other the way a husband and wife should, but neither of them was made that way. Still, it wasn't a hardship to be married to your best friend and maybe one day they'd both find the elusive "one" for them.

"Any exes in your past that might come out of the woodwork now you're famous?" Lucas asked.

"No exes, no. A few one-night hookups, but I'm guessing if they were in the same condition I was in, my face would be as blurry to them as theirs are to me. God that sounds...awful."

Lucas couldn't help laughing at the mortified expression that stole over Ryan's face. "Ah, the drunken hookups. Well, if they do remember you, be prepared for it to be splashed all over the trash rags. 'Ryan Lowe did me in the broom closet,' that kind of thing."

Ryan coughed and spluttered the beer he'd been trying to swallow. "The broom closet," he finally managed. "I'm all class, mate; we always went back to their place." Ryan gave Lucas's arm a little punch to reinforce his mock outrage at Lucas's accusation of broom closet hookups.

Somehow they'd wound up on the sofa together, so Lucas could feel heat radiating from Ryan's body again. "Yeah, all class. Can you tell me any names?"

Lucas laughed when Ryan's cheeks flushed even redder, and he dropped his gaze. Ryan was so beautiful when he blushed; hell, Ryan was beautiful all the fucking time.

At twenty-nine, Lucas had six years on Ryan, but he still remembered his teenage years, the anonymous hookups, the desperate fumblings with only the need to get off staving off the disgust at finding himself on his knees in an alley somewhere. It had stopped when he'd married Anna and landed a part on *Tides*.

When the urge became too strong these days, he used a very discreet agency, as did Anna. They were both young, with healthy appetites, and they'd sorted that out when they first decided to get married. They'd killed two birds with one wedding. Anna was safely out of her abusive family home, and they both had the cover their agent insisted they needed to make it big in Hollywood.

They talked for a little longer, Lucas very conscious every second that he was leaning in closer and closer to Ryan. He could feel lust bubbling away under his skin, boiling his blood, and he was painfully aware of how much he wanted to kiss him, touch him, hold him. He needed a break; he needed space, before he did something fucking stupid.

"Hey, um, it's getting late and I'm an old man compared to you, so I think I'm gonna call it; otherwise I won't be able to get up in the morning." Lucas stood as he spoke, trying to keep his eyes off Ryan. One more look and he didn't know if he'd be able to hold to the promise he'd just made to keep his hands to himself and walk away.

"Sure, old man. Hey, you mind if I have a shower before I go to bed?" Ryan was standing now, too, and again, he was somehow too fucking close.

Lucas stepped away, gesturing for Ryan to follow him. "Sure. There's a bathroom attached to your guest room. Towels on the shelf. Help yourself." He stopped at the door to Ryan's room and flicked the light on. He still couldn't risk looking at Ryan.

"Thanks, mate." Ryan clapped him on the shoulder as he passed. It felt like a hot brand on Lucas's skin, so he fled with a muttered "good night" over his shoulder.

It took him hours to finally drift off, the image of Ryan just down the hall, naked under the shower, kept sleep far out of his reach.

Chapter Three

Samdom hanging out offscreen??? They are so perfect together!

RYAN

It was quite possibly the most comfortable bed he'd ever slept on. Pity he had to be up in about five minutes to get ready for his day on a luxury cruiser. Merely thinking the words had him shaking his head in disbelief. The idea he'd be sailing on a boat that belonged to Maria and Antonia Curzon was unbelievable. He reached down and pinched his thigh, just to be sure. If the old wives' tale was true, he wasn't dreaming.

Ryan allowed himself another shower. He'd never been under a rainfall showerhead before, but after his shower last night, he was quickly becoming addicted. The water was as hot as he could bear, and as the name suggested, water literally rained down over his body. It was amazing. No one could start the day in a bad mood if they had this to wake up to. He was low maintenance but hadn't been sure what they'd be doing today when he'd packed his overnight bag, so he had a few outfits on hand. Definitely shorts and a tee for a day on a yacht. Other than the Sydney ferries a handful of times, Ryan had never been on a boat before, but he loved the water, so he was looking forward to it.

What did rich folks do on a cruiser all day? Fish? Drink? Talk shop? He had no idea what to expect; like much of his life lately, it would be a complete mystery.

Lucas and Anna were waiting on the sofa by the time he dragged himself out of the shower and dressed. Lucas wore a pair of tan chinos and a vibrant green T-shirt and Ryan just knew it would highlight the startling green of his eyes. A Seattle Thunderbirds cap covered his messy black hair, and he hadn't shaved this morning, so Ryan could see light stubble coming in. He looked fucking gorgeous.

Anna wore a sheer cover-up dress and Ryan could make out a dark-toned bikini underneath it. A wide-brimmed sun hat covered much of her face, but when she peered up at him, Ryan could tell she had no makeup on. Anna wasn't at all one of the stick-thin starlets that seemed to haunt every square inch of Hollywood. She had these delicious curves Ryan loved and she wasn't afraid to be her natural self. She was one of the most stunning women he'd ever met.

"Ready?" Lucas asked.

"You bet. I'm so excited," Ryan answered, sounding for all the world like an excitable twelve-year-old boy allowed out with friends for the first time.

There would be no car service for them today, so Lucas was driving them to the marina. Ryan could tell it was a moderately priced car, not the fancy overpriced monstrosity he might have expected. As successful and famous as the Everses were, it seemed as though they had managed to keep their feet planted firmly on the ground.

Ryan sat quietly in the back seat while Lucas navigated the car through the LA traffic that was still ridiculously heavy despite it being a Saturday morning. Coming from a small town, Ryan had little experience driving in heavy traffic and was under the impression Lucas would need his silence in order to concentrate and successfully manage the bumper-to-bumper nightmare that was the gridlock of LA highways.

"You okay, back there?" Lucas eventually asked.

"Yeah, just can't get over the traffic here. It's...terrifying."

Lucas let out a tinkle of laughter. "What, they don't have traffic 'down under'?"

"Oh we have traffic, sure, but this is something else, especially coming from where I did. So...um, where will we be sailing to today?"

Anna turned to face him from the passenger seat as she answered. "No idea. Maria and Antonia often just let their captain have free rein. Sometimes we head out to one of the islands, but usually they're happy to cruise aimlessly. They're surrounded by people constantly, so I think it gives them some much-needed peace and quiet. They are lovely women, but tough as nails when it comes to business." Anna chewed on her lip for a moment and it looked to Ryan as though she were debating whether or not to say her next words. "Look...umm...you know the story with Antonia, don't you?"

Everybody knew about Antonia Curzon. She was one of the most famous transgender people on the planet. Her complete and unashamed honesty had been a watershed moment for the transgender community at a time when fear and hatred was abundant. Of course, there was still plenty of it, but Antonia had made a difference and there was even talk of her dipping her toes into the world of politics. "Yeah, of course, I know. It doesn't bother me at all, if that's what you're wondering." Ryan couldn't help the tinge of annoyance in his voice. He didn't give a rat's ass about stuff like that. If people were happy, then go for it. Wasn't that the much-talked-about goal in life—to find happiness—and who the hell was he to dislike the fashion in which others found it? As long as it was consenting adults and all that, why should he care? Ryan had seen enough small-mindedness to last him a lifetime and couldn't fathom the need some people had to stick their noses into everyone else's business.

"Sorry, Ryan, I didn't really mean it that way. I just...they're good friends of mine, and obviously, Antonia has had to deal with a lot of bullshit, so I get a little overprotective." Anna explained. Ryan understood narrow-minded assholes and admired Anna's concern for her friend.

"Of course. Sorry. I didn't..."

"Hey, let's not worry about it okay? We've got it out of the way and we're good. We'll be there in roughly ten minutes." Lucas interjected.

They spent the next ten minutes talking about random stuff, mostly Anna and Lucas sharing stories of past trips on the cruiser. Apparently the Curzons often had other guests with them and Lucas and Anna never knew which big star they might find aboard. It promised to be an interesting day.

Lucas left his car with the valet. *A valet at a marina. What kind of world have I stepped into?* Then the three of them made their way down to the berth where the *Put a Curz-on U* was docked. The boat—or was it a fucking ship?—took Ryan's breath away. It was enormous and stunning in its magnificence. Fuck it. He felt underdressed in his boardies—hell, a fucking tuxedo might have been more appropriate. Anna led the way across the gangplank and Ryan soon found himself standing aboard the teak aft deck of unadulterated luxury on the water.

"We're on the sun pad, hon," a voice called out.

"Stay there. We'll come out," Anna called back. "Drop your bag there, Ryan." Anna pointed beside a loveseat inside the cabin.

Ryan took a step inside to put his bag down and took in the cream leather sofas and gorgeous wood paneling with wide eyes. It looked so expensive and pristine, Ryan was almost afraid to breathe.

"Come on, this way," Anna called. Ryan followed behind Lucas as they made their way to the front of the cruiser.

It was a little slippery and Ryan held on to the railing as he did his best to look as if he belonged on the craft. As he cleared the cabin and came out from behind Lucas, he could see three other people standing on the sun pad. Maria and Antonia Curzon were both in sundresses and enormous broad-brimmed hats. They were both smiling, and if Ryan didn't know better, he would have sworn they were identical twins. Anna had approached them and was drawing one of them in for a hug while Lucas was doing the same to the other. It was then Ryan took note of the third stranger. Was that...?

"Jesus fucking Christ, you're Harrison Cooper!" The man—the legend as far as Ryan was concerned—turned at Ryan's outburst with *that* smirk on his face and his hand extended. Ryan *must* be dreaming, but he was determined to get a handshake in before he woke up, so he strode forward with as much speed and bravado as he could muster.

It was only seconds, but Ryan would swear black-and-blue the whole nightmare had lasted hours as he tripped over something on the sun pad, probably his own damn feet, and lurched forward, narrowly missing slamming into Mr. Cooper. He screamed a manly scream immediately before his forward motion took him over the railing and into the refreshing waters, from which he almost wished he'd never emerge.

Unfortunately, he did emerge and peered up at five faces staring over the railing at him. "I'm okay," he called out and waved up at his audience. He thought he saw relief on the faces watching him, mixed with an understandable hint of amusement. He didn't think he'd hurt anything except his ego. He swam around to the rear of the boat and climbed onto the little deck that sat at almost water level. Ryan then gathered his courage and climbed up.

Lucas was there, concern and amusement jockeying for prime position in his expression. "You okay, Ryan?"

"Physically yeah, but...Jesus, Lucas, I just swore at and then almost fell into Harrison Cooper, before falling overboard in front of him." Ryan peeked up at Lucas's face and could see the amusement winning out and finally Lucas burst out laughing. "It's all right, go ahead and laugh. I must have looked like a complete dick." He managed to say before joining Lucas in laughter.

"Are you kidding? Maria and Antonia adore you already, and Harrison said it was the 'best goddamn introduction' to someone he'd ever had. I mean we're all laughing our asses off, but in the best way," Lucas soothed.

Ryan rolled his eyes, though he could definitely see the funny side. "Why did it have to be Harrison fucking Cooper? I mean he is...he is perfection—"

"I've been called plenty of things before but never perfection." Came the voice of the man himself from behind them.

Oh, Jesus, maybe if he sat down and shut up, he'd make it through the rest of the day without either setting the man on fire or vomiting his lunch all over him.

"Good to meet you, Ryan. You make quite an impression."

"Thanks. I'm so sorry about that. I clearly haven't gotten my sea legs just yet. I'm a big fan and it is equally wonderful and mortifying to meet you." Ryan shook hands with Harrison Cooper. *Harrison fucking Cooper.* Despite the embarrassment of moments ago, Ryan allowed himself to enjoy the exchange and felt an actual tingle as he touched one of his first-ever crushes. Any person alive who claimed they didn't crush on Harrison Cooper was either a liar or dead inside as far as Ryan was concerned.

They were soon joined by the three women, and Ryan finally got to meet them in a more dignified manner. Despite the inauspicious beginning, Ryan soon found himself immersed in the little group and having the absolute time of his life.

By the time they'd anchored in a quiet little bay for lunch, Ryan was feeling comfortable and had almost forgotten, or at least come to terms with, his earlier humiliation. He joined Lucas up on the flybridge with a beer and some kind of amazing seafood salad.

"Hey. You doing okay?" Lucas asked as Ryan sat on the cushioned bench beside him.

"Are you kidding? I'm having the time of my life. I can't thank you enough for inviting me, Lucas." He took a swig of his beer before continuing on, too excited to rein in his words. "I mean I've never done anything like this before and not just the boat or meeting Hollywood royalty. I've never spent a day with friends before. You guys are great, Harrison's great, Antonia and Maria are divine. I can't...pinch me." He thrust out his arm.

Lucas snorted out a laugh. "Pinch you?"

"Yep. I'm just not sure this is real, and I've already pinched myself and I felt it, but maybe it has to be somebody else pinching me to be sure I'm not dreaming. So pinch me." He held his arm closer, but Lucas pinched his thigh instead, gently. Ryan still felt it. In fact, Ryan felt it as a zap whenever Lucas touched him.

"Ryan, why'd you have no friends growing up? I mean you're just...you're terrific. I can't understand it." Lucas's grin had fallen away, and as much as Ryan didn't like even thinking about his youth, he answered the genuine inquiry.

"We were poor and my dad was the town drunk. I often had no food or proper uniform or books or whatever I needed for school. I was always running around with a runny nose and too small shoes, ratty clothes. I was the obvious target for bullies. None of our neighbors wanted their kids to play with me. We were *that* family everyone whispered about, but no one bothered to help. And when I got older, I was...the kids thought I was pretty. They started calling me gay or girly. I never fought back, mostly because I just didn't care. I mean I don't think either of those things are insults for one thing, so I kept to myself. It was easier. By then, I would have been too ashamed to have anyone at my place anyway...with Dad and all. I'd realized it wasn't normal to have beer bottles all over the house, no food in the fridge, and your father passed out wherever he'd fallen."

Lucas's hand was suddenly on Ryan's knee, patting, comforting—burning him. "Shit. I'm sorry, man. That sucks."

Ryan knew he'd had a shitty childhood, but he also knew there were far worse, and he'd made it out. He didn't think about it too often and he didn't let himself wade into the murk of bitterness and resentment. "It did suck, but I'm away from there now and...well, just look at me. I'm on a sixty-foot cruiser; actually, I fell off a sixty-foot cruiser in front of Harrison Cooper. None of the assholes back home can claim that." Ryan laughed and was glad when Lucas joined in to break the slight cloud of the past that had formed over them. "Plus I've met you...and Anna, of course. You're the closest thing I've ever had to a friend."

Ryan kept his gaze down, feeling awkward about the honest, raw statement, but Lucas and Anna had been so good to him they had to know how much he appreciated it.

"I'm not the closest thing you've ever had to a friend, Ryan. I *am* your friend."

Chapter Four

The Witches' Hammer! Samdom *is rising!!*

LUCAS

"What do we talk about?" Ryan asked the group, and Lucas could see mild panic on his face.

"I guess we'll be talking *Samdom,* mostly," James snapped. Lucas turned to Ryan, who had paled beside him. Was that their problem? Eloise and James were the main couple of the show, but talk of the growing *Samdom* fandom had been bandied around the set. Lucas knew scenes were being rejigged to give Sam and Dominic more screen time to capitalize on the popularity. Talk of it usually made Lucas chuckle. The *Samdom Fandom*—it was perfect. It was so conveniently named it made Lucas wonder if the author had chosen his character's names with that ship in mind.

"But...I don't... There is no *Samdom,* yet. We haven't even filmed the kiss," Ryan stuttered out. Their characters of Sam and Dominic didn't act on their attraction until the final episode of the season.

"You can't be that naïve, Ryan. Sam and Dominic are popular already. Haven't you read how perfect you two are together? Seen the YouTube videos? You'll want to renegotiate your pay for next season." James's tone still held a snippy, bitter quality, and Lucas would be damned if he'd let it fall upon Ryan. Ever since Comic-Con, a protective streak a mile wide for Ryan had opened up inside Lucas and he was coming out swinging.

"That's enough," he barked. "If Sam and Dominic are popular, that can only be a good thing for the show and for each of us. We can all renegotiate our pay. You two need to keep your egos in check. It's not Ryan's fault he's so popular." He glared across the table at his two costars. If he had to rate them, he'd say that he, Eloise, and James held the same level of fame—they were all stars of the small screen. He was the oldest of the three, so he hoped that gave him a modicum of respect from the other two. Though in this industry, they probably believed that at twenty-nine Lucas was over the hill and on his way out.

James glared at Lucas, for just a brief moment, and then put his head back down to concentrate on his tweeting. The entire main cast of seven sat around a large table in one of the meeting rooms. The sixth episode was currently airing, and they were each expected to twitter and talk while watching it as part of Mike Faraday's social media bombardment.

Lucas could see Ryan's hands moving over his iPad as he sat beside him doing his best to tweet. Ryan hadn't had a clue what to do, so Lucas had given him some tips. He advised him to tweet mostly about how great other cast member's scenes had turned out, or any little bits of trivia about shooting a scene. He warned Ryan to never, ever tweet how he thought he looked on screen or how bad a job he thought he had done. Fans didn't want to hear actors putting themselves or their performance down. Savvy fans knew it for what it actually was most of the time: a desperate attempt by the celebrity to get a compliment to boost their fragile ego.

The show was already a global hit, but the studio wanted more—hence the social media blitz. Who'd have believed a show about modern day witch hunters, using the fifteenth-century book, the *Malleus Maleficarum*, or Witches' Hammer, as their guide would be so popular? Of course, they had the book series to thank for that. A few years ago it had been vampires and werewolves and then zombies...now it was witches and witch hunters. He wondered what the next fad would be.

Across from him, Eloise and James sat practically huddled together now and seemed to be content to whisper to each other and work on their posts together. Between him and them were Sean Fielding, Katarina Stewart, and Emmeline Reeder. They were the older of the regular cast members and played the show's main villains. Lucas enjoyed working with them, even if Eloise and James were being a bit dickish at the moment.

"We'll be live streaming in ten minutes, folks. Be ready." Mike called to them.

It was a short ten minutes because suddenly Lon burst in the door, counting them down for the live feed. Lucas didn't have a chance to see what kind of impact the small altercation had made on his two annoyed costars, or how Ryan had taken it. Instead, he spent the next thirty minutes making nice with his castmates, answering questions fans tweeted, and doing his best to ensure the viewing audience saw a happy, friendly cast. He occasionally glanced at Ryan, sitting next to him, judging how he was reacting to the whole thing.

James had been correct and a lot of tweets were directed toward the *Samdom* storyline. Readers of the book series already knew they ended up as a couple, and though they hadn't shared a great deal of screen time together, in the third episode, they had met, and the writers had made sure to add a little something to plant the seed of an attraction between Sam and Dominic. Every episode after had seen them spending more and more time together and the chemistry between them was palpable. It was also a sweet and realistic budding relationship, and as much as the fans were screaming for the kiss, they also loved the "domestic" moments between Sam and Dominic.

Lucas heard laughter from Ryan several times. He may not believe it of himself, but Lucas could tell Ryan was a natural with fans. There was an honesty and vulnerability to him that was incredibly appealing. The man was completely guileless. It was delightful to hear his excitement and enthusiasm for the show.

It was a late night by the time they'd wrapped up and Lucas was glad, not for the first time, that the studio provided a driver. He and Ryan had decided to share a ride home tonight. With their shooting schedules, it didn't always work out that they could go home together.

Their usual driver, Chris, was waiting for them, heat running on this unusually cool LA evening. Ryan hopped in first and Lucas admired his perfect jean-clad ass as he bent to get in the car. It was damn hard enough to keep his hands off, but it was asking the impossible to keep his eyes off him.

When they were both in and comfortable, Chris got them moving. Ryan turned to Lucas immediately. "You didn't have to defend me, you know."

Oh, so he was annoyed about earlier with Eloise and James. "I know I didn't, Ryan, but I can't stand that kind of bullshit. It's not that I didn't think you couldn't stand up for yourself."

Ryan appeared distressed and Lucas wondered if he'd misread the whole thing. "No, I didn't think you thought... Let me start again. Nobody has ever been on my side before. No one has ever spoken up for me and I appreciate it. I really do. I just meant you didn't have to do it and get yourself on their bad side." Ryan looked so earnestly thankful for simply being treated as a human being that it almost broke Lucas's heart.

"I'm on *your* side, Ryan. I like Eloise and James, even if they are being dicks right now. But you...you're my friend, and I stand right beside my friends. Always. You may not have had that before, but you've got it now.

Me…and Anna—we're on your side." Christ, it was could have been a line out of the show, but Lucas meant it with everything he had. Lucas desperately wanted to hug Ryan to make up in a small way for all the people who should have loved him.

This big, gorgeous, funny, sweet, unsophisticated Australian had become important to Lucas. Very important.

For what should have been an uncomfortably long period of time—but wasn't—he and Ryan held eye contact. Lucas was also pretty sure they were edging closer together, and for an insane second, he wondered if he was going to kiss Ryan, or if maybe Ryan was going to kiss him, before sanity prevailed and they pulled back from each other. It had been a near thing, though.

"Is this where we hug it out and cough awkwardly to cover our discomfort at sharing our feelings 'cause, you know, we are manly men and all." Ryan smiled, but it was a tentative, nervous smile and then he did do a sort of half cough, half giggle. He could tell Ryan had picked up on the almost kiss and was uncomfortable about it.

Lucas was going to do his best to ease the awkwardness. "Nah, man. This is where we punch each other on the arm and compare our sexual conquests and fighting prowess."

Ryan boggled at him before sheepishly mumbling, "Well, that won't take long." The tension was instantly dissipated with their humor, and Lucas relaxed back into his seat.

"So, um would you rather have to twitter every day and be hugely famous or never have to do that tweeting shit again and nobody ever remember your name?" Ryan asked.

"Oh, I'd rather everybody forget my name. The fame never drew me. I just love to act."

"Yeah? What is it that you love about acting?" Ryan's luminescent brown eyes smoldered almost gold with the passing lights, and Lucas marveled at how beautiful he looked every time the lights illuminated his face. The man was fucking breathtaking.

"It's freeing. I can be lots of different people and not worry what anyone thinks. And it's very…satisfying when you do a scene well and move people. I wanna make people laugh and cry and get angry and be scared to death. All of it, I just wanna make them feel. What about you? How did a small-town Aussie boy wind up wanting to act?"

Ryan shuffled around a bit on his seat, as though embarrassed by his coming answer. "A little of the same as you, but I love the challenge. It's hard for me. Most of the time I'm shit-scared while I'm doing it, but in a sick way, I guess that's the appeal. Crazy, huh?"

"No. Not crazy at all. It's like an adrenaline thing for you. I get it."

"Sort of, yeah. I'm not a junkie, though; no jumping out of planes or whatever. I just enjoy the thrill of performing. When I was growing up, life was, not boring—it can't be boring living with an alcoholic—but routine, I guess. Except this one time when I volunteered for the school play. When I got up on stage, it was...bam, this is amazing and hard and addictive. It didn't come easy to me. I was shaking the entire fucking time I was on stage, but I loved every minute of it. The teacher running the show told me I had raw talent." Ryan suddenly chuckled. His face was lit up with joy and he was so striking that it was so exceedingly difficult not to reach out and cup his beautiful face.

"I don't know why I listened to her; she wasn't a drama teacher...she taught math. But once she told me that, I thought, that's it—I've got talent, I'm off to Hollywood. Bloody stupid to be honest, but here I am, and one day I'm gonna have to thank the crap out of Miss Wolfe."

"I think lots of people will be thanking Miss Wolfe one day, Ryan. Hell, I'd give a shout-out to her now—she got you here." *To me*—Lucas thought but left unsaid.

"Did, um, did your parents support you wanting to act, or did they try to ship you off to be an accountant or something?"

"Accountant? Shit, I'd fail at that. Numbers and I are not the best of friends and math and I...well, we're not on speaking terms." Lucas said as Ryan tossed his head back and laughed. Every one of Lucas's senses went on high alert when Ryan was around. His entire body sparked to life. The sight of him, the sound of his laughter, and the scent of him was an onslaught to Lucas's defenses. If Ryan touched him right then, Lucas was pretty sure he would capitulate immediately, pull him into his arms, and prove just how much he wanted Ryan.

"My parents were very good about it, really. They did talk to me about finding a more 'appropriate career,' but in the end, they were okay with me rolling the dice. They're very fucking happy with it now." Lucas's entire family was well taken care of—maybe too well—if he were to be honest, but he enjoyed being generous.

"So you get on well with your family then?"

"For the most part. I don't see them much right now; I'm so busy with work and all. We had it pretty good growing up, and I get on all right with the sibs. Matty and I clash a bit, but I think it's because we're closest in age...a year apart. They're all trying to get into the industry too. Our last big knock-down, drag-out fight was because Matt thought I should be using my influence to get them jobs, but it doesn't always work that way. Family, huh." Lucas shrugged and then could have kicked himself. Complaining about his family to Ryan, who only had a deadbeat dad to claim as blood, was not the most empathetic thing he'd ever done.

"Yeah, family." Ryan grimaced.

"I'm sorry, Ryan. I know you've...well your family situation is shitty. I shouldn't complain about mine."

"You weren't complaining, Lucas. I asked about them and you were telling me. We're all fighting our own battles. Besides, I haven't given up on family."

"You mean your dad?" Lucas clarified.

"No, not him. He's a lost cause. I mean I haven't given up on having a family. It seems to me if the one you're born into is utter shit, then there's nothing wrong with making a different one of your own. I believe people are drawn to one another as friends or lovers and sometimes as family. Blood doesn't make you family; that's only a fluid in your body. Love and respect and fierce loyalty...that's family."

Ryan's humility and sweet nature did nothing to alleviate the growing crush Lucas was developing. Ryan was spot-on. Some people were drawn to others and Lucas knew he was being pulled toward Ryan like a fucking magnet.

Chapter Five

Shooting for season one ends. Will we get our Samdom *kiss??*

RYAN

Ryan couldn't believe he was a rising star in Hollywood! He couldn't walk around the block now without someone approaching him or catching the knowing glances people gave him. It was taking time for him to get used to it, and he still shook with nerves in a large group of people.

He'd also started receiving some fan mail. Most of it came through the studio, but a handful of letters and packages had come directly to his home address. Ryan found it disconcerting to think complete strangers, many of whom claimed to have a crush on him—and to be honest seemed to be a little disengaged from reality—knew where he lived.

Most of the mail had been pleasant: congratulatory letters of support, in truth, but a handful had disturbed him. One set of letters, in particular, had gone into meticulous detail of what the writer wanted from him, which was frightening in itself, but it was the writer's vivid description of the tiny scar on his neck just below his right ear that gave him pause. That scar was seldom visible in photos or on film, which led Ryan to the troubling conclusion that the writer either knew him or at some point had gotten close—too close—to him.

Maybe he'd mention it to Lucas and ask for his advice. Lucas had far more experience with celebrity than he did and would hopefully be able to help him.

Lucas greeted him as he always did when he was picked up to go to the studio today. Ryan did his best not to let the anxiety of his growing celebrity or the fan mail that came with it show, but apparently, Lucas knew him too well already.

"What's up?" Lucas asked as soon as he'd situated himself next to him in the car. "You seem nervous. Is it because we're filming the kiss today?"

Sure he was nervously excited for the kiss, but it was the fame that was really doing his head in. "Have you ever gotten fan mail?" he asked and immediately castigated himself for his stupidity. Of course Lucas had gotten fan mail; he was a bigger star than Ryan fucking Lowe.

Lucas laughed softly. "Yeah, sure, I've gotten some. Why?"

Ryan fumbled around for words. He always felt comfortable around Lucas, but that didn't mean he didn't feel lost sometimes. He'd never had friends or someone close he could talk to. It was a new and novel experience. "It's just that...um, I've gotten a few things sent to my place that freaked me out a bit."

"Threats?" Lucas's tone was cold and hard, nothing close to the warmth Ryan was used to.

"No. No, not at all. Just creepy. There was one, though, that mentioned the scar below my ear. It's hardly visible and I ...it was a little disconcerting, that's all."

Lucas didn't laugh at him, which Ryan was incredibly grateful for. "Look, fans can be scary, Ryan. Some of them don't seem to get we're people, too, or that we aren't our characters, and you'd be amazed at what they can find out about you. If you get a bad vibe from it, though, hold on to the letter. I won't lie, it could escalate, but then it could be nothing. Maybe you could get security to take a look."

Ryan didn't want to overreact. Maybe he'd put it aside and forget it. It was likely just a harmless person looking to connect with him. "Thanks. I'll hold on to it. I'm sure it's nothing. Just freaked me a little because the scar is tiny and... I'm fine. It'll be fine," he finished, feeling more and more embarrassed for letting such a little thing bother him.

"You're gonna be fine with this. I know it's a little overwhelming, but I'm here for you. Whatever you need, okay?"

Ryan nodded and did his best to put thoughts of his increasing fame out of his mind so he could concentrate on today's shoot. Today they were wrapping up the final scenes for the midseason and Ryan was more nervous than he'd been at any time before. This was the episode where he and Lucas would finally kiss—after ten episodes of UST.

Ryan knew if he was watching the show he'd be screaming for Sam and Dom to hurry up and do it already. Nearly every scene they were in featured some longing gaze or a straight-out hint that they wanted each other—the sexual tension was killing them all. It wasn't hard to act in those moments. Ryan could feel the pull toward Lucas; his raw sexuality was intoxicating and Ryan felt more lit up every time he saw Lucas.

Shooting the scene today would be different. It wasn't that he was nervous about kissing Lucas, exactly. The two had become good friends, certainly the best he'd ever had. Being in Lucas's atmosphere had almost become a compulsion, and Ryan planned to hold on to it with everything he had.

His nerves were mostly over getting the kiss right for the fans. Sam and Dominic were one of the most popular couples on screen, and the fans were clamoring for more from them. It was insane. After weeks of tension and will they-won't they, by the time this episode aired, Ryan hoped people would be salivating for the kiss, as he was...and it had to be a good one.

Despite being warned against it, he'd searched all the stuff people had put online. The YouTube videos where they'd mashed up scenes of him and Lucas, focusing on all the touches and looks they'd shared, and set them off to romantic or sexy songs were amazing and yet oddly disturbing. He was slightly surprised that, first, people had time to do it and, second, that they could be bothered.

He'd clearly underestimated people's connection with their fandoms.

His personal favorite was a compilation set to "SexyBack." He couldn't deny he loved watching Lucas strutting about in his shirtless scenes, looking much finer than anyone had a right to. He cringed at his own shirtless swaggering but had to admit the training had done wonders for his abs.

"Marks, people." Lon's voice thundered through the room and Ryan moved to his mark. He couldn't see Lucas yet but knew he was just off set, waiting for his cue. They'd done the read through and had blocked the scene to find their marks, but they hadn't done the kiss. Lon wanted the first time captured on film for authenticity. "Action."

Ryan wiped at the tear that slipped down his cheek, surprised at his ability to conjure them from nothing. He heard the door slam and glanced up to see Lucas storm into the room, fully made up as Dominic. He looked all avenging angel and hot as fuck as he stormed toward him, stopping too close to be anything but intimate.

"Sam," Lucas purred. He reached out and wiped at a tear with his finger. That was unscripted, but as with so many of Lucas's touches in character, Ryan went with it, leaning in to the touch.

"What the hell are you doing here, Dom?"

"I'm not letting you do this, Sam. I can't watch you do it." They held eye contact. Ryan had always wondered how actors managed to hold eye contact for so long without pissing themselves laughing or getting extremely uncomfortable—eye contact was difficult for him. With Lucas, though, he found himself more often than not completely lost in the green of his eyes. Lucas's pupils were blown so wide only a thin rim of the amazing green was visible. The expression in Lucas's eyes was intense and heated, and Ryan almost wished they weren't acting. He'd kill for someone to look at him that way for real.

"Why, Dom? Why is it so hard for you to watch me go out with Mia? You've already told me we're only friends, that you don't want anything else from me. You don't want me, but no one else can have me. Is that what you want?" Ryan pulled away and moved to his next mark. They were back across the room from each other now and this was the moment. They held eye contact across the distance between them for the count. And then Lucas was moving toward him again with purpose. Ryan's heart felt as though it would thump right out of his chest as he watched Lucas stride toward him, and he did his best to brace himself for what he knew was coming.

Lucas gripped his shirt in his fists and yanked him closer. It was a possessive declaration. The distance in height was negligible at this point and Lucas tilted his head slightly before pressing his lips to Ryan's.

"Turn a little more; keep your nose down a bit, Lucas," Lon's instruction broke the intensity, relieving Ryan, who'd almost been overwhelmed by the touch of Lucas's lips on his.

At the same time, though, Ryan wanted to block out the directions being barked at them and just experience the kiss, but it was impossible. There was no way he could mistake this for anything other than what it was, a technical movement between the two of them to make the most visually pleasing kiss possible.

"Okay, pull back a little and gaze at each other...good. Now back in for another kiss," Lon instructed, and Ryan was ready to walk over and punch him in the face. Then he wanted to kiss Lucas properly...privately. "Okay, and pull back."

Lucas leaned away from Ryan, a tiny smile on his face, and then he pressed his forehead to Ryan's. More improvising. Lucas's instincts when it came to Sam and Dom were spot-on.

"I lied to you, Sam. You're mine and I want everything with you." Lucas pulled his head away from Ryan's; finding eye contact again, he then reached out and tucked Ryan's hair behind his ear. He rubbed his index finger down Ryan's cheek when he finished and Ryan couldn't help the grin that crept onto his face. He wondered if Lon would keep all of that in the scene—the little touches of intimacy that had crept into both his and Lucas's performance.

Ryan tried his best to finish the scene and thought he'd made a pretty good job of it. Lon had them do the whole scene twice more, despite being pleased with the first take. When Lon finally called it, Ryan was unaccountably exhausted. It was an emotional scene, sure, but he'd done a few of them before and had never felt quite so drained afterward. Perhaps it was the fight he'd had to wager with his own body to keep his reaction to Lucas's proximity under control that left him so exhausted.

Lucas walked with him back to the makeup trailer to wash off the day.

"What did you think?" Lucas asked and Ryan could hear the hesitation in his voice.

"Well, I think it went great. Lon seemed happy with it. It was...not what I was expecting, though." Beside him, Lucas stopped walking and Ryan turned to look back at him. He could see something in his eyes...doubt, fear?

"What do you mean, not what you were expecting?" Lucas asked.

"I just meant it didn't feel romantic at all, you know. With Lon shouting directions at us... I dunno. I guess I thought we'd walk in there, kiss, and that's it. It was more technical than I expected."

"Oh," Lucas murmured and resumed walking.

Ryan quickened his pace to catch up with his perplexing costar. "So, you're flying out tomorrow?"

"Yeah, filming starts the day after. I'm a little nervous." Lucas flicked a quick glance at him. "They're adding a fair bit to my part and it's my first movie role. There's some big names in it and I'd hate to let them down, ya know."

"Hey, you've got this, Lucas. You're a great actor. You're going to be great." Lucas had landed a supporting role in a big-budget flick, and they'd called him back in to film some extra scenes during their show's hiatus before they released the film. Clearly, he'd impressed the studio enough that they'd wanted to expand his role. While Ryan was happy for him, he knew he'd miss him like crazy while he was away on set.

Ever since that first weekend he'd stayed at Lucas's, he'd spent most weekends at Lucas and Anna's. Most of the time, if they weren't on the Curzon's boat, they just sat around drinking, talking, or watching dodgy movies and even trashier TV, but it was fun and he would miss it. Anna had already told him he had to visit her while Lucas was away, but he wasn't sure how much was politeness and how much was a genuine willingness to hang out with her husband's on-screen lover.

"Listen, Anna's gonna come out to visit me on set. You could come with her if you wanted. I mean if you don't have any other plans for your break."

Did he have other plans? He'd half-heartedly thought about traveling a bit, seeing some more of the US. Perhaps he'd do that rather than crashing his best mate's reunion with his wife. "Thanks. I...um... I think I'm gonna do a bit of traveling. I'm dying to see the Grand Canyon and some other...stuff."

"Some other stuff? Wow, sounds as if you've got your itinerary all planned." Lucas snickered.

"Shut up. I'm more of a free spirit. Just gonna go where the wind takes me."

Lucas gave a full-bodied laugh then, and Ryan loved the sound of it. The unaffected laughter was contagious and had him chuckling too. "Ryan, you have to study the planned route whenever we go out on the Curzon's boat so you 'have a rough idea' where we're going. Free spirit my ass."

"Yeah, yeah. Well someone should be responsible for where we're heading in that thing. Didn't you ever watch *Gilligan's Island*? A three-hour tour, mate, and they were lost for years. And I don't know about you, but my building a cabin out of palm trees and woven reeds skills are not exactly stellar," Ryan argued.

"So much wrong with that show, Ryan. Don't even get me started. I mean how did Gilligan wear the same clothes every day for years and never get a tear in them, and the shit the professor did with a coconut, a bit of wire and a safety pin? Nah-uh." Lucas was on a roll, and as much as Ryan enjoyed it, they'd arrived at the makeup trailer and Ryan feared an hour-long lecture from Lucas about the inaccuracies of TV shows.

"Okay, okay. You've gotta suspend disbelief a little, my friend," Ryan tried. Too late, though, because Lucas was on his high horse and Ryan did spend the next hour trying to keep a straight face as Lucas expounded the ridiculousness of the Mork from Ork episodes of *Happy Days* and don't get him started on when Satan came to Salem on *Days of Our Lives*.

Ryan spent much of the time wondering how the hell he was going to make it through the next few weeks without Lucas.

They shared what Ryan knew to be a bro-hug when Lucas dropped him off at his place later that day. Ryan promised to keep in touch with Anna for him and that he would consider joining her when she came to visit. Ryan stood at the entry to his apartments and watched Lucas being driven away. He could sense the icy touch of loneliness already, and he was not even five minutes into their separation. He couldn't face going upstairs just yet.

Almost a block away, there was a bar he had visited a few times since he'd moved in and a drink sounded perfect right about now. He walked the short distance, trying to divert his mind from the constant thoughts of Lucas. Despite the popularity of their show, Ryan had managed to avoid too many encounters with fans so far. He supposed it helped that he didn't really go anywhere aside from the studio and Lucas's place.

The bar was pretty full. Most of the tables were taken, but there were several empty stools at the bar. Ryan took one at the end before signaling for the bartender. He ordered bourbon neat and settled in while his order was prepared. Most of the patrons looked as though this might be the first stop of a night out with many of them dressed far out of the code this bar would require. The music was turned low and sounded like a mix of classic rock and pop. There was no dance floor, and the food selection was mostly fries in a basket, with or without Buffalo wings.

Nothing and no one in his immediate vicinity made any sort of impact on the hold Lucas had on him though. He could feel eyes on him, but as he looked around, no one seemed to recognize him, or if they did, they didn't give a fuck. It didn't stop a shiver from tearing through him as he once more bore the heavy weight of somebody's stare upon him.

When his bourbon was placed on a coaster in front of him, the barman wandered off to take his next order. Ryan reached out and grabbed the snifter, putting it to his lips. He could feel the burn of the bourbon in his nose hairs and braced himself for that first scorching sip. They got smoother after the first mouthful.

When he finally woke the next morning, Ryan had only vague recollections of the night. He knew there'd been a woman in there somewhere; he could still smell her perfume, but somehow he'd made it home without her. He also knew from the gaps in his memory, the spinning in his head, and the roiling of his stomach that there'd been way too many bourbons.

He spent what was left of the day dreadfully hungover and scared to death some photos of him buck naked except for a cowboy hat and with some woman's bra in his teeth would wind up in a tabloid—or worse, a YouTube video.

But apparently, the fear and nausea weren't awful enough and hadn't clawed their way deep enough into his psyche to stop him from doing the whole thing all over again only a few nights later.

Chapter Six

First pics. How hot does Lucas Evers look in his new film role?

LUCAS

"Shit, Luke. You scared the hell outta me. You're like a ninja sneaking around here." Anna threw herself into his arms and he didn't hesitate to catch her in a warm embrace.

Lucas had made it back to his hotel room just in time to see Anna walking through the door. He'd left a room key at the front desk for her, knowing he'd never get off set in time to get to the airport to pick her up. He'd stuck his foot in the door as it was closing and used it to kick it open and follow Anna in.

"Missed you, babe." He pressed a kiss to her forehead.

"Missed you, too," she replied. "Which room is mine, left or right? I wanna dump my bag and grab a drink, shower, and something to eat, not necessarily in that order."

"Right one. Take a shower and I'll order some room service. The usual?" he called to her.

"Yeah. Biggest burger they've got. I've been good all week and I need it after... I just deserve it, Lucas."

Lucas called in their order. He suspected Anna was referring to his family being the reason she needed a burger, but he didn't want to fight with her. Anna insisted his family was using him, but family took care of each other. His siblings would get their shot one day, and his parents had worked hard to raise him and his brothers and sister. He felt they deserved to be looked after.

She'd sounded both pissed and fed up when she'd called before her flight. He couldn't blame her. His family could be...difficult for her to deal with, which is essentially what she had to do whenever he was away. It was especially difficult as she also had to deal with his and Anna's move to San Francisco now filming for *The Witches' Hammer* had been officially relocated to the city.

Room service arrived just as Lucas heard the water turn off in the shower. He put the food on the table, oddly pleased neither he nor Anna were the type to eat only rabbit food in order to preserve their figures.

"Smells so gooood," Anna dragged out the sound of her pleasure with the meal he'd ordered for her. "How've you been, Luke?"

"Great. It's been amazing these last few weeks. The cast that had to come back are great, and the crew is awesome. Making movies is totally different to filming a weekly television show, and so far, I'd have to say I prefer television. Not that I'm not having a great time and learning a lot, but with the exception of the slight jealous bump in the road, we had over screen time, working on *The Witches' Hammer* is like going to play every single day with my best friends." Lucas missed everyone from the show, but missing Ryan was a little aching throb in his heart.

At some point, in some way, Ryan had become that person who made him realize there was something more than just himself to this life. He had become the person Lucas thought of first in the morning and last at night. He was Lucas's comfort. It was an unfair burden to place unwittingly onto Ryan's shoulders, but he'd done it anyway. They'd texted and even Skyped a few times, but Lucas couldn't feel Ryan's heat through the devices, nor could he inhale that alluring woodsy and mint scent that was distinctively Ryan.

"But the location here is...stunning." He pulled back the curtains as he spoke, so Anna was able to fully experience the amazing view he had. From his sixteenth floor room, he looked out over the ever-changing color palette of the ocean. The sandy white where the waves broke blending into a light aqua and then the deeper blue of the ocean proper, had given Lucas hours of delight as he'd stood on his balcony admiring the majesty of Mother Nature.

"It is beautiful. You know, you should think about buying a place out near the beach. You've always loved it, Luke. You could get a little place, for weekends if you wanted to stay closer to work during the week." Anna joined him at the window, burger in hand. Nothing came between Anna and her burgers.

"You mean a *little* place so my family couldn't stay, right?" Lucas and Anna's relationship was perfect as far as he was concerned, but the one thorn in their paw was his family. Hers, they had nothing to do with, and if she'd let him, Lucas would have had them up on charges years ago, but she'd just wanted to move on and forget them, and he respected her wishes.

Anna had always liked his family, but once he'd become successful, her opinion had changed. They were still civil to each other, but there was a distance between them that bugged him.

"Lucas, I don't want to fight with you, but have you looked closely at your finances lately? They each spend more every month than you do, and now Matthew is asking for a new car so he looks more successful when turning up at auditions. The car he already has is better than yours. Your mom and dad are talking about remodeling and the apartment you bought them is only a few years old. I mean, come on. I'm not saying cut them off, I just think you should rein in their spending. That's all."

Anna had full access to his finances; she took care of paying bills for them, but she rarely used his money for herself. She'd earned a fair amount herself with various parts and advertising contracts. Anna was one of the most sought-after plus-size models, a term which Lucas found to be ludicrous. Anna had a stunning body and healthy size, but somehow she was considered plus size? Crazy. She used her own money for personal items, despite his offer for her to spend his. Lucas was whatever the opposite of a money-hungry person was. He knew he had it, and he appreciated that he had it, but he wasn't terribly interested in it.

"They really are trying to get work, you know," he tried pleading his family's case, knowing Anna didn't buy it for a second, and even he was starting to wonder just how keen his siblings were to support themselves.

"Okay, Luke. We're in paradise and it's too beautiful here to argue, so let's drop it. Have you heard from Ryan?" The question took him a little by surprise. Anna liked Ryan, he knew, but she rarely asked about friends of his, most likely because he'd never made a friend like Ryan before. Stardom was a weird thing, where you were often completely surrounded by people and yet utterly alone. Fake, fake, fake, fake—that's what he was used to with the *friendships* he'd made in Hollywood.

"Yeah, we've texted and I've talked to him on Skype. Why do you ask?"

"How did he seem?"

What was Anna getting at? Had something happened? "He seemed fine. I ask again, why?"

"I know you like him a lot, Luke. And I think he's great. I really hope something works out between you two. I just thought...well a couple of my friends saw him the other night and he was in a bad way—"

"What do you mean 'a bad way'? Wait, what do you mean you hope something works out between us?"

"I mean they said he was quite drunk, like could hardly stand up drunk and some starlet was all over him. Apparently, they put on quite a show. I'm sorry, Luke."

Fuck. Lucas had seen Ryan drink before. Hell, they usually had a few together, but he'd never been drunk, not like that anyway. Was fame getting to him? Lucas knew how intoxicating it could be. Had something happened? Was it boredom now there was a break in shooting? Lucas knew how difficult it was not to let the adulation go to your head and give you an overblown ego.

Lucas felt this overwhelming need to have Ryan with him. He'd missed Ryan and he'd endured a low simmer of yearning to be by his side since they'd been parted, but that had suddenly turned into the shrieking need of a boiling kettle.

"Starlet..." Did that mean Ryan was straight? They'd never discussed it openly and Ryan had evaded any hint of the sex of his past partners. Everyone assumed Lucas was straight because of his marriage to Anna—but what about Ryan?

Lucas had been attracted to Ryan from that first day when he'd auditioned with him and that had deepened into friendship—more than that hadn't really seemed like an option. Faced with Ryan's apparent heterosexuality, Lucas found himself feeling—bereft. Those sentiments he'd put a pin in and hadn't wanted to look at too closely had suddenly slipped from his grasp. "I guess that means... Doesn't matter. Do you think he's okay?"

"Why don't you give him a call? Can't hurt to check. And for the record, Lucas, I don't think this means he's straight. There is such a thing as bisexuality, Luke, and I've seen the way he looks at you...the way you watch each other, and I'm not talking on the show." Anna finished with a knowing smirk on her full lips. Had he been that obvious with how he'd looked at Ryan? He'd assumed he'd covered up his attraction—he was an actor, after all. Perhaps the lust had slipped through his mask.

"I'm aware there's such a thing as bisexuality, Anna, but what are the chances?"

"Lucas, you two can't help touching. You brush up against each other as you pass—even if there's a mile of room to get by, you sit too close on the sofa and even give affectionate little taps and pats. You're drawn to one another. It's like you can't help touching. Not touching each other is what's unnatural for you, and clearly neither of you even realize you do it."

Did they do that? Lucas tried to think back. Lon had told him once that he loved the extra little touches they threw into their scenes, the affectionate little touches, he'd called them. He'd said that was what made Sam and Dominic so believable as a couple. Had that connection on-screen spilled over into real life? Was that all it was or was there something more there?

Lucas had read comments from fans about how obvious it was he and Ryan wanted to be together in real life, especially when they saw snippets of them together offscreen. They only had to glance at one another and the fan base seized on it, claiming they could be a couple outside the show too. He'd dismissed it as the deluded and hopeful ranting of the more "crazed" fans. Though the truth was he had caught himself many times too close to Ryan or with his hand somehow, somewhere on Ryan.

"Okay," Anna started before licking at her oily fingers now that she'd devoured her burger. "I'm going to grab a beer and sit out on the balcony and soak in this location of yours." She brushed past him and grabbed her beer from the kitchen. She stopped in front of him on her way back past and stretched up on her toes to kiss his forehead. At five-foot-ten, she didn't have too far to stretch. "Call him." She winked and stepped onto the balcony, closing the door behind her.

Lucas went into his room and opened up his laptop. He wasn't huge on technology but knew enough to get by. He'd been taught about Twitter and Instagram because connecting with fans via social media was the way of the future. It was a painstaking and disagreeable part of his job as far as Lucas was concerned. A necessary evil.

It was almost seven at night where Lucas was, making it close to ten back home. Ryan should still be awake, and if not, at least it wasn't too late to wake him. Of course he could be out drinking and...whatever.

The ring of his Skype call trilled in the room as Lucas settled back on his bed. He was nervous; he had no idea what he was going to say to Ryan. He really had no business sticking his nose into Ryan's life like this, but regardless of every other emotion swirling inside him, Ryan was his friend, and he couldn't sit back and do nothing if his life was spinning into the bottom of a booze bottle.

"'llo." Ryan's muzzy voice came through the speakers as his image filled Lucas's screen in that jolty way Skype had. "Lucas? That you?"

Lucas could see Ryan's shirtless torso filling much of the screen and did his best to keep his eyes looking up, locked with Ryan's own. "Yeah, Ryan, it's me. Did I wake you?"

"Nah, mate. I was just heading to bed. What's up?"

"Nothing much. Just thought I'd check in, see how you're doing. What've you been up to?"

Ryan yawned wide and scratched at his chest and Lucas fought harder to keep his gaze away. "Gym, mostly. Gotta stay in shape while I'm on break or I'll lose my form. I'm bored mostly. When are you back?"

"Shooting's running a bit over, so I probably won't be back until a few days before the Teen Choice Awards. I guess Mike called you about our nomination?"

"Yeah." Ryan laughed the genuine laugh Lucas loved so much. "Something about best chemistry and best kiss, or liplock, I think they call it. Guess we pulled that one off then." They'd pulled it off all right. The kiss had aired a couple of weeks ago and the reaction of fans had been phenomenal. Think Bella and Edward at the peak of Twilight mania, but the gay version and no vampires.

"We did. Have you seen some of the YouTube videos? I like the crack ones myself. Some talented folks out there." Lucas laughed.

"Yeah, I saw that crack one where every time you looked at me that squeally voice would go 'Oh yeah, oh yeah, that's what I'm talking about.' That was hysterical." Ryan's image froze for a moment on the screen, catching him mid-laugh. He was fucking gorgeous.

"Listen, Ry, I just... I wanted to make sure you were okay. Anna's here—"

"Yeah, I'm sorry I didn't come with her, Lucas. I thought I should let you guys have some couple time. I'm all right here anyway."

"No, it's okay... It's just Anna mentioned some friends of hers seeing you out one night and you were...you weren't in a good way. I mean it's none of my business, but I wanted to make sure." Ryan would either appreciate Lucas's concern or tell him to fuck off and mind his own business. He watched a flush creep into Ryan's cheeks and his gaze drop. Fuck, he hadn't wanted to humiliate him.

"Oh. Yeah. No, I'm okay. Just had a few too many one night. Stupid. At least I didn't end up on YouTube. I'm not really sure why I did it...or what I was thinking."

"Ryan, you don't owe me an explanation. Like I said, I just wanted to make sure you were okay."

"Why?" And wasn't that the big question. Why did he care so much? Why had he pried into Ryan's personal life?

"I care about you, Ry. That's why. We're friends, aren't we? That's what friends do—they care."

"You're calling me Ry now? Do I get to call you Lu?" Ryan's smirk was back and Lucas couldn't be more grateful for the change of pace. It had gotten altogether too serious, too intimate.

"Ah, that'll be a no on the Lu. Luke will be perfectly fine, thanks. So um...you really are okay?"

"I'm good, Luke. Promise."

Lucas nodded his head. "Okay then, well...um..." Christ, he had no idea where to go to from here. He'd just have to use their fallback. "So...would you rather fall overboard meeting one of your heroes or live out the nightmare where you turn up to work naked?"

Ryan's laugh was thick and hearty and it almost felt as though his warmth was spreading to Lucas through two screens and two-and-a-half-thousand miles. "Asshole," Ryan finally got out.

They spoke for another hour, mostly nonsense, but Lucas felt better afterward about...everything. Ryan seemed fine, if a little lonely. It was only a few more weeks until Lucas headed home and he'd tried again to convince Ryan to fly out for a visit. He'd declined, but Lucas hoped maybe he'd change his mind. He'd said he wanted to see more of the US, and Hawaii was part of the US as Lucas had pointed out.

Anna was still on the balcony when he walked back out of his bedroom. She'd had a few more beers and was sitting and staring out at the now black ocean.

"You should talk to him, Luke," she said as he took the spot next to her on the lounger.

"I just spent an hour talking to him, Anna."

"Not what I meant. He makes you happy, he lights you up. Talk to him about how you feel."

"Lights me up? What the hell, Anna. I thought we agreed we didn't do that kind of romantic bullshit." He reached over to tap the neck of his beer against hers as he spoke, hoping against hope she wouldn't see through him. It was meant to be a toast to their shared anti-romanticism view of the world, but she pulled back from the action.

"It's not bullshit if it's real, Luke."

Chapter Seven

Oh my god, it's happening. It's happening. Everybody stay calm.

RYAN

Another heave and Ryan finally emptied the contents of his stomach. Damn, he shouldn't have had that last shot. He was in that awful in-between time when the buzz of his drunkenness had worn off and reality was creeping back in. It was during this sliver of time that guilt always threatened to drown him.

Ryan Lowe had more than he'd ever wanted. He was one half of the most popular couple on television. His character, Sam Dawson, and the character of Dominic Simmons were the most popular ship out there—everybody shipped *Samdom*. Ryan had more fame than he'd believed possible and was on his way to a bigger fortune than he could ever spend. He loved his job on *The Witches' Hammer* and he liked the people he worked with.

In fact, his castmate, Lucas Evers, had become his closest friend. He'd heard horror stories of other actors who had played close friends or lovers, and yet hated each other in real life and it sounded awful.

So if he had everything anybody could hope for, why the hell was he drowning his sorrows in the bottom of a bourbon bottle? Why did he feel so...empty?

Gingerly, Ryan dragged himself from the floor, where he'd wrapped himself around the toilet bowl. He grabbed some toilet paper and wiped at the spit and puke that had been trailing down his chin, dropped the paper in the toilet, and flushed. He groaned as he walked over to the sink and turned the cold tap on. Ryan was disgusted to see his hands shook as he cupped them under the cool water and splashed his face. After a few times, he rubbed his hands back and forth over his face and up into his hairline.

The lighting was dim in the large marble bathroom—mood lighting his realtor had called it, but he could still make out the pallor. The sallowness of his skin was in sharp contrast to the bright-red lines that snaked through the whites of his eyes. The delicate skin beneath his eyes had tinted dark-purple, undeniable evidence of his sleepless nights. He appeared much older than his twenty-three years. He slid his glance to the reflection of the side of his head, marveling that he couldn't actually see the skin there pounding outward with each throb of his headache. If his fans could see him now...

He couldn't allow this to be a regular thing. He'd grown up watching his father's spiral into alcoholism. That couldn't be him.

What was he drinking for? He didn't know if he was drinking to mask the loneliness or the growing fear of his fame. He'd become too afraid to go out his front door and risk running into a crowd. And what totally galled him was that in the harsh glare of sobriety, or almost sobriety, he had no fucking clue what he had to whine about. His show was a hit; he was a success, but fame was not turning out as he'd expected. This afternoon was meant to have been a quick trip to buy some groceries, but instead, he'd wound up having to hide in the men's room until store security had been able to clear out the mob that had descended once word had spread that he was there.

He could still hear the screaming—women, and a few men, young and old—calling for his attention, begging for him to notice them. To what end? What did they want from him? He could feel the press of bodies as they'd closed in on him, phones out, desperate for a selfie with him, regardless of whether or not he was willing. He imagined there were hundreds of shots floating around now of his face, pale and sweaty, a twisted look of terror contorting his features while the other faces in the shot were smiling widely, as they'd experienced one of the best moments of their lives, oblivious to the torment he was in.

The entire time he'd been terrified the person who knew his scar so well was in that crowd.

Would they look at his face in those images and recognize the distress he'd been in? Would they even care that Ryan had been screaming inside, pleading silently for help? Did the fact he'd chosen to be an actor preclude him from any sense of privacy? Any sense of safety when out on the street? He'd known fame was a possibility when he'd pursued acting, but had he truly considered what it would be like? How awful he'd find it? It wasn't the fans, individually, who bothered him. So far, he'd encountered some delightful people, but when they formed a group—a mob—and that mentality took over and they no longer saw him as a real person is when he felt hemmed in, trapped. Maybe he'd get used to it—he hoped.

"Come on, fucktard, stop whinging like a punk and get your shit in a pile." It was a slightly different spin on the same old pep talk he gave to himself every fucking day. He must be doing it wrong because it sure as hell wasn't working.

Ryan tsked at himself, shook his head, and considered punching the mirror. He was almost sober, though, so common sense prevailed, and instead of using his hands to take out vengeance on an innocent inanimate object, he used them to continue washing his face and brushing his teeth. He finished off by scarfing down a couple of aspirin with a glass of water.

If he managed to fall asleep now, he'd get maybe four hours before he had to be up. He was catching a commercial flight with Lucas. It was a risk, leaving the flight so late. They wouldn't have even had to fly if shooting had remained in LA, but San Francisco locations were needed for season two and it was cheaper, apparently, so the whole production had been moved.

If there was any delay, they wouldn't make it to the awards in time, but the truth was, he wouldn't mind being late. The red carpet would be the most difficult part of awards shows for Ryan. He hadn't been to any, certainly never as a nominee, but he was pretty sure he wasn't going to be a big fan. He and Lucas were up for two categories at the Teen Choice Awards: Choice TV: Chemistry and Choice TV: Liplock.

According to...well...everyone, they were a shoo-in to win. The first season of their show, *The Witches' Hammer,* finished airing four weeks ago and after a season of playing cat and mouse, with building sexual tension, Sam and Dominic had finally acted on their feelings and kissed. The reaction from fans had been...shocking, at least to Ryan. He'd foolishly watched copious YouTube videos of fan reactions as they'd watched the episode, and he could easily admit the screaming and the exclamations of the fans that they were *dead* had scared the bejesus out of him. It was the crying that had really done his head in, though. People had literally shed tears of joy that Sam and Dom had finally kissed. What the hell would they do if there was a more intimate scene? Something he knew was in the cards.

Even before the kiss episode, otherwise known as the "Oh, my God, it's happening" episode, Sam and Dominic had been popular characters. They had, by far, eclipsed the lead couple, Ella and Chase, in the popularity stakes and it showed in the screen time given to them toward the end of the season. Eloise and James had finally come around after an initial bout of jealousy and now they were all enjoying the spoils of starring in the number-one-rated show...worldwide.

Sleep was calling to him and Ryan fell into his king-size bed in the sweats he'd had on since yesterday morning. Best guess, he'd be out in maybe fifteen minutes.

THREE HOURS LATER, the brutal blare of his alarm successfully woke him and undid all the good work the aspirin and sleep had done for his headache. Lucas and their driver would be here in half an hour. At least all he needed was a shower and a bit of gel in his hair and he'd be good to go. He hadn't seen Lucas for weeks, so he was at a crossroads between feeling nervous as shit and over-the-top joyful at seeing him again.

The shower was as hot as Ryan could bear and he stayed under the spray far longer than he should have. Ryan and Lucas had decided to wear their suits on the plane; they only had to endure an hour-and-a-half flight, so he only had to slip his bespoke new suit on and he was ready. Thankfully, Ryan had packed an overnight bag yesterday, so he was, for once, organized.

Lucas's wife wouldn't be joining them tonight. He and Anna got on well and she was very understanding, considering it was his job to kiss her husband. He had been hoping she'd be there tonight on the red carpet because he knew Anna was adept at handling both the screaming fans and the media. Tonight would be his and Lucas's first public appearance at an awards show since this craziness had started.

His phone's message beep trilled through the room and Ryan reached for it to read his text. It was from Lucas: *Downstairs in 5*.

He texted back a quick thumbs-up and slipped his shoes on. He did a hasty check around his apartment; it was huge compared to what he was used to, but he only used a few of the rooms, so it didn't take long. Then he grabbed his bag and headed out the door.

By the time Ryan got downstairs from the twenty-seventh floor, the black town car was waiting in the pickup bay. Ryan recognized their new San Francisco driver standing at the back door, ready to open it for him to get in.

"Hey, Josh. How's it going?"

"Good, Mr. Lowe. Yourself?"

"It's Ryan, Josh. I've told you already." Ryan smiled as he moved past Josh and sat in the back seat next to Lucas. He could hear Josh's laughter as he shut the door and walked around to hop back in the driver's seat.

"He'll never call us by our given names, Ry. Did Chris teach you nothing?" Lucas chuckled. Ryan loved how Lucas had taken to calling him Ry. It was intimate; the shortening of a name was the hallmark of a close friendship as far as Ryan was concerned.

He had the unsettling urge to reach over and hug him, maybe even plant a welcome-home kiss on those soft, full lips.

He'd known he'd missed Lucas while he'd been away, but the full weight of the loss hit him as soon as he suddenly had him back. His emotions were jerking him around like a fucking schoolboy, and Ryan would give anything for a drink right about now.

"Yeah, but I can keep trying. I hate the whole Mr. Lowe crap, especially because two years ago I was doing Josh's job." It was true; two years ago he was driving limos and flipping burgers and waiting tables and whatever other work he could get. He'd come to the US from a less-than-a-dot-on-the-map town in Australia with a little over four thousand dollars in his account, a bag full of threadbare clothes, and ridiculously unrealistic dreams. But somehow he'd made it, and now everyone knew his name. And the idea of that terrified him.

"Well, those days are over, my friend. You are the less handsome half of, soon to be officially, the most popular couple on TV. We are the most shipped ship on the planet."

Ryan still had trouble understanding the whole idea of shipping, but if it kept the fans watching and the ratings high, then he was all for it. "How's Anna?"

"She's...yeah, she's good." Ryan could hear the tension in Lucas's voice but wasn't sure it was his place to pry. If there was something wrong, surely Lucas would tell him if he wanted him to know.

"Didn't change her mind about coming, then?"

Lucas kept his head turned from Ryan, watching the world go by outside the tinted windows of the car. "Nah. She had an audition to prepare for." Anna had had a few bit parts and recurring roles in several shows, and she was a stunning model, but she hadn't achieved the same success as her husband. Not only was Lucas's career soaring, thanks to his role as Dominic, but his supporting role in the low-budget flick was already generating Oscar buzz. Lucas Evers's star, which had already been shining bright, was about to go supernova.

"Oh yeah. Good role?"

"Not sure, to be honest. She hasn't really told me much about it." Lucas lacked the usual enthusiasm and joy that wove through his tone; instead, he sounded bland and disinterested. It wasn't the welcome back Ryan had been hoping for.

"Everything okay, Luke?" Ryan's hand jutted out as though he was going to rub Lucas's arm in comfort, before he realized what he was doing and pulled it back. He'd become acutely aware that sometimes something Sam would do on the show blurred into his reality and he touched Lucas more intimately than was probably acceptable offscreen. It was something he had to try to rein in.

"Yeah. Yep. Sorry. I'm just tired, I guess. I need to pep up before we get to LA. I 'spose the hordes of screaming fans will wake me up soon enough though." Lucas sounded convincing. He was an exceptional actor, so he would have convinced someone who didn't know him like Ryan did. But Ryan could hear the wobble in his voice, the hitch that caught on the lie.

The ride passed in a blur and they arrived just in time for check-in to avoid having to wait around at the airport, but their own cleverness bit them in the ass. Of course, wearing their flashy suits would garner attention, and it only took one person to recognize them and they found themselves surrounded by well-wishers, fans, and the just plain curious. Ryan pinned a smile on his face as he signed a few items and posed for several selfies, but he couldn't prevent the tremble in his limbs or the quickening of his breath. As more people closed in, he could sense something pulling at his inner calm, threatening his sense of safety—he wasn't entirely sure the crowd wasn't going to crush him either accidentally or maliciously. He pressed himself tighter against Lucas, using his body as a touchstone to ward off the panic. He felt a warm hand grab one of his and squeeze, and he knew, purely from the zap when they touched, that it was Lucas.

Thankfully, airport security came to break up the ruckus and escorted them to their flight. Ryan wasn't sure how much longer he'd have been able to breathe among the press of all those bodies. Dealing with crowds was supposed to get easier the more you did it. Didn't seem to be working that way for him, though.

Lucas was quiet again once they boarded, and like a chameleon changing its colors to match their environment, Ryan's mood mellowed to complement it. They shared some idle chitchat and observations of the people around them, but they spent most of the trip in silence or taking photos with several fans on the flight who found the courage to approach them.

Ryan only saw Lucas flare into the lively, fun man he remembered as they pulled up at the red carpet outside the Forum. Even though their limo was supposedly soundproof, Ryan could hear the screaming already. He would never get used to this.

"Ready to do this, Ry?" Lucas asked, keeping his gaze fixed out the window of their limo. Ryan suddenly realized Lucas had hardly looked at him all night.

"Yeah, Lucas. Let's go."

As soon as the limo door opened, Ryan's world ignited with the flashes of hundreds of cameras. It was so blinding, Ryan shut his eyes for just a moment before he stepped into it. Lucas had stepped out ahead of him and Ryan could make out his silhouette, standing tall, facing toward the crowd of fans with both of his arms raised, hands waving madly. Another roar went up from the crowd when Ryan emerged from the limo and took his spot beside Lucas. His entire body shook like a leaf and his lungs worked hard to draw enough air into them. Jesus, fuck, he couldn't do this. He could feel the anxiety squeezing him, crushing his airway so simply breathing became fucking difficult.

He joined Lucas in waving to the fans, doing his best to try to block out the flares of the cameras, the rumble of the crowd, and the sudden fear there was not enough room left for him on this fucking planet.

It was so bright Ryan couldn't make out anything beyond the flashes. He knew the crowd was there only from the noise and the blurry outline of their bodies. Out of the corner of his eye, he saw Lucas turn away from the fans so Ryan knew he could now safely turn away from the crowd that threatened to crash over him like a wave, shattering his fragile body beneath its might. The long stop-start walk up the blue carpet awaited him, but the crowd was at least thinner there. Reporters would be lined along it, screaming their names, hoping to draw their attention to get a brief interview. Oh god, he hoped he got used to this part of his job quickly.

They walked together. Most of the media lining the carpet were familiar to Ryan. He'd made it his business to learn about the reporters who usually covered these events. The first in line was Abe Waller, but there was no way Ryan was going near him, not after the way he'd treated other stars. Sherry Scott stood on the other side of the carpet and Ryan made a beeline for her, hoping Luke would follow him.

"Ryan, Lucas...a few words please?" Sherry beckoned them over and fired off questions before they'd even reached her. "You two are the couple of the year. Your popularity has been unlike anything we've seen for some time. What do you attribute that to?"

"Hey, Sherry. I think it's a mix of things. First of all, the books were wildly popular, so we're kind of riding on the coattails there. And I think Sam and Dominic are fundamentally flawed characters, but they're doing the best they can in a violent world while falling in love with each other. People want to cheer for them to get their happy ending." Lucas's answer was flawless, yet Ryan could tell he lacked his usual spark; perhaps he hated dealing with the press too.

"And the chemistry between you two is...sizzling. People love watching that. And you have to know there's a legion of fans for not only *Samdom* but *Lovers* also. How do you feel about that?"

Ryan waited for Lucas to answer. What the fuck was *Lovers?* Jesus, was it Lowe and Evers mixed to create another ship? What the fuck? Ryan turned to Lucas and took in the expression on his face. He couldn't read it. Was it sadness? Nervousness? Lucas looked almost...despondent. Whatever it was, there was no answer forthcoming from him.

"Ah...um the chemistry comes from the great friendship Lucas and I have built. He's an amazing actor and a great friend, so I think that comes through in our performance. It's wonderful that fans support Sam and Dominic. Sadly, for the rest of us, this man here is happily married." Ryan did his best to laugh off the whole *Lovers* idea, he could feel the sweat trickling down his back and beading on his forehead. He was becoming more and more anxious the longer he was on the carpet, especially with Lucas seemingly checked out beside him.

"What is it like, as two heterosexual men, to kiss each other?"

"It's the same as kissing a woman, except for the stubble." Ryan laughed, allowing her assumption to pass him by. "Actually, it's technical and not romantic in the least when the director is giving instructions in your ears."

After that, it was a long tedious walk up the carpet for Ryan. Just once, he wished someone would ask him something different other than the usual: Who are you wearing? What do you think of your chances tonight? Can you tell us what's in store for Sam and Dominic next season? What's it really like getting to kiss Lucas Evers? Other than the "who are you wearing" question, Ryan tried to mix up his answers a little. He'd much rather be on set, working his ass off, covered in dirt and sweat.

A few more times he and Lucas were interviewed together, but Ryan could tell by Lucas's answers there was something not right with his friend tonight. He'd sensed it all evening, but Lucas's half-hearted responses to the questions thrown at him had been the final nail in the coffin.

As soon as they'd cleared the carpet, they both made a beeline for the bar. Ryan ordered his usual, but Lucas asked for water. Lucas certainly didn't drink like he did—especially not lately—but he usually had a few.

"You sure you're okay, Luke?" Most of the guests were already seated; the show would start in five minutes, so there was no one around to overhear them. Lucas finally turned to face Ryan and their gazes locked for the first time that night.

"Ryan...I." Lucas closed his eyes, drawing in a deep breath and Ryan knew whatever he was about to say wasn't what he'd wanted to say. "I'm fine. Just tired. Honestly." Lucas patted Ryan's shoulder in the typical way to indicate everything was fine, even though it clearly wasn't.

"Well, I'm here to listen if you need me, okay?"

"I know, thanks, Ryan. Let's find our seats and pick up our awards." Lucas smirked.

Their table was close to the front of the auditorium; their show was up for several awards and was expected to win most of them. Most of the cast was present tonight along with the director, producer, and other crew, so they were spread over two tables. After greeting the rest of the table, Ryan and Lucas sat together, with only moments to spare before the lights dimmed and the show began.

An hour and a half and several bourbons later, it was finally time for the awards Ryan and Lucas were up for. Knowing the cameras would be on him, Ryan tried to sit with a certain amount of nonchalance. He didn't want to seem too eager to win, while at the same time, he wanted to show his fans how thrilled he was they had voted for him. It was a balancing act made more difficult by the bourbon coursing through his system, making reality a little fuzzy.

When they called his and Lucas's name for the Liplock award—why they couldn't simply call it best kiss, he didn't know—Ryan stood and turned to Lucas. Ryan was taller, but Lucas was strong as an ox, and Ryan found himself being pulled into a fierce hug. He could hear the teen audience at the back of the auditorium going batshit crazy. It was a surreal moment, even though Ryan's whole life had turned to the bizarre the second he was hired for the role of Sam Dawson.

Lucas released him and they made their way to the stage. It was oddly dreamlike as Ryan reached for his surfboard trophy, shook hands with the presenters and followed Lucas to the podium. Even though he'd been assured they would win, Ryan hadn't prepared anything at all to say, so he was quite happy to let Lucas take the lead. He held on to Lucas's surfboard as he took the podium.

"Thank you. Wow!" Lucas began but was drowned out by more screaming. "Thank you, guys. Um, I guess thank you to Lon Greenway, the best director ever. Mike Faraday and Sally Worth our producers. Thank you to the entire crew and the fabulous cast. There are way too many people to name, but every person who works on the show should be thanked. It's a team effort. Thank you to the fans—" More screaming drowned out Lucas's voice, though it wasn't just wild, unfocused screaming this time.

The teen crowd was chanting something, and it took just a moment for Ryan to register what they were screaming: Kiss. Kiss. Kiss.

The crowd was asking them to kiss, as though they were a real couple. It was like when the royals were on the palace balcony after their wedding for chrissake. Did these people not understand the difference between the real world and the fantasy of their show? The noise wasn't abating and Ryan suddenly realized Lucas was staring at him. Did Lucas want to kiss for them? Should they? Wouldn't that—Oh God. He was in Lucas's arms again, but this time Lucas was pressing his soft lips to his, moving gently. It was a chaste kiss, but there was definitely passion simmering underneath and it was so, so good. And then Lucas deepened it, their mouths parting slightly and Ryan was caught up in it. He slid his tongue out, just grazing Lucas's lips as he pushed his tongue inside Lucas's hot mouth, tasting and exploring, licking into the warmth. With his arms busy holding their awards he couldn't wrap them around Lucas's strong body like he wanted to, and Ryan felt it as a loss. What the actual fuck?

As they pulled away from each other, the noise inside the auditorium was deafening. Ryan tried to catch Lucas's gaze, but he'd already turned back to the microphone and Ryan couldn't have repeated what Lucas was saying under pain of death. His head was spinning and it had nothing to do with the bourbon.

Chapter Eight

OMG! Is it really real?? Lovers?? I'm dead.

LUCAS

"What the hell was I thinking kissing Ryan like that, Anna?" It was more than a week after the Teen Choice Awards and Lucas was still reeling from the impromptu smooch with the person he'd considered a good friend and secret crush for most of the past six months. He hadn't spoken to Ryan, other than at the cast table read-throughs, since that night, so he hoped he hadn't fucked things up too badly with him.

When he'd held Ryan in his arms and kissed him in front of thousands last week, every person in the audience and every person watching at home on their screens disappeared and Lucas's body had gone up in flames so hot he thought he'd burn. He'd experienced lust before, desire, but this time he'd felt it deep in his very bones. He'd never before been so consumed by the existence of another human being. The intensity of his need for Ryan in that moment had frightened him.

After they'd left the stage, Lucas had offered Ryan an apology for just planting one on him like that, insisting he was giving the crowd what they wanted, but he should have checked with Ryan first. Ryan had seemed...dazed. He'd told Lucas it was fine and the crowd loved it, which they had. There were thousands more YouTube videos of *Samdom* out there now with "that" kiss in them.

"It's like I told you, Luke, you can't keep your hands off him, so when the crowd offered you an excuse to get even closer, bam! You took it. Stop beating yourself up about it."

"I meant to pull away from him. Putting some distance between us, not trying to climb him like a fucking tree and jam my tongue down his throat."

Everyone had enjoyed the kiss: the fans, the producers, who had said it was genius; even his wife had congratulated him on single-handedly boosting the ratings for *The Witches' Hammer* when it returned in a couple of months. But how did he feel about it? And what about Ryan? Lucas couldn't even answer the question of whether he'd done it because the crowd was screaming for it or if he'd kissed Ryan simply because he'd missed him so damn much and he hadn't been able to help himself.

"It was good, though, wasn't it? It sure looked like it was good." Anna laughed.

"Yeah, it was good. Fuck, Anna, it felt right. It felt like a he's-the-person-I'm-supposed-to-kiss-every-damn-day-for-the-rest-of-my-life kiss."

"Then talk to him. My god, man, I can't make it any clearer. Open that pretty mouth of yours and speak the words." Lucas could hear the frustration in Anna's tone.

They were due back on set tomorrow and Lucas was nervous. He wasn't entirely sure what kind of reception he would get from Ryan. Even though Ryan had been completely caught off guard by the kiss, it had only taken a moment for him to catch up before the kiss had turned—insanely fucking hot.

Their kiss on set had been purely technical to make sure it looked good on film, but this kiss had been spontaneous, and Lucas had...well, to say he'd enjoyed it was the understatement of the year. He'd fucking loved it. It had been a damn good kiss. Carnal. Sensual. All the things a kiss should be.

Didn't matter though, did it? You could share a good kiss with someone and it didn't have to mean anything.

Yes, Lucas had been with plenty of men before, and he found Ryan incredibly attractive, but Ryan was straight and they were friends, nothing more. Nothing more. Nothing fucking more. He'd been telling himself that for months.

Perhaps if he said it often enough it would somehow magically become true.

His movie, *Over the Oceans,* was due to be released in weeks and the Oscar buzz that was already flitting around was amazing to him. Talk of him being up for Best Supporting Actor didn't fit into any sort of reality he could imagine. Now was not the ideal time for any scandal in his private life.

"I'll think about it, Anna. Okay? It's...it's just a big risk. I don't want to ruin our friendship."

"I know, Luke. It is a big risk, but what if...just what if it pays off?" Anna winked and left him alone with his thoughts...and his computer.

As much as he told himself not to, Lucas turned to his laptop again. He went straight to YouTube and clicked on his favorite video. Jesus, what was wrong with him? Was he some kind of masochist who enjoyed the torture of watching him and Ryan together? He sat there, like the absolute creep he was, and watched the spliced images of him and Ryan set to quite possibly the most sickeningly, wonderfully beautiful romantic song ever, "Turning Page." He'd watched this video an embarrassing number of times and couldn't seem to get enough. He'd become one of those crazed fans he'd rolled his eyes at not too long ago, but worse. He was one half of that couple who looked so beautiful together and looked so lovingly at each other that he swore to god it almost brought a tear to his eye. And if a tear actually fell, he was chucking his fucking laptop over the balcony.

His other favorite was set to "Wicked Game," the Ursine Vulpine version. It was slow and seductive and Ryan looked hot as fuck moving in slow motion against the background of the sensual song. Lucas especially loved the part where whoever had edited the video had slowed down their kiss at the Teen Choice Awards. It looked blisteringly hot, especially the little peek of their tongues dueling once the kiss had truly gotten going, and it never failed to get Lucas hard every time he watched it. And every time he watched it and got hard, he ended up jacking off.

But, always, the brief moment of pleasure that afforded him soon passed, and he was left hollow and alone because it wasn't real. It was all fucking make-believe and he was left wanting something that was so temptingly close he had actually tasted it, and yet it was so very far out of his reach.

This had to stop. He'd become ridiculously caught up in the magic of *Samdom*, or *Lovers* as some fans had started referring to them, ludicrously pleased their real-life surnames of Lowe and Evers combined to form the moniker *Lovers*. The fans, especially those who made the YouTube videos were weird, wonderful, and his bread and butter. Without the fans, there would be no show and without a show no job for him.

Now he had months of torture to look forward to—enduring being close to Ryan again. Allowed to touch and kiss Ryan as Dominic, but definitely friends only as Lucas. Perhaps he should try harder to ease back a bit, try to put some distance between himself and Ryan. Could he do that though? He'd failed miserably the other night. Jesus, Ryan had come to mean so fucking much to him. He was his best friend, really. How could he risk losing that? But he knew being so close to Ryan and yet having to keep his distance was going to fucking kill him.

It was after midnight by the time Lucas finally felt his lids drifting closed. He'd spent hours foolishly watching himself and Ryan in countless YouTube videos. He pushed his laptop to the side of the bed and curled down into the covers, desperately hoping sleep would come quickly and he wouldn't spend what was left of the night tormented with dreams of someone who wasn't his.

IT WAS RAINING when Lucas woke. All the scenes he would be shooting today were indoors so it wouldn't affect his schedule at all. In fact, from what Lucas could remember, he was shooting in the studio all week, and most of his scenes were with Ryan. The storyline was picking up pretty much from where it had ended last season and that meant Sam and Dominic would be spending whatever time they had not fighting witches, figuring out their newly minted relationship. And that included exploring their physical relationship. How in the hell was Lucas going to make it through this?

Lucas was dressed and downstairs waiting for his car ahead of schedule. Anna was headed back to LA for work over the next few days and he'd miss her company. He wondered how he'd manage when or if Anna finally left him, or he left her. He knew they'd always be friends; he had that comfort at least.

The black luxury car pulled in right on time, and Lucas opened the back door before the car had even come to a complete stop. Much like Ryan, he too hated the whole star treatment bullshit. He greeted Josh and buckled in. Ryan's place was only about ten minutes away, so Lucas used that time to wrestle back control of his emotions.

By the time Ryan stepped into the back seat with him, Lucas had taken every bit of the desire and yearning he felt for Ryan and shoved it so far down he'd probably need to go spelunking to find those feelings again.

"Morning, Luke. Ready to get back into it?" Ryan spoke as he settled himself into the seat.

"You bet I am. How's your week been?"

And so, polite conversation went on for the thirty-minute ride to the studio. It was friendly and easy, and if it hadn't been for the blazes of warmth, and the flickers of electricity that shot through him every single time his eyes locked with Ryan's brilliant brown ones, Lucas would have thought he could have gotten out of this mess in one piece. Instead, he suspected by the time Ryan Lowe was finished with him his heart will have been shredded.

The one thing about working on *The Witches' Hammer* that Lucas hadn't missed was the lengthy visits to the makeup chair. He didn't mind the makeup at all; in fact, he kind of liked the way it made him look: exotic and almost literally magical. It was the time it took for the transformation that bothered him.

The cast and crew he would be working with today were waiting for him by the time he'd made it to the set. He knew they would have shot some scenes he wasn't required for, so it wasn't wasted time, but still, he hated keeping people waiting.

The first thing he noticed on set was how Ryan looked in his witch-hunter gear. Tight black leather clung to firm, bulging thighs and followed the curve of his perfect ass. A black T-shirt, tight enough to show the lines of his ripped abs, stretched at the arms where Ryan's biceps bulged with every movement. Lucas could tell Ryan had bulked up in their downtime. Christ, Lucas thought he might actually be drooling.

"Marks," Lon called, and Lucas hurried to stand on the mark from which he would make his entrance. "And action."

Lucas burst through the door, allowing it to hit the wall, and ran toward Ryan. He stopped short of pulling Ryan into him, gripping his upper arms tightly enough it would probably leave marks, but Lucas knew if this was reality and Ryan had just done something stupid that nearly got him killed like his character Sam had, he'd be gripping on to Ryan as tightly as he was in character as Dominic.

"Sam, oh god, Sam, are you crazy? Do you know what could have happened to you?"

Ryan reached up and cupped Lucas's face, dragging him closer. "I'm fine, Dom, and I had to do something. There were children there, and I couldn't..."

Lucas drifted even closer so their foreheads were touching. "I can't lose you, Sam. I can't. I know you have to do your job, but please, please don't risk yourself." He allowed the desperate pleading to trickle into his tone.

"Hey." Ryan pulled his head back to regain eye contact. "You're not gonna lose me, Dom. I'm not going anywhere." When Ryan's lips pressed to his, Lucas tried so hard to focus on his director's voice and keep the kiss technical. Instead, he found himself kissing Ryan as though it was really him that he'd nearly lost, not their fictional characters, and the kiss turned bruising. To add to his horror, he felt himself getting hard. His entire body was fitted against Ryan's with not an inch between them, so he knew Ryan would feel his erection.

Somewhere in the background, he could hear Lon, but his words wouldn't register. What the fuck was happening to him?

Abruptly he pulled away from Ryan and tried covering his hard cock with some sleight of hand—a bit of look over here while my hard-on, which I don't want you to see, is going on over there. He spluttered and coughed and bent over, mimicking the actions of someone caught in the middle of an irrepressible coughing fit. Once he had himself under control, he stood and spluttered, "I'm so sorry. I had a tickle in my throat and I couldn't—" He coughed again. "—couldn't help it."

"Here." Ryan shoved a glass of water into his hands.

"Thanks."

"Are you all right, Lucas? Need a break for a minute?" Lon asked. Lucas shook his head and sipped at the water. "Well that kiss was...a little *more* than what we needed, but it looked great, so we'll keep it. When you're ready, we'll pick up from when you break apart and start with the lines there."

"Sure," Lucas grunted and took more sips of his water, dragging out the time until he had to go back into hell all over again and get up too close and too personal with a man he wanted beyond reason. Guess he hadn't pushed those fucking feelings down far enough, after all. Fuck his life.

Chapter Nine

Now this is what we been asking for!! Samdom *is my OTP*

RYAN

"Oh my god, today's the day," Henry gushed. "Sam and Dom coming together in the biblical sense. Oh, my fucking god, I cannot wait."

"I know, darling. The day has finally arrived," Catherine replied with just as much delight, if a little less enthusiasm than Henry.

Ryan laughed as the two continued dressing him for the big scene. Today they were shooting *Samdom's* first time, and Ryan was nervous. It wasn't a terribly explicit scene; after all, their largest audience demographic was teenagers, but it would involve plenty of kissing, touching, and a hint of nudity. The fans were...eager for this moment in the storyline and Ryan was worried. He didn't want to fuck it up, but the thought of, god, even just the idea of make-believe sex with Lucas was distracting.

After the scene with Lucas last week, Ryan had been shaken. Ryan knew Lucas had gotten caught up in the kiss; they both had. Lon's directions had gone unheeded as lust ruled them, though thankfully, he'd seemed pleased with the end product. Lucas had gotten hard. Ryan had felt his sizeable length against his thigh, and it had done nothing but inflame Ryan, searing him more than the kiss already had.

"What do you think? Is this what Sam would wear to seduce his man?" Henry had apparently designed the easy access shirt Ryan/Sam now sported with just this moment in mind. As far as Ryan could tell, it was a pretty standard royal-blue button-down, though he didn't possess the creative eye Henry and Catherine had for clothes. His trousers were dark sandy-colored chinos. They wouldn't be coming off but had been custom-made to be loose around the waist to show a bit of peek-a-boo of the band of his briefs, yet they were firm across his ass.

"Henry, darling, nobody is going to care what he's wearing as long as it comes off, and quickly. We're all salivating for these two to make love."

Ryan had never heard Catherine curse or use any other less-than-ladylike words.

Henry clapped his hands together, his glee remaining unbridled. "Make love. Oh god, Catherine, they're going to fuck good and hard. That's what'll be happening in my little head, anyway." Ryan couldn't help laughing at his wardrobe people. Polar opposites, and yet they got on like a house on fire.

Ryan wasn't a vain person, but he knew he looked pretty good in the outfit. He wondered what crazy outfit Lucas would be in. With his character's flair for fashion, and Henry and Catherine's interest in this scene, Ryan knew it would be something interesting.

"I look great. Thanks, you two."

"Yes, yes, of course, you look great; now off you go and get that man." Ryan wondered if Henry realized it was make-believe or if, like so many others, he believed there was a *Lovers* in real life.

Ryan had admitted to himself weeks ago he had a tiny crush on Lucas, but Lucas was married and not remotely interested in him. Why was it that so often people fall for someone who was so obviously wrong for them? Why hadn't the crush burned itself out by now? He'd had plenty of unrequited crushes before, but this one confused him. It had dug its way in and didn't seem to be letting go of him anytime soon. It was somehow *more* than all of the others.

Perhaps it was normal for actors to develop a crush on their on-screen lovers. Who could he ask? He had no friends other than Lucas and Anna, and he could hardly ask the object of his crush—or the man's wife. And if he asked his other costars, well, that was giving away his secret and asking for trouble.

By the time he was dressed, made up, and on his way, Ryan was just eager to get it done. As he entered the set, which was effectively Dominic's bedroom, two things caught his eye. First, the bed covered in black silk with a mass of pillows in all sizes and shades of red that couldn't possibly be comfortable to sleep on, and second, Lucas. He was facing toward Ryan while he was talking to Lon. He had on an aquamarine silk button-down that highlighted the green of his eyes and accentuated his flawless skin perfectly. The shirt was embroidered with gold strands in patterns that almost looked like fireworks. Lucas wore it untucked, and underneath it appeared as though he only wore black leggings which clung to every curve and muscle of his toned legs. His dark hair, which he'd had to grow even longer, in keeping with his character, sat in almost shoulder-length waves, wisps of his fringe falling into his eyes. He looked smoking, fucking hot.

He could do this. He could. There was no reason why he couldn't smooch the shit out of Lucas and then pretend to take him to bed, all while not being affected by it. No reason at all. Tonight he could go home and do whatever the hell he wanted with the memories of today, but for right now he was an actor, and he was going to act the hell out of this scene and do his best to remember it was just that—an act.

"Hey, Ry. You ready?"

Ryan hadn't even noticed Lucas approaching, but now that he was standing in front of him, Lucas was all that Ryan could see. "Yep. Love the outfit, mate."

"Yeah, Henry called it the shirt you wear when you're expecting fireworks. He and Catherine were...creepily excited about today." Lucas hadn't moved his gaze from Ryan's face but now he let it slide down Ryan's body and his scrutiny was so intense it almost felt like a caress. "Color suits you."

Speaking of color, could the green of Lucas's eyes be any more fucking perfect? He could be poetic and describe it as the color of emeralds, but frankly, it reminded Ryan of the tree frogs they used to get back home. Well there was a pickup line if he ever needed one. The aquamarine of the shirt drew the green out, making it pop, though it didn't really need any help. Ryan's gaze dropped to Lucas's mouth, drawing attention to his slightly parted lips and his tongue as it flicked out to lick at his bottom lip. Ryan bit his own tongue to stifle a groan. Fuck, this was gonna be harder than he thought.

Ryan couldn't think of a goddamn thing to say to Lucas's compliment, so he chose the awkwardness of silence instead. Lucas was still looking at him—staring—essentially, and Ryan knew his cheeks would be flushing a brilliant pink. "Umm...ah...Lon's not quite ready yet?" Oh, god. Weak.

"No, something's up with the lighting. Should be no more than five more minutes. So...um would you rather be a Jedi or a Sith?"

"Come on, Luke. At least make them challenging. I'd rather be Han-fucking-Solo." Ryan grinned. Thank Christ for the would-you-rather game; it'd saved their tongue-tied asses more than once. He used it when he was feeling particularly nervous around Lucas. "You?"

"I'm gonna roll with a Sith because they've got the red lightsabers, and everyone knows red things are faster and infinitely more badass than green or blue." Lucas smirked.

"Oh, I dunno, green is pretty epic." Lucas's eyes were a dynamic green that, when the lighting hit them just right, reminded him of fucking lightsabers, and if that didn't just make his geeky little heart throb. "Okay. Would you rather have the Imperial March play every time you entered a room or be able to talk like Vader at will?"

"Imperial March. I mean, what a fucking entrance. You don't need the Vader voice when you've already established you're a badass with your entrance." Lucas smirked one of his evil smiles. "You?"

"Same. God, you'd feel ten-fucking-feet tall walking into a room with that music playing."

"Okay, we're good. Marks." Lon's deep voice echoed in the relative compactness of the area where they were filming.

Ryan moved to his mark, trying not to ogle Lucas, as he took on Dominic's saunter and moved across the room. The man made it damn hard not to, though.

"Action."

Ryan pushed off from the wall he was leaning against and stalked toward Lucas. Once he reached his on-screen lover, he wrapped his hands behind Lucas's neck as he sucked Lucas's lower lip into his mouth, using his bigger body to force him backward until Lucas's back hit the wall. It was Dominic who typically instigated any physical interactions between the characters, but apparently Ryan's less experienced Sam was sick of waiting. Today he'd be doing his best to seduce Lucas/Dom. No! Fuck, he had to keep Lucas separate. This was all fiction; there was no seducing Lucas.

"What was that for?" Lucas panted once Ryan pulled back and released him, stumbling a little against the wall, as though he'd been thoroughly debauched from the kiss and his legs couldn't quite hold him up.

"That was just because I wanted to, Dom. I've missed you and you're back and I get to touch you again." He leaned in for another kiss, less demanding and sweeter this time.

This time it was Lucas who pulled away and stepped around Ryan. "Sam, we have to... We need to stop—"

"Why?" he demanded.

"Because if we don't stop now, I may not be able to, and I don't want to rush this...not with you." Lucas had caught him in the tractor beam of his gaze again, and unscripted or not, Ryan leaned forward, wanting to be closer and closer to Lucas. He dipped his head and took another kiss.

When he pulled back this time, he cupped Lucas's cheeks, again forcing him to hold his gaze. "Dom, I want you. I want this...please." Ryan heard Lucas let out a groan before closing the distance to reach Ryan's mouth. Lucas took control of this kiss, spinning Ryan so that his back was now pressed against the wall and all Ryan could do was hold on.

"Tilt a little to your right, Lucas... Good. Ryan, bring your hands up into Lucas's hair. Fist it a little... Perfect..."

Fuck, Lon's voice was ruining it. No, wait. There was nothing to ruin; this wasn't real. Lucas wasn't kissing the shit out of him. This was Sam and Dominic. Nothing more.

"Okay, now Lucas, work on his shirt. Remember, you're desperate for each other. The shirt's an obstacle to getting what you want."

Ryan was losing it. His mind was spinning out of control as he fought to concentrate on Lon's words, on what he should be doing. Lucas had pulled back from the kiss and had him pinned to the fucking wall with his gaze alone. Then Lucas was pulling and tugging at his shirt until the buttons gave and his shirt flew open. Lucas's hands went immediately to his bare skin, his touch hot enough to burn.

Ryan once again was on fire in a room full of people as Lucas touched and nipped and kissed his way down the column of his throat and over his chest. Ryan's head dropped back and thumped on the wall behind him. Lon was still babbling...something, but Ryan was lost. He vaguely recalled having to get to the bed, but he couldn't remember how he was supposed to be doing it. Lucas's body and scent were the only things keeping him grounded, which was weird, because they were also the things that were making him fly.

Lucas's lips were on his neck again, just below his ear, and then he heard Lucas whisper, "Any time now, Ry. Throw me on the fucking bed." Lucas's breathy words shot tingles through his skin and right to his dick.

Damn, he'd missed his cue. They should be on the bed by now, but he'd been too caught up, so Lucas had needed to remind him. Fuck.

Ryan fisted his hands in the shirt Lucas still wore and then stalked forward, pushing Lucas back with his bigger body until Lucas's legs hit the bed. Ryan adjusted his grip on Lucas's shirt and pulled upward, lifting it over his head. *That* hadn't been in the script, but he figured it was only fair for Lucas to lose his shirt, too, and he wanted skin on skin. Besides, Lon hadn't called a halt to...anything, yet. In fact, the room around him seemed eerily quiet.

Once Lucas stood before him, torso as bare as his own, Ryan gave him a none-too-gentle shove and Lucas fell back onto the silk sheets, bouncing a little as he landed. Ryan wasted no time covering that perfect fucking body with his own and taking those fucking flawless lips again in a kiss that quickly spiraled out of control. Lucas's hands were on his back and in his hair, trying to pull him closer, though he couldn't have gotten any closer without actually being inside of Lucas and... Oh fuck, that thought tore a moan from him that should have embarrassed him, but he frankly couldn't care. He was hard as fucking steel and knew Lucas would be able to feel it pressing into his thigh, but he could feel Lucas, too, and he had his own erection to contend with.

"Cut." It wasn't Lon's usual bellow, but it was enough to knock some sense of reality back into Ryan and he pulled away from Lucas, rolling to his side. He lay beside Lucas for a moment trying to gather his composure and will his cock under control. He shut his eyes, and now that the torrent of lust was easing, the shame was starting to creep in. He could hear Lucas breathing heavily beside him, but no one else in the room had made a sound.

Once he'd calmed, Ryan stood and turned to find himself face-to-face with his shocked-looking crew. Did he say something? Did he run screaming in embarrassment from the room? Lon's eyes were darting between him and Lucas, who was still lying on the bed, one arm thrown over his eyes. He'd pulled the cover over his lower body to try to conceal his still noticeable erection. Shit. Was he angry? Upset? Had Ryan crossed a line?

"Ah...um, good job. I think we... Why don't we take ten and we can come back and finish the last bits of the scene? I'm just gonna... I think I need to check what we got on film. Just to... Okay, break." Lon sounded confused, a little dazed.

Ryan didn't wait around once Lon had spoken. With a last glance at Lucas, who remained on the bed, he fled the room, his thoughts pinballing through his head. The only clear belief he had—and it was flashing at him like it was in neon lights—was that somehow, some time over the last few months, he'd started falling for Lucas Evers more than a simple crush, and everything was monumentally fucked up because of it.

Chapter Ten

Wtf? Is Samdom *sinking?*

LUCAS

"You okay, Luke?" Anna's voice broke into his thoughts, a welcome respite from the constant loop of worry and what-ifs.

There was really no other way to describe it: Lucas's life was fucked. He was fucked. Everything was fucked. The scene last week with Ryan had... It had screwed him the fuck up. Ryan had been aggressive and sensual and so fucking hot. The sensation of Ryan's body against his, the way he moved, the little sounds he made... Jesus, he'd nearly had Lucas coming in his pants like a teenager—in a room full of people.

The hell of it was they'd both been hard, which meant Ryan had reacted to the whole thing too. Lucas tried desperately not to read too much into it. There'd been friction and men got hard from that. Maybe Ryan had been imagining some woman to get him in the right frame of mind, although Lucas could have sworn when they'd been looking into each other's eyes Ryan had only seen him.

"Yeah...no. Not really. We're shooting the big 'I love you' scene today, and I'm nervous as fuck." Lucas had told Anna all about what'd happened last week and she'd thought it was awesome. She'd seen it as another sign that maybe something more than friendship could develop between him and Ryan. In her quiet yet resolute way, she'd tried to convince him to talk to Ryan about it, but he couldn't risk it. What the hell was he supposed to say?

"What have you got to be nervous about? You're an excellent actor, Luke, and you've done these scenes before... Is it because it's Ryan?"

Of course, it was Ryan. How could he not be nervous about saying words to Ryan that skirted close to the edge of truth? He wasn't in love with Ryan, not yet, but god, he was close. He'd been falling hard for a while. "It's Ryan. I don't know how I'm gonna do the scene with him, Anna. Just thinking about what happened last week gets me all messed up. I need to keep my distance."

Lucas had started pulling away from Ryan. He hadn't invited Ryan to come over on the weekend and he'd started sitting away from him if they had a break together, which they often did. On set, he'd also consciously started trying to rein in the touches that had come so intuitively before. It was exhausting to actively battle to control his body every second he was around a certain person.

"You need to talk to him, Lucas. Come on. I've never seen you like this before. Something's happening here between the two of you, and it could be good—so good if you would only give it a shot."

"He's straight, Anna."

"How do you know? You can't just assume somebody's sexuality, Luke. Has he been with anyone you're aware of since you've known him? Other than that starlet, of course, and he was drunk that night. Have you asked? I watched that episode, Lucas, and I thought the TV was going to burst into flames, and it wasn't just you. My god, the way he looked at you... I'd kill for someone to look at me like that. If the expression eye-fucking wasn't already in use, it would have been coined after that scene."

"It could have just been acting," he tried.

"Well, if that was acting, then that man is going to win a fucking Oscar every year for the rest of his acting life. Why can't you just talk to him? What are you afraid of?"

Wasn't that the big question? What was he afraid of? "I'm scared of losing him, losing his friendship. Maybe that's all I can have with him, and I'd rather that than nothing."

Anna smiled sadly and reached up to put her hand on his cheek. "Aren't you losing him already by pulling away?" Dammit, he hated that smart people were always making him think. Anna was right and he would lose Ryan if he kept pulling away, but he just didn't know the right thing to do.

"Shit, I'm gonna be late. I'll see you tonight, babe." Lucas fled out the door, even though he had plenty of time before his car arrived. He'd simply needed an out, an escape from talking about the mess he'd landed in.

As the car pulled up, his phone trilled and he glanced at the screen to see it was his father. He'd been expecting and dreading this call. He'd left a message last night asking his dad to call him back to discuss finances. After looking things over, he'd decided Anna was right, his family was taking advantage. He didn't mind helping them out at all, but his siblings, in particular, were too young to sit back and retire.

"Hey, Dad."

"Hey, Luke. What's up? You needed to talk?"

"Yeah, look. I'd rather do this in person, but I can't get down to LA right now. I'm concerned over what's going on in the family with money." He took a deep breath, gathering his courage to continue. "I think that if I keep handing out money, there's no real incentive for Matt, Craig, and Kayla to try even harder to get work. So, I um... I'd like to sit down and discuss a budget."

There was no immediate response from his father, and the silence had his nerves on edge. "So you're not going to be helping us anymore?"

What? "What? No. I'm not cutting anyone off, just cutting back. I want them to find their own success. Obviously, I'd help out if anything major happened, but to be fair, Dad, you all individually spend more than I do."

"I'm sorry. I didn't realize." Lucas could hear the wobble in his father's voice. This hadn't gone as he'd hoped. "I'll tell the family."

His father hung up before he could formulate a response, and he didn't answer when Lucas called back repeatedly. Fuck. He didn't think he'd been unreasonable at all. Maybe he'd give his dad time to cool down so he'd see the fairness in what Lucas had said.

It could also be he'd embarrassed his father. The man had a lot of pride and they'd never been a family to talk about things like money. Lucas had just done what he did for his family without discussion. Perhaps his father had been humiliated because his son had been taking care of everyone in the family. Dammit. He was messing up all over the place.

By the time Ryan joined him in the back seat of the car, Lucas was confident he'd gotten himself back to normal, or normal-ish. He would do this scene; he'd stay friendly but distant with Ryan; he'd put the altercation with his father out of his mind, and everything was gonna be okay.

The heat from Ryan's body and his familiar scent assaulted his senses and challenged the tight rein he had on himself as soon as he'd settled in beside him. He'd have liked nothing more than to pull Ryan to him and spend the entire car ride kissing and petting. Oh, this was so not going well.

"What're you up to this weekend?" Ryan asked.

"Not much. Actually, Anna and I might go away...somewhere."

"Oh." Lucas could hear the disappointment in Ryan's tone, as yet another weekend came around without his usual invitation for Ryan to spend it with him. It fucking sucked knowing he was upsetting Ryan, and he knew his pulling away from their friendship was hurting the man.

They exchanged pleasantries for the ride, but Lucas felt the loss of closeness in their friendship like a rip tearing at his very soul. They walked together to makeup and wardrobe with minimal words spoken between them, only the occasional suggestions regarding the shoot today. Ryan seemed every bit as nervous as Lucas felt.

Lon was waiting for them by the time they got to the set. Yesterday they'd finished shooting a large-scale battle sequence that had required the entire cast and crew to shoot at several outdoor locations over the past few days. Today's scene was set on the balcony of Dominic's high-rise apartment. Naturally, it was being shot on the ground in a sound studio with green screens for the nighttime cityscape that would be edited in later.

Lucas and Ryan moved to their marks. It was shortly after the battle that the Witch Hunters had come close to losing, and Sam and Dom had been separated during the fight, neither knowing if the other had survived until they'd found each other at the very end. They'd both been injured and Dom had brought Sam back to his place to help patch him up. Ryan had a few bandages and some blood smears strategically placed all over the top half of his body. The fear of nearly losing each other would prompt the declarations of love. Lucas knew this, understood the motivations, and knew how to play the scene. He could fucking do this.

"Action."

Ryan grabbed onto Lucas's upper arms, squeezing a little too tightly. "Dom, I thought... I thought I'd lost you. I couldn't find you, and I just... I was so frightened."

"Shh, it's all right. We're all right. I was scared, too, but we're okay, Sam. We're okay." Lucas let the words drift off as though Dom had finally convinced himself they really were okay. The words were coming and Lucas braced for the impact.

Ryan squeezed a little tighter and stepped in a little closer. When he spoke, his voice was soft, awed. "I... Dominic, I love you. I am so in love with you and I can't lose you."

The lines had been perfectly delivered, too perfectly, and Lucas felt them slam into him with the impact of a freight train. Fucking hell, he was in a whole new world of misery. He swallowed and gritted his teeth, preparing to reply. "I love you too."

"Cut... Lucas, come on. Dominic is telling the love of his fucking life that he loves him, too, not that he's got a fucking venereal disease. A little less distaste in your tone, please," Lon chastised.

Distaste? Shit, he hadn't been going for that at all. Lucas geared up to try again. He raised his gaze to Ryan's dark-brown eyes and repeated his line, hoping this time he'd nail it, and they could move on from this nightmare. "I love you too."

"Cut," Lon bellowed again. "Is epic, out-of-control, take-your-breath-away true love too boring for you, Lucas? Again."

Lucas had rarely been on the receiving end of Lon's criticism. Sure, he'd had to do several takes in the past, and Lon had offered some suggestions when he hadn't been one hundred percent happy with his performance, but he'd never had this before. He'd witnessed Lon's scathing reproaches directed at others and sympathized with them. Apparently, today he was the one who was drawing Lon's ample fire.

"Everything all right, Luke?" Ryan's tone was concerned as he turned his worried face toward Lucas.

"Yeah. Sorry. I just can't seem to get it." What else could he possibly say to Ryan? That the "I love you" line Ryan had spoken had clawed its way under his skin? That it had felt too real? That he desperately wanted it to be real? That it had screwed him up?

"You'll get it, Luke. Relax...it's just me." Ryan smiled. *Just him.* Yes...but that was the problem.

It was another seven takes before Lon finally called it. He told Lucas he was satisfied with the final take, but Lucas could tell from his flat tone he was less than impressed. This was a pivotal moment in the show, the scene the fans had been clamoring for, and Lucas had fucked it up. He couldn't bring himself to even glance Ryan's way. With any luck, Lon might let him have another shot at it if time allowed.

UNFORTUNATELY, LUCAS NEVER got the chance to have another go at it, and when the show aired only a few weeks later, it was the start of a panic among fans, many of whom feared *Samdom* was sinking to the bottom of the ocean. What's happening with *Samdom*? What went wrong? Are *Lovers* over? There were angry tweets and Facebook comments and even handwritten letters to the studio, all asking the same thing. Is the romance between Sam and Dominic finished? And didn't the studio know that *Samdom* was endgame?

Of course, those who'd read the books knew that Sam and Dom got their happily ever after, but Lucas couldn't blame them for wondering. He'd watched the "I love you" episode and had cringed at the bland look on his face and almost monotone delivery of his line when he'd told Sam that he loved him. And he'd had to look away when the most awkward kiss ever followed it up.

At the live stream after the episode, he'd been too ashamed to sit with Ryan, and for the first time ever had sat across the table from him, hardly daring to glance his way, let alone talk to him. Naturally the ever-vigilant fans had pounced upon that as further evidence of the "growing discord between the world's most-shipped couple." Why were they sitting apart? Why couldn't they look at each other? What was going on? Question after question bombarded the twitter feed.

Lucas loved the fans, knew that without them his career was dead in the water, but right now he wished they'd all disappear and take the enormous spotlight they had shining on him and Ryan with them. It was an ungrateful notion, but his head was too fucked-up to care right then.

Chapter Eleven

A stalker? Leave our Ryan alone.

RYAN

"Marks." Came the familiar call from Lon, and Ryan watched as the actors took their place on set. Eloise had returned from a touch-up and was now standing back-to-back with James. She had two knives in hand, while James held a sword aloft. "Action."

Ryan watched, transfixed, as the action swirled before him. Without background music, he could hear every grunt and slap of skin. As "fake" as it was, the entire sequence looked spectacular. Ryan's gaze returned time and again to Lucas, despite his efforts to ignore him. Lucas's actions were fast and agile; the intensity on his face was breathtaking. It became increasingly difficult for Ryan to drag his gaze away until he eventually threw in the towel and openly stared as Lucas dodged and deflected, and then attacked with grace and a litheness Ryan knew would look mesmerizing on-screen.

Things were different between him and Lucas and had been since the Teen Choice Awards and that bloody onstage kiss. He recalled returning Lucas's kiss with enthusiasm; in fact, if Lucas hadn't pulled away when he did, Ryan wasn't sure how things might have ended up.

He was petrified his feelings were seeping through his pores, visible for anybody to see. Shooting their love scene had been a humiliating mess, despite how well the scene had turned out. He'd tried to downplay his reactions during filming as enthusiastic and committed acting, but he wasn't entirely sure anyone had bought it. He couldn't pinpoint when the longing looks from Sam to Dominic had morphed into being from Ryan to Lucas.

They'd been back on set for weeks, and while Lon seemed happy with his work, his relationship with Lucas seemed off. The little extra touches Lucas had put into his performance last season and earlier this season had dried up. Lucas still picked him up every morning, but he hadn't invited him over for the weekend; of course, he'd also been busy with his upcoming movie release, but the closeness was gone and Ryan knew why—he'd freaked Lucas the fuck out.

They'd always shot plenty of scenes together, but only a handful of them as a couple since the out-of-control scene where Sam had seduced Dominic. The fans had been blown away when that episode aired. There had been a growing RPS, or real people ship, as Ryan had discovered, for him and Lucas, and Ryan felt awful about it, especially for Anna. Even though Lucas had insisted Anna understood and didn't mind, it must still suck to have so many people actively imagining your husband with another person.

Of course then had come the "I love you" scene and after that aired, fans started wondering what was wrong with *Samdom*. It was like being on a fucking seesaw, the highs and the lows, the love and the hate from the fandom. Lucas had been off that day and even Ryan had noticed the bland performance. He knew where to lay blame, though...directly at his own feet. For Ryan, the declaration of love had seemed almost real—natural—and he'd let his own growing emotions bleed into his performance. It could have been him and Lucas, not Sam and Dominic, and Ryan would have confessed his feelings with the same depth of emotion, the same fervent longing to be loved back. Clearly, that had thrown Lucas off. Ryan had stepped over the line, blurred make-believe and reality, and it had distressed Lucas.

There was a lot going on in the storyline and plenty of action scenes to shoot. It kept Ryan's mind off whatever was happening with him and Lucas. Except for times like now, when he was waiting around the set, unable to start shooting his scenes until Lon finished up with whatever scene he was currently directing.

Ryan was the only main cast member not shooting right now. He couldn't face quiet, alone time—too much rattling around in his head. Instead, he stood back a little from Lon and watched the fight scene.

The entire cast had learned FMA, which was basically a fighting style that incorporated swords, sticks, knives, and empty hands. Ryan preferred the knife fighting, and fortunately, that was the style his character Sam preferred. He was sitting out the fight today, but he came to watch, knowing it was essentially an all-in knife fight.

Ryan watched as Lon called cut and the step coordinators did some last minute tweaking between takes. He tried his best to put thoughts of Lucas out of his mind. Too bad the man himself was ten feet away in his black fighting leathers, looking hotter than sin and slowly working through his moves with their costar Sean as the step coordinator watched on. Sean and Lucas were equally matched heightwise, but Sean had far more muscle bulk than Lucas. Lucas had speed, though; at least his character, Dom, did. At the start of the sequence, Sean would have a blade and Lucas would not; he'd be fending off Sean's attacks with the knife by pushing his forearms to Sean's to block him. It wasn't dangerous in that Lucas could get cut, but they went at it hard to make it as realistic as possible, and Lucas and Sean would both likely have bruises by the end of the day.

During practice, the cast unhurriedly progressed through their movements, but with each run-through, they sped up. When the cameras rolled, they would work fast, and hopefully, the learned movements would innately flow through their bodies, giving the scene authenticity.

Lucas looked good. Better than good. His leathers were tight and accentuated his long, toned legs and tight ass. The material stretched and gave as Lucas shifted, and the lighting added tone and definition with each agile movement. Lucas wore a loose tunic top, in keeping with his character's flashier dress style. It didn't highlight Lucas's broad back, taut abs, or well-defined arms, but every now and then it would flare up at the hem with Lucas's movements, and Ryan would catch a glimpse of smooth, dark skin. Ryan had seen Lucas shirtless plenty of times, and whatever view the tunic covered up, his imagination supplied.

Fuck. He had to stop lusting after his very married, very straight best friend. Ryan never labeled himself and had never thought of himself as gay, straight, or anything else. He allowed himself to experience everything he felt, and if that included attraction to a man, then so be it. He'd only ever slept with women, but the ferocity of the desire he felt for Lucas wouldn't allow him to slam the door on that option.

Jesus, how had his life gotten so messy? The only positive for him at the moment was that he'd received no letters from his weird scary fan in weeks.

Lon called action again, and before the fight had reached its conclusion, Ryan's phone was vibrating in his pocket. Months of working with Lon had taught him the value of having his phone on silent while on set; an untimely phone call wasn't worth risking Lon's wrath. Unwillingly, Ryan turned and strode from the set to ensure his call wouldn't disturb them.

Once he found a secluded spot his swiped his finger to answer the call. "Ryan Lowe."

"Mr. Lowe. It's Jared Farmer, head of security. We have a Leighton White at the front gates. She is insisting that she's your girlfriend and wants to be let onto the lot. You haven't given us her name to authorize entrance, but given the veracity of her claim, and her unwillingness to move along I thought it best to confirm with you."

There was silence over the line as Ryan tried to parse what Jared was saying. He didn't know any Leighton White or any variation of either of those names, and he certainly didn't have a girlfriend. It was probably only a fan trying to get in. Did he go up there and meet her, sign an autograph, take a photo with her so she would leave satisfied, or did he stay the hell away?

"Mr. Lowe. You there?"

"Oh, ah sorry. No...um, no, Jared, I don't have a girlfriend, and I don't know anybody by that name. Should I come up there?"

"No. You stay where you are. We'll take care of this. Sorry to bother you."

Jared had hung up before Ryan could even reply. He guessed this was probably a fairly regular thing for security to deal with. People were oddly fascinated with celebrities and he was sure more than a few had tried to sneak into the studio in the past.

Ryan put his phone back into his pocket and returned to the set. From the looks of things, they'd started yet another take. Ryan took his spot near Lon and settled back to watch.

It took another hour before Lon finally called it, and by then, the incident with the fan had completely slipped from Ryan's mind. He'd once again fallen into Lucas's orbit, the pull of it so intense Ryan struggled to break out, the world outside forgotten.

As the crew began dismantling unnecessary set pieces or repairing anything dislodged during the filming, many of the cast spoke casually with each other. Comments about the shoot were exchanged along with a lot of backslapping for the success of the scene. Ryan joined them and offered his congratulations to all for a job well done. He was talking to Sean about the knives when an unfamiliar voice called his name.

Ryan turned to see Lon standing with a man he recognized as one of the security team on the lot. They had twin looks of concern on their faces as they waved him over. As he headed toward them, Ryan felt a presence come into step beside him and knew without looking that Lucas had joined him. He could smell the citrus fragrance that always seemed to cling to Lucas, mingled with sweat and heat from his well-exercised body. It was intoxicating and Ryan fought to resist the urge to lean closer and breathe him in deeply.

"Everything okay?" Lucas whispered.

"No idea. Hope so," Ryan quietly replied.

"Mr. Lowe. I'm Jared Farmer. We spoke earlier." Jared was a bear of a man. Tall, broad, long hair pulled back in a hair tie and a full but neatly trimmed beard. He was imposing and Ryan couldn't help thinking he'd definitely chosen the right profession. Ryan would be amazed if anybody was willing to take Jared Farmer on.

"Of course. It's good to meet you in person. Everything okay?" he asked, mirroring Lucas's words of just moments ago.

"I'm afraid not. We had some trouble with the woman who was here earlier, claiming to be your girlfriend. I wondered if you'd mind coming through to my office and have a look at some footage, see if you recognize her?"

"Sure, yes. What kind of trouble?" Ryan felt cold. He knew celebrities often attracted stalkers, and he also knew some had paid for their fame with their lives. Hopefully whatever this was wouldn't escalate to those extremes.

He could feel Lucas beside him shifting uncomfortably, and he spoke before Jared had the chance to answer. "What do you mean? What happened earlier?"

It was Lon who answered Lucas, obviously having been briefed on the situation, and Ryan was glad for the chance to collect himself while the others spoke. "It seems a lady turned up earlier claiming she was Ryan's girlfriend. Jared called Ryan, but he didn't recognize the name and has no girlfriend. Jared asked her to move on. Let's just say she didn't go quietly."

Ryan looked to Jared whose focus was on him. He continued on for Lon, "She hurled abuse at me, which frankly, eh, I've had better. I've been called every name you can think of and then some. She eventually walked away and I thought that was that, but she came back moments later in her car and repeatedly rammed another car that was waiting at the gates to be allowed in. No one was hurt, thankfully. She reversed and drove off, but we got her plates and the police have been called."

The cold that had seeped into Ryan's body dropped by degrees and his limbs were actually shaking. He had no idea what to do or how to handle this. A warm hand fell to his shoulder and squeezed, and Ryan could have cried with the comfort it provided. Lucas.

"Hey. It's all right, Ryan. Let's go and have a look; see if you can identify the woman and then the police will handle it. You're safe here." Lucas's voice dripped with reassurance. Ryan straightened and nodded and then turned to follow Jared to his office. He'd never been to the head of security's office before, had never had the need.

The studio lot was huge, so they drove in a couple of the golf carts, getting them there in only five minutes. It was a large well-appointed room, befitting the person responsible for the safety of so many. Jared ushered Ryan behind his desk, where he could see a large computer monitor with a frozen image taking up the entire screen. Lucas stood at his side, and he could also sense Lon's presence behind him.

"Okay. I'm not going to show you the entire exchange, but I'll run a few minutes from the start of our interaction with this lady. Listen to her voice; look closely at her face and body. She may have changed her appearance—you'd be surprised how a simple haircut and change of hair color can disguise someone." Jared advised.

Ryan hunched a little to get closer to the screen as the recording began. Leighton White, or whoever she was, was an average-size woman, light-brown hair, pale skin, maybe in her midtwenties. There was absolutely nothing memorable about her, aside from her eyes. They were a dark brown, almost black, and looked...crazed. There was something off about them, or her, and Ryan could see it clearly in her eyes. Even more terrifying, though, the eyes seemed vaguely familiar.

After a few minutes, Jared halted the recording. "Anything?"

Ryan thought for a moment. He didn't *know* her, but bizarrely, he felt as though he did recognize her. He certainly couldn't place her or offer her name, but there was a niggle in his mind that he'd met this woman. "I don't know her, but she seems familiar, like I might have met her somewhere, but I can't remember."

Jared turned to Lucas. "What about you? Or you, Lon? Either of you recognize her?"

"No. I've never seen her before. I don't think so anyway," Lucas replied.

"Nope, never. I don't know her." Lon answered adamantly. "What happens now?"

"Well, like I said, the police have been called and we'll hand over what we have to them. Her image and name will be circulated to ensure she doesn't get through the gates here. Mr. Lowe, do you live in a secure building?"

Ryan nodded numbly, disbelieving of the situation he found himself in.

"Good. I'll print out an image to give security there. Take extra precautions: try not to be alone anywhere, be aware of your surroundings, and if you do come across her, don't engage with her." A ringing phone interrupted Jared, and he held a finger up and stepped away to answer the call.

Jesus, how had this happened? Ryan could feel the shaking return, so he moved to one of the seats in the office. Lucas followed and rested a reassuring hand on his shoulder.

"Mr. Lowe, I made some calls after the encounter and that was Clare from the office getting back to me. As you may know, any mail goes through her and the studio also monitors any electronic mail that comes in. Unfortunately, it seems Leighton White has attempted some previous correspondence with you. Now, it's not threatening as such, but Clare found it sufficiently disturbing not to pass on to you and has kept a record of it all. This isn't the first time we've had to deal with inappropriate fans. In most cases like this, the person simply moves on. Unfortunately, there are the exceptions. If this is a stalker, we want to get on top of it immediately. These types of people may never physically hurt you, but they still can ruin your life anyway by aggressively insinuating themselves into it. I'm sorry; I know this is difficult..."

"Not your fault." Ryan managed to squeak out. "Thank you."

"Sure. Has anything unusual or out of the ordinary happened lately? Phone calls, maybe? Anyone harassing you?"

"You had those letters a while back. The ones that mentioned your scar." Lucas jumped in before he could answer.

"Letters?" Jared asked.

"They weren't threatening, but they creeped me out a little because they mentioned a scar that's not easily visible. I've also had some hang-up calls, but I wasn't worried about them" Ryan explained.

"Okay, look, I'm going to step out to meet the police at the gates. Stay here, take a moment, and I'll bring them here to talk to you as well."

Ryan tried to respond, even if just with a nod in Jared's direction, but he found himself virtually paralyzed. Was this a different person to his letter writer? Should he have told Jared about those almost intimate letters? Oh, how he wanted his anonymity back. He heard footsteps and voices and then the door shut and he was alone with Lucas.

Lucas squatted in front of him and placed his hands on Ryan's knees. "Hey. You okay?"

"No. Shit, Lucas, what do I do?"

"Whatever the police and Jared tell you. Look, Ryan, it's likely nothing. I mean we've all had fans go a bit crazy from time to time; hopefully this will blow over quickly." Lucas was rubbing his hands along Ryan's thighs now, soothing him. "But, it might not, so you need to prepare yourself for that eventuality as well. Maybe look at private security. I know the studio will provide some for you. I mean, come on, you're their second biggest star." Lucas winked.

Ryan couldn't have been more grateful for Lucas's attempt to lighten the mood. "Second biggest? Oh I suppose you, Mr. Oscar-buzz-movie, are their biggest star?"

"But, of course." Lucas's expression was all pretend arrogance; Ryan knew he had no genuine conceit.

"Biggest ego, I think you mean," Ryan mocked, and suddenly he could manage a grin to replace the frown.

One of Lucas's hands moved to curl around the back of his neck and he pulled Ryan forward so their foreheads were touching. It was a move Lucas had done so many times in character but this time was real. "Nothing's going to happen to you, Ryan. I won't let it."

In the silence that followed Lucas's promise, all Ryan could hear was the thudding of his heartbeat.

Chapter Twelve

Ryan Lowe taken? Is our Sam off the market?

LUCAS

It had been two weeks since the incident with Ryan's crazed fan and so far there'd been no further physical encounters. Lucas knew dozens more letters from Leighton White had been sent to the studio, but they seemed to have mostly been creepy professions of love—no overt threats. The hang-up calls had continued, although they were sporadic. The studio had come to the party by providing extra security, but even though Ryan himself had claimed it was unnecessary, it wasn't enough to ease Lucas's worry. Lucas still picked up Ryan every morning, but now he hung around the lot, even if he'd finished for the day, waiting for Ryan so he could travel home with him. The only times that didn't work out were when Ryan finished his schedule before him. On those days, he tried to invent ways for Ryan to have to stay until he was ready, but it didn't always work.

A couple of times he'd had to halt the shoot so he could call Ryan at the time he estimated he should be getting home, just to be sure. He couldn't concentrate on a fucking thing until he knew Ryan was home safely. He didn't think Ryan had twigged yet, but it wouldn't take long for him to see through to Lucas's overprotective ways.

The police had found Ms. White's car but not the woman herself. As far as they'd been able to ascertain, Leighton White had a clean history. No arrests, no evidence of prior stalking, no mental health concerns recorded—nothing. For all intents and purposes, she was a normal twenty-six-year-old nail technician who hadn't shown up to her job or dwelling since the day she'd come to the lot. She was from Los Angeles and it looked as though she'd traveled to San Francisco the day before her appearance at the lot. The police had found a few friends and even less family, but none had anything negative to tell police about her, though they were getting concerned as they hadn't seen or heard from her either.

It was a Sunday, a no-work day, and Lucas had invited Ryan over. Much to Anna's amusement, Lucas had even canceled a few upcoming weekend trips to promote his movie so he could be in town to spend time with Ryan. He needed to be here, needed to have Ryan close. They were heading over to Paris in a few weeks to shoot some scenes on location and Lucas couldn't wait. Maybe he could breathe easier when thousands of miles separated Ryan from his stalker.

Ryan would be here in half an hour, so Lucas was reading through next week's script while he waited. When Anna's shouts echoed through the living room, Lucas dashed into the media room where he knew he'd find her.

When he entered, Anna turned her pale face and wide eyes to Lucas. "Oh my god, Luke, I think he's in big trouble." Her tone was flat, wary.

Lucas turned to the screen and found himself gazing into the eyes of Leighton White. Anna had frozen the image, but he could read the ticker at the bottom. "Ryan Lowe's girlfriend speaks out."

"What the fuck is this?" he roared. "Shit, sorry." He apologized immediately. He wasn't angry with Anna. He was just...alarmed.

"It's okay. Come and sit down. I'll show you the whole thing." Anna wiggled a little, edging herself farther over on the sofa to make room for Lucas. He sat, eager to find out what on earth was going on.

The entire interview lasted for approximately twelve minutes. It was twelve minutes of lies and bullshit and terrifying delusions. With a beaming smile on her heavily made-up face, Leighton White spoke of her whirlwind romance with currently one of the world's most popular stars, Ryan Lowe. She spoke of meeting him in a bar, how they had gotten to know each other, and how their love bloomed. She also droned on about her hopes for the future with Ryan, including marriage and children.

What frightened Lucas the most was the intricacy of her delusions and her unwavering belief in them. It wasn't just a lie that had popped into her head; she'd constructed a thorough, almost believable life with Ryan. And somehow, her delusions had been accepted by this program, which was kind of like a knockoff *Entertainment Tonight* but with no authenticity or apparent willingness to verify facts. By the time the interview had finished, Lucas was sitting in stunned silence, unable to parse what he'd just listened to.

"What do we do, Anna? I don't know...how do I help him?" He turned to his wife, knowing she knew how he felt about Ryan, how much he cared.

"I don't know, Lucas, but we'll figure it out. Surely the studio will know what to do, how to react. The publicists, higher-ups. Can't be the first time some psycho has been sprouting shit about one of their stars." Anna dropped her hand to Lucas's thigh and rubbed, reminding him of his similarly consoling gesture he'd used on Ryan only weeks ago.

The buzzer of their intercom blared through the room, making them both jump. It had to be Ryan. Did he just tell him? Show him? How could he keep him safe? They both stood, and Lucas walked to the intercom to buzz Ryan up.

"How about I go and get some beers for us? I'm thinking we may need them."

"Thanks, Anna." Lucas pulled her to him and wrapped his arms around her before dropping a kiss to the top of her head. "I'm glad you're here."

"I'll do whatever I can to help, Lucas. You know that. You need to think about...you need to think about your feelings for him and how you want things to go. We promised each other when we first decided to marry that if one of us fell in love—"

"I'm not—"

"Luke, it's me." She pulled back and gave him her brilliant, cocky smile. "Just think about things, okay?"

In love. In love with Ryan. Was he? He knew he was deeply in lust with him, and where there was desire, he suspected it was like a flashpoint waiting for a spark that would set it alight, transforming it into something more. Into love. But had he gotten there yet? Having no experience with this kind of love, he wasn't sure. Did it even matter? As far as he knew, Ryan was straight and while, yes, he had physically reacted to Lucas during several of their scenes and that goddamn kiss at the Teen Choice Awards, that didn't necessarily mean anything. A brisk wind could make some men's cocks harden; maybe Ryan was just...easily aroused.

"Lucas..."

"Huh." He turned to find Ryan standing close, a concerned look on his face.

"You okay? I called your name, like three times." A little half-smile graced Ryan's perfect lips, but a full twinkle gleamed in his eyes and Lucas knew. He knew he was in love with Ryan Lowe, sickeningly and irrevocably in love. Fuck his life.

"Sorry, man. Come in. Want a beer? Anna's just gone to get some. I'll go help. Your usual? You look good…I mean, ya know, you're looking well. How've you been? Probably not much changed since I saw you on Friday. I'll just go help Anna. Take a seat. Be right back." Lucas went to brush past Ryan after that humiliating verbal hemorrhage, but Ryan reached out and grabbed his arm, twisting him a little so they were eye to eye.

"Lucas, what the hell's going on? You okay? You don't seem… You seem off."

At least showing Ryan the clip of Leighton would buy him time to sort through his fucking feelings and decide how he was going to handle this clusterfuck.

"Ryan. Something's happened. Take a seat." Ryan followed him and they both sat on the sofa. Anna walked in with their beers, and after a brief greeting to Ryan, she took the footstool and dragged it closer, sitting on it just near Ryan's legs.

"Okay. You two are freaking me out. What's happened? Please, tell me."

"Ryan. I'm so sorry, but that woman, Leighton White, she's been on *Early Entertainment*, telling the story of how you two met and fell in love."

"What?" Ryan bellowed as he stood. "I don't know her. She's not my girlfriend. Fuck."

"We know, Ryan. She's clearly got an agenda. I've got the footage if you wanna—"

"Yes. Show it to me." Ryan collapsed back down and Lucas played the interview for him.

Lucas endured every hateful second of the twelve minutes it took for them to watch the disturbed woman fantasize about her life with Ryan and was thrilled to be able to hit stop once the horror story was done. He immediately turned to Ryan, ready to offer…anything. Anything Ryan needed. He found Ryan sweating beside him, a slight green tinge to his pasty pallor.

Ryan glanced at him briefly and then hung his head, resting it on his palms. He was rocking slightly, and Lucas thought he could hear puffy little breaths of "Oh fuck" being repeated constantly. "Ryan?"

"I know her. I know her. Oh fuck. What have I done?" Enormous, scared brown eyes peered up at Lucas, who had gone still and silent at Ryan's words. "I know her, Lucas. Oh Jesus, oh fuck. She was the girl. She was…oh fuck."

Lucas snapped out of his shock and reached for Ryan, wanting to comfort him. "How do you know her? What girl?"

Ryan stood and paced a little while constantly streaking his fingers through his hair so violently that, for a moment, Lucas worried he might rip it right out of his scalp. "That night at the bar back in LA. The night when you left me... I mean after we finished shooting season one and you were going to make *Over the Oceans*. I went to that bar and...fuck, I...we...I slept with her. I was drunk and she was the girl. I swear it's her. Jesus. She's gonna go all bunny boiler on me, isn't she?"

Ryan's eyes were pleading with him as he looked at Lucas. Was this woman going to go all Alex Forrest on Ryan? Seemed like it. Should he admit that to Ryan? Probably. Did he want to add another log onto the fire of fear currently burning its way through Ryan? Fuck no. He wanted to grab him and hold him and run off somewhere safe with him.

That night when you left me—was that how Ryan thought of it?

Lucas moved toward Ryan, and without any real thought, pulled him in close, wrapping his arms around him and probably holding him too tightly. He felt Ryan's head turn and rest on his shoulder, and he could feel little puffs of his breath on his neck.

Neither seemed inclined to let go, but Lucas knew the embrace could turn awkward very quickly, so he reluctantly pulled away from Ryan and guided him back over to the seat. Anna was still sitting on the footstool and she immediately took hold of Ryan's hand when he sat.

"I'm so sorry, Ryan, but even if you did sleep with her, she shouldn't be doing this crap."

"Thanks, Anna. I feel awful and I just...I don't know what to do." Ryan shook his head; disbelief, fear, and sadness were evident in his expression. Lucas suspected he felt every bit as bad for having a one-night stand with the woman as he did for the predicament he now found himself in.

"We're gonna give Mike a call. The studio will know how to deal with this. Whether to comment on it, and how, and what to do regarding security. They'll have procedures, Ryan, and we'll help you. Maybe you should stay here tonight. I can take you home to pack a few things..."

Ryan fidgeted, his gaze darting around the room as he seemed to be thinking about Lucas's suggestion. "No. I think...maybe I should go. I can't start changing things, living out of fear. Thank you for the offer, but I think..." Ryan stood and Lucas knew he was getting ready to leave right that second and he couldn't bear that.

"Stay for lunch, at least. That was the plan anyway." He desperately tried. He wasn't ready to have Ryan out of his sight, wasn't ready for the fear of not being able to see Ryan, not knowing he was okay, to start soaking into his bones.

"Yeah. Of course. Sorry, that was the plan. My head's a little...shaky."

"Sit down, Ryan," Lucas couldn't help the dominant tone creeping into his voice. "Drink your beer. I'm going to give Mike a call." Lucas left Ryan sitting with Anna and went to his room for some privacy while he made the call.

Mike answered on the second ring. "I was expecting this call, Lucas. Is Ryan with you?"

"Yeah. What the fuck, Mike? Did they even try to check their facts before airing? Did they pay that woman to spew her lies?"

"Look, Lucas, I've already got legal on it. We'll get a statement together for Ryan. This won't necessarily hurt his public persona—"

"I don't give a fuck about his public persona. Is he safe? That's all that matters."

"I know and you're right. I'll be honest—we are concerned about the potential for physical harm to Ryan. How's he holding up?"

How was Ryan holding up? He was shaky, upset—understandably so. This was his first encounter with one of the less appealing consequences of fame. "He's nervous. He slept with her, Mike. She was a one-night stand after he'd been drinking. He's just put it together now. He doesn't really have any experience with this kind of thing. Up until now, it's all been positive for him. I think he'll be okay, though."

"Right. Okay. Look, I'm gonna organize a meeting for first thing tomorrow with...everyone, actually. We'll get a plan together; get the experts in to talk to him about what he can be doing."

"It's fucked-up, Mike. Why does he have to do anything? She's got no right—"

"Calm down, Lucas. You know many stalkers are suffering from some form of mental illness. It's likely she has no real understanding of the impact she's having on Ryan. It's either that or she's after a big payday. We'll do what we can from our side of things, okay?"

Lucas gritted his teeth. He knew Mike was right, but it still rankled. Ryan didn't deserve this. "Yeah, okay. It's frustrating, you know. I wanna help, but I don't know what to do."

"That's what we'll sort out tomorrow. Now, go and enjoy the rest of your day off. I'll text meeting details once it's sorted."

Lucas finished his call with Mike, knowing there would be a flurry of behind-the-scenes activities going on to try to sort out this mess. He returned to where Anna and Ryan were waiting for him. "Mike's got it covered. He's gonna rally the troops and we'll have a meeting tomorrow. For the rest of the day, though, let's not think about it. How about some trash movies? What are you two up for?" Lucas tried a smile—it likely appeared more as a frightening grimace, but he was doing what he could to help ease Ryan through this.

"Well, I don't know about you guys, but I always find a *Jaws* marathon therapeutic. I know I know...the original is a classic, but they go downhill from there. I mean *Jaws: the Revenge*...come on." Anna was already up, no doubt preparing to organize one of her fabulous movie marathon feasts, and Lucas loved her just a little bit more for being so good for Ryan right now.

"I'm ashamed to admit I've never gotten past *Jaws 2*, so I'm in. Lucas?"

"Oh I'm in, all right. It's winter so I won't need to go in the ocean for a while anyway. Anna and I'll get the food organized. Ry, you get the room ready—we need blankets, pillows, and pajamas. You can borrow some of mine." Lucas was thrilled to see a genuine smile gracing Ryan's handsome face. He'd do anything to keep it there.

Chapter Thirteen

Is Leighton real? Are they together?
Is she really good enough for our Ryan?

RYAN

"Stay, Ry. Come on, we'll have another sleepover. You've already got pajamas on," Lucas begged.

Ryan was scared shitless of the person who was officially stalking him, and if things had been different, he would have loved to stay with Lucas. He would have loved to have Lucas's arms wrap around him and for Lucas to whisper to him that he was safe and everything would be all right.

Failing that, he'd need a stiff drink—a few of them. He was flirting dangerously with drinking. He'd always sworn he'd never end up becoming his father. He should stay; it was safer that way, but staying exposed him to other dangers—such as his feelings for Lucas.

He had to get home. "Thanks, both of you, but I can't let this run my life. I'll be fine, honestly." He could see the worry in Lucas's eyes—and Anna's—and he could see their genuine desire for Ryan to stay, but he needed to go. Lucas wasn't his. He said goodbye and fled.

The Jaws-a-thon had been awesome, with him and Lucas on the sofa and Anna sprawled out on the chaise beside them. It had been comfortable and fun and every-fucking-thing Ryan wanted with Lucas, but the realization that he couldn't have it became unbearable and Ryan had run.

The minute he walked into his apartment he downed a shot to steady his nerves. After that, he sat in the dark and proceeded to try to drink away his fear and self-loathing.

The terrible truth was he was falling in love with Lucas—a married man. But what about Anna? Even if he didn't know Luke's wife, he'd still never go after someone else's spouse. He'd concluded weeks ago that if he had to apply a label to himself, he was definitely bisexual. He'd never been in love with a woman, but he'd slept with a few and enjoyed it, although it had been nothing close to the desire that consumed him when Lucas was near, or hell, even when he merely thought about the man.

His life had become so tangled: his feelings for Lucas, his shame at having those sentiments for someone else's husband, and now this stalker injecting her own brand of chaos. To be fair, he'd been the one to bring her into his life, but did one drunken hookup mean he had to pay such a steep price for it? He knew what stalkers were capable of and it terrified him.

The lights of the city had long ago lit up the night sky and Ryan stared at the shimmering beauty of San Francisco as he polished off his fourth...maybe sixth drink. If he was losing count, he'd probably had enough, but the buzz he needed just hadn't hit him yet, so he poured himself another. He heard the vibrations of his phone ringing again on the kitchen counter, but still didn't get up to answer it. What if it was it her? Or could it be someone checking to see if he was all right? Who'd check on him? He had no family to care. Lucas and Anna might check, but he didn't think he could handle speaking to them.

An hour and maybe two more bourbons later, Ryan had worked up a nice buzz. Actually, if the last time he'd gotten up to use the bathroom was any indication, he'd moved past a nice buzz and was happily coasting into drunkenness. His phone had stopped ringing, and the city outside seemed quiet. Ryan was pretty sure he'd drop off to sleep at any moment.

Too bad some fucker banging the shit out of his fucking door was putting paid to that. Ryan stumbled out of his seat and made his way on wobbly legs to his front door. Without thought, he threw it open hard enough for it to bounce off the wall.

"Luke, what the hell are you doing here?" Ryan could hear the slur of his words but didn't have the ability to give two shits right then.

"Did you even look out the fucking peephole, Ryan? And why haven't you been answering your fucking phone?" Lucas roared at him before pushing his way past and making his way into Ryan's living room.

Ryan pushed the door shut and followed Lucas into the room. He couldn't work out what was wrong with Lucas. What the fuck was he screaming at Ryan for? "It's a secure building, asshole. They're not gonna let anyone up here who shouldn't be. And my phone...my phone's... I didn't wanna talk."

"Didn't want to talk? You've got a stalker who's already been violent once and is clearly delusional, and you don't *want* to answer your phone when I call to check on you? You selfish prick. I was worried... We were worried!"

"You aren't my father, Lucas, and Anna isn't my mum. I'm a fucking adult and I can come and go as I please!" he roared back, thankful the headache he knew would come hadn't kicked in yet.

"You're fucking drunk, which apparently makes you fucking stupid. I mean this whole fucking mess started 'cause you got drunk and slept with a fucking nutcase."

Ryan saw red—literally saw a red fog descend. "Fuck you, Lucas. Fuck you. Get the fuck out if I'm such a sloppy mess."

Ryan watched the color drain from Lucas's face and his eyes widen in shock at what he'd just accused Ryan of. "Shit, Ryan. I'm sorry. I'm so sorry, I didn't mean that. It's just... Fuck..." he roared. "I was scared. You didn't answer your phone and I was so fucking scared."

Lucas approached him; hands outstretched, and through the haze of alcohol, Ryan could tell Lucas was shaking, even as he was trying to placate Ryan. Lucas had said the wrong thing and he knew it. His life until this point had been full of loneliness and lacking any real relationships. Did Ryan want to lose the most important relationship he'd ever had over words said in anger and fear? Because Ryan could plainly see Lucas had been afraid—for him.

"Ryan, I'm sorry. This isn't your fault—none of it—and I should never have said that. I need to know you're safe. When you didn't answer your phone...I panicked. I thought maybe..." Lucas shook his head and Ryan wondered if he was trying to dislodge whatever unpleasant thoughts he'd formed in his mind.

"I'm all right. I only had a few drinks and I didn't... I didn't think you'd be worried if I didn't answer."

"What? Why would you think that?"

"Nobody's ever really been worried about me before," Ryan lamentably admitted.

Lucas moved closer and rested his hands on Ryan's shoulders. "Well someone's worried now." He tipped his head so their foreheads were touching for barely a moment before pulling back and wrapping Ryan in his arms.

Lucas's body was strong and warm and he held him so tightly Ryan could have wept at the security he experienced in his friend's embrace. Oh god, he smelled so good. There was no way Ryan was getting out of this tangle of emotions unscathed; he was falling and he knew the impact would be brutal.

"Well." Lucas cleared his throat as he pulled away from Ryan. "Now I've made sure you're safe, I should probably get going—"

"Stay," Ryan barely managed to whisper. "Just for a little while, Luke, stay with me?" It was the closest Ryan could get to admitting how terrified he was of his stalker.

Lucas studied him for a good long while, long enough for Ryan to start shifting uncomfortably, before Lucas nodded—almost in defeat, it seemed to Ryan. What battle had he lost?

"I'll give Anna a call and let her know you're okay and that I'm gonna stay for a while."

"Sure," Ryan replied and turned into the kitchen to give Lucas some privacy. He'd felt awkward and shy when he'd asked Lucas to stay, but he hadn't been ready for him to leave. He was troubled by both Leighton White and his feelings for Lucas, so the smart thing would have been to let Lucas leave. Maybe it was the bourbon or maybe just the longing, but for whatever reason, he hadn't been ready to let Lucas go yet.

It was stupid and foolish, but Ryan chugged a quick shot while Lucas was on the phone. It settled quickly in his belly, spreading its warmth and fuzziness. Whatever sobriety he'd achieved with Lucas's arrival was gone; sunk back under another swig of booze.

"Drink?" he offered Lucas when he walked into the kitchen.

"Just one, thanks."

Ryan could sense Lucas watching him closely as he poured each of them a drink. Lucas hadn't been happy about finding him drunk tonight, but he was a grown-ass man, and if he wanted a drink or six, he'd damn well have them. Besides, that last shot was giving him a nice little hit of bravado.

Ryan handed Lucas his drink and walked over to the sofa, plopping himself on one end and sprawling his legs out. If Lucas wanted to sit with him, then he'd damn well have to maneuver himself around Ryan's limbs. He was being a tipsy asshole; he knew that. He'd asked Lucas to stay and now he was getting snarky with him. What was wrong with him? Too much booze? Too many emotional whirlwinds wreaking havoc within him?

Lucas glanced at him before grabbing his ankles and yanking his legs off the sofa. He sat in the recently vacated spot before Ryan could manage to get his legs back up there.

"So, you guys were worried, huh?" He daren't look at Lucas, while he asked the question, afraid the answer may have changed.

"Frantic. Anna was ready to raise the alarm." Lucas huffed a little laugh. "She's like a pit bull, that one. Grabs on to something and won't let go. Even if I hadn't already been getting ready to come to check on you, she'd have made me. You're lucky you didn't have a SWAT team at your door."

Frantic. No one had ever been frantic over him before; hell, no one had ever been mildly concerned. Ryan was regretting the shot and the half-finished drink he was cradling in his hand. The alcohol was fanning the flames of emotions creeping through his body and he needed to get the fire under control. There was no way he could, or should, spew his emotional shit all over Lucas.

"*Hemlock Grove?*" he asked and chuckled at Lucas's puzzled expression. "Do you wanna watch some *Hemlock Grove* with me? I didn't get to watch much TV before; I was always working and going to auditions, but I'm trying to catch up a bit and I've just started on *Hemlock Grove*. One episode and then you can go. Okay?"

"All right. Bring it on."

Ryan fussed around with his Netflix and dimmed the lights—no point watching a scary TV show with the bright lights ruining the atmosphere. He considered another drink and quickly dismissed the idea because he was already fighting with everything he had not to jump into Lucas's lap and kiss the shit out of him. He didn't need any more booze to fuck with his inhibitions.

During the opening credits, Ryan did his best to catch Lucas up a bit on the show, explaining characters and who was what and what had happened so far. Ryan had always enjoyed scaring the shit out of himself in the safety of TV and movie viewing, but the reality of being frightened of something in the real world was...not so entertaining.

"Hey, that's the guy who's gonna be in the new *It* movie, right?" Lucas asked.

Bill Skarsgård was suitably creepy as Roman Godfrey, but the stills of him as Pennywise were downright disturbing. "Yeah, that's him. He's creepy as shit, but those Skarsgård brothers...damn."

Ryan chanced a glance at Lucas and found him watching him, confusion all over his face. "You find them hot?" Lucas asked.

Ryan was suddenly uneasy. He didn't think for a second that Lucas was homophobic at all, but still, he wondered if admitting to finding men attractive would make things uncomfortable between them. Curse his inebriated tongue. "Yeah. Yeah, I think they're all...great looking men."

Thankfully, Lucas let it go and they sat silently watching some creepy shit on the small screen. Ryan could feel his eyes drifting shut every so often. Now that he'd stopped drinking, the alcohol in his system was dragging him into that too-tired-to-even-move stage, and he just wanted to close his eyes and sleep. He stretched out a little more on the sofa, aware of, but not really caring, when his feet ended up in Lucas's lap. He dozed.

Sometime later, or maybe only a few minutes, he couldn't tell, he felt Lucas lift his legs and wriggle out from under them. He kept his eyes closed but listened as Lucas moved around the room. He heard him getting closer and then Lucas's warm hands were under his head, lifting it, to put a pillow under him. Keeping his eyes closed, because there was no way he could do this if they were open, Ryan reached out and searched for one of Lucas's hands. When he found one, he grabbed it and tugged a little. Lucas seemed to get the message and bent down; Ryan felt his breath feathering over his face.

"Don't go," he whispered. Ryan heard a groan fall from Lucas's mouth and then the entire top half of his body was being lifted as Lucas sat on the sofa and gently lowered him back down so that his head was resting on Lucas's pillow-covered lap. Ryan hardly dared move. He kept his eyes shut, feigning that state of being drowsily asleep and not really knowing what he was doing so that come morning he could excuse this...whatever was going on.

Once again, the remaining alcohol in his system was pulling him into sleep, and then Ryan felt a strong hand ghosting through his hair, over and over. It felt so good, so intimate. Ryan had never been touched this way before.

Fuck. All he wanted to do was drift off with the warmth of Lucas around him and the tender sensation of his fingers carding through his hair, but he could think of nothing but Anna. Ryan wouldn't do anything that might potentially hurt her. Nor could he risk doing anything that might harm his relationship with Lucas. Since Leighton showed up, his friendship with Ryan had gotten back on track after awkwardness and distance had crept in. One false move now and it could all blow to hell again.

He knew what he had to do. He had to get the fuck up and let Lucas leave. Then he had to get into his own fucking bed, jerk off to images and sense memories of Lucas, and then go to fucking sleep. His mind knew that, his heart knew it but was pretending it didn't, and his dick didn't give a shit—it was too busy enjoying Lucas's touch.

Just as he was preparing to "wake up" and let Lucas leave, he felt Lucas's hand drift down to cup his face and softly rub his thumb over the apple of his cheek. Soft breath breezed over his face as Lucas lowered his head closer to his own. "I'm not gonna leave you, Ry. Never." The words were a whisper, a mere puff of breath, but they resounded through Ryan's brain like a marching band. He was so screwed.

Chapter Fourteen

What's wrong with our Lucas? Is he sick?

LUCAS

"Luke, I'm fine, okay. I'm home. Safe." Ryan's voice sounded through the phone.

Lucas had no idea how much longer he could last like this. It was getting harder and harder every day to leave Ryan at his place, knowing he'd spend the next ten or so hours with Ryan out of his sight, and knowing he'd spend almost every second of those ten hours wondering if Ryan was okay, all while imaging some nutjob coming after him, hurting him.

"Okay. Well, you know you can come over, or I'll come to you if you need me. And make sure you call if there's anything…if anything seems off." Lucas knew he sounded totally overprotective, but he couldn't help himself.

"Luke, I promise, okay? I'll be fine."

It had been two weeks since the interview with Ryan's stalker and things had intensified, at least privately. The woman had sent copious emails and handwritten letters to the studio demanding to see Ryan, some of them claiming the studio was responsible for keeping Ryan from her. She'd sent her worn underwear, locks of her hair, fingernail clippings. Ryan had tried to laugh it off by claiming she was sending herself to him one tiny piece at a time, but he hadn't fooled Lucas.

The media had also received emails and letters from her, decrying the situation she was in: cut off from the love of her life just as he was from her by the "nefarious machinations" of the studio. Fortunately, most media organizations she had contacted had given her story limited coverage, some even refusing to report on it at all—recognizing it for what it was. Lucas was pretty sure the studio had put pressure on media outlets not to report on Ryan's crazed stalker.

Lucas, Ryan, and other cast members had been to several meetings with studio heads, police, and security experts. The fear had expanded to include practically everyone from the studio who were involved with the show, given the stalker's assertion they were keeping Ryan from her. Security had been doubled and the studio was considering hiring extra bodyguards for when the cast was out and about.

When Lucas's brain gave him a moment's respite from his frantic concern for Ryan, his thoughts always drifted to his other feelings for Ryan. He'd been surprised when Ryan had admitted to finding the Skarsgård brothers attractive, not that it meant Ryan was gay or even bi. Plenty of straight people could admit someone of the same sex was an attractive person. Still, the confession had given Lucas pause, maybe even hope that he may have a shot with Ryan. He'd sat on that fucking sofa with Ryan's head in his lap for over an hour that night, and the sheer force of will it had taken him not to lean down and kiss Ryan had left him exhausted.

Between that and the lack of sleep from worrying about Ryan, Lucas was shattered. He was barely keeping his shit together. Filming would end in a few weeks for a short hiatus and Lucas couldn't wait for the break. The Oscar nominations came out in a little over three weeks, and the talk was still buzzing that he'd be up for Best Supporting Actor. It was incomprehensible to him.

"Luke?"

"Yeah, Anna," Lucas answered, putting his hand over the mouthpiece of the phone.

"I need to talk to you. Can you spare a minute?" She took his hand and started leading him to the sofa, not giving him a choice.

"Anytime for you, Anna. You know that." He smiled at her before putting the phone to his ear again. "Gotta go, Ry. I'll see you later but remember..."

"I promise, Luke. See you later." Ryan ended the call and Lucas turned his attention to his wife. She'd been spending a lot of time in LA recently, which helped solidify the suspicion he'd already had that she was seeing someone.

"Lucas, I love you. You know that don't you?"

"Sure, I love you too." He squeezed her hand reassuringly as he spoke.

"So when I tell you to stop being a dumbass you'll take it with all the love that's intended?"

"What? What're you talking about?"

"Lucas, you're pale, you've lost weight, you've got bags the size of Texas under your eyes, and you're so jumpy you're about ready to come out of your skin. You. Need. To. Talk. To. Ryan. I can't make it any clearer." She was so beautiful, so kindhearted, and not for the first time, Lucas had that little niggle of regret that they couldn't be what they wanted for each other.

"I talk to him every day, Anna. In fact, I just hung up from talking to him." He tried the smartass approach, knowing Anna would take him down a peg for it.

"Don't try it, Luke. You are so in love with that man I'm surprised your heart hasn't burst gooey romantic confetti all over him. You need to tell him. I've never known you to be a coward, so please don't start now. Where is the man who marched into my parents' house, put my dad on his ass, and told them both that they'd never lay a finger on me again?"

Hell, where was that man Anna remembered? Because if he was gonna do this with Ryan, he'd need him. "He's here...somewhere, just been taking a rest."

Anna leaned forward and dropped a kiss on his forehead. "Well, wake him the fuck up, because you deserve to be happy, Lucas, and Ryan Lowe might be your happiness, wrapped in a smoking-hot package I might add."

Could he do this? Should he do this? Something had to give; he knew that much. What if he laid his heart bare and Ryan trampled it? What if he didn't?

"I can see the cogs turning, Luke. Just get up and do it. Stop overthinking."

"Just do it. Is it that easy?" He asked, more to himself, but Anna answered for him.

"It can be. I'm here for you, Luke, no matter how it goes. And think, if it goes well, you're off to Paris in a couple of days, and you can't get much more disgustingly romantic than that for a first date. Now get the fuck up and get over there and tell that man of yours what's what." She actually smacked his ass as he stood and moved past her.

Twenty minutes later, he was pacing in the lobby of Ryan's building, security and the doorman both watching him with a wary eye even though they knew him well.

Just breathe and just do it. He set those words on a loop in his head and made his way to the elevators. He couldn't fight it anymore; he was worn down—his nerves frayed. He had to tell Ryan how he felt about him—staying quiet was killing him.

The ride up in the elevator seemed even shorter than usual, and too soon, he found himself standing at Ryan's door. He'd spent the drive over thinking over what he'd say, but he could tell the words had fled him, leaving him to wing it as he waited for Ryan to open up.

Ryan answered in a pair of jeans. Nothing more. No shirt, no shoes, no socks, and Lucas felt his mouth go dry. He looked so fucking sexy. The urge to trace his fingers down Ryan's chest was almost irrepressible, and Lucas put his hands in his pockets to tame them.

"Luke. Come in. Everything okay?" Ryan asked as he gestured for Lucas to walk past him.

"Yeah, it's good, Ryan. I just... I need to talk to you."

"Sure. Sit down. I'll grab us a drink."

Ryan walked through to the kitchen and Lucas took a seat trying his best to get comfortable, but he was nervous and fidgety and his body couldn't relax, so Lucas moved to Ryan's balcony instead. Ryan's view was spectacular, looking out over the city, the bay to the left, and if he craned his neck, he could catch a glimpse of the Golden Gate Bridge. It was dusk and lights were on but not yet fully glowing. In ten minutes, the city would be fully lit up and look astonishing.

He felt Ryan move up next to him and turned, reaching for the beer Ryan had in his outstretched hand. "Thanks, Ry." Delay. Delay. That's all he could think of as he took a swig.

"Yeah. Cheers, mate."

Feeling like a creep, Lucas watched as Ryan swallowed his mouthful. The muscles of his throat pulled taut while they worked. He'd have given his right arm to reach out and lick up the column of that throat right then.

"So. You wanted to talk to me. Is everything okay?" Concern flashed in Ryan's eyes, so Lucas assumed he thought he was here to deliver bad news.

"Nothing bad, Ryan... Well, maybe it is. I dunno... No, it's nothing bad. Look, um... I haven't been completely honest with you."

"About what?" The concern and puzzlement intensified on Ryan's gorgeous face.

Lucas took another swig and a deep breath and then let everything tumble out of his mouth, uncontrolled and unstoppable. "I don't want to hide anymore, Ryan. Not from you. My marriage to Anna is not...it's not a real marriage. I mean, it's real, but it's fake."

Utter confusion graced Ryan's face. "What? I'm not sure I understand."

"Anna came from an abusive home. We married to get her out of there. But it wasn't the only reason. I'm...I'm gay, Ryan. Anna and I have never...consummated our marriage, nor will we ever. I've never been with any woman. It's a marriage of convenience to get her away from her family and to hide the fact that I'm gay and she's bi."

Lucas watched Ryan the entire time and saw the confusion slowly change into a pinch of understanding as he nodded his head. "The first agent we had said that even though times have changed, it would still be easier for us to launch our careers if we were seen to be a married, straight couple. So that's what we've done...until now." Lucas heaved in a huge breath, knowing he was coming to the real game-changer. It was this next confession that could make or break his happiness.

"If I hadn't met you, I would probably have been content to live out my life as Anna's husband. I love Anna—as my friend, but it's not enough, not anymore. I want so much more. I want to love someone fiercely. I want it to be like...like if we're apart it actually hurts, but then when he comes back to me, the ecstasy I'll find in his arms will burn me...consume me. I don't want to be just content anymore. I want to burn, Ryan." As much as he'd wanted to turn away from Ryan as the vulnerability of his confession ripped through him, Lucas couldn't. He was held transfixed by Ryan's gaze.

Carefully, as though he were approaching a startled animal, he put his beer on the balcony ledge and reached out, letting the backs of his fingers graze down Ryan's cheek.

"It's you, Ryan. You're that ecstasy; you're the one who lights me up, makes me burn. I'm falling in love with you, utterly in love. I think I started falling the day you fell off that boat in front of Harrison Cooper and I haven't stopped falling yet." Ryan still hadn't spoken and Lucas didn't know if that was good or bad. Had he disgusted him with his confession? Had he ruined everything?

He let his fingers drift around the back of Ryan's head and tangle into his hair. Waiting.

"No one...no one's ever told me they love me before," Ryan whispered.

"Anybody who's ever known you and hasn't loved you or hasn't told you they do is a fucking idiot." He itched to pull Ryan closer, press his lips to Ryan's. "Look, please don't freak out, Ry. I just... I needed to tell you. I'm breaking apart at the seams. I'm so worried about you, and I've hardly slept, and Anna said I should tell you. So I've told you." He was blabbering, uncomfortable now his feelings were out there, exposed and blowing in the breeze. "I don't expect anything from you, and more than anything I hope this won't ruin our friendship because you're my best friend, too, and I don't wanna lose that but I—"

"Shut up, Luke." Ryan smiled, and then he moved. Like lightning, Ryan gripped Lucas and pushed him backward until he hit the wall. Ryan's gaze never left his and Lucas swore he saw heat in his eyes, desire. "Do you have any idea how many times I've dreamed of you saying corny shit like that to me, Lucas? I've lost fucking count. I've wanted you for so long, but I thought I was screwed because you were a happily married man." Ryan shook his head, and then before Lucas could take a breath, Ryan sealed their lips together.

If he'd thought his body had burned from Ryan's touch before, it was nothing to the conflagration that blazed through him now. Ryan's lips were soft and warm and demanding, moving with Lucas's until he was dizzy with the passion. Lucas licked at the seam, demanding entrance, and once he had it, he pushed his tongue into that warmth, licking and exploring. Lucas tried to pull back to get some air, but Ryan sucked on his tongue, not allowing him to go anywhere. Who the fuck needed air anyway?

Lucas's eyes rolled back in his head as he imagined Ryan sucking something else with those fucking lips of his. Finally, Ryan released him, but he didn't let him go far, their faces so close their breaths were mingling just as their tongues had, moments ago. They were both breathing hard.

"I'm falling in love with you, too, Luke," Ryan whispered.

Lucas pressed his mouth to Ryan's again, but it was sweeter, softer, a gentle acknowledgement of the words they'd spoken.

"Can we...? Come and sit down, Luke. We can talk some more." Ryan grabbed his hand and didn't let go, not even once they were seated on the sofa together, even closer than usual, their bodies turned so they could face each other.

"Shit. I... I don't know what to say now," Lucas spluttered out. "I didn't really think much past my big announcement." He laughed, feeling a lightness that had been missing for months.

"How 'bout I talk for a bit. I probably owe you an explanation too." Ryan kept his gaze on their joined hands, gently playing with Lucas's fingers while he spoke.

Lucas would have been content to sit and stare at the stunning man across from him like in some cheesy romance movie, but hopefully, once the confessions were out of the way, they could start working on a real relationship.

Chapter Fifteen

*Samdom heads to Paris. Producers promise
action for them in the city of love?*

RYAN

He had to be dreaming. That was the only logical explanation Ryan could come up with to explain the fact that Lucas Evers was sitting across from him on his sofa, their hands entwined, moments after both admitting they were falling for the other.

For the briefest of moments, as Lucas had explained his marriage to Anna, Ryan had considered it may have been a ploy to try to get Ryan into bed. But he knew Lucas better than that—much better—and he'd dismissed the idea immediately, ashamed of ever having it. What Lucas had told him rang true. Lucas and Anna clearly loved each other, but Ryan had never seen romantic affection between them—no kissing, hand-holding, loving gazes into each other's eyes. Nothing.

Still, Ryan needed to talk to Anna before things went any further with Lucas; it was the right thing to do. Hopefully, Lucas would understand.

For now, though, he needed to get everything out on the table.

"Um...so I guess the first thing I should tell you is I've never been with a man. I don't...I'm not really big on labels, so I've never given myself one. I've never felt like I needed to define my sexuality. I've been attracted to men, but nothing's ever come of it. I've been with a handful of women but nothing even close to love." Ryan couldn't help marveling at how relaxed this conversation with Lucas felt. What could have been a potentially awkward chat was flowing with surprising ease, but that was one of the things he loved about his relationship with Lucas from the beginning—he'd been comfortable around him.

"I've never been in love before either, Ry. It's... I mean, I literally hate letting you out of my sight, and I don't mean that in a controlling sort of way, which it totally sounded like. I mean I miss you the same as I'd miss air when you're not with me. I've never felt that before." Lucas's face was so earnest and in awe as he spoke that Ryan had to fight the urge to lay another kiss on those soft, warm lips.

Hell, just the memory of Lucas's tongue in his mouth, the groan he'd let out when Ryan had sucked on it, almost had this conversation derailed then and there.

"I know. It's... I haven't had much love in my life—none really, but I get now why everyone raves about it. This is not because of the show, is it? I mean we've had to act falling in love, but acting is not what this is, is it?"

"No. It's not that. It's real, Ryan. This is real."

Ryan nodded, acknowledging the truth of Lucas's words. "I'd like to... I know you're not out but would you have dinner with me sometime? I want to do this properly. I'd like to date you." Did he sound too pathetic? Would Lucas scoff at him? Ryan had never dated before, but this was important to him. Back home, most couples got together after a quick root in the back seat of a car, and Ryan didn't want that with Lucas. He wanted something more closely resembling the fairytale.

"I'd love to date you. In fact, I've got an idea...well, it was kind of Anna's," Lucas admitted with a sheepish expression on his face. "We're off to Paris on Tuesday. I'm not sure if you've been there before, but I've been a couple of times, and I would love it if you let me take you out while we're there."

Ryan's pathetic heart fluttered like a hummingbird's wings. Paris. A first date with Lucas. Oh, he was all over that. "I'd love it. Um...there's another thing I need to ask. I'd prefer to talk to Anna myself, if that's all right. I care about her a lot and I need to speak to her about all of this," Ryan said, spinning a hand around in a gesture to encompass what the "all of this" referred to. To his surprise, Lucas threw his head back and laughed.

"Oh, I'm sure Anna'll love that. She'll no doubt tell you every one of my mortifying secrets. I'll ask you not to judge too harshly," Lucas said with a playful grin on his handsome face.

Ryan joined him in laughing, feeling lighter than he had in months. The weight of his life no longer pressed him quite so far into the earth. "I can't wait to hear those stories. There could be nothing more embarrassing than the Great Harrison Cooper Debacle of 2017, however, surely."

"Oh, you have no idea."

Fuck, Lucas was so beautiful that Ryan couldn't keep hold of his control. He lurched forward and pressed his lips to Lucas's.

Despite getting close to Lucas during filming, Ryan was still getting used to the feel of a man's hard body pressed tightly against his. The scrape of Lucas's whiskers was a little shot of pleasure. Lucas reclined back on the arm of the sofa so that Ryan was practically lying on top of him. His body was hot and solid, no hint of softness; in fact, nothing about kissing Lucas could have confused his brain into thinking he was kissing anyone other than a man.

Ryan's lips moved down the length of Lucas's throat, kissing and nipping at the skin there. His nose was pressed into Lucas, just below his ear, and his scent—the citrusy scent Ryan thought might be his most favorite in the world—was so strong there that it had Ryan reeling. His senses were quickly becoming overloaded with all things Lucas, and Ryan knew he had to pull away before he had Lucas naked beneath him.

Despite the onslaught of sensations and the draw of Lucas's body, Ryan somehow managed to stop. He stood from the sofa and paced the room, willing his almost out-of-control libido to calm the fuck down. He'd never been so wild for anyone. Lucas followed him to his feet and reached for him. Ryan put a hand out in a universal gesture of stop. "No. Stay there, Luke. I just need a minute to...to calm down. You're so fucking hot that you've got me all worked up. I wanna rip those fucking clothes right off you but we can't yet...so stay back."

Lucas's lips pulled up into a wicked smile, but thankfully, he made no further move toward Ryan.

Not only did Ryan want to speak to Anna before this progressed, he also had no real clue what to do. Natural instinct was screaming at him to just get Lucas naked and go from there, but his inexperience worried him.

"Have you been with a lot of guys, Luke?" The question burst out of him before he'd given it any thought.

"Um...a few," Lucas hedged.

"Like, more than or less than say...ten?"

"Do you really want to know?"

Did he? The thought of Lucas with anyone else was difficult to even consider; the image of another man's hands on that perfect body had Ryan clenching his fists. The simple truth was he felt vulnerable about his lack of knowledge in the man-on-man sex department. He'd be almost a virgin all over again, and it was bloody awful the first time around. "Just ballpark. I just... I don't know anything about it and I'm worried—"

"Ry, you've got nothing to worry about. When you're ready, it's going to be fucking awesome. I promise you. We'll go at your pace, and if there's anything you're uncomfortable with, we can take it off the table. Okay?"

Ryan nodded, reassured by Lucas's understanding.

"And I don't have an exact number for you, but it's less than thirty." Lucas stalked a little closer. "And I can guarantee you, Ry, once I have you, those others will be wiped from my memory. I've never wanted anyone the way I want you." The look on Lucas's face was pure seduction, causing Ryan to feel his control slipping away again.

Clearing his throat and gathering his resolve, Ryan padded over to where Lucas stood and then wrapped himself around him. After a moment he pulled away, placing a gentle kiss on Lucas's forehead as he went. "Right, okay, well. That's enough of that then."

Lucas chuckled, probably at his discomfort, but Ryan didn't care. His cock was hard again, so he had to get Lucas out of there—the temptation was too fucking much.

"All right. Tell you what. I'm gonna go. We've got no filming tomorrow, so why don't you come over in the morning, have your chat with Anna, and then you can pack in the afternoon. Maybe get some sleep before we go, because I promise you, Ryan, once I get to have you to myself, it's not gonna be a quick wham, bam, thank you, man. I'm gonna need hours with you. I wanna learn every inch of your body and find every little sensitive spot you've got. Do you understand?"

Lucas's bright green eyes had darkened while he spoke, his body drifting closer and closer to Ryan's. Holy shit, he'd never had this before; he'd never experienced desire so strong. Ryan's mouth was desert dry when he attempted a response. "Ah...um...yeah, okay. Morning, packing, sleep. I can do that. And then...then the rest...that'll be—"

Lucas cut him off with a last kiss, one so hot and intense Ryan's knees went weak, and no matter how hard he tried, nothing more coherent than *oh my fucking god* swam around in his brain.

Before anything resembling normalcy returned to him, Lucas was out the door and Ryan could only stand where Lucas had left him, panting humiliatingly with his dick so fucking hard it would need to be taken care of before Ryan could even attempt sleep.

RYAN WAS UP early the next morning and at Lucas's door at a time too early to be decent. It couldn't be helped; he'd hardly slept a wink last night. After jerking off in the shower, he'd attempted to get some shut-eye, but if it wasn't the copious erotic thoughts of Lucas playing on a loop through his head keeping him awake, it was the moments of shock that zapped through Ryan when he remembered exactly what had happened last night.

Love. Lucas was falling in love with him and it was un-fucking-believable. This shit didn't happen to Ryan Lowe, small-town boy, outcast, unloved loner. For the longest time, Ryan had thought of himself as unlovable. After all, how could anybody love someone whose own father couldn't be bothered with him? Now, thanks to Lucas, he had to rethink everything he'd believed. Lucas loved him or was falling in love with him. How the fuck had it happened?

These thoughts chased him all the way to Lucas's front door at a ridiculously early hour and were still flittering through his mind when Anna opened the door. Before he could even get a word out, she'd pulled him to her and wrapped him up in a warm embrace.

"I'm so glad you're here, Ryan. Come in," she graciously invited. "Go sit in the living room and I'll make us a coffee."

Ryan had been here enough times to find the living room on his own. He chose to sit on one of the cream-colored sofas, sliding down a little to make himself appear far more relaxed than he felt. His gaze wandered around the room while he waited, and he could see several photos of Anna and Lucas on the wall. Not one of them was at an awards show or similar. Instead, they were mostly of the pair when they were younger or in casual clothes, looking relaxed and happy.

He wondered if Lucas was awake, and if so, would he come and join the conversation or hang back and allow him and Anna to hash things out.

"Here you go. Strong black, as you like it." Anna handed him the mug and then moved to sit on the sofa. She sat forward as though eager to get this show on the road. "So, I'm guessing you're here to get my approval to sleep with my husband."

Thank god the coffee was too hot to have taken a sip, otherwise he would have sprayed it all over the place with Anna's words. "Shit, Anna, don't sugarcoat it or anything."

A wicked smile pulled at her lips. "Ryan, Lucas is my best friend, but there has never been anything between us, nor do I ever want there to be. I love him, and I swear if you hurt him, I'll pull your fingernails out one by one, but he's not mine and I don't want him in that way. Go forth and fuck like bunnies with my blessing, young man."

Ryan couldn't suppress the boom of laughter that rushed out of him. When he was back under control, he returned his gaze to her, doing his best to allow his sincerity to show in his expression. "Anna, I won't ever hurt him. I swear. He means more to me than anyone ever has. I'd as soon chop off my own leg than hurt him."

"I'm gonna hold you to that." She smirked. "Seriously though, Ryan, I have been pushing for this. I could see the way you two looked at each other. You both care very much and you make Luke happy. He deserves that. If you need my assurance you aren't stepping on any toes here, then you've got it. Besides, I've got a little something of my own brewing." The smirk turned wicked and Ryan knew there was a story there.

Before he could ask a single question, Lucas walked into the room. He wore nothing but sleep shorts that did little to hide his mouthwatering bulge. "Hey," he greeted drowsily. "Guess I owe you a twenty, Anna."

"Yes, you do. You should be aware by now I'm always right." Anna turned from Lucas and fixed her gaze back on Ryan. "Luke didn't think you'd be here this early. He thought he'd be okay to sleep in, but I knew you'd be here." She winked.

Lucas walked toward him and Ryan didn't know where to look: his gorgeous face with those stunning green eyes, his perfectly toned arms, his broad, firm chest and ripped abs, or that enticing bulge that was completely indecent in those shorts. Once Lucas reached him, he leaned down and pressed a kiss to Ryan's lips. A shiver of lust rippled through his entire body, but it was chased by a sliver of uneasiness. Despite her assurances, Ryan still felt a tiny bit uncomfortable kissing Anna's husband right in front of her.

"Well, while the idea of watching you two...doing whatever you're going to do is certainly tempting, I've got plans this morning. Ryan, if I don't see you, enjoy Paris. And please stop worrying. Lucas is all yours." She smiled and pecked him on the cheek when he stood with her to say goodbye.

Once Anna was gone, Ryan was alone with Lucas—Lucas and his barely covered bulge that seemed to be growing while Ryan stared at it.

"If you keep looking at me that way, Ryan, I'm gonna throw you down and suck your brains out through your dick." Lucas's husky voice broke through his bulge-induced daze, the words he spoke hooking into his brain until all he could think about was Lucas's lips wrapped around his cock.

"Is that a threat?" He winked, briefly looking into Lucas's eyes before returning his gaze farther south.

"That's a fucking promise."

Before he knew what the hell was happening, Ryan was back on the sofa, landing with a *whooff* when his breath was knocked out. Lucas knelt before him, spreading Ryan's legs so he could fit between them and then moving his hands to the zipper of Ryan's jeans. Shit.

"And I always keep my promises, Ry."

So carefully, Lucas unbuttoned and unzipped him before commanding him to lift up and then pulling his jeans and briefs down when Ryan lifted his ass off the sofa. His cock was rock-hard, but Lucas didn't go straight for it. Instead, Ryan was pushed farther back into the sofa when Lucas surged up and kissed him. The kiss was brutal and needy. There was desperation to it and Ryan knew if Lucas had wanted him for as long as he'd wanted Lucas then he must be damn near starving.

All Ryan could do was hold on as best he could, while Lucas kissed the fuck out of him, before pulling back to stare into Ryan's eyes. A sinful grin spread across Lucas's lips before he licked them and then bent and took Ryan's cock into his mouth. Ryan jolted and let out a curse when he felt the head of his dick hit the back of Lucas's throat. Fucking hell, there was no way he was going to last long.

"Shit, Luke. Fuck!" Ryan's hips moved with helpless little thrusts. The warmth of Lucas's mouth, the suction as he pulled back was too much. He ran his fingers through Lucas's hair, not wanting to grip it but needing the grounding of the touch. He'd had blowjobs before, but nothing had even come close to this. Just when he thought he had himself under control, Lucas hummed around his cock and Ryan could barely get out a warning before he shot down Lucas's throat.

Lucas sat back on his knees with a smile as he licked at the little trail of come seeping from the corner of his mouth. Ryan stared in awe as he realized Lucas was touching himself, working his hard cock in almost a blur. He shifted his gaze to Lucas's eyes and watched as he stared intently at Ryan. Almost before he could drop his gaze back down to what Lucas was doing to himself, Lucas let out a desperate moan and came.

Jesus fucking Christ, if this was what it was going to be like being with Lucas, he wasn't at all confident he'd survive it.

Chapter Sixteen

Lovers snapped out and about in Paris. Are we sure they aren't real??

LUCAS

"Ryan!"

"Lucas!"

"Over here! Ryan! Lucas!"

Fuck, so much for sneaking into San Francisco airport. Lucas didn't even know if it was the media or the public calling to them. All he knew was he could feel Ryan trembling beside him as the crowd closed in. He tried to smile. Give them a little something so they'd move on, but it seemed this was a crowd of scavengers and he and Ryan were the carrion they were determined to pick over.

"Lucas, where's your wife?"

"Ryan, where's Leighton? Is she your girlfriend?"

He could hear Ryan's breathing hitch beside him, so he turned to look at him. Ryan looked terrified. Lucas knew security would be here soon; he just had to help Ryan get through this fucking crowd.

"Lucas! Ryan! Look this way!"

Why did they have to fucking shout at them—they were right there. Lucas was losing his cool. Wave after wave of tension was rolling off Ryan, and his obvious distress was making Lucas angry. He grabbed Ryan's elbow to guide him and pushed his carryon in front of him, using his considerable strength and the bag to barge his way through the surrounding throng. He knew his face was like thunder and it would be captured on film, but he didn't give a fuck. He only wanted to get them out of there.

Lucas had made it a considerable distance when he saw security coming—and plenty of them. They quickly had the mob rounded up and on their way. Lucas, still holding onto Ryan's elbow, made a beeline for the nearest family restroom. One security member was hot on their heels, so Lucas knew they'd have a small measure of privacy to collect themselves once they entered the restroom.

"Jesus," Ryan puffed out. "Lucas." It hurt to hear his name falling from Ryan's lips as a broken sound. Clearly, Ryan didn't manage well with crowds yet.

"You okay?" Lucas pulled him into his arms as he asked the question. He felt Ryan nodding against his shoulder.

They stood wrapped together for a few minutes before reluctantly pulling away.

"Sorry, Luke. I'm still getting used to that."

Lucas pressed a gentle kiss to Ryan's lips and cupped his face. "It's okay. You'll get there." Lucas hoped like fuck he was right about that. He couldn't help thinking that celebrity was no place for someone so anxious in crowds.

They stayed in the restroom for a few minutes while Lucas talked nonsense to Ryan to help calm him. The security guard was waiting for them when they eventually exited and he escorted them to their gate, where they were, mercifully, able to board with no further trouble.

IT HAD BEEN several years, but Paris was exactly as Lucas remembered it. The only difference was the last time he was in the beautiful city it had been summer, and now there was a light snow falling. The weather was far colder than Lucas was used to but he loved it. He loved being snuggled up in his woolen overcoat with his scarf, gloves, and beanie accessorizing his winter look.

As soon as they'd stepped on the plane out of San Francisco, Lucas could tell Ryan felt as relaxed as he had. There was no Leighton White to worry about now, and though she'd not caused trouble, other than her ridiculous interviews with the trash rags and bombardment of emails and letters, it was still a relief to know they wouldn't have to look over their shoulders for her while they were away. They also had more anonymity in Paris, and even though they'd been recognized a handful of times, it was nothing compared to being in the US.

They'd been here for two days and had completed the shoot for the show this morning. Most of the crew who'd come to Paris had left a short while ago, eager to get back to their families now that the job here was finished. The upcoming scenes of Sam and Dom on Parisian streets and a fight sequence in Sacré Cœur would look amazing; Lucas had no doubt of that. The timing of the shoot couldn't have been more perfect for Lucas and Ryan to enjoy the city together.

They weren't due to fly out until tomorrow and that left tonight and most of tomorrow for Lucas to wine and dine Ryan. After the impromptu blowjob the other day, they hadn't had much of a chance to be alone, and jetlag and a hectic schedule had robbed them of time their first day here. Lucas couldn't fucking wait to get his hands on Ryan again. He could still taste Ryan on his tongue, and the way Ryan had responded to him had been so hot—his helpless moans and whimpers had been such a fucking turn on. He couldn't wait to try more—everything—with him.

He'd tried to avoid the clichéd romantic Parisian date when he'd planned this evening, though he fully intended to take Ryan up the Eiffel Tower tomorrow. Lucas much preferred the trip up and view from Notre-Dame. The gargoyles at the top were magnificent and the view out over Paris from Montmartre to the Eiffel Tower was outstanding. He hoped Ryan was okay with heights and tight spaces. The stairwell was close-fitting in places.

Afterward, they'd find an out-of-the-way café to eat in before he'd take Ryan to Le Caveau des Oubliettes. He couldn't wait to go back there. It was a music venue often referred to as a jazz bar, even though the musical acts could vary to include rock, soul, and sometimes even punk and other mixes of music. Tonight though, jazz was on the menu. The room downstairs where the musicians played was a dungeon-come-wine cellar and was essentially a cave. The acoustics were sensational and would provide a unique experience.

It would be a simple date, but Lucas knew Ryan. He knew a three-star restaurant on the Michelin Guide that cost more than what most people earned in a week would never impress Ryan. His down-to-earth attitude was one of the things Lucas loved about him.

There was no way Lucas could have stayed away from him any longer, so he arrived at Ryan's door ten minutes early for their date. When Ryan answered on the second knock, all of Lucas's plans flew from his head. He'd have been happy to spend the rest of the afternoon and evening ensconced in Ryan's hotel room with the man who'd answered the door wearing nothing but an enormous towel wrapped around his trim hips and water trickling down the hard planes of his torso. His wet hair was plastered to his head and he looked fucking edible.

"Shit. I'm late. Sorry, Lucas. Come in."

"Relax, I'm early." Lucas gave serious thought to ripping the towel away and plastering himself to Ryan's body, but he wanted more than just the lust. He wanted a relationship with Ryan, not just sexual satisfaction; though he knew he'd certainly get that as well.

Ryan closed the door once Lucas entered and moved past him, gesturing for Lucas to take a seat while he finished getting ready. Lucas used the time while Ryan was out of sight to get his horny fucking body back under control. No matter what way he cut it, Ryan was a temptation and Lucas found it damn near impossible to keep his hands to himself whenever he was near. It had been difficult before, but now that he was allowed to touch Ryan—all bets were off.

"So jeans and a sweater are all right?" Ryan called from deeper in the hotel suite. Lucas had already given the dress code, but Ryan was probably as nervous, if not more so, than him.

"Perfect. Casual, but warm. It's freezing out there." Snow had begun falling lightly earlier in the day, but it had petered out and wouldn't be near enough to blanket the city in white. Lucas loved the snow, and as he waited for Ryan, he had thoughts of him and Ryan going somewhere with heavier snowfall. Not a city, though, but perhaps a lodge somewhere where they could enjoy the beauty of the snow from the warmth of a fully windowed room with a roaring fire to settle in front of.

Allowing a tiny chuckle to escape, Lucas couldn't help laughing at himself. For years he and Anna had laughed at the romantic gestures of others or mocked what they had called the ridiculously sappy movies that hit the screens every year without fail. And now, suddenly, Lucas found himself in one. Whenever thoughts of Ryan popped into his mind, which was often because he couldn't get the damn man out of his head, feelings of sentimental romance seemed to accompany him. Lucas really needed to rent a few of those movies he'd laughed at because he had no fucking idea how to actually do romance.

"Ready," Ryan called from behind him and Lucas stood up and turned. Fucking hell, the man was exquisite and absolutely stole Lucas's breath away.

Lucas moved closer and took a kiss, gentle and sweet. Now was not the time to kiss the fuck out of Ryan like he wanted to, or they'd never get on this date. "Let's go, then."

They walked to Notre-Dame. The earlier snow had eased into a clear afternoon with the sun just starting to sink in the sky. With luck, they'd be at the top of Notre-Dame just before twilight, and the city would appear almost magical with the growing dark and lights starting to flicker on.

Once they stood before Notre-Dame, Lucas watched as Ryan stared in awe. As incredible as the cathedral was, Lucas kept his gaze fixed on Ryan, though. The wonder in his expression was striking and Lucas would much rather enjoy that view than the thirteenth-century cathedral before him.

"Wow. It's stunning," Ryan offered.

"Yes, it is," Lucas replied, not referring to the cathedral at all. "Come on. We'll look inside—the stained glass is spectacular—and then we'll head up. You're okay with heights, right?"

"Yeah, I'm okay with heights. The view must be awesome from up there." Ryan started moving forward as he spoke and Lucas hurried to catch up.

"It is. It's the gargoyles that really make it worthwhile, though. They are stunningly spooky. Gothic architecture at its best. I've been to a few of these churches...or cathedrals—St. Paul's, St. Peter's—the big ones. But Notre-Dame is hands-down my favorite so far. Wait till you see the stained glass windows, especially with the sun setting behind them like it will be now. Amazing."

They spent a good twenty minutes wandering inside the cathedral, with Lucas pointing out a few things he'd learned from his last visit. Ryan seemed mesmerized by the stained glass, especially the Rose windows.

Eventually they climbed the towers that turned out to have a hidden bonus Lucas hadn't even considered: the view of Ryan's tight ass as he climbed the stairs ahead of him. Paris treated them to perfect weather to enjoy a clear view over the city.

"Oh god, Luke, the gargoyles are amazing. Look at that one." Ryan pointed to one of the stone gargoyles that had a long stone tongue rolling out of its mouth looking as if it was licking a banana or corn—or was that a...nope, surely not. "Look at the tongue. Oh my god, that's awesome." Lucas watched the boyishness sweep over Ryan's features. His enthusiasm ensnared Lucas in its grasp, as always.

"No, no, look at this one with the horn. It almost seems to be perched over the city, watching...guarding it." Ryan continued on. They both chose a favorite gargoyle and hoped they'd be able to buy a copy from one of the many souvenir shops below.

Darkness was falling on the city as they stood on the walkway between the two towers. There weren't many others up here at this time, braving the cold of the coming night, so they found themselves suddenly alone. There was no way Lucas was passing up this opportunity to stretch his romance legs, so he took Ryan into his arms. He kissed him sweetly, chastely, and yet still managed to have both of them panting when they broke away.

During filming for some of their scenes for *The Witches' Hammer*, they were both supposed to have been looking at each other with love, and until this moment, when he broke the kiss with Ryan and pulled back to look intently at him, he'd thought they'd nailed it. But the brightness that shone from Ryan's warm brown eyes, the unbridled affection that glimmered in them was unlike anything Lucas had ever seen. It was as if he'd pulled the drapes open so everyone could see the love there. He wanted to see that look every fucking day from now until he took his last breath.

"You look so beautiful tonight, Ry," he whispered and was rewarded with a shy smile and flushed cheeks. He could have stayed here all night with Ryan, but if they wanted to get to the jazz club before the crowds, they needed to leave.

The jazz music was already thrumming when they arrived at Le Caveau des Oubliettes. The cave was packed, despite the chill of the night but not so crowded that it was intolerable. They'd grabbed a quick bite in one of the cafés they passed on their way here. It was a small place in a narrow street and they'd braved the weather and sat at one of the outdoor tables, quickly scarfing down some dinner so they could get back indoors.

Once they'd entered the music venue, they found a spot to stand away from the bulk of the crowd, and Lucas got them both a beer. Ryan's foot was tapping along to whatever tune was playing. Lucas enjoyed jazz but was certainly not an aficionado; in fact, he'd be hard-pressed to name more than three jazz musicians. It was too loud to talk without yelling into each other's ears, so they sipped their beers and enjoyed the music.

As the evening wore on, Le Caveau des Oubliettes became more and more crowded, and soon Lucas's body was pressed tightly against Ryan's. Lucas could feel Ryan behind him, his leg still tapping away to the tunes, but then the band played a slower tune and Ryan put his arms around Lucas's waist and swayed them both. Lucas could feel Ryan's cock hardening and rubbing over his ass.

"It's called "Moonlight Serenade," Lucas," Ryan's throaty voice murmured in his ear and suddenly it was time to go, for two very insistent reasons. First it was getting uncomfortably crowded, and Lucas knew crowds weren't Ryan's favorite thing, especially if they were recognized. More urgently, though, was the length of Ryan's body pressing up against his while they moved to the music, and that sexy, fucking voice in his ear had him so fucking turned on he could feel his dick pressing demandingly against the zip of his chinos. He needed some relief. He needed Ryan.

It was crazily cold out when they left the venue, but they'd both dressed appropriately and were more than happy to walk back to their hotel. Lucas took a risk and grabbed hold of one of Ryan's hands, linking their glove-covered fingers. He'd have to do this again one day without the wool barrier between their hands.

"It's a beautiful city," Ryan's soft words pierced through his reverie.

"Amazing, isn't it? The architecture is fantastic. There's so much history here, too; in fact, right across Europe everywhere we turn we run into history. Have you ever been before?"

"No. I've always wanted to. Especially Italy: Rome, Venice, Florence. I never had the money. I had to work my ass off to get the money to get me to LA and tide me over until I found work. Now I've got plenty of money, though, so maybe I'll get a chance," Ryan said, and Lucas wondered if the wistful expression on his face was because of the money he now had, the fact he was in Paris, or that he was holding another man's hand.

Would it be too presumptive to suggest a trip together while their show was on hiatus? Lucas was lost when it came to relationship stuff. Sure, he'd been married for almost a decade, but it wasn't truly a marriage. He knew Ryan had never had a relationship so they'd be teetering on that tightrope together. And oddly, he knew neither would let the other fall.

"I've seen a bit of Rome, but I've always wanted to go back and spend time there. I remember when I first saw the Pantheon I actually felt teary. I mean, I was standing in front of this building that is almost two thousand years old, and it knocked the wind out of me. I kept imagining the people of the time. Did they even think for a moment that two thousand years later people from all over the world would come to see their building? It's extraordinary."

"It's hard to believe something we built could last that long. I mean, I can't imagine the Sydney Opera House still being around in two thousand years. It's kind of eerie in a way," Ryan added.

"Perhaps..." Lucas swallowed, grabbing hold of his courage. "Perhaps we could go together. I'd love to see it again and I'd love to see it with you, Ryan."

He felt Ryan squeeze his hand and turned a little to sneak a peek at him. There was a large, genuine smile on his face. "I'd love that."

They spoke of other places they both wanted to visit as they continued their way back to their hotel. A light snow started falling as they approached the lobby and it simply added to the magic of the evening.

When they got to the elevators, Lucas was very aware they'd reached the awkward part of the date. Whose room did they go back to? Did they go together or share a good-night kiss and head to their separate rooms? Lucas knew what he wanted but Ryan was so much more innocent than he was, and he was determined not to push him and scare him off. The blowjob the other day had been well received, but they hadn't really talked further about what Ryan was and wasn't willing to try. However, he knew that any deal breakers Ryan might have would be okay with him. It was the entire package Lucas was after with Ryan, not just the body—as fucking gorgeous as that was.

They stepped into the elevator, and coward that he was, Lucas stood back to allow Ryan to press the button. They were only one floor apart and Lucas sighed when Ryan pressed his floor. It hadn't answered his question. Was Ryan going back to his room alone and expected Lucas to press the button for his own floor? Or were they both going back to Ryan's room?

"I'd um...I'd love it if you came up to my room, Luke. I'm not ready for this night to be over," Ryan shyly offered.

Lucas put a hand on Ryan's cheek and pressed a gentle kiss to his lips. "I'd love that," he breathed.

Chapter Seventeen

Lovers *rising*

RYAN

"Good. So that little awkwardness is settled. We might as well get it all out of the way... I'd like you to... I *want* you to stay tonight, Luke. I want to..." Ryan's courage faltered. He knew Lucas was letting him set the pace, so it was up to him to be as clear as possible with Lucas about what he wanted—and he wanted everyfuckingthing.

"Wild horses, Ry...wild fucking horses couldn't keep me away. We'll just see where the night takes us, huh?" Lucas smiled one of his perfect smiles, his green eyes flashing, and Ryan knew exactly where he wanted the night to take them.

The date had been everything he could have hoped for. There'd been no flashiness to the evening and that suited Ryan perfectly. Lucas was fun and entertaining and had chosen places Ryan would have picked to go himself if he had any knowledge of the city at all. Ryan loved jazz and the cave-like structure of the music venue had enhanced the acoustics perfectly. The food in the little backstreet café had been authentic and delicious, and Notre-Dame had blown his mind. His first date ever, and it had been wonderful.

Ryan had also been acutely aware of Lucas's presence all afternoon and into the evening: the heat radiating from his body, his intoxicating scent, and the luminescence of his extraordinarily green eyes under the lights of the Parisian night. Ryan had been half-hard all fucking night, and as nervous as he was, he wanted more from Lucas. And he wanted it tonight.

Once they reached his room, they removed coats, gloves, scarves, beanies, and sweaters. After that, Ryan gestured for Lucas to take a seat on the large sofa.

"Drink?" he offered.

"Beer, thanks. Whatever you've got."

The room was larger than any hotel room Ryan had ever stayed in and it offered a kitchenette spacious enough for some basic cooking if the mood took him. So far, he'd been more than happy with room service. He grabbed a couple of beers and handed one over to Lucas. He then settled himself comfortably next to him, enjoying the companionable silence as they sipped their drinks.

Ryan wasn't quite sure what to do next; he'd never tried to seduce a man. Hell, all Lucas would have to do to seduce him was wink and nod, but Ryan wasn't sure what he needed to do. This was a different world opening up to him. *Well, nothing for it but to dive in.*

"So, thank you for tonight, Luke. I had a great time."

"I did too. I wasn't sure. I've never been in this situation before. I've never really dated. It's kind of weird, especially because I've known you for a while now and we were friends first."

"It was good, though?" Ryan grinned when Lucas nodded in response. "Well, I bet we can make it even better." He tried for some semblance of a sexy, come-on face but supposed he probably failed dismally. He sucked at this. Perhaps he should try for honesty rather than trying to play at being suggestive and seductive.

Ryan shifted forward in his seat and put his beer bottle on the coffee table. He turned to look at Lucas. "Luke, I...I want to be with you tonight. I want you... This—whatever it is—between us... I want it."

Lucas moved quickly, putting his own beer down before gently grabbing the sides of Ryan's face and kissing the holy hell out of him. His lips were far warmer than Ryan had expected, and the scrape of his scruff twisted knots of desire in his belly.

"You sure?" Lucas whispered during a break in his relentless assault on Ryan's mouth. Ryan nodded, hoping Lucas understood because he wasn't at all sure he was capable of words. "Ryan." Lucas pulled back from him and stared into his eyes with an intensity that should have scared him, but all it did was make his dick fucking harder.

Ryan stood and grabbed one of Lucas's hands, giving him a firm tug so he understood he was meant to stand and follow him. Ryan walked toward the bedroom; he would have run if he didn't think that would have looked too pathetically desperate. But before he could walk through the door, Lucas yanked on his hand, forcing him to stop. He turned to face Lucas, terrified that maybe he'd changed his mind.

"Ryan, I need you to tell me." Lucas didn't need to elaborate; Ryan knew what he was asking.

He pulled Lucas to him and kissed his lips, softly, tenderly. "I want this," he murmured as he turned them and backed Lucas into the bedroom. Ryan didn't stop until he felt Lucas bump into the Egyptian cotton sheet-covered bed. He fisted Lucas's shirt and used that to push him onto the bed. Ryan followed him down, pressing his lips to Lucas's as they went. Lucas's tongue swept into his mouth, dueling with his own, causing Ryan's eyes to roll at the sensation. He was hot all over, tingly—desperate. For more of Lucas, for everything.

Lucas rose to his elbows and scrabbled backward toward the middle of the bed. Ryan chased after him, not allowing any separation of their flush bodies. He bent to kiss Lucas again but this time was different. The anticipation of what was to come, the sensation of lying on a bed, the feel of Lucas's pliant body under his own, all swirled together into a raging storm of passion, making Ryan suspect he couldn't get close enough.

His lips moved to Lucas's neck, trailing nips and kisses down its length, occasionally sucking the smooth skin between his lips to leave Lucas marked. *Mine.*

He was so fucking hard already from the touch of Lucas's cock against his own, both of them moving their bodies, seeking out the friction they needed. Ryan groaned as the hard lengths rubbed together, even through the material of Lucas's chino pants and the thickness of the denim he was wearing.

The thought of the cloth barring him from the naked skin he craved had Ryan moving. He pulled away, kneeling with his legs on either side of Lucas's trim hips, his ass resting on Lucas's thighs. With one sure movement, he ripped his Henley over his head, tossing it somewhere over his shoulder. As soon as it was gone, Lucas reached up and traced his torso with warm fingertips. Every ridge and dip of muscle was explored. Lucas left no part of him untouched. And then those long fingers were pulling at the button of his jeans and fumbling with his zipper.

Ryan couldn't stop the loud groan when Lucas reached in and pulled his cock free. It was only the second time this man's—any man's—hand had touched him there and the pleasure was unbearable. He needed to get his jeans off but had no clue how to do it with even a tiny bit of grace. Before he could manage any sort of movement, he felt himself being flipped so he was now on his back with Lucas straddling his body.

Lucas squirmed backward, gently pulling at Ryan's jeans as he went. When he reached the end of the bed, he stood, leaving Ryan's jeans pooled at his ankles while struggling to get his shoes off. Once they were gone, the jeans and briefs quickly followed. Ryan then lay spread out naked on the bed, watching as Lucas's gaze tracked all over his body, his pink tongue peeking out to lick at his lips. He felt no self-consciousness at being naked in front of Lucas, the lust and desire he could see in Lucas's eyes giving him the confidence he needed. But Ryan wanted Lucas as naked as he was, so he sat up to reach for the buttons on Lucas's shirt. But Lucas gently pried his fingers off and eased him back down. "Uh-uh," he whispered.

"Not fair, Lucas," Ryan replied, though he wasn't disappointed for long. Lucas unbuttoned his shirt slowly, his gaze never leaving Ryan's, and the heat and lust Ryan could see blazing in the green orbs had him squirming with need. Once the torturously unhurried removal of his shirt was complete, Lucas's hands moved to his pants, slowly unzipping and then sliding them down his perfectly muscled legs. Ryan watched as he stepped out of his pants.

All Ryan could see—all he could focus on—was the fucking flawless body before him. Lucas was every wet dream he'd ever had.

Lucas crawled back over Ryan and leaned down, close enough they shared breath. "I fucking love stripping for you, Ry." There was no possibility of replying because Lucas's lips were on his again, tasting him, teasing him. Ryan's cock grew impossibly harder at the sensation of Lucas's now bare body rubbing against his.

For a moment, a flash of Lucas's vastly superior experience unnerved him, but Ryan could feel the evidence of his effect on Lucas, who was thick and hard against his thigh. He had this. They both wanted this.

Ryan pressed a hand between their bodies, searching. When he found Lucas's cock, he grabbed ahold and groaned at the feel of the silky flesh-covered hardness. He'd never touched another man—anywhere—except platonic hugs and the occasional slap on the shoulder, but this was entirely different. His stomach fluttered, a kaleidoscope of lust and passion and anticipation. He tentatively moved his hand over Lucas's length, rubbing his thumb over the crown, dipping his nail gently into the slit. Lucas's entire body bucked against his, and the sounds he was making had Ryan practically humping beneath him.

"What do you want?" Lucas whispered against his ear.

"I don't—oh fuck, I don't know." Ryan barely managed to get his words out. *I want whatever you can give me.*

"Well I know what I want, Ryan." Oh Jesus, Lucas's breathy whispering in his ear was doing all sorts of things to him—all of them good. "I want to go for a ride." Lucas's lips were back on his almost before he'd finished the last word. Ride. Did that mean...?

Ryan couldn't think straight. His mind was a whirlwind of lust and desire so strong it threatened to sweep him away. He wanted something... needed something, but he was too inexperienced to understand what it was.

"Fuck, hang on," Lucas blurted and then jumped up from where he'd lain over Ryan's body and fled the room. Moments later, he dashed back, a giant grin on his face and a condom and small sachet of lube in his hands. "I used to be a boy scout." He winked.

Lucas tossed his supplies on the bed close to Ryan's head and then knelt over Ryan's body again, knees on either side. He pressed kisses to Ryan's inner thighs, nipping and tugging with his teeth every now and then. He worked around Ryan's cock, making Ryan nearly fly off the bed when Lucas finally licked a path up his hard shaft. Ryan's hands were fisted in the sheets, his head thrashing side to side as the pleasure flooded through his overheated body.

"Fuck...oh fuck, Luke. I won't... I'm not gonna..." Eloquence was lost to Ryan, and Lucas had clearly not gotten the message that he wasn't going to last long because he took the head of Ryan's cock into his mouth, sucking hard. Ryan knew he couldn't take much more and reached down to fist his hands in Lucas's hair, tugging gently. This time Lucas understood and pulled off, favoring Ryan with a wicked grin, before lowering his head again to lick a line from Ryan's navel to his collarbone.

"Oh god," he groaned.

"You are so fucking hot, Ry. Those noises you're making...the way you smell... Jesus, you're turning me inside out."

"Lucas, please."

"I've got you, baby," Lucas whispered to him. Ryan couldn't stop his body from squirming, searching for something...relief, more, he didn't know. Lucas sat up, depriving Ryan of his sinful lips while he fumbled for the lube. Ryan watched as he tore the packet open and dripped some of the contents onto his fingers. Then Lucas reached behind his own body and Ryan could only imagine what those fingers were doing, the moans falling from Lucas's lips painted an accurate picture, causing Ryan's hips to continue to roll. He was helpless to stop his movements as his body frantically searched for release.

Other than closing his eyes on a moan, Lucas hadn't looked away from Ryan as he worked. He finally brought his hand back and broke open the condom, rolling it onto Ryan's length. Then he drizzled more lube onto his fingers before one of his big hands grabbed Ryan's cock, stroking so the lube was coating him. Ryan could feel his dick twitching in Lucas's hand, and he had to bite his lip in an effort to stop himself from coming.

"Okay, baby, I'm gonna ride you now. You might wanna hold on." Lucas's voice was husky, his eyes glazed over, and his grin fucking filthy. He rose to his knees, putting Ryan into flux between fascination and complete pleasure as Lucas slowly lowered himself onto Ryan's cock until his ass was resting on Ryan's pelvis.

Ryan watched as Lucas's eyes drifted closed, and he leaned forward to rest his palms on Ryan's pecs. For a moment, he didn't move, nor did Ryan, despite the urge to do so almost shattering him. Suddenly Lucas's eyes opened and he shifted, raising himself up and lowering back down. The fit was exquisite: so tight and warm. With each downward slide from Lucas, a groan slipped from his lips, his entire torso writhing as though trying to wrangle in the pleasure.

It was a visual and visceral spectacle different to anything Ryan had experienced before. Pure instinct took over as Ryan's hands moved to Lucas's hips, gripping him tightly and holding him steady. He took control and thrust up hard into Lucas's heat, over and over. His rhythm was chaotic and frantic as he became consumed by the overwhelming need to come. The sounds they made were indecent and lewd, and somewhere in the chaos of his thoughts, he wondered if his neighbors could hear them.

"So fucking tight, Luke. Oh fuck...yeah," Ryan ground out.

Lucas had one hand on Ryan's chest, the other wrapped around his own dick, jacking in time to Ryan's thrusts.

A growl unlike anything Ryan had ever heard tore from Lucas's mouth as he began coming all over Ryan's chest, some of it even hitting Ryan's chin. Ryan watched as Lucas continued to pull lazily on his dick as he wrung out the last of his release. "You look so fucking beautiful, Luke," he managed to breathe out; at least he hoped he did, because right then his own orgasm slammed into him, darkening his vision and ripping a similar roar from his own mouth.

Lucas eventually collapsed and lay panting on top of him. They stayed that way for an indeterminate period of time until Ryan felt his cock soften and slip from Lucas's body. Lucas lifted off, moving to stretch out beside him. Ryan reached down to remove the condom, tie it off and chuck it in the direction of the can beside the bed. On jelly legs, he stood and walked into the bathroom, wet a facecloth, and cleaned himself up. He grabbed another and took it into the bedroom.

Lucas's eyes were closed when he walked back in and gently began cleaning him. When done, Ryan tossed the cloth and lay back on the bed, pulling Lucas so his back was lined up to Ryan's front. Ryan had never cuddled after his past encounters, but he couldn't have walked away from Lucas now at gunpoint.

In his sleep, Lucas wiggled a little, subconsciously settling himself against Ryan. He cinched his arms more tightly around Lucas and pressed his lips to his hair. "I fucking love you, Luke," he whispered as his eyes closed and sleep took him.

Chapter Eighteen

Was it an accident? Will he be okay?

LUCAS

Paris had seemed like a dream—a wonderful, magical dream, one that Lucas had never woken from, and he was slowly coming to realize he didn't need to wake—that the dream was actually his reality.

Since they'd flown back from Paris, he and Ryan had spent most nights together, and Lucas thought he was doing a pretty good job keeping his promise to learn every inch of Ryan's body. That little spot where his thigh met his hip that got him every single time Lucas nipped at it was his favorite. God, just thinking about Ryan: how responsive he was, the sounds he made. He was fucking perfect.

Lucas knew Ryan had been uncomfortable, at first, staying at his place with Anna there, but with her warmth and openness directed at Ryan like a spotlight, he'd soon realized his presence simply wasn't an issue. There were no unresolved romantic feelings between Lucas and Anna; they were friends—close friends—but nothing more.

The nights they'd spent away from each other had been miserable. Lucas had missed the strength and heat of Ryan's body every second they were apart. Sleep was hard to pin down when cold sheets and a gaping hole where Ryan should have been were all he had to cuddle up to.

Ryan's stalker had gone quiet and the general consensus was she'd lost interest. The media were steering clear of her, and Ryan had refused to acknowledge her in any fashion after the initial statement had been given on his behalf. The studio was maintaining security, but she hadn't been heard from in a while.

It had been weeks since he'd had contact with his family. He knew they hadn't been thrilled about the budget they'd been put on, but it wasn't as though he'd cut them off completely. Besides, he wasn't an enabler, and his siblings had to at least start partially supporting themselves. He hoped they'd come around soon, because he did miss them, and he wanted them to meet Ryan. He'd give them another week to stew and then he'd make the first move to reconcile with them.

It was an unusual day today. For once, Ryan had an entire day filming while Lucas wasn't required on the set at all. Anna was in LA again, and he was at loose ends. Ryan was coming straight home from work, so he decided to do something special. Lucas hadn't cooked anything more complicated than eggs on toast for years, but today he was in the mood to challenge his culinary skills.

Ryan's taste in food was as understated as his taste in most things. No matter what level of success he achieved, Lucas could not imagine Ryan ever wanting the fanciest and most expensive anything. He knew Ryan liked all things meat—he chuckled to himself at that thought—so he decided on a simple meatloaf. The fact Lucas made it from scratch would be enough to impress Ryan, he hoped.

The recipe seemed simple enough, but Lucas knew he didn't have any of the ingredients, and he probably didn't have the utensils and other equipment he'd need either. He made a list—it wasn't a long one—and decided to drive to the local market. He wanted to stock up on some beer and other things and didn't relish the idea of walking home lugging all of that.

The six-year-old Buick Enclave he drove, while not top of the range and clearly out-of-date according to some who changed their cars as frequently as their underwear, had never given him any trouble. He loved the color, he loved how it handled, and he was comfortable driving in it. He couldn't fathom driving anything flashier. He pulled out of his underground parking and merged into the busy San Francisco traffic. The Noe Valley Whole Food Market was a little farther than the Safeway up the road, but Lucas was willing to drive the extra distance.

He made it two blocks in fairly good flowing traffic and was just bursting into what would be an unfortunate sing-along to "Baby Got Back," of all songs, when he heard the roar of an engine and the furious blasting of several horns. Lucas turned barely in time to see a car hurtling at him through the intersection. He had mere seconds to react. Collision was unavoidable, so the best he could hope for was for the impact to be survivable. Lucas did his best to relax into it, turning the wheel so, hopefully, the impact would hit the rear of the car. When the other vehicle hit him, though, every thought flew from his head aside from one last question as unconsciousness took him—will I ever hold Ryan again?

RYAN

"Cut. Take five, folks," Lon boomed.

Ryan usually checked his phone during breaks, but today for some reason, as soon as Lon called "cut," Ryan was desperate to get to his phone.

As soon as he pulled it from his pocket, he found four missed calls, all from Anna. Ryan's stomach plummeted as he hit "send" to return her call.

"Ryan, thank God. It's Lucas. Oh damn—" Anna broke off and Ryan could hear soft crying and deep breathing while Anna tried to get herself under control. Meanwhile, Ryan wanted to scream through the fucking phone. What the hell had happened to Lucas? Ryan doubled over; putting his head down before he did something stupid like faint. Something bad must have happened, and Lucas would need him, so he couldn't afford to be passed out on the fucking ground. "Sorry, Ryan. It's Lucas; he's been in a car accident. I'm not sure, I don't know the details. All they said when they called is that he'd been brought in unconscious. The other driver was killed. Oh, Jesus, it must have been bad. They've taken him to USFC. I'm on my way to the airport to fly back. Ryan, I'm so sorry. Can you get to him?"

Ryan listened to Anna with an unwilling ear; if he didn't hear it, then maybe it wasn't true. This wasn't make-believe, however, and he had to get to Lucas. "Fuck. Okay. Fuck. Anna, I'm on my way to him. Be safe and I'll see you when you get here, okay?" Anna breathed a simple "See you soon" before hanging up, and Ryan ran back to Lon.

"Lon. I've gotta go. It's Lucas. There's been a car crash. I have to go." He didn't care if they thought he was oddly upset or if they wanted him to stay and finish the shoot. He was out of there. He needed to be with Lucas.

"Shit. Okay, Ryan, calm down for me. What hospital is he at? We need to get on top of this before the press finds out."

The press. Ryan hadn't even considered that. Surely they'd stay away while Lucas was...he didn't even know what...recovering, lying in a coma, dying. He had to get there. "USFC. I'm sorry, Lon, I have to go. Anna's in LA. Someone needs to be there with Luke."

"Okay. Look, you go...with a driver, Ryan. I'll sort things out here. I'll see you at the hospital."

Ryan only just caught Lon's last word because he'd already turned and was running toward the exit.

He'd never be able to say what happened on that trip to USFC while he sat in the back seat as Josh sped him toward Lucas. He knew his phone was ringing but he was sure it was either Lon or Mike, and he couldn't face talking to them. He didn't want to hear how they'd decided to spin this...whatever it turned out to be. There was no way he could deal with that with any kind of equanimity.

His thoughts were pounding in his brain, each throb a new and horrifying scenario of what he might find when he got to the emergency room. He hadn't heard again from Anna but didn't expect to—she'd be on her way from LA. He spared a thought for Lucas's family but Ryan had never met them, and he knew things were strained between Lucas and them right now. He trusted Anna would contact them; they needed to know regardless of the current state of their relationship.

Josh walked him into the emergency department after he'd managed to park the car close by. Ryan would happily pay the fine or tow charge if it was in the wrong spot. He was just glad the man was there because his legs were wobbly and he needed the support.

They approached a desk where a kindly looking man sat behind a monitor. "Excuse me," Ryan ventured, "could you tell me... I'm here for Lucas Evers. Could you tell me where he is?"

"And you are?"

"Oh...um I'm Ryan Lowe. I'm his...." What was he? Boyfriend? Partner? Work colleague? Probably none of those titles would get him in to see Lucas. Fuck, he hadn't even considered that.

"We know who you are, Mr. Lowe. Mr. Evers's wife has already given permission for you to go back to be with him. Your friend will have to stay out here, but if you follow me, I'll take you through." Carl—according to his name tag—offered him a sympathetic smile and Ryan could have kissed both him and Anna right then.

"I'll wait over here, Mr. Lowe. You give me a call when you're ready to...when you need me." Josh offered.

"You should go, Josh. I don't know how long... It could be a while."

"I'll be here." And Ryan was hit with another sympathetic smile. He wondered how many more he'd get before this nightmare was over. He nodded and turned to follow Carl.

This hospital seemed no different to any other Ryan had been in, though that number was fortunately few. Carl led him through a series of corridors until he was taken into a small room that had little floor space left since it contained a bed and numerous machines and IV stands. On the bed, with his stunning green eyes closed to Ryan's scrutiny and his skin paler than Ryan had ever seen it, lay the man he loved. He wouldn't gloss over it, deny it, or try to rationalize it—he was spectacularly in love with Lucas Evers, and the sight of him on that hospital bed punched a hole in his guts, making Ryan radiate fear he may lose him far too soon after only just finding him.

Carl walked away after guiding Ryan to the room, and for a brief moment, Ryan was alone with Lucas. All he could think of doing—the only thing he had to offer Lucas was his touch. He moved to stand beside the bed and linked his fingers with the hand that rested along Lucas's side. His hand was so cold to the touch that if it hadn't been for the beeping of the machines playing the music of Lucas's life, Ryan might have thought he'd lost him already.

He heard someone enter the room behind him. "Mr. Lowe?"

"Yes," he answered without turning to look.

"I'm Francine, Lucas's nurse. You can call me Fran. Doctor will be here shortly to discuss Lucas's condition with you. Is there anything I can tell you in the meantime?" From her voice alone, Ryan pegged her to be in her fifties, graying hair and with the quintessential appearance of a grandmotherly caregiver. When he turned to her, he found he couldn't have been more wrong. Francine would be lucky to be thirty; she had hair dyed an amazing shade of purple, and a line of studs ran up both ears. The only thing that fit the image he'd had was that her face exuded kindness and compassion.

"Is he going to be all right?" It was the only question that mattered.

"The next twenty-four hours will tell us more. He's suffered trauma to his head, and some bruising from the airbag. He has some swelling, but the doctor will give you more detail when she gets here. I'd be optimistic if I were you."

"I heard... His wife told me that the other driver was killed?"

"I'm sorry, I don't really know too much about it. I can tell you that the police are here to talk to Lucas; obviously, I've denied them entry."

"Do you mean that it was his fault? Is that why they're here?" Poor Lucas. If he'd killed someone, regardless of how accidental the circumstances, Ryan knew he'd be devastated.

"I'm sorry. I don't know."

Ryan could only nod and turn his attention back to his lover. He'd give everything he had, and would ever have, to see those gorgeous green eyes open right now, or to hear Luke laugh or call him Ry.

It must have been half an hour before the doctor arrived, but she really didn't have much more to tell him than Fran had, other than giving a name to Lucas's condition. Diffuse Axonal Injury. The doctor told him Lucas's brain had basically lagged behind the movement of his skull while it was flung about in the accident. There was talk of shearing and tearing and nerves and lesions, but all Ryan understood was Lucas's brain had been hurt, and no one could tell him if it would be his Lucas who eventually woke up. They were waiting for the swelling to ease and Lucas to regain consciousness before they could tell anything more. God, if he would only wake up.

Sometime after the doctor had left them alone again, Ryan's phone beeped. It had been quiet for a while after he'd ignored several calls, so Ryan pulled it from his pocket to check. It was a text from Anna letting him know she'd landed and would be at the hospital within the hour. Ryan couldn't wait to see her. He needed someone else here to help him shoulder the worry. After shooting off a quick reply, he returned to his silent vigil at Lucas's side.

It was only minutes later that he heard a commotion in the hall. He did his best to block it out, hoping it couldn't possibly have anything to do with him, until the door burst open and Fran gestured for him to step out of the room. He came face-to-face with two men in suits and one in a police uniform. The fuck? Even if the accident had been Lucas's fault, which he didn't buy for a minute, surely they weren't going to attempt to arrest him while he was still unconscious.

Fran glowered at the men before ushering the four of them into a small waiting room so they could talk privately without disturbing anyone.

"Mr. Lowe?" One of the suited men asked as soon as Fran left them alone.

"Yes."

"I'm Detective Holland; this is Detective Bourke and Officer Shilton. We need to speak with you."

"Me? I wasn't in the accident."

"We're aware, sir. Do you know a Leighton White?"

Oh god, Ryan's legs almost buckled and he must have lost color, because one of the detectives, he couldn't remember which at that moment, took his arm and guided him to a group of chairs. He was vaguely aware of his head nodding as he finally managed an answer. "Yes. She... I... We had a...a one-night thing and then she started stalking me. Why?"

"Mr. Lowe, Leighton White was the driver of the car that hit Mr. Evers's car. We were called to the scene when they found some troubling things in the wreck of her vehicle. We'll need you to come down to the station—"

"No, I won't leave Lucas. We'll have to talk here." Oh god, this couldn't be happening. Lucas was hit on purpose? It was his fault and the idea of that was enough to make him sick. Ryan wretched into the trash can in the room, unwilling to care about the detectives hovering over him.

When he was done, one of the men handed him a paper cup of water and some tissues. He cleaned up as best he could and turned to face the detectives.

"Look, come in once Mr. Evers's condition has stabilized, but we do need to speak to you as soon as possible. We should tell you we believe this was a targeted attack on Mr. Evers. And we believe Mr. Evers may still be in danger," the taller one, maybe Detective Bourke, said.

"Why? I thought... I was told the driver had died."

"That's correct sir, Ms. White is deceased. Unfortunately, from what we found in the wreckage, we don't believe she was working alone."

Chapter Nineteen

It was Ryan's girlfriend?? That bitch best be dead!

RYAN

Anna arrived ten minutes after the detectives left, finding Ryan in a state of utter shock and distress. She listened with dawning horror as Ryan told her what he knew. Leighton White had tried to kill Lucas. Leighton White was dead, but the police were still concerned for Lucas's safety. Because Leighton White hadn't been acting alone. None of it made any sense. Why had she gone after Lucas? Who else would be working with her and why?

"Ryan?" Anna's soft voice broke into his thoughts.

"Sorry?"

"I asked if you wanted a coffee. I sure as hell need something." Anna's eyes flashed with what looked like fear.

"No. I... Thanks, Anna, but I'm okay." Ryan didn't move from the chair he'd pulled up next to Lucas's bed. He still had Lucas's hand in his, and if Fran thought it strange that Lucas's wife and he were both holding Lucas's hands, she never showed it.

"I don't understand. She was obsessed with *you,* and since when do stalkers join forces with someone else? Did the detectives give you any idea who?"

Ryan shook his head. "All they had so far were some photos of Lucas's car and a phone they found in her car with messages to and from another number about the...about what she should do to Lucas because apparently he was the reason she and I weren't together. It was a burner, untraceable. The texts, Anna... I mean, Jesus, she was hounded to do this—manipulated. There were countless messages about how bad Lucas was, how he had to die so she could have me." Ryan shook his head again, disgusted by the entire nightmare. "They're trying to track down where Leighton has been, where she got the car. It was an old junker, Anna, no airbags. She had to have known she might be killed when she rammed Luke."

Ryan knew people did appalling things, and yet he was still shocked by their behavior, each and every time. Leighton had been manipulated and clearly had some problems, so he tried to find room in his heart to grieve for Leighton White, but all he could manage was a tiny sliver of sadness. She'd very nearly taken the only person Ryan had ever truly loved away from him.

In the chaos, Ryan had forgotten about Lucas's family. It had been hours; surely they should be here by now, unless Anna hadn't told them. He couldn't imagine her being spiteful, despite knowing her concerns over them using Lucas. "Anna, what about Luke's family?"

"I called them. Would you believe they are currently on vacation in Spain? So much for supporting themselves. I think Matthew and Craig are in the States, though. Luke's dad was going to call them." Anna huffed and shook her head. "Money fucks people up, Ryan. Who knows if they'll even show? I mean, they're good people, but I can see how money is changing them. They've got to stop using Lucas."

Lucas's finances were none of Ryan's business, but he hated the idea anyone was taking advantage of his generous nature.

The door creaked open again and Ryan turned to see Fran poking her head in once more. "Ryan, there's a few people out here who've asked to see you. They're from your studio. Want me to tell them to get lost, or do want to speak to them?"

"I better come out and see them, Fran, otherwise they'll never leave." He hated walking away from Lucas, but he knew Mike and Lon were probably out there and he knew how stubborn they both could be. "I'll be right back, Anna." Ryan leaned down and dropped a kiss on Lucas's lips, completely oblivious, and honestly uncaring, of Fran's reaction. From the soft smile on her face, he didn't think she minded one little bit.

Fran led him back through the maze until they reached a small room just off of the much larger waiting room where he'd left Josh some time ago. Inside was, well, too many people for that little room, causing Ryan to visualize them being disgorged from it like a clown car when this meeting was over. He found Mike among the faces and locked on, needing the strength that exuded from the calm man.

"How is he, Ryan?" Mike asked as soon as he stepped into the quiet room.

Ryan heard the door snick shut after Fran left and turned to address the people waiting for his reply. "Still not conscious. Doctor says we'll know more once he wakes. There's a lot of swelling, but brain function seemed okay on the EEG. He looks... He's all bruised and banged up. Doesn't look like himself." The words choked out of his throat. Every time he assumed he had a handle on what had happened, he'd hear words such as brain function and swelling and it would knock the wind right out of him again.

"The police have spoken to us. I don't... I can't believe what's happened. I'm aware this isn't really the time, but we need to make a statement. The press is already here being fucking vultures. Some asshole took pictures of Lucas in the wreck, and they've already hit social media. And they know your stalker was the other driver."

It wasn't so much that Ryan was angry, more that he felt incredibly sad that a statement to the press even had to be considered at this point in time. He was angry about the photos, though. Was Lucas not entitled to some dignity in his most vulnerable moment? "Honestly, Mike, you guys would know best what to say. I don't think Anna is even thinking about it at this point. I don't know... How do you even explain this, and what about the accomplice? Do you even mention that? I just... I don't care right now. Do what you think is best."

"Look, Ryan, this involves you too. We're drafting a statement, but we'd like you to be there when Lon reads it to the press."

"No. Absolutely not. Why? No." Apart from being away from Lucas for too long, Ryan knew he wasn't a good enough actor to be able to disguise his feelings for Lucas if he had to stand in front of the media and discuss the horrible events of that day. No way.

"Ryan, I know this will sound really callous, but you and Lucas are...you're a business, a brand. Your fans, viewers, and the studio heads will all want to see you. You need to show your face."

Ryan liked Mike, but right then he wanted to lash out and put him on his ass; either that, or he needed a big fucking drink. Instead, he settled for advancing on Mike until there were mere inches between them. He gritted his teeth to prevent his words from tearing out of his throat. "Lucas is not a fucking business. Our fans will just have to accept that I'm not leaving Lucas again while he is in that room fighting to come back to me. And the studio can go fuck itself if they can't understand that. Excuse me." He didn't bother looking around to see any of the reactions he knew would be sweeping over every face in the room. The studio could fire his ass, but he belonged in that stark, white room with the beeping machines and the man he fucking loved. There was not one other place on the planet he needed to be right then, so he stormed out.

Everything had changed in Lucas's room when he finally managed to find his way back to it; most terrifying was the missing bed and the man who had been in it. Ryan felt his stomach drop, and terror must have flashed across his face, because Anna jumped up and came over to him, grabbing onto his forearms.

"He's fine, Ryan. They just took him for another scan. He's fine." Anna rubbed his arms soothingly, and Ryan heard the whoosh of relief expel from his lungs.

"Shit. I thought… That was everyone from the show. Mike says they're going to make a statement to the press and he wanted me to be there." Anna nodded in response; having lived with the beast that was fame and celebrity longer, she understood it better than him. "I can't do it, Anna. I know I'll lose my shit, and I won't leave him. I have to be here when he wakes."

"Of course. You don't have to explain yourself to me. I am so glad he has you. He deserves to be happy." She took hold of both of Ryan's hands and gave them a little squeeze. "He saved me you know, not just when he married me but before that. When Mom…when Mom and Dad would knock me around, I'd sneak across the road and into his room and he always made me feel better—every time. He begged me to report them, and even said he was going to, but I begged him not to. They were my parents. As an adult, I can see how stupid that was, but when you're a kid you just…you love your parents unconditionally, even if they don't love you back."

"I'm so sorry, Anna. I know what it's like to have shitty parents. Dad didn't knock me around, but I was never on his radar; he never ever thought of me. I don't think he'd have noticed if I was dead in a ditch somewhere." Ryan could see the sadness of a ruined childhood reflected in Anna's kind eyes, and he reached out to embrace her, dropping a kiss on the top of her head. "Hey, but we showed them, right? Look at us now. We're successful, we're gorgeous, and we've got one thing they will never have, and it's the best fucking thing in the world. We've got Lucas."

"We do," Anna whispered and then pulled out of his hug to look him in the eyes. "Ryan, I'm going to be asking Lucas to divorce me and come clean about our relationship—"

"Anna, you don't—"

"I'm not just doing it for you and him. I've…well, I'm in love with someone, too, and she's asked me to marry her. She knows everything about Lucas and our arrangement, but she wants me, Ryan. She wants to be with me, officially." Anna beamed. How had he missed that incandescent glow of love shrouding her?

"Anyone I know?" Ryan asked, expecting a negative response.

"Yes, actually. You know her quite well, and you just love going out on her boat."

"Maria Curzon? Holy shit, Anna. That's great." Ryan could see Anna shaking her head.

"Wrong sister. It's Antonia."

"Shit. That's...fucking great, Anna. I wish you both every single bit of happiness you can grab onto." He pulled her in for another embrace just as the door flung open again. Two young men stood at the door, and though Ryan had never met them, he knew instantly who they were. Matthew and Craig Evers. The likeness to Lucas was both unmistakable and painful for Ryan to see, especially having to look into bright green eyes that were similar but just not the ones he wanted to see.

Ryan felt Anna tense in his arms, but she still turned to the brothers with a sympathetic smile on her face and gave them each a hug. "It's good to see you both here. I'm sorry for the circumstances."

"Where's Lucas?" The taller of the two asked.

"They've taken him for some tests. Matthew, Craig, this is Ryan Lowe." Anna introduced him and though each brother offered to shake hands with Ryan, he could feel it was under sufferance and they weren't terribly interested in him at all.

"What have the doctors said?" Craig asked. Matthew had yet to utter a word, other than his mumbled hello to Ryan.

As Anna finished explaining what she knew of Lucas's condition and the accident, the door opened again and Lucas was wheeled back into the room, closely followed by Fran and Doctor Kalman. Fran fussed around Lucas, so Ryan stood back to allow her to get him situated. He stood with Anna as she introduced Matthew and Craig to Doctor Kalman and gave the doctor permission to discuss Lucas's condition in front of them.

"Well, there isn't much more to report. He's just had another EEG and brain activity continues to look good. His pupils are reactive and he's a ten on the Glasgow Coma Scale. These are all good, positive signs. He's on steroids to try to get the swelling down, but it's up to him now. We just need him to regain consciousness," Doctor Kalman said in her calm, measured tone that Ryan thought must be part of the training to actually become a doctor.

"How long do you think he'll be out?" Ryan asked.

"I really can't say. Typically, if it's a moderate injury, it can be at least six hours. We've passed that mark, so while I don't expect permanent brain damage based on the EEG, I wouldn't be surprised if there are some temporary issues."

What the hell were temporary issues? "Like what?" Ryan pressed.

"Sometimes there can be problems with speech, coordination, memory, or even personality changes. A broad spectrum can be affected, and with these types of injuries, the damage is often microscopic so we can't see it all on the scans. I know this is very difficult, but we just won't know until he wakes up." Doctor Kalman patted his shoulder, and after a few more words of comfort to Anna, left the room. How, in this day and age, could they not know anything? Didn't they realize that was Ryan's future lying on that bed, shut off to the world around him?

Craig moved to stand beside Lucas's bed and gave his hand a squeeze. Matthew remained at the foot and made no move to speak to or touch his brother. Ryan could feel anger boiling in his gut; surely, cutting back his money wouldn't cause him to hate his brother.

It was all Ryan could do to try to dig his fingers into the unyielding wall to stop him from moving forward and doing something that would give away his relationship with Lucas. Anna moved to the other side of Lucas's bed, sparing him an apologetic grimace.

The entire uncomfortable encounter lasted only half an hour before Matthew declared he was exhausted and asked Anna if he and Craig could stay at her place, not missing the opportunity to have a dig that they couldn't afford a hotel. Anna wasted no time calling a nearby hotel and booking the best room available, clearly not wanting the brothers around. Neither brother had spoken to him since their introduction, nor had they shown much interest in the knowledge that this had purposely been done to their brother. It appeared as though money really did fuck people up.

"Well, they were...something." Ryan managed once Lucas's brothers had left the room. "They were cold, Anna. I mean Craig seemed to care the bare minimum, but Matthew looked like he couldn't give a shit. Have they always been that way?"

"No, well, not that bad anyway. They were always an odd family. Close, but not really under the surface, you know. It's hard to explain. They kind of stuck together and cared, but in some of them, it seemed to be a shallow kind of love. If you were outside looking in, you'd say they were tight-knit but once you got on the inside...not so much."

Ryan could finally move back where he belonged, at Lucas's side. He grabbed Lucas's hand and pressed a soft kiss to each of his knuckles. He couldn't smell his Lucas underneath the stench of antiseptic and the lingering odor of blood from the gashes Lucas had sustained in the crash. He'd give anything to smell that citrusy scent that was his Lucas.

Time past achingly slowly as they waited for Lucas to wake, making Ryan fidgety. The silence was suddenly disturbed by the buzz of Anna's phone. She'd fallen asleep in her seat, with her head resting on Lucas's bed, but came awake at the sound. Ryan did his best not to listen as she took her call.

"Ryan, that was Antonia. She's here and suggested I pop home for a shower and something to eat."

"Sure, yes, go on, Anna. Get some rest."

"Will you be all right? I can stay."

"I'll be fine. Go, really."

"Okay, I'll catch a nap and a change of clothes. Can I bring you anything?"

Ryan wasn't leaving the hospital. Short of being physically dragged out, he was staying right here at Lucas's side, but he didn't want Lucas to wake up to a smelly, disheveled mess. "Change of clothes would be great. I have a bag in Lucas's room; you could bring that back for me, please. And could you grab my toiletry bag, too?"

"Okay. I won't be long. Call me if anything...for anything." And with a quick hug, Anna left.

Relieved at finally being alone with Lucas, Ryan allowed his gaze to wander unfettered over his lover. The bruising on Lucas's face was purpling, and the swelling made him almost unrecognizable, but this was still his Lucas, so Ryan let his hands gently roam. His fingers trailed over the features of Lucas's face, slowly tracing the edge of his lips and up into his hairline. It was only a butterfly touch, with Ryan agonizingly aware of the damage that lay beneath his fingertips. He bent down and brushed his lips over Lucas's, before moving them to his ear and whispering, "Wake up, Lucas. Please, please come back to me." For the first time since he'd heard the news, Ryan allowed the tears to slip from his eyes.

Chapter Twenty

Has Ryan even left the hospital? Lovers *is real!!*

RYAN

"Okay, Luke. Would you rather fight a hundred men the size of little gray garden lizards or one lizard the size of a man?" Ryan looked hopefully at Lucas. He'd lost count of how many *would you rather* questions he'd asked in the last two days, and he hadn't received a single answer yet. Lucas's eyes had remained steadfastly closed, the startling green concealed behind his lids. Ryan hadn't left the hospital and had refused to take calls from Mike or Lon or anybody from the studio.

Anna had come and gone several times, and Craig had made another visit, without Matthew, but he'd been far friendlier this time around. Ryan could see that in better circumstances he'd probably like Craig and could even see them becoming friends. But the one voice he wanted to hear, the eyes he wanted to look into were closed to him, and the loss was painful, despite his constant reminders that it was a temporary loss.

Detectives Holland and Bourke had tried to make contact, but nothing he had to say to them was urgent since he didn't know anything. The only urgency, as far as he was concerned, was Lucas waking up.

Ryan looked at the beautiful face again, willing those stunning eyes to open. Then he kissed Lucas's knuckles and laid his head on his chest. He could hear Lucas's heart beating strongly against his cheek. "It's beating with mine, Luke. We're apart but your heart is beating with mine, so now all you have to do is wake up and come back to me, and I'll give you that ecstasy you wanted. I promise you."

He felt the rise and fall of Lucas's chest and the small puffs of air on his face, but it wasn't enough. "Okay, how about this one? Would you rather live comfortably in the wild, far from civilization, or live in the city as a homeless person?"

"I'd rather live wherever you are, Ry."

The words were spoken so quietly that for a moment Ryan thought his imagination was supplying the answers he wanted to hear. He had to be sure, though, so he lifted his head and turned to look at Lucas and found bright-green eyes staring at him. The mouth that had been so quiet for the past two days had spread into the hint of a smile, and if Ryan wasn't so conscious of Lucas's injuries, he would have thrown himself on top of him in relief. Thankfully, he had the presence of mind to restrain himself, so instead, laid a palm on Lucas's cheek.

"Luke? God, you're awake. I have to call Fran. We need the doctors." Ryan reached for the buzzer, pressing the call button for a nurse, knowing Fran was on duty. "How do you feel? Are you all right? Do you remember anything? I...oh, thank god, you're awake."

"I'm okay. What happened? I don't... I feel funny, but I think I remember a car hitting me and then...um..."

"Everything okay in here, Ryan? Oh, well, Lucas, you're awake." Fran moved to Lucas and quickly checked him over, flashing a light into his pupils and asking him to squeeze her hand. "I'm just going to pop out and page Doctor Kalman, and then I'll be right back," Fran said with a big, genuine grin on her face.

"Ry, what happened?" Lucas's voice was raspy and soft—unused for several days—but Ryan would have heard it anywhere.

"The car...it crashed into you, and you've got a head injury. You've been in a coma for almost three days, but the rest of your injuries were minor, abrasions and bruises, really. You were lucky, Lucas. She hit you hard." Ryan bore another stone of guilt settle in his guts every time he remembered it was *his* stalker who had tried to kill Lucas.

"She? Was the other driver...is she hurt?"

Before he could answer Lucas and tell him the entire sorry story, Fran walked back into the room and took charge as only nurses can do. Ryan was ordered to stand at the end of the bed, out of the way, while Fran asked Lucas a battery of questions and again took his blood pressure, pulse, and whatever else they seemed to monitor every half hour. Before she'd finished, Doctor Kalman entered the room.

While she, too, asked a barrage of questions, Ryan took the opportunity to call Anna, who answered on the second ring. "Ryan, everything okay?"

"He's awake, Anna. Just woke up, just like that." He snapped his fingers even though Anna probably couldn't hear it.

"Yes!" she yelled, and Ryan could imagine the fist pump she was likely doing. "I'm about ten minutes away. I was gonna stop at Starbucks to grab us some real coffee, but that can wait. I'll be right there. Is he...is he him, Ryan? Is he our Lucas?"

Ryan swallowed past the lump in his throat, knowing Anna had had the same fears as he had—that they wouldn't get their Lucas back. "Yeah, I think so, Anna. I think so." He heard Anna clearing her throat and then a barely audible "See you soon" before she hung up.

"Ryan, we're going to take him for a couple of scans. An orderly will be here shortly to take him down." Doctor Kalman squeezed his bicep as she leaned in a little closer. "It looks good, Ryan. Very good." She smiled and left the room. Fran followed close behind her, leaving Ryan alone again with Lucas.

Ryan didn't bother to wipe away the tear that slid from his eye as he turned back to Lucas. He walked closer and then bent down and pressed his lips gently to Lucas's. When he tried to pull away, Lucas grabbed the back of his neck to hold him there, keeping their faces close together.

"I love you. God, I love you. Don't cry. I'm okay. I promise."

They'd danced around the admission, claiming they were falling for each other, but the writers were correct, if ever there was a time to confess love for another person, it was in the moments after nearly losing them— and mercifully getting them back. He should have done it much sooner. "Lucas, I've never been so fucking scared. I kept talking to you, and you wouldn't wake up, and the doctors didn't know how you'd be when you did wake up. I was terrified, but oh god, I love you, too, so fucking much. And if you ever do this shit to me again, I'm gonna spank your ass. Hear me?"

Lucas chuckled and nodded, but even though it was only a tiny movement of his head, he still winced.

"Try not to move your head too much, Luke. It took a battering, and it's gotta be sore."

"Worst fucking headache ever," Lucas confirmed.

Before Ryan knew it, one of the orderlies had come in and rolled Lucas away. It didn't seem fair; he'd only just gotten him back and now he was gone again.

Anna arrived before Lucas returned, so Ryan told her what he knew, which really wasn't much other than Lucas was awake and seemed like himself.

"Ryan, I know you haven't been paying any attention, but you should be aware the press is going nuts. They know it was your stalker who hit Luke's car. And now it's been leaked that she wasn't working alone. That's just the mainstream media. Fan sites and entertainment channels are far more interested in the fact you haven't left the hospital since Luke's accident and what that means for *Samdom* or *Lovers*."

"It wasn't a fucking accident, Anna. She hit him on purpose." Ryan broke in, frustration and anger replacing his naturally calm manner. He admitted he'd had no real idea of what celebrity truly meant, and as much as he loved his job, he wasn't in the least sure he was okay with the fame that came with it.

"I know, Ryan. Look, I know how hard this is, but you need to be prepared for the shit storm you are both going to be walking into when you set foot outside this door. I've been sneaking in and out as best as I can, but they've caught up to me a few times. I've said nothing to them and nor will I, but be prepared."

"Sorry. You're the last person I should be yelling at. It's been a long few days. So what... I mean, are people happy this has happened because they get to see the romance of *Lovers* develop? That's just...sick."

"Yeah, it is what it is. Welcome to celebrity. Look, the studio has declined to comment on anything since they gave their initial statement that Lucas had his...was attacked. They've given updates as to his recovery so far but nothing more. People are coming to their own conclusions. The *Samdom* shippers have decided you two are together in real life now—not that they're wrong"—she added with a wink—"and they are disturbingly happy about it, considering that Lucas is supposedly happily married to *moi*."

As much as Ryan wanted to get the hell out of that hospital with Lucas, he couldn't help wondering if they'd be better off staying put until the storm blew itself out. Whatever happened, though, he'd be doing everything he had to do to shield Lucas from as much of it as he could.

"Mr. Lowe, we hear Mr. Evers is awake." A deep, cranky-sounding voice boomed from behind him. Who the hell had told the cops that Lucas was awake?

"Detective Holland. Yes, he is, but he's away having some tests; perhaps this could wait," Ryan suggested.

"Mr. Lowe, we're not the enemy here. Somebody tried to kill Mr. Evers. Even though that person is dead, we are absolutely certain she was not working alone. This means there is someone still out there who may wish to harm Mr. Evers."

Shame pierced through Ryan. He knew everything the detective had said was true, and yet, until Detective Holland actually spoke those words, he'd somehow refused to put two and two together. "Shit," he mumbled. "Of course. I'm sorry. I should have been helping you. I've just been so worried about Lucas."

"Look, we understand, Mr. Lowe. But now that Mr. Evers is awake, we really must speak to him." The other detective, Bourke, spoke for the first time. "Mrs. Evers, good to see you here too. I know we've spoken already, but maybe you've thought of something else to add." He acknowledged Anna and moved to shake her hand.

"Detective Bourke. I don't have anything new, but I will ask you to take it easy with my husband; he's only just woken up."

"Of course. As we said, we're not the enemy here."

Ryan spent the next twenty minutes telling them what he knew about Lucas's attack, which was pretty much only what they'd told him when it had first happened. He knew of no one who would want to hurt Lucas and tended to agree with the detectives' suspicion it was another crazed fan who had trouble separating fiction from reality and wanted Lucas out of the way to get to Ryan. The guilt pulled at his guts, making him sick with it.

By the time Lucas was brought back to the room, Ryan was heavy with both guilt and worry. It was one thing to be worried for yourself, but it was almost paralyzing to worry about someone you loved.

Ryan walked over to Lucas, took his hand, and kissed his lips as soon they had him situated comfortably. The nature of his relationship with Lucas would be plainly evident to the two detectives, but he didn't care. They'd need to know anyway.

"Uh, Mr. Lowe, could you confirm the nature of your relationship with Mr. Evers for us please?" Detective Holland asked.

"Ryan's my boyfriend." It was Lucas who spoke, so loud and so clear, leaving no room for misinterpretation, and Ryan couldn't help the little flutter in his heart that Lucas's straightforward declaration elicited. The two detectives shared a look and Ryan didn't miss the glance that Detective Bourke sent to Anna. Neither commented further, perhaps dismissing the situation as the crazy, freewheeling lifestyle of Hollywood celebrities.

"That probably would have been handy to know before now." Detective Holland glared accusingly at both Ryan and Anna, who merely shrugged as though she believed it should have been obvious to the detectives.

Ryan sat at Lucas's side as the detectives filled him in on their investigation so far. The grip Lucas had on his hand tightened as the story unfolded. Ryan hadn't had a chance to soften the blow before the detectives told Lucas all about Leighton White and her attempt on his life. By the time they'd finished and started asking him questions, Lucas had visibly paled and was shaking. Anna moved to stand on his other side and rubbed his arm soothingly.

"I don't know of anyone. I can't think of anybody who'd want to kill me. I...as far as I know, I don't have a stalker, at least not one who's made contact with me. And I don't think I've pissed anyone off so much that they'd want to kill me."

"We've spoken to your agent, studio, and what family we could locate, and they all confirm that they've received no correspondence that concerns them or know of anyone with a grudge. Nothing has raised any alarm with them." Detective Bourke confirmed.

The detectives left shortly after getting all to agree they understood the serious nature of the threat and would take appropriate precautions.

"Have my family been here, Anna?" Lucas asked once the three of them were alone again.

"Ah, your folks and Kayla are in Spain, but they should be back soon. Craig and Matthew have both been here, and I've called them to let them know you're awake, so I guess they'll be in soon to see you."

Ryan found the lackadaisical attitude of Lucas's family to the attempt on his life to be incomprehensible. Had he been thousands of miles away when Lucas had been hurt, he'd have moved heaven and earth and the fucking stars themselves to get to Lucas. Yet here it was closing in on three full days after the attack and his parents were still not here. They were only in Spain, not another fucking galaxy.

"Stop overthinking, Ry. You're here and Anna's here. That's all I need." Lucas tried a smile to match the lightheartedness of his words, but it fell flat. "They'll get here when they get here. Now, what the fuck else has been going on since I've been out of it?"

Ryan glanced at Anna, wondering if she was going to share her news with the newly awoken sleeping beauty. He watched her draw in a deep breath and reach for Lucas's hand. "Actually, Lucas, there is something I should have told you months ago. I'm going to be needing that friendly divorce we agreed on."

"What? Who is it?" A sly grin spread on Lucas's gorgeous lips, nothing but happiness for Anna shining in his eyes.

"Well, Antonia has asked me to marry her. We've been seeing each other for a while and I love her so much, Luke. And as an added bonus when I kick your ass to the curb, you and Ryan will be free to come out if that's what you want, and let's face it, that's gonna make millions happy—*Lovers* is real and all that. I am not kidding—you guys are gonna be bigger than *Brangelina.*"

There had been times over the last year Ryan had found himself wondering what parallel universe he'd stepped into when he thought about his life or heard people speak about his celebrity or the *Samdom* ship. Surreal didn't even begin to cover it, and now they were considering going public with their relationship and Ryan knew Anna was right. Things would get even crazier for him—for them all.

"I'm so fucking happy for you, Anna. Just tell me where to sign, and you are free to marry that gorgeous lady of yours."

Anna leaned down and kissed Lucas's cheek before snuggling her head under his chin to give him a hug. Ryan didn't even feel a pang of jealousy. "Thanks, Luke. I'm gonna... I'm just gonna give Antonia a call. Her people want to start working on a press release. Obviously, you'll have to okay it first and nothing will happen until we are all ready. If you want to leave Ryan out of it, that's fine. Okay. But think about it. It's time for us to stop hiding." She kissed Lucas again and squeezed Ryan's arm before slipping out the door and leaving Ryan alone with Lucas again.

"What do you think about us coming out?" Lucas's voice was low, hesitant, as though nervous about Ryan's response.

"I'm yours, Lucas. That's the only thing I know for sure in all this craziness. But I'd like to be yours walking down the street holding your hand, and yours when we share a kiss while we're waiting for our dinner in a less-than-fancy restaurant somewhere, and yours when we hug goodbye at the airport if one of us absolutely has to leave the other—because that's the only way I'll be leaving you. If I absolutely have to." Ryan sat on the bed at Lucas's waist and bent down to kiss him.

This wasn't a gentle peck like they'd exchanged since Lucas woke up; this kiss was proprietary. Lucas might be his, but Lucas also owned Ryan completely and utterly.

"Hey, look who I found wandering around," Anna broke in, her voice pulling Ryan away from the warmth of Lucas and their kiss. He turned just as an older couple entered the room behind Anna.

"Mom? Dad? Hey, good to see you both."

Ryan was unceremoniously usurped from his place beside Lucas as Mr. and Mrs. Evers moved in to hold their son. Mrs. Evers whispered quietly in Lucas's ear, and Mr. Evers stood back once he'd hugged Lucas and gave his wife some room to be with her son.

"I'm gonna go make that call. Back soon," Anna said and then almost fled the room.

"How're you feeling, Lucas? We were told you were in a coma. What's going on?" Mr. Evers boomed.

"Hey, Dad. I'm feeling good. I woke up not long ago. Everything seems to be okay. Anna said you guys were in Spain. I didn't even know. Sorry you had to come racing back."

Ryan couldn't help the snigger he let out at Lucas's words. Three days was hardly racing back.

"Ah Mom, Dad, this is Ryan Lowe. Ryan this is my dad, Samuel, and my mom, Megan."

"Good to meet you, Ryan." Samuel Evers shook his hand while Megan smiled and waved, refusing to move from her son's side. "You're on the show with Lucas...Sam...you play Sam?"

"Yes, sir. I'm sorry about the circumstances, but it's good to meet you both."

"Mom, Dad, Ryan's not just my castmate. This is not quite how I was going to tell you, but we're together."

"Oh. Well. How is Anna with that? I mean I know your arrangement with her, but she's okay? But how will all of this impact your career? Are you sure you should be doing this?" Megan spoke loud enough for Ryan to hear her for the first time.

"Anna's fine, Mom. She's got someone too." Lucas didn't add anything about his career and how it would be affected by coming out.

"Well, I guess we'll get to know Ryan while we're here."

"You won't need to stay long. I feel really good and the doctor seems pleased with me and my medical tests. Honestly, book a ticket back to Spain and finish your trip. Hey, I thought...wasn't Kayla with you?"

"Oh we've got our ticket back, and yes, Kayla was with us, but she stayed behind with her new *friend*."

"Um, I'm going to pop out for a few minutes and give you guys some time alone," Ryan excused himself and sent a smile to Lucas before fleeing.

"You okay, Ryan?" Anna was leaning on the wall a little way down the hall. Her phone in her hand but her other hand covered the mouthpiece.

"What the fuck is up with them?" was all he could manage.

"Ah, the pretend closeness of the Evers family?"

"Yeah. Jesus, they didn't rush to get here, they already have their ticket back to Spain, and Kayla didn't even bother coming back to see her brother who was in a fucking coma. I don't get it. And they seemed more worried how Lucas coming out would affect his career rather than his happiness."

"Look, they care, Ryan, but it's a lip-service kind of caring. They say the words, but they don't back it up with the actions. It's frustrating, I know, but they've always been that way. Lucas and Craig are probably the only ones in that family I'd rely on."

Anna's apparent easy acceptance was no doubt born from years of dealing with the Evers clan. Ryan couldn't imagine ever feeling okay about the family's...apathy toward each other, but wherever they might let Lucas down, Ryan would do his best to prop him up.

Chapter Twenty-One

Lucas heads home—with Ryan in tow??

LUCAS

"Anna?" Lucas tried not to sound panicked as he called out. It was the first day since his accident Ryan had gone back to work and he'd only agreed to go because Anna would be at home with Lucas. He'd regained consciousness three days before and the doctors had finally released him after a barrage of tests and intrusive observations to ensure he was fine. "Anna?"

"Yeah, Luke. I'm here," she answered as she poked her head into the kitchen.

"Anna, can you smell this for me?" He held the bottle of milk toward her, a sense of desperation creeping up his spine.

"It smells fine, Luke. It's not off," she replied after taking a sniff.

"But you can smell the milk?"

"Yes, of course, I can smell it. Smells fine." Confusion was clear on her face. "You okay?"

"I can't... I can't smell it, Anna. I can't smell anything." He turned as he spoke and reached into the fridge pulling out anything that should have a detectable odor. Where there should have been the robust stench wafting from his tuna salad, there was nothing, and his block of dark chocolate failed to emanate the warm, comforting scent it was usually so rich with. In desperation he leaned into Anna, searching for the familiar floral fragrance of her perfume, but she, too, had been stripped of any scent.

"I can't smell anything, Anna. There's nothing. I didn't even realize while I was in the hospital, and I mean...the food tasted funny but I assumed it was the medication, but I can't smell anything."

"I'll phone Doctor Kalman to find out what's going on. Don't— Try not to worry just yet." Anna left the kitchen and Lucas threw open the pantry door searching out more strongly scented foods to test, but by the time

Anna returned, he'd found nothing that could stir any sense of smell. It was gone. In the scheme of things, he knew it could have been so much worse, but he was shaken.

Lucas considered calling Ryan. He needed him, wanted him with him. The studio had already rewritten scripts incorporating the disappearance of Dominic into the storyline to allow Lucas time off to recover. Ryan's character would be minimally in the show while he was off desperately searching for Dominic and generally losing his ever-loving mind because of his lover's disappearance. The studio had been good to them both, so Lucas put thoughts of calling for Ryan out of his mind. He'd be home tonight, and hopefully, Lucas would understand more about what the hell was going on by the time Ryan got back.

"Luke, I spoke to Doctor Kalman. She said that loss of smell can be caused by head injuries like you suffered. She wants to see you tomorrow, so I made an appointment with her for right after your physio exam, okay?"

"Thanks, Anna. Did she say if it was permanent?" Lucas knew he'd come out of his attack very well, all things considered. He was seeing a physiotherapist more as a precautionary thing than a necessity. He had to be wary of symptoms such as headaches, nausea, forgetfulness, and any one of the other myriad of problems that can arise as the result of head injury. Other than that, though, he appeared to be relatively unscathed.

"It can be. She said there's no real way to tell. I'm sorry." Anna hugged him and he drank in the warmth of her comfort. As wonderful as it was, it wasn't the hug he needed though.

Lucas spent the rest of the day trying not to think too much about what he might have lost. Anna didn't leave the apartment at all. She sat with him and watched movies, all painfully bad comedies in a desperate attempt to keep his mind off what had happened. The tuna salad he had for lunch tasted bland, different from how he knew it should taste, and he wondered if that was as a result of his loss of smell, or if his sense of taste had diminished too. He wasn't a huge food lover, but he hoped he wouldn't be faced with only flavorless meals for the rest of his life.

They heard the key in the lock earlier than expected, so they both rose to greet Ryan and Anna whispered a few quiet words to him before retreating to her room. Lucas was left to drink in the sight of this man who meant everything to him. Ryan looked tired and disheveled; he'd no doubt had a rough day back on set.

They both took a few steps toward each other and then he had Ryan back in his arms. He dropped several gentle kisses to Ryan's lips, forehead, eyelids, and all over his face, all while rubbing his nose over Ryan's smooth skin as he went, inhaling deeply, searching for, but never finding, the woodsy-mint scent that was Ryan.

"I can't smell you anymore, Ry," he whispered. "You always smell of the woods and mint, but now there's nothing. Jesus, you always smell so fucking delicious and now... I can't."

Ryan pulled his head back and locked his gaze with Lucas's. "What do you mean?"

"I can't smell anything. Nothing. I hoped... I thought maybe I'd still be able to smell you. I could have picked your scent out of anywhere before, but I can't smell you now. There's nothing."

Ryan's head was shaking in denial. "You can't smell anything? Why? What does this mean? Should we go to the hospital, Luke?"

"Shh, it's okay. I'm okay. Anna spoke to Doctor Kalman and she said this can happen. It could be permanent...or not. I'm going to see her tomorrow after the physio, so hopefully I'll find out more then. Don't worry. I'm fine. Really."

Lucas took Ryan's hands in his, pulling him along until they reached his bedroom. Lucas tumbled to the bed, pulling Ryan down with him. As they lay facing each other, Lucas reached out with his hand, allowing his fingers to roam over Ryan's beautiful face.

"All day, I've been thinking about you, wanting to do this. I missed you." He pressed a kiss to Ryan's lips and then pulled back while his fingers continued their exploration.

"Fuck, I've missed you too. It's not the same on the set without you there. The media's still camped out here and at the studio. It's a fucking nightmare. They know I'm here, Lucas, and I think we need to make that statement soon. It looks bad, you know."

Lucas did know. As far as the world was concerned, he was happily married to Anna, and now the man who portrayed his lover on-screen had virtually moved in with them. People would be talking. Maybe it was time for him to talk, too, and set the record straight. Leap right out of the fucking closet.

"We will. Soon. Right now, let's forget all that shit. I only want you. I want to hold you, and if I had my way, I'd never let you go." A sweet little grin stirred on Ryan's lips and Lucas couldn't help kissing that sweetness.

When he pulled back, Lucas wiggled around so Ryan was spooning him. He played with Ryan's fingers for a short time. "So...um I've been thinking about this one all day... Would you rather have to look after crying baby triplets for five hours or go without food and water for twenty-four hours?"

"Easy. The triplets," Ryan answered without hesitation.

"The screaming triplets? Seriously?"

"Yeah. I love my food too much to give it up; plus, I adore kids."

"You love kids? So you...would you...do you want them someday?" How had this turned so serious so quickly? But Lucas needed to know.

"Yeah, I do. Two girls and a boy. I didn't have siblings growing up and it was lonely. I don't care if I adopt or have my own but I know I can give kids a good life and I want them." Ryan stopped suddenly, and Lucas turned to see an expression of horror dawning on his face. "Oh shit. Have I scared the bejesus out of you? Did you...do you want kids?"

"I do. I hadn't quite got it down to the number and sexes, but I definitely want them one day, so relax, I'm not gonna run away screaming." Lucas laughed before dropping another gentle kiss on Ryan's lips. He watched relief lighten the warm brown of Ryan's eyes and knew he'd found that little piece of himself that had been missing all his life.

It was that elusive piece everybody is born without, because the love of your life had it with them. The ache of longing and wanting only eased when that piece was found. He'd found it now—with Ryan, and he wasn't letting it go. He'd wanted to love fiercely, but until now, he hadn't understood in the least what that meant. He would love Ryan with everything he had, because if he lost him, then he knew he'd be losing that essential piece of himself again. He couldn't live without it, not now he knew what he'd been missing.

He had no idea how long they lay there, gently petting each other, nuzzling and kissing, before they drifted off to sleep.

Chapter Twenty-Two

Samdom's *back and OMG Lon tweets that they're gonna DANCE!!*

RYAN

The media circus wasn't folding up their big top and leaving town; in fact, they were basically camped outside Lucas's apartments. Josh drove into the underground parking garage every day now to pick Ryan up, and Ryan was no expert, but he thought the tint on the car windows was a little darker than it had been. Other than the hospital a few days ago, where he'd undergone more tests for his loss of smell, Lucas hadn't left the building. His parents had popped in a few times, and they'd stayed for dinner last night before flying back to Spain this morning. Ryan didn't think he'd ever be their favorite person, but they got on well enough, and for his part, Ryan genuinely liked them, despite his initial annoyance with their almost blasé attitude to Lucas's injuries. Craig and Matthew had also returned to LA shortly before their parents had left. His opinion of them hadn't changed much: he liked Craig but found Matthew offputtingly quiet—standoffish.

Today would be Lucas's first time back on the set. It would be a short shoot for both of them to ease him back into the story, but Lucas would have to do a few catch-ups over the next few days. They were shooting Sam and Dom's reunion after Dominic had been found, and it included, of all things, a romantic dance together. Lon wouldn't tell them which song they were dancing to, only that it would be slow and sensual, and they should dance accordingly. Whatever the fuck that meant. Ryan couldn't dance, not well anyway, but he figured if it was slow they would just sort of sway together.

"Thinking about that dance?" Lucas whispered from behind him, startling him out of his thoughts.

"How'd you know?"

"You're an overthinker, Ry. I know you're worried, but don't be. I can dance—" Lucas pressed a kiss to the side of his head. "—so I'll make sure I make you look good, baby."

Ryan snickered. He'd missed working with Lucas and despite his nerves, shooting a romantic scene with him would be no hardship. "You'd have to be, um...shit...I don't know...John Travolta, to make me look good dancing."

"Oh, I've got one. Would you rather be able to dance like Baryshnikov or sing like Presley?" Lucas asked as he moved away and grabbed his bag so they could leave.

"Sing. I love singing, would hate not to be able to. Besides I've seen what some people call dancing and I can do that; it's just wiggling my ass—"

"Fuck, I'd love to watch you wiggle that ass. Naked, of course. How 'bout you show me your moves tonight? And wait...what? You can sing? How did I not know this?"

Ryan laughed at the thought of showing his moves to Lucas and then reconsidered and thought it might not be such a bad idea. They hadn't made love since Lucas had gotten home from the hospital, and Jesus, he fucking missed it. They'd petted and kissed—a lot—but Ryan missed being inside Lucas's tight body. He'd been so afraid of hurting him, though, that he'd balked at any hint Lucas had given that he was ready. Maybe a bit of a lap dance tonight would get the ball rolling.

"I can hold a tune. I have a lot of secret talents you're unaware of, Mr. Evers. Maybe if you're lucky, I'll show you some of them one day."

"Show me now, show me now," Lucas called in the singsong voice of a six-year-old child.

"All right, you big kid. I'll show you one." Ryan walked to the end of the hall and then turned to face Lucas. He started walking back toward him and then he widened his steps, put his weight slowly down on one heel at a time and proceeded to walk toward Lucas in slow motion. He knew he looked exactly as if someone had slowed the speed on the film of his life, and judging from his reaction, Lucas loved it.

"That's amazing. Oh my god, you look amazing. How did you learn that?"

It's interesting what you can learn when you have no friends to hang out with, no money to go places, and a bit of free time where you needed to keep as busy as possible to keep your mind off not having the first two.

"Self-taught from YouTube, the magical place of great, weird, and wonderful things." He laughed. "Now let's go before we're late on your first day back."

"Wait, wait. What else can you do? Come on. Boyfriends shouldn't have secrets," Lucas pleaded as they entered the elevator.

"You have no patience, Luke. I'll show you what I can do with a couple of cupcakes tonight." He winked and then found himself pressed back against the wall of the elevator car. Lucas's solid body pressed up tightly to his, barely an inch between them, and Lucas was nibbling at his neck.

"I had patience waiting for you, Ry. I'd have fucking waited forever," he whispered before returning to nip little kisses down the column of Ryan's throat. "And what the hell can you do with a cupcake? Come on, you can't make me wait for something as mysterious as that."

Lucas kept up the questioning and the onslaught of kisses and touches determined to wear Ryan down, all the way to the studio. If Josh hadn't suspected about them before, he damn well knew for a fact now.

"Lucas, so good to have you back. How are you doing?" Eloise was the first to greet them, with James not far behind, and Lucas spent the next fifteen minutes explaining how he was doing to anyone who asked as they walked by and thanking them for the flowers and various other get-well gifts and messages he'd been sent.

Once they were made up and costumed, they headed to the set. The craving to take Lucas's hand as they walked itched, and Ryan had to grit his teeth through it. The sooner they released their statement and could live their lives openly, the better.

"Okay," Lon called out once he noticed their arrival. "This is a short scene to ease Lucas back in. We'll do one walk-through for the lead-up to the dance and then we'll shoot. We're gonna put the music on and see what these two can do with it."

Fifteen minutes was all it took for them to rehearse the scene and then Lon was calling "Mark."

Ryan and Lucas stood wrapped in each other's arms as Sam repeatedly kissed Dom, whispering over and over again how glad he was Dom was home. They were on the "balcony" of Dom's place, and when the episode aired, a star-filled night would be added. Inside the apartment, candles were scattered around the room, and in the background, music was coming from a stereo. When they danced, the volume would increase.

"I love you, Sam. I'm sorry I scared you." Lucas put his hands on Ryan's cheeks and held him still as he pressed their lips together. This was the moment they would start to dance. Neither would ask the other, they'd just start moving to the background music as though their bodies couldn't help themselves.

Suddenly the volume increased and Ryan could clearly hear music, which he couldn't help moving to. It was a soul ballad, almost like something from the 50s or 60s, with a throaty female voice singing.

The music was a backdrop though; the real magic was in Lucas sweeping Ryan into his arms and swaying both of their bodies. Not for a second did they break eye contact as their bodies swayed and their breaths mingled. Ryan could have stayed right there forever. In the background, the singer crooned of having love on the brain, and it couldn't have been more appropriate if the song had been written specifically for them and this moment.

Even as the song ended, Lucas kept them moving, holding Ryan firmly in the steel grip of his gaze, occasionally dipping forward to press kisses to Ryan's lips, nose, forehead. Someone somewhere was calling out something, and then the music was playing again, and Ryan was lost—completely, totally and utterly lost in the magnetism of Lucas.

Some kind of commotion stirred at the end of the second run-through of whatever song it was, this time too much for them to ignore. Reluctantly, they moved away from each other and turned to face the crew, some of whom appeared shocked, while others looked smug and knowing. Their secret, the tatters that were left of it, wouldn't last much longer.

"Lucas. Happen to remember the nominations coming out this morning?" Lon boomed.

The Oscar nominations were being read out this morning, and not only had Ryan completely forgotten about it, Lucas hadn't mentioned them either.

"Totally forgot, Lon. Are they out?" Lucas calmly replied, his gaze still resting on Ryan.

"Oh, they're out, and somebody we know is off to the Oscars." Lon was not a smiley person, but an enormous grin graced his face now.

"You're kidding."

"I most certainly am not. Our very own Lucas Evers is nominated for Best Supporting Actor in a Motion Picture."

Ryan turned to Lucas and was immediately hit by his moving body as Lucas grabbed him and twirled him around. Though Lucas was not a small man, Ryan was considerably bigger than him, and the strength it took for Lucas to lift and twirl him did nothing to abate the hard-on their slow dancing had provoked.

The crew moved in to congratulate Lucas, but they would have to wait their turn as Ryan kissed the hell out of him once he was back on solid ground—out of character, in front of god and everyone. "I'm so fucking proud of you, Lucas." Ryan managed to get the whispered words out before Lucas was swooped up in a wave of handshakes, hugs, and congratulations—their kiss either forgotten or tactfully ignored by the crew.

"Well, congratulations, Lucas." A deep, thunderous voice boomed through the revelry. Ryan turned with the rest of the group to see a man he recognized but had never actually met. Philip Moyers was the head of the studio that made their show—the same studio that had produced *Over the Oceans*. Mr. Moyers would no doubt be thrilled with his giant star in the making.

"Mr. Moyers, thank you. I didn't know you were here." Lucas shook the man's hand, seemingly not intimidated by the studio bigwig whatsoever.

"I suspected congratulations would be in order and wanted to be here personally, so I flew up last night. I also wanted to see how you were doing after what happened to you. And I, uh, also need to discuss a few things with you and Ryan."

Ryan's stomach plummeted, knowing what probably needed to be discussed. He'd made peace with coming out to the world, and Lucas had seemed to as well, but who knew what the studio might think about it all? Even in 2018, irrational fear and prejudice still thrived.

"Let's pop into the office, shall we?" Philip Moyers commanded, not requested, and Ryan had no choice but to follow.

The office was enormous. Ryan had been in Mike's office before, but it was the size of a broom closet compared to this overwhelming monstrosity. The room was easily larger than the crappy apartment Ryan had first lived in when he'd arrived in the US. It might even be a similar size to the shitty duplex he'd shared with his father, growing up. An enormous desk, shelves, conference table, and sofas did their best to fill the space but they could have easily doubled the furniture and still had plenty of room left over. Philip gestured for them to take a seat on one of the sofas. Lon and Mike Faraday had joined them, though they sat on the other side of the coffee table with Philip, and Ryan could have sworn he was back in the school principal's office about to be lectured over pulling his socks up, working harder, and doing the right thing.

"So let's get to it, shall we?" Philip took immediate control as Ryan would expect. "First off, we're thrilled with your nomination, Lucas. You deserve it and we are actively seeking more movie roles for you with the studio. Obviously, we are also thrilled with the work you are both doing on *The Witches' Hammer*. Number one show in the world currently, and you and Ryan have finally knocked off that Isak and Even from the Norwegian show as favorite on-screen couple. What I need to know is what is happening personally with you two. Has the on-screen romance flowed over into real life and how can we use that for everyone's benefit?"

Use that? Use them? Ryan couldn't believe what he'd heard. They weren't a circus act to trot out and perform on command. Or were they? Was this the price of being in this industry? Ryan was flummoxed, completely unable to get out any words. Beside him, he felt Lucas stiffen and wondered if he felt as...insulted as he did.

"Mr. Moyers, thank you for acknowledging our hard work for your studio." Lucas stood as he addressed the group of men sitting opposite. "However, our personal life is not something to be used or managed for anyone's benefit. You do need to know the truth of the whole situation though. Anna and I have never had an actual marriage. We married as a cover for each other and to help with a personal matter I won't go into. We will be divorcing in the coming weeks and releasing a statement. She is, and always will be, my best friend.

"As for Ryan, I am wholeheartedly and unconditionally in love with him, and I hope to fuck he feels the same, because I intend to shout it to anybody who wants to listen. Hell, I'll sing it and tap dance along if I need to so people know he is it for me. And then I am going to take him out in public whenever and wherever we want to go, and I am going to hold his hand and hug him and kiss him, if the mood strikes while we're out there, because I couldn't be fucking prouder to have him by my side and know that every other fucker in the world is pea green with envy because he's all mine. Now, I'm not sure if any of that fits into your plans to *use* the situation, but that's what I'll be doing." Lucas sat back down and pressed a kiss, not a peck, but a sweet yet passionate kiss, to Ryan's lips.

For his part, Ryan was still floundering, utterly unable to find the words to articulate the feelings and thoughts spinning around in his head.

For a few moments, there was nothing but silence in the room. "Well, that answers that for me. Lucas, Ryan, the studio is behind you one hundred percent. We'd like to make a joint statement with you, acknowledging your relationship and how happy we are for you. I would suggest delaying the announcement until the news of your nomination settles down. And my apologies; 'use' wasn't the correct term." Philip nodded at both Lucas and Ryan, and with the arrogance of the truly powerful, expected the apology would be accepted and that was the end of that.

"Now the other issue I want to consider is your safety. I'm fully aware of the incident and Mike has informed me the police are still actively searching for another person they believe was involved. When this"—Philip waved his hand around gesturing to the two of them—"comes out; when you two come out, your popularity is going to skyrocket. Everyone's favorite ship is real. Christ, we couldn't make that shit up." He grinned wolfishly and Ryan couldn't help thinking he was still too greedily joyful about their situation. "But we need you safe. We'll be paying for security. We'll keep up the bodyguards and get some permanent live-ins for continuity. This person has gone after one of you once, we're not risking them getting another chance."

Bodyguards, Oscars, making announcements about their relationship, ongoing threats to their lives. It was all so much—too much. Ryan had never expected, never been prepared for, any of this. He'd never given much thought to what would happen if he achieved his dream of becoming an actor. He'd either never really believed he'd make it so big, or he'd thought his laid-back nature would afford him some defense against the pressures of fame. The reality was beyond what he'd expected, and unhappily, he realized it was too late to turn back. His anonymity was lost for the foreseeable future, at least.

"Thank you. We're happy to take whatever steps we need to keep safe. Right now, though, I'd really like to go home and celebrate with Lucas."

All Ryan wanted was Lucas. To be alone with him, hold him, love him, and be so fucking proud of him that he felt like the pride was going to burst right through his skin. Ryan stood, as though on autopilot, when Lucas stood and spoke the obligatory words. He shook hands as protocols dictated, but in his head, he was already on his way home with Lucas.

"Come on. Let's go home." Lucas whispered and took his hand, leading him back to the car and home.

Chapter Twenty-Three

OMFG! So hot! Samdom *have hot bodyguards!*

LUCAS

It was obvious the whole drive home Ryan had been freaked out by the meeting with Philip Moyers. Actually Lucas had been wondering for a while when Ryan's freak-out would come. Ryan had so far had an up-and-down battle with fame, but there was a lot he'd had to deal with on top of that, not least of which was falling in love with another man. Some kind of freak-out was inevitable.

As soon as they got back to Lucas's apartment, Ryan had excused himself and gone for a shower. And though Lucas considered following him into the shower, he thought it best to give him some space. Instead, Lucas stood on his balcony, overlooking the lights of the city in the distance, and waited. Ryan had been in there for close to twenty minutes now, and Lucas was starting to rethink his strategy. Maybe he needed to go in and remind Ryan of what they had, how much they had to hold onto...to fight for.

Just as he made up his mind to go into that bathroom, two strong arms caged him in against the balcony railing. Ryan's muscular body pressed against his, and his nose trailed up the length of Lucas's neck before he nuzzled at his ear.

"Would you rather me be inside you—" Ryan began and then bit at Lucas's earlobe. "—or you be inside me?"

Lucas's entire body stilled at Ryan's words. Ryan had rarely hinted at wanting Lucas to have him and Lucas had never pushed, though the thought—the dream—had always been there, hovering at the edge of his fantasies. Lucas turned in Ryan's arms, needing to see those warm brown eyes, though he didn't get much of a chance.

The moment he faced Ryan, he was caught up in a searing kiss. It was as though Ryan was trying to consume him. It was wild, it was ferocious, and it was the best damn kiss he'd ever had. Even as it continued, Lucas began moving forward, forcing Ryan to back up as he strove to get them into the bedroom without relinquishing contact.

There was fumbling and bumping into furniture and Lucas knew they weren't going to make it to the bedroom. "I'll have you another time, Ry." He wanted his first time inside Ryan to be special, not fast and desperate as he knew this encounter was going to be. "Pick a surface," he ground out as he took a breath.

Ryan answered him by steering them to the kitchen. Kitchen bench it was. When Lucas's back hit the bench, they tore their lips apart and the desperate tearing off of clothes began. All Lucas had to do was tug off the towel Ryan had wrapped around his hips and he had him gloriously naked. Ryan had to work harder for it, though, pulling at Lucas's T-shirt and fumbling with the zipper on his jeans until he finally had them pooled around his ankles.

Lucas found himself unceremoniously spun around and his torso pushed down onto the kitchen bench. He reached across and held onto the other side, intuiting that this was going to be a hard, desperate fucking, and loving every second of it. Ryan's body was draped over his as he nipped and sucked his way over the planes of Lucas's back. His tongue slowly trailed down Lucas's spine until it just touched the crease of his ass and Lucas's entire body shivered at the sensation. Lucas was so fucking turned on he was worried the slightest touch to his dick would have him coming too soon.

"Fuck, Luke. It's been too fucking long." Ryan's voice was thick and hoarse with lust as he moved back up to whisper in his ear. Lucas could feel Ryan's hard cock nestling in the crease of his ass. He was every bit as frantic as Ryan and nodded his consent. "Not enough. Say it," Ryan commanded.

"Fuck me, Ry. Hurry up and fuck me." Lucas felt Ryan pulling back and knew immediately what he was after. "Bottom drawer."

Ryan's big body moved away from his as he bent down to grab the lube and condoms Lucas had the foresight to keep handy in most rooms of the apartment. In moments, the heat of Ryan's body was back and he heard the snick of the lube opening and closing just before Ryan's fingers were playing at his hole. He moaned as one of Ryan's thick fingers entered him. Seconds later, a second finger breached him and Ryan crooked his fingers, finding that spot inside that eliminated any remaining discomfort the minute Ryan's fingers brushed over it.

"Come on, Ry. Fuck...please." Lucas wasn't too proud to beg. He needed Ryan inside of him. He needed to be filled so fucking full that there was no room for any fears or worries to linger.

When Ryan pulled his fingers free, Lucas could hear the crinkle of the condom wrapper shortly before Ryan's hands grabbed his hips, pulling them away from the bench a little, giving him more room. Lube drizzled over his hole and a finger spread it around, the tip dipping inside just enough to tease. Then he felt the head of Ryan's dick pushing at his entrance.

Lucas forced his body to relax, helping to ease Ryan's way and before long Ryan was fully inside, his groin pressing against Lucas's ass. This was the moment; this was when the noise in his head was silenced as his body was commanded by Ryan's, ordered to take its pleasure as Ryan pounded into him from behind. His torso skated over the surface of the bench, back and forth as Ryan slammed into him again and again. Dirty talk was lost to grunts and groans as Lucas did his best to stave off his impending orgasm, wanting to come with Ryan.

"Fuck, oh fuck, Luke. It's so fucking good," Ryan mumbled against his back as he lay his body back over Lucas's and changed the tempo to a slow grind of his pelvis against Lucas's ass. A big hand grabbed at Lucas's swollen dick, tugging in a tormentingly slow pace. But Lucas needed more.

"Harder...fuck me harder." The warmth of Ryan's body drew away as he stood again, one hand still on Lucas's cock, the other back on Lucas's hip. Ryan picked up the pace again, tilting his angle slightly to peg Lucas's prostate every few thrusts. Lucas knew it wouldn't be long now.

Ryan panted above him, the strain of his ferocious pace showing. "Luke, fuck...come, Luke, come for me."

That was all it took, that simple order, and Lucas was coming over the kitchen cabinet, jet after jet of come streaming out of him. The final one just as he felt Ryan stiffen and jerk inside of him as his own orgasm took him. With a last moan and shudder, Ryan collapsed over Lucas's back, his lips worrying at Lucas's neck as they both tried to calm down after what was for Lucas the orgasm of his life—so far. There would be plenty more moments of pleasure with Ryan; he knew that for certain. Lucas was no inexperienced virgin but, Jesus, it had never been like this before. It was almost as though love took the pleasure and amplified it by a million. How the fuck was he expected to survive this?

"Love you, Luke," Ryan whispered into his ear.

"Love you, too, baby."

PHILIP MOYERS HAD left several messages during the morning while Lucas was busy reacquainting himself with Ryan's body. He'd left the address of a security firm where he had made an appointment for them to meet potential bodyguard teams. The ones they were currently using were attached to the studio and had only been a temporary solution until they all knew what was happening with Ryan's stalker. They all knew exactly what was happening now, and Lucas was equal parts astounded and terrified.

"We need to get going, Luke. You ready?" Ryan called to him. Lucas turned and found his lover attempting to put his boots on while walking toward Lucas on the balcony.

"I'm readier than you are." He chuckled.

"Ha-ha. I'd be on time if you hadn't despoiled me that last time...after I'd already showered, so I had to shower again."

"Despoiled you? I despoiled you? If you recall, Ryan Lowe, it was you who ended up balls deep in me after we got out of the shower. Something about not being able to keep your hands off me..."

Ryan had finally managed to get his boots on and was standing close enough that Lucas could see the golden flecks in the deep brown of Ryan's eyes.

"You okay, Luke?"

"I'm okay. I'm...a little scared, I guess. I've never had anyone try to kill me before. It's weird, ya know, to think someone hates you enough to actually want you dead." Lucas knew everything about his attack, and the police had shared the knowledge that Leighton White wasn't working alone. Yet he still found it inconceivable somebody had already tried to kill him once, and if the police were correct, would likely try again. He couldn't see how it could be true.

"They're not gonna get you, Luke. We're going to go meet these bodyguards and they are going to stick to you like glue...well not too close. I mean they won't be anywhere near your bedroom or your bathroom, and I have fond memories of us naked in the kitchen, so maybe that's out too."

Ryan could always manage to pull Lucas out of the bog of despair. He threw his head back and laughed. "I get it. They'll be around, but they're not getting in the way of us...despoiling each other."

Ryan leaned forward and dropped a kiss to his lips. "No one's getting in the way of that. The important thing is that we're gonna get whoever we need here to do whatever they have to do to keep you safe because I'm not losing you. I've waited almost twenty-four years for you and these last few months with you just aren't enough for me—a lifetime wouldn't be enough."

"Fuck. You start sweet-talking me and we're not gonna make it out of here. Let's go meet these hunky bodyguards."

"Hunky? What? No way. I'm sure they'll have a nice mature gentleman for—"

"I can work with a silver fox," Lucas said as they began moving toward the door.

"He'll be bald and very old...you know wrinkly and...and saggy. All his muscles will have turned to flab and...he'll just be yuck."

"He'll be yuck? That's shallow of you, Ryan. I expected better."

Lucas had learned it was necessary to balance the nightmarish part of their lives with the levity and happiness their company gave each other, so by the time they arrived at Krispin Security, Lucas was feeling more relaxed and he could see the sheen of worry on Ryan's features had lost some of its luster.

They were led into a meeting room that was beautifully appointed with a huge, dark-oak conference table and the most comfortable office chairs Lucas had ever sat in. They were left with water and coffee while they waited for Patricia and Roger Krispin to meet with them. They didn't wait long.

The Krispins seemed more owners of a mom and pop hardware store than one of the most reputable and successful security agencies on the West Coast. Both had silver-streaked hair and, while their clothes were professional and expensive looking, they weren't over-the-top power suits. They looked friendly and sweet, but Lucas could see brilliant intelligence and sharp fierceness in their eyes. They were not to be messed with.

"Mr. Evers, Mr. Lowe. Good to meet you both." Roger Krispin extended his hand to shake both Ryan's and Lucas's when they stood to meet him. His wife, Patricia, was not far behind. She gestured for them to take a seat, after the initial greeting, and Lucas settled himself back into his chair next to Ryan. The Krispins sat on the opposite side of the table.

"Phil has made us aware of your situation, so we have taken the liberty of putting two teams together and also a plan of what to expect and how we foresee things playing out." Patricia spoke with the clear authority and assurance needed to instill confidence in potential clients in this business. Within five minutes of meeting them, Lucas knew he'd trust them to guard his life, and more importantly, Ryan's.

"How will it work? I mean, I understand it will be the same men rotating so we are familiar with them and vice versa, but will they be living with us? Do they go home at the end of a shift? Do we need them around the clock?" Ryan had never been a pushover, but Lucas admired the assertiveness that was creeping into his character when it came to their safety.

"It's all negotiable, Mr. Lowe. It will depend on your wishes, available space, how willing you are to have this intrude upon your lives. Our bodyguards are trained to be discrete, invisible. The idea is that you know they are there and that you're safe, but at the same time, you are unaware of their presence. If that makes sense," Roger supplied.

"Perfect. May we meet them?" Lucas asked.

"Of course. As my wife said, we have two teams for you to meet today. It's important that you feel comfortable with your guards. Ask them questions, get to know them. We'll get some more tea or coffee in here, so take your time, until you feel good—or not—about the teams we've chosen."

Things happened quickly after that. Several people wheeled in a cart loaded with a coffee urn, a carafe with hot water for tea, and various condiments. Cups and saucers were stacked neatly and the shelf below was filled with pastries of every imaginable kind. While this was being set up, Lucas watched six men and two women file into the room and take seats.

Looking at their clothing, Lucas thought they could be octuplets. Each and every one of them had on a black suit with a light-colored shirt and a varying shade of blue tie. The women and three of the men had their hair pulled back in tight buns. The group looked formidable.

If he was honest, Lucas knew he expected all of the men to be giants. At least six-foot-five and muscles on their muscles. Two of them fit that mold. The others certainly weren't small men, with the exception of one who looked maybe five-eleven at a stretch, and though not skinny, would be on the thinner side. He chided himself that he hadn't expected the women at all. They looked exceptionally fit and could likely easily put him on his ass.

Lucas wasn't quite sure what to do or say next. Fortunately, two of the men stood. One was the six-foot-five giant and the other stood around Ryan's height of six-two. They looked fierce, serious...scary. The taller one spoke first.

"Mr. Lowe, Mr. Evers. I'm Ethan Stone. This is my team: Gavin Holburn, Christina Waller, and Max Hart. Patricia has suggested my team for your protection, Mr. Evers. I'll let Billy introduce his team and then please feel free to ask any questions of us." After shaking their hands, Ethan Stone resumed his seat, so Lucas turned his attention to Billy.

"I'm William Merrow, Billy. My team: Ben Cronin, Paulina Moss, and Harry Boyd. We'd be very happy to take up security for Mr. Lowe." As with the first team, their handshakes were all firm and confident. Lucas liked both teams immediately. They talked a little while they had their coffee, but it was Ryan who took the initiative to stand and move around the room, talking to the men and women present. Lucas had noticed long ago that Ryan was more comfortable standing in meetings and gatherings, and in this instance, it worked out well.

Lucas spoke to Ethan Stone, a little off to the side of the rest of the group.

"Any questions, Mr. Evers?" His voice was as big as you would expect from someone of Ethan's size.

"Actually, I wanted to ask about Billy and his team." Lucas watched the confusion, and then realization, dawn on Ethan's handsome face.

"If you'd be more comfortable with Billy's team, I'm sure it'll be no problem. It's imperative you have confidence in your team. If we've let you dow—"

"No. No, shit. Sorry. That's not... I'm very happy with your team. What I want to know is if Billy's team is the best. Are they good enough to keep Ryan safe? I can't... Nothing can happen to him." These people would find out soon enough the nature of his relationship with Ryan, and Ryan's safety was too important to him to worry about being outed.

"Mr. Evers, I would trust Billy and his team with my life. Billy is ex-marine. Paulina and Harry are army and Ben..." Ethan turned his gaze toward Ben, and Lucas watched a tiny grin pull at his lips. "Well, don't let Ben's size fool you. Out of everyone in this room, he's the most...lethal."

Lucas looked across the room at Ben, who stood talking to Ryan, the difference in their size noticeable, and wondered if he could really protect Ryan. Ethan had called him lethal. He certainly didn't look it—not with his head tipped back in laughter at whatever Ryan was saying to him. The delight on his face made him appear especially young, almost adolescent. He was a handsome man and he definitely seemed to have hit it off with Ryan.

A splinter of jealousy spiked Lucas as he stood watching his lover laughing with the handsome man, and Lucas unconsciously moved toward their direction. "Come meet Ryan," he managed to say to Ethan before he walked away. He felt, rather than saw, Ethan's giant frame move into step beside him and wondered if this was how it would be from now on, his every move shadowed by a giant sentinel.

Before he reached Ryan's side, he caught his eye and any jealousy disappeared when Ryan's true smile adorned his lips—just for him.

Ben spoke first as they approached. "Oh my god, Ethan. You gotta hear about when Ryan met Harrison Cooper. Fucking hilarious, man."

"Ben!" Ethan snapped, though Lucas didn't miss the indulgent twitch threatening to pull a smile from the professional, serious Ethan Stone.

"It's okay, Ethan. Ryan wants to be called Ryan and he swears almost as much as I do. You gotta unclench, buddy." Ben's handsome face was stretched into a broad grin, but it couldn't hide the flinch when Ethan excused himself and walked away.

Another half hour spent mingling with this group of men and women made Lucas more than satisfied that this whole round-the-clock guard situation could work. These people were smart and had flawless backgrounds either in military or law enforcement. By the time he and Ryan left the building, Lucas was convinced any one of them could easily save his or Ryan's life, get the bad guy, and bake a cake all at the same fucking time.

Chapter Twenty-Four

Did Lovers *almost kiss—in public?? Hell, yeah, I'm here for that.*

RYAN

"Ryan, come on. You look fucking gorgeous. Let's go."

Ryan could hear the frustration in Lucas's voice as he called out to him from the front door. He'd let Lucas think he'd come back into the bathroom to fix his hair. He didn't want to worry him.

"You okay, Ryan? Maybe I should get Lucas." Ben's voice was thankfully quiet, so at least Lucas wouldn't overhear the worry in his tone. They'd been under full-time protection for three weeks now, and while Ryan liked each of the members of both security teams, Ben was by far his favorite. He was relaxed and fun to be around. He stood on no ceremony with either Ryan or Lucas and had been the first to call them by their first names and watch a movie with them while he was off the clock. Ryan knew Lucas's team leader, Ethan, wasn't overly pleased with Ben's laid-back demeanor, but it suited Ryan perfectly.

"No. No, Ben. I just need a minute." Fuck, he had to get it together. It was getting harder and harder for Ryan to leave the house lately, and he couldn't be sure if it was fear of what—or who—might be out there waiting for them or something else. He was fine going to and from the studio; mainly because he knew once he was through the gates, he was safe again, sheltered—the crowds couldn't get to him there.

"Don't you think you should tell him?" Ben persisted.

How did he tell Lucas how anxious he was getting each time he had to leave the house? Despite no formal statement, rumors were rife about their relationship and fans were growing both in number and in their audacity in approaching both him and Lucas on the street.

Two days ago he'd been mobbed when he and Ben had walked down to a nearby Safeway while Lucas had been doing a promotional interview for his movie and Oscar nomination. Ben had needed to use a chair as if it was a battering ram to get people out of his way so they could make it to the restroom. Once he'd made it there, Ryan had suffered a panic attack. Thankfully, Ben had been there to keep anybody from coming in and finding him on his knees, shaky, sweaty, and struggling to catch his breath.

"I'm good, Ben. Really. Let's go."

After discussions between him and Lucas, Anna and Antonia, and finally with the studio, they'd decided to start dipping their toes in the pool of public appearances together. There'd be no PDA until a statement had been made, but they could certainly go to a basketball game together. That's how Ryan ended up sitting with Lucas in the back seat while Ethan drove and Ben sat in the front passenger seat for the drive to Oracle Arena.

Ryan had followed the Sydney Kings while living back home but had thrown his support behind the Lakers once he'd moved to LA. Tonight, Lucas had managed to get them courtside tickets to the Lakers vs. Golden State Warriors game.

Once they arrived, they were shuffled through the VIP entrance and taken to their seats. Fortunately, Ryan could avoid contact with most of the crowd, though he couldn't avoid hearing the screams of their names once they were recognized.

It was loud in the arena, the atmosphere inside vibrating with expectation, and Ryan couldn't believe how close they were to the court. The players were right there—he could hear them breathing hard as the game continued, and Ryan was pretty sure, at one point, beads of sweat flew from Nick Young and landed on his cheek. Nick Young was an awesome player and pretty hot, but if the sweat had come from Jordan Clarkson, Ryan might never have washed his cheek again.

By halftime, Ryan knew he should have eased up on the beers. There was no way he'd make the end of the game without a trip to the restroom.

"Luke, I've gotta go to the bathroom. Be right back," he whispered in Lucas's ear.

"Take Ben with you," Lucas ordered, as though Ben would have let him out of his sight.

Ryan rolled his eyes. "Yes, *Dad.*" The instinct to lean forward and plant a kiss on Lucas's lips had become so natural to him that he'd made it far more than halfway before he remembered and pulled back. He'd gotten awfully close and there could be no confusion about what he'd been going to do for anyone who'd been watching; hopefully, no one had witnessed the near miss.

A roar went up in the crowd and Ryan looked around for what might be causing the ruckus. He expected maybe a three-pointer or a slam dunk; instead, his gaze caught on the big screen and he watched himself in slow motion leaning into Lucas who wore a grin and obvious look of affection on his gorgeous face. When Ryan pulled slowly away, the whole thing started playing over again, to the delight of the cheering crowd. Fuck. His mistake had been witnessed all right—and was being replayed over and over for the entire crowd to see.

"Shit, Luke. I'm so sorry." He turned to Lucas, terrified of seeing anger on his face. Instead, he was met with a laughing Lucas.

"Don't worry about it. It's all gonna come out soon and until then...well, we've just made the front pages of the trash rags. Honestly, don't worry. Now, go pee and hurry back to me."

Ryan tried to brush it off as easily as Lucas had, but he struggled, knowing the entire stadium had watched an almost intimate moment between them and were likely still watching them now. As he stood, Ben stood with him and followed as he made his way out of the court and headed toward the restrooms.

He knew every pair of eyes present were on him as he walked, and his breathing became labored and heavy. He strained for breath until he felt as though he couldn't get enough air into his lungs. Once they'd cleared the courts and were in the outside passageways, Ryan felt a strong hand on his elbow, guiding him and pushing him forward. His vision had darkened, but he could still see the group of a dozen or so people coming toward him, calling his name. He was suddenly turned one-eighty by that hand on his elbow, but even more people were converging on him from behind. Ryan was pressed against a wall with Ben's solid body standing in front of him, doing his best to cage him in and shield him from the crowd.

The wall was solid at his back but it offered him no comfort and he could feel his entire body trembling and his knees buckling. Oh god, he was going to die here. He was fucking terrified. He couldn't get out, couldn't get away from the noise of people screaming his name. What did they want? He was in trouble. His body wasn't doing what it should be doing. He couldn't hold himself up anymore, and he couldn't fucking breathe. The noise...the fucking noise. And all of these people were stealing the air, leaving nothing for him.

Somehow, he ended up on the ground, his knees pulled up to his chin. There was a body in front of him and he did his best to hide behind its legs. Faces were peering at him from around the body and flashes of light were blinding him. It'd be over soon; there was very little air left now. The noise was too much—the commotion unbearable. Shouted, garbled words and some kind of banging assailed his ears. He couldn't clear a path through the chaos that circled around him and worse—inside of him.

"Breathe," a soft voice instructed him, but didn't this idiot know there was no air left for him to breathe? "Come on, breathe for me. Big breath slowly in and...let it out."

Ryan tried to do it, tried to listen to the voice and do what it told him. His vision had darkened so much he couldn't see the owner of the disembodied voice, didn't know where to look. What if the voice wanted to hurt him, not help him? He was so hot and his heart felt like it was trying to beat right out of his chest.

"Ry...Ryan, it's Lucas. I need you to breathe for me. Nice and slow, big breaths. With me, okay? Look at me, Ryan. Please. I need you to look at me."

He knew that voice. He loved that voice. It would never hurt him. The voice was so peaceful—so safe. Warm hands were on his face dragging his head up. Through the dimness, he saw two bright-green orbs, and as the panic gradually eased and rational thought returned, he realized he was looking into the concerned face of his lover.

The crowd he knew had been around him was gone, and standing behind Lucas's kneeling body were Ben and Ethan. Ryan became aware that beyond them several other men were forming a barricade around them. They looked to be security men, maybe from the stadium. It was coming back to Ryan now: where he was, what had happened. Shame slithered through his body like a skulking lizard. How could he have lost it like that...here? In public?

"Ryan?" Lucas's voice was anguished. He hated that he'd been the cause.

"I'm sorry, Lucas. I'm so fucking sorry."

"Don't you dare. There's nothing to be sorry for. Are you all right? You scared the shit out of me."

All Ryan could manage was a nod. Lucas might claim he had nothing to be sorry for but Ryan couldn't absolve himself that easily.

"Lucas, if you're ready, we've got a clear run to the car. They've brought it around front for us. Just a couple of steps, Ryan, and we can get out of here, okay?" Ethan's tone lowered, almost as though he were talking to a child when he spoke to him. Ryan thought he heard Ben mumble something to Ethan but couldn't catch it.

Again Ryan nodded; he wasn't sure who he was nodding to, but he wanted out of there. Now.

Lucas stood first and held out his hand to Ryan, who took it, grateful for both the strength and comfort it provided. Lucas moved beside him and put an arm around his shoulders, walking him toward the exit. Ethan strode in front of them, blocking them from view while Ben brought up the rear. The arena security men walked with them at a respectful distance, but near enough they could further shield the little group from view.

Ryan was efficiently bundled into the back seat of the waiting car, followed by Lucas. Ben jumped in the other side and once again Ethan drove. Lucas's arm was back around his shoulders and his other hand had hold of one of Ryan's.

As they sped back to Lucas's place, Ryan rubbed his thumb over the knuckles of Lucas's hand. He was still too mortified to offer any sort of defense for his behavior. No one spoke. At intervals, Lucas pressed a kiss into his hair and trailed his nose down the line of Ryan's throat. As he rubbed Lucas's knuckles, he could feel the skin was scratchy, rough, and he looked down to see they were raw and bloody. He gasped and pulled back from Lucas.

"Lucas, your hand. What happened?"

"Nothing, baby. It's nothing." Lucas did his best to brush off the question and play down the condition of his knuckles, but Ryan could tell it was definitely not nothing.

"Lucas. Please. Tell me what happened." Ryan watched as Lucas glanced at Ben, he could also see Ethan's eyes flick back at them through the rearview mirror.

"They wouldn't leave you alone, Ry. You were...you weren't breathing right, and you looked terrified, and they wouldn't leave you alone. I couldn't get to you and this one guy." Lucas shook his head, anger stomping its feet over his features. "He was trying to take photos and he wouldn't stop. Wouldn't get out of my way...so I hit him. Popped that fucker right in the nose."

"Yeah, ya did," Ben commented and slapped a high five to Lucas.

Ryan couldn't have heard right. Lucas wasn't a violent person, ever. But he'd hit someone...because of him. How could he have put Lucas in this position? What the fuck was wrong with him?

Lucas leaned in and pressed a kiss to Ryan's forehead. He trailed his nose down Ryan's face, rubbing it against Ryan's own before pressing a kiss to his lips. "Why didn't you tell me, Ry?" They rested their foreheads together.

"Tell you?"

"About the anxiety. About the panic attack the other day. I'm so sorry. If I'd known..."

Ryan reached up and held on to Lucas's face with both hands, his gaze boring into Lucas's so he could see the veracity of what he was about to say. "Please...please don't. None of this is your fault. It's mine. I... I'm weak. I don't... I'm struggling with so much right now. It's not what I expected. Fame. It's so much worse. I'm sorry I scared you. I'm sorry I didn't tell you... I should have. But I love you, Luke. With everything I have, I love you."

Lucas pulled him forward, and although it was awkward being in the back seat of a car, it was the most-needed hug Ryan had ever had. "There's nothing weak about you," Lucas whispered into his ear.

Ethan drove into the underground parking garage and the residual tension in Ryan finally eased. It was secure here and they'd be able to walk up to Lucas's apartment with privacy. Ethan and Ben stayed close, but as promised, their presence was not at all intrusive.

Once they were safely inside the apartment, Ryan was ushered into the shower while Lucas went to make them both a cup of tea. For a brief, idiotic moment he considered booting up his laptop to see how much damage he'd done. He was fairly confident his meltdown and Lucas's subsequent violent outburst would have been captured by dozens of people falling all over themselves to be the first to upload it to YouTube.

Ryan tried to let the hot water ease the ache in his body from the shaking he'd done earlier. He couldn't stop worrying. About everything: Lucas, the studio, the show, his fans. So much rested on his shoulders, the weight of it was pushing him deeper and deeper into the ground.

By the time he got out of the shower, Ben and Ethan had both made themselves scarce and Lucas was waiting on the sofa with piping hot tea and a plate of his favorite Chips Ahoy. Ryan climbed onto the sofa and into the lap of the man he adored. He held on desperately as Lucas soothed him, petting his hair, and whispering into his ear how much he loved him. But, could it all be okay as Lucas was promising?

Chapter Twenty-Five

Oscar night...Lucas better win!

LUCAS

"You're gonna pace a hole in the carpet, Lucas. He's gonna be okay," Ethan advised, though until he saw and heard for himself, he would still be crazy worried about Ryan.

Lucas would have given anything to go with him today, but Ryan had insisted it was something he needed to do by himself. He should be back any moment, and Ben had called Ethan to let him know everything was going fine, but Lucas still worried.

As soon as he heard the door open, he was moving. In moments, he had Ryan wrapped in his arms and then he practically dragged him to the sofa, pressing him back into it before sitting next to him. "So..." he encouraged.

"So, it went well. Doctor Bowen was great. He did a full assessment but is leaning toward an anxiety disorder. He thinks it's mostly crowds that are the problem. Like I feel as though I can't get away from them and the...all the air is being sucked up by the crowd until I feel like I can't breathe."

"Jesus. That must be terrifying."

"Yeah. It's stupid—"

"It's not stupid." Lucas interrupted.

"I mean...I know logically I can breathe, but I can't seem to get my head to believe it. We spoke about medications and other treatments. He gave me some breathing exercises to practice when I can feel a panic attack starting up. He wants to see me again next week and then regularly until..." Ryan's eyes never left his and for that Lucas was grateful.

After the incident at the basketball game three nights ago, Ryan had barely been able to look at him. Lucas knew he was ashamed and embarrassed by his behavior, despite Lucas's assurances that he had nothing to be ashamed of. The truth was Lucas could understand where

Ryan was coming from; if roles were reversed, he'd probably be a little embarrassed too. It was never easy falling apart in front of those you love.

"Until...when?"

"Just until. There's no cure, Luke. This'll be an ongoing thing I'll have to manage. I uh...I'm starting on Ativan. I know...I don't want to be on medication, but the Oscars are two weeks away and I need to be there...for you. I want to be there. Hopefully, the Ativan will allow me to do that."

Ativan. Jesus. Lucas hated the idea of Ryan on medication. "Ry, you don't have to. I mean, I understand you don't want the drugs, so if that means you can't be there at the Oscars, I understand."

Ryan took both of his hands in his and brought them to his lips, kissing each knuckle gently. "I won't have mastered the breathing or any other exercises that may help me in time. The Ativan will, hopefully, allow me to get there and not freak out. After that, I can re-evaluate things."

"What about side effects?"

"That's why I don't want it to be a long-term thing. I know there's some fairly normal ones such as sleepiness and nausea and even some forgetfulness, but there can be some more serious effects too."

"Like what?"

"Depression, suicidal thoughts, delusions—"

"No. No way, Ryan. That's...it's too..."

"It's short-term, Lucas. I swear. And those more serious ones are mostly if it's used the wrong way. I'm going to do my best to learn to control the anxiety, but I want to get on top of it and I think the Ativan will help me to level out so that I can learn other techniques to help me."

"I wish I... I wish I could fix this for you, Ry."

Ryan chuckled and leaned in to press their lips together. "There's nothing to fix. I just have to manage it...we do. I need you. I will need you to be there with me. Can you do that? Do you want to do that? It's not exactly what you bargained for."

"You're what I want, Ry. You're who I want. I'll be right beside you...always. You just promise me...promise you'll talk to me and tell me what you need. No more hiding." He tried to twist his face into a stern, authoritative expression, but with the love of his life looking so vulnerable before him, he knew he probably looked more of a goofy lovestruck buffoon.

"You got it. I am sorry I tried to hide it from you. You must have been terrified when you saw me like that."

Lucas had been terrified when Ethan told him at the basketball game that Ben was calling for help. As they'd been running to Ryan's side, Lucas had no idea what had happened and wave after wave of scenarios, each more horrifying than the last, had crashed through his imagination. He was wholly unprepared for finding Ryan crouching on the ground, shaking, terrified, and struggling for breath. Ethan had charged their way through the crowd gathered around and taken up sentry with Ben, while Lucas had tried to calm Ryan, but not before he'd punched that fucker in the nose. He smiled every damn time he thought of it, the satisfaction of his hard fist connecting with the softer cartilage of the nose of the man who was tormenting his lover. It was sublime.

Shockingly, no police had arrived at his door and no footage of that part of the incident had landed on YouTube or anywhere else for that matter. The man had never come forward to report Lucas. The studio had handled the other footage of Ryan with a simple statement claiming he hadn't been well that evening. End of statement. Once again the studio had their backs and was willing to stand behind Ryan, and Lucas, in whatever way was needed. It seemed they were right behind their number one couple from their number one show. Lucas couldn't help wondering how much support they'd get if their popularity slipped. He'd been around the business long enough to see how it all really worked.

"I've never been so fucking scared. Never." He pressed kisses to Ryan's lips, nose, cheeks, every place he could reach. He couldn't imagine he'd ever be articulate enough to put into words how this man made him feel, the depth of emotion that swamped him at just the thought of his lover, but he could show him—that he was good at.

LUCAS WAS FULLY supportive of metrosexual men and manscaping and all of that, but it wasn't him. For his Oscar event spruce-up, he'd settled for a haircut yesterday. That left him the day today with nothing to do until the limo came for him and Ryan this afternoon. They'd flown down to LA late last night and made their way to The Four Seasons. They'd opted for the luxury hotel, rather than staying at Lucas's LA residence, simply because they were both feeling lazy and preferred not to have to worry about cooking or tidying up.

A few nights ago, a press statement had been released about Lucas and Ryan. It was important that it went out before tonight, especially because not only would Lucas and Ryan be attending as a couple, but Anna and Antonia would also be attending together. Lucas knew the story had aired, but neither he nor Ryan had wanted to follow any of the fallout so had avoided news and social media. The time was fast approaching when they would no longer be able to avoid fans' reactions, but for a short time, they could hide away.

"Morning," Ryan called as he approached where Lucas was sitting on the balcony. "Thinking about your acceptance speech?"

Lucas enjoyed the kiss Ryan pressed to his lips and smirked at his lover. "No guarantee I'll be accepting anything, Ry."

"Oh, I'm pretty sure the Academy won't overlook an amazing talent such as yours. I'd definitely have a speech ready if I were you."

Lucas did have a speech ready, though he was by no means certain he'd need it. "What do you wanna do today? We've got hours."

"Trash movies?"

There were an enormous sofa and large television in their suite, and Lucas could imagine nothing better than curling up with Ryan and whiling away the hours in each other's arms until the limo came. "Perfect. Suggestions?"

"Okay, in keeping with the shark theme, it's got to be *Sharknado*. We can get through at least the first two before we have to get out of here."

They stayed in their pajamas, ordered some ridiculously overpriced room service, and settled in to watch some of the best "so bad they are good" movies ever.

They shared a shower and blow jobs and were downstairs waiting for their limo on time, accompanied by their bodyguards for the evening, Paulina and Gavin.

Lucas couldn't take his eyes off Ryan; he looked so fucking hot in his tux. He knew he was nervous, but the Ativan seemed to be helping, and Ryan was also using the breathing techniques he was learning. He'd had no adverse reactions in the two weeks he'd been taking the medication.

"You nervous about this?" Ryan asked.

"What? The Oscars? Not really. How about you?" The limo was huge, with room for at least another six people, but they were huddled into the corner as though every other seat would burn them.

"A little. The Ativan is helping. Once we're inside, I'll be all right. But I meant are you nervous about being out as a couple for the first time?"

"Not at all. This—you and me—is the most natural thing in the world to me. If we lose fans because of who we love, I'm okay with that. I'm never hiding again, and no amount of fame or money could make me deny you. You're it, Ry. We're it. Us, together, is all I want...all I need."

They spent the ride to the Dolby Theater holding each other and enjoying the last of the peace before the madness returned.

The crowd and commotion of the red carpet were unlike anything either of them had experienced before. It was alarming for Lucas, so he could only imagine the terror Ryan must be experiencing. The sheer volume of people in and around the carpet was astonishing, and if Lucas thought he'd seen photographers before, it was nothing to this. They were five or six deep at least, each of them with enormous lenses that zeroed in on Lucas and Ryan as soon as their feet hit the red of the five-hundred-foot long carpet.

Each click of the camera shutters combined with the others to create a roar of sound. Lucas could hear the cheers of the crowds and occasionally, through the lull, his or Ryan's name being called. There were even a few "*Lovers*" shouted out. Lucas didn't let go of Ryan's hand the entire time, not even if a photographer called for a solo photo. Tonight, more than ever, they were a package deal.

Amazingly, that was the easy part. The interviews were to come. Mercifully short, they would nonetheless be excruciating to bear. Unlike many others here tonight, Lucas and Ryan chose not to have hangers-on. No publicists, assistants, or umbrella holders. Their security discretely stuck to the background, and Lucas and Ryan faced the line of interviewers as though they were interrogators rather than media professionals.

"Lucas, Ryan, or should we call you 'Lovers'?" The first woman they approached asked, looking terribly pleased with herself for the rather obvious and banal lead-in.

Lucas smiled and laughed as the well-trained actor he was, all while secretly wishing time sped up and this night—at least this part of it—was over. "Hi, how are you this evening?" He tried.

"How am I? How are you? That's the question of the night. First-time Oscar nominee and some very big news in your private life announced recently. What an exciting time to be you, Lucas."

Jesus, was there a question in there somewhere? Lucas flicked a glance to Ryan, who kind of half smiled while boggling his eyes, clearly as uncomfortable as he was, but holding it together. "Yeah. It definitely is. I mean, I'm so honored to be nominated among some amazing actors this year. *Over the Oceans* is such an amazing and poignant film and I hope I've done justice to the role. As far as my private life goes...well, I can sum it up pretty succinctly. I couldn't be happier."

"And what about you, Ryan? You must be proud of your man."

"Absolutely. Lucas works harder than anyone I know and puts his all into his acting, so he deserves this acknowledgement of his talent."

"And who are you both wearing tonight?"

On and on it went, many of the same questions, many different ones, some easy to answer, and some completely unanswerable. By the time they made it inside, Lucas was exhausted.

"You all right, Ry?" He asked as soon as they were in the theater and away from the blinding glare of fame. Lucas could feel a tremor running through Ryan's body and hear his deep breathing, but his face seemed calm. Ryan had been amazing on the carpet and Lucas couldn't be prouder.

"I'm doing okay. Glad that bit's over." Ryan nuzzled his nose against Lucas's and Lucas pulled him closer, wrapping him in his arms.

"If you want to go—at any time—tonight, you just say the word and we're gone. Okay? I know this isn't easy for you, and I can't tell you how proud I am that you are on my arm tonight, but I'll go as soon as you need to." Lucas spoke quietly into Ryan's ear.

Ryan pulled out of the hug and dropped a gentle kiss to his lips. "I'm good, Lucas. I promise, and I'm the one who is proud of you. Sometimes I just... I can't believe where I am—or who I'm with...a fucking Oscar winner for chrissake."

"I haven't won yet."

"Details. It's only a few hours away, so I'm calling it now." Ryan grinned and Lucas felt that familiar desire burn through him at the sight. "Now let's find our seat and get this show on the road."

RYAN HAD LUCAS'S hand in a death grip when his nomination was called, and Lucas wondered if he'd have to take Ryan on stage with him if he won, because he wasn't at all sure Ryan was letting go anytime soon.

"This is it," Ryan whispered as the envelope was opened.

"And the winner is...Lucas Evers for *Over the Oceans*." Somebody, Lucas had forgotten who, in the mayhem of the moment, read out. Lucas stood and marveled as time slowed around him. He turned and pulled at

Ryan, who'd also stood to applaud, bringing him into his arms. He kissed him, tenderly and lovingly, and then pressed their foreheads together.

"So fucking proud of you, Luke," Ryan said through his enormous smile and all Lucas could do was nod.

Reluctantly, he moved away from Ryan and made his way toward the stairs. He could see Anna and Antonia standing on the other side of the aisle, applauding along with the rest of the room, so Lucas made a beeline for them. He swooped Anna into his arms, laughing as she kissed his cheeks.

"Well done, Luke. About fucking time."

"Thanks, babe." He gave Antonia a hug before finally making his way to the stage.

He kissed and thanked the young woman who'd presented his category, whose name still escaped him. Lucas did his best not to consider the millions of eyes on him as he stood at the podium to deliver his speech.

"Um, thank you. Thank you so much. As we all know, there are so many people to thank when you make a movie, and I am never going to get through them all. So my heartfelt thanks go to every cast and crew member who worked on *Over the Oceans*. It is a beautiful story brought to vivid life under the amazing direction of Frank Waller. Thank you also to Mission Studios for giving me a chance in this film. I know the music will start playing me off soon, so I'd like to say thank you to Anna, who has always, and will always, be my best friend and supporter. Love you, Anna. My family for always being there for me and supporting me. Love you guys. You know life throws so many different forks in the road of your life, some you take, and some you bypass. I must have chosen all the right forks so far because my life has led me to the most beautiful and amazing man in the world. Ryan, I love you with my entire heart, and regardless of the question the answer always...*always* is I'd rather be wherever you are."

Chapter Twenty-Six

How hot did Lovers *look in their tuxes please?! They are so soft.*

RYAN

Even now, almost three hours after Lucas's acceptance speech, Ryan could still feel the tingle up his spine, the flutter in his chest every time he recalled the words Lucas had spoken about him, and to him, in front of the entire world. If there was anyone who hadn't heard about them from the statement the studio released, they knew now. Lucas—and he—had unequivocally come out.

The press had kept Lucas backstage longer than usual, every one of them desperately clamoring to get more out of him—to get the dirt. Ryan knew they could expect a tidal wave of interview requests in the coming days and wondered how Lucas felt about that. Should they put it all out there in an effort to satisfy curiosity? Or should they retain some mystery to their relationship? Would their fandom's curiosity ever be satisfied?

It was dimly lit and incredibly crowded in the ballroom, but it took less than three seconds for Ryan to catch Lucas's gaze across the room. Though he couldn't see the green from this distance, his eyes were nonetheless a beacon calling to Ryan and he couldn't look away.

As ever, Ryan was enthralled by Lucas's beauty. Here he was surrounded by the elite of Hollywood, some of the most beautiful people in the world, in a stunning ballroom, with delicious food, exceptional champagne—which he wouldn't indulge in now he was on Ativan; one of the pluses of being on medication he guessed was that he'd had to cut out alcohol—and the most stunning man in the world on his arm, and all Ryan wanted to do was get the fuck out of there, take Lucas somewhere private, and pound him into the fucking mattress.

Ryan grabbed the glass of water for himself and the champagne he'd gone to get for Lucas, and made his way back. Lucas was talking to—fuck was that—it looked like Helen Mirren. Ryan didn't think he'd ever get used to mingling with people who'd always been his idols.

Though the room was crowded, Ryan didn't feel that sensation of almost being robbed of breath. No one in this room was paying the least bit of attention to him, unlike on the red carpet when Ryan had been furiously counting backward over and over to stave off the leftover panic the drugs couldn't deal with.

By the time he'd made his way to Lucas, he was standing alone again, though Ryan could see people getting ready to move in, have their turn with the man of the night. Too bad for them that Ryan wanted his turn with Lucas. Just for a few minutes, he needed to be alone with him, even if it would be in an overcrowded room.

As he drew near Lucas, that singular, indescribable connection they shared must have alerted Lucas to his approach because he turned those bright green eyes on him.

"Thank you. How're you doing? Ready to get the fuck out of here and help me celebrate properly?" Lucas's smile was dripping with pure want and unadulterated filth. Clearly, they were on the same wavelength, and if Ryan wanted his first time having Lucas inside of him to be in a broom closet, he'd drag him into the nearest one right now. He'd keep that little fantasy for another time, though; because tonight he wanted Lucas to have him in their room, on their giant bed, where they were both free to scream the place down.

Emboldened by Lucas's attitude and their public outing, Ryan leaned in and brushed their lips together. Lucas didn't let him get far though when he tried to pull back, instead, grabbing him with one hand on the back of his neck and deepening the kiss. A flicker of tongue and nipping teeth had Ryan's cock filling. He needed to get them the fuck out of there before their coming-out evening turned into something far more public than anybody wanted.

"Let's go, Luke," he growled against Lucas's lips, fighting to hold onto his control. He felt Lucas nod and that was all he needed. Ryan watched Lucas down his champagne, his throat working as he swallowed, and all Ryan could think about was the other thing he wanted Lucas swallowing. He felt his hard-on twitch, so getting Lucas out of there became a frantic urgency.

Ryan took the glass from Lucas, planning to dump it somewhere on the way out. His other hand grabbed Lucas's and dragged him toward the exit. He could focus on nothing but getting Lucas naked. People passed by in a blur and despite being in a room full of some of the world's most recognizable faces, Ryan couldn't have named a single one they passed on the way out.

They didn't have to wait long for the limousine and Ryan thanked the universe their hotel wasn't too far away. Paulina and Gavin squeezed in the front, leaving Ryan and Lucas alone in the back.

Every second, the want for Lucas was growing and he was losing the battle to keep his hands to himself until they were alone. He made the mistake of turning to look at Lucas. The green of his eyes, the flawlessness of his skin, and the way he sprawled in the corner of the seat, his legs slightly spread in invitation, mingled together into a whirlpool of lust that pulled him under, dragged him into that spot—his spot—between Lucas's parted thighs. Thank fuck, they were in a limo, giving him room to kneel there and then tilting his face up to Lucas, silently begging for the kiss he knew would both fan the flames of desire and start to ease the ache of need.

Lucas didn't disappoint. The kiss was hard, demanding, and almost animalistic in its desperate urgency. Their teeth gnashed together as their tongues fought for dominance. It was a punishing brand of Lucas's lips upon his. He knew he'd be bruised and swollen from it, but he'd never wanted anything more.

Ryan reached down and palmed Lucas's hard-on while their lips continued their battle. Ryan's own dick was rock-fucking-hard and he was astounded at the idea he might actually come from kissing alone. Lucas pulled away, panting fast, and held Ryan's head still in his hands. "Fuck, Ry. We've...we've gotta stop. I'm gonna fucking come and neither of us has got one stitch of clothing off yet. When I come tonight, the first time, I want us both naked and both of us so fucking desperate for it we'll be screaming, and then I am gonna finally get inside that tight fucking ass of yours and pound you until you can't fucking take anymore. And then, only then, will I let us both come." Lucas ended his promise with a lick to Ryan's lips that forced out the groan he'd held onto while Lucas had said such dirty things to him.

Ryan pressed himself back into the opposite corner—the only chance he had of keeping his hands off Lucas until they got back to the hotel. That was where they spent the last five minutes of the ride home, each in their separate corners but with their eyes never looking away from each other, the need and want sparking between them as though they were live wires.

The ride up to their room was a blur, with Ryan's entire focus split between keeping his hands to himself and maintaining the marathon eye-fuck they were currently engaged in. Ryan wanted to get to the proper fucking.

They had only managed two steps into the room before Ryan had Lucas pushed up against the closest wall. Thankfully, just as they'd been promised, their guards had discretely disappeared. Ryan's body was flush with Lucas's, allowing him to feel every hard ridge and plane. Like a scene out of so many movies, they fumbled with their clothes in a burning need to feel skin moving against skin. Lucas was naked in no time. Ryan loosened his tie, quickly removing his shirt. By the time he reached his own pants, Lucas had joined him in getting the rest of his clothes off—all except his bowtie, which still hung loosely around his neck.

"Leave it on, Ry. I want just you and the fucking tie." Lucas ground out.

"Jesus, Luke. Bed... I need the bed. I need you in me now."

Lucas stopped writhing against him and pushed Ryan's head back so he could look into his eyes. "You sure that's what you want? You don't have to. I mean, I would love to get into that ass of yours but what we've been doing is fucking awesome."

"No. I want this, I want you, Luke. I want every inch of your fucking gorgeous cock inside me. And I want it now." For the second time that night, Ryan grabbed Lucas by the wrist and dragged him where he wanted him. Forethought was a magical thing and it allowed them to get down to it without having to search around for lube or condoms. They were there, on the bed where Ryan had put them before they'd left earlier in the day.

Ryan lay on the covers, spreading his legs a little to make room for Lucas. Lucas crawled over him, slowly, licking and kissing his way up Ryan's body. Ryan shuddered uncontrollably when Lucas nibbled at his inner thigh, kissing right into the juncture of his groin. He continued his upward movement, ignoring Ryan's throbbing cock, and pressed kisses over Ryan's torso. By the time Lucas reached his lips, Ryan was panting and writhing, desperation coursing through every inch of his body.

Lucas lifted up and held himself over Ryan's prone body with his arms. Ryan watched as Lucas's gaze trailed over his length and his pink tongue poked out to lick at his lips. "You are so fucking gorgeous, Ry. Every fucking inch of you is perfect, every fucking inch." And then he said no more because his mouth was busy again, worrying at Ryan's heated flesh.

"Luke, please. I need...more."

"Okay. Roll over for me." Ryan complied without thought; he was all sensation now. Everything had become about his senses, his body one enormous nerve ending, feeling every single thing Lucas was doing to it.

Once he was on his stomach, Lucas gripped his hips and lifted a little before placing a pillow under him. Ryan felt exposed, with his ass tipping up in the air, but nothing would stop him from sharing his body with Lucas.

Ryan heard the snick of the lube and tried not to tense when Lucas's finger rubbed over his hole. Lucas had played with his ass a little before and Ryan had loved it. When Lucas's long finger finally dipped inside, Ryan breathed through the slight discomfort, knowing the good part would be here soon. Lucas added another finger, crooking them and finding that spot inside of him that blew his fucking mind.

After tormenting him for a while, Lucas pulled his fingers out and curved his body over Ryan's back, his lips brushing Ryan's ear as he spoke. "How do you want it, Ry?"

"Just like this, Luke. I want you all over me. I wanna feel your body completely blanketing me while you're inside of me. Please, Luke."

"Shh. Okay, baby. Tell me if you need to stop, okay?"

Ryan could only nod. Anticipation had his nerves standing on end so that every touch, every breath of Lucas's that gusted over his skin felt intense enough to make him come. His hips were rolling of their own accord, searching, and he couldn't quite catch his breath. He listened as Lucas tore open the condom packet and rolled it down his length. He heard the lube snick open and close again. And then he felt the head of Lucas's cock pushing at his hole, insistent, determined.

"Relax. Let me in."

Ryan willed himself to relax; he wanted this—needed it. He felt Lucas moving again, easing his way in until his cock popped through the ring of muscle and Lucas kept pushing forward until Ryan could feel his pelvis against his ass. Ryan was so fucking full, so overwhelmed, and now that the initial discomfort was easing, so fucking good. Lucas hadn't moved again since fully seating himself inside Ryan.

"Jesus, Luke. Ah fuck, you need to move. I need...I need it."

Rather than the thrusting he was expecting, Lucas rolled his hips a few times before rocking—no—grinding against Ryan's ass. It felt so fucking good and with Lucas's body on top of his, not a millimeter of space between them, and their hands linked above their heads, Ryan felt caged in—owned. In this moment, he was Lucas's completely and utterly.

Suddenly Lucas's torso lifted off and he released Ryan's hands, moving his own to grip Ryan's hips. Lucas pulled out and slammed back in, rocking the bed and shoving Ryan forward with the force. Ryan's eyes rolled back in his head as Lucas's cock brushed his prostate as he moved inside, thrusting into him over and over, unrelenting, despite the punishing rhythm.

Ryan felt the tingle brewing in the base of his spine, and in desperation, he squeezed his hand under his body, searching for just a little more friction on his throbbing dick. Lucas's thrusts were enough to force his cock through the grip he managed to get on himself, and Ryan knew he was moments away from a blinding orgasm.

"Gonna...oh, fuuuck," he drew out as Lucas slowed his pace and started grinding into him again. Lucas gripped his bow tie and gently pulled so that Ryan's head lifted and he turned his face to accept the kiss he knew Lucas was chasing. "Gonna come, Luke. Fuck."

"Do it, Ry. Fucking do it."

Ryan roared through the release that quickly followed Lucas's command and only just retained the wherewithal to feel it when Lucas tensed and spilled inside of him. Ryan's entire body shook as he tried to coax it down from the high of orgasm and he couldn't even move when he felt Lucas rise from the bed and eventually return with a warm, wet facecloth.

Lucas cleaned him with all the tenderness to equal the passion he'd unleashed on Ryan's willing body. Ryan found it difficult just to keep his eyes open and eventually gave up when Lucas hopped back into bed and spooned against his back.

"You good, Ry?"

"Better than good. That was...I don't even know how to describe it. The best fucking thing ever, maybe."

"Yeah, it was," Lucas replied, trailing and nuzzling his nose over the back of Ryan's neck, around his ear. "I wish I could fucking smell you, Ry—smell us, together. God I miss the smell of you and sex. While we're fucking, I used to be able to smell your skin, your arousal. I can touch you and feel you, but I can't fucking smell you." He pressed a kiss behind Ryan's ear.

"Doc said it might come back, Luke." Most people never gave much thought to their sense of smell or losing it. Through Lucas, Ryan had learned it was a painful loss. Lucas's taste was all out of whack and Ryan knew what Lucas meant about not being able to smell him. So many times, when they'd been lying around together, Ryan had subconsciously searched out Lucas's scent. A quick whiff to comfort him, arouse him, even connect him to Lucas, but Lucas had lost that with Ryan. It may not be the worst loss Lucas could have faced, but it was a loss, nonetheless.

Ryan made to move off the bed and clean them up when Lucas's arms tightened around him, pulling him closer. "I haven't finished with you yet," Lucas growled into his ear, his words and gravelly tone sparking another flame of lust with Ryan's well used and sated body.

Chapter Twenty-Seven

WTF is going on with Lovers?

LUCAS

Last night had been amazing. A fabulous, amazing, unfuckingbelievable night. Yes, he'd won an Oscar, and that alone was more good fortune than Lucas had ever believed would come his way. But the real prize was the man lying beside him, now snoring softly so fucking adorably. Being inside Ryan last night had been...well, Christ, better than he ever could have imagined. It had been perfect. The tightness, the heat, the sounds Ryan had made, the helpless little movements...everything had been perfect.

Lucas begrudgingly eased away from the warmth of Ryan's body. He was determined to surprise Ryan with a delicious breakfast in bed. Max and Harry were sitting in the living room of their suite. Paulina and Gavin had won the draw to accompany them to the Oscars last night and Lucas could tell from the looks on Harry and Max's faces that they'd heard all about it and were jealous as hell that they'd missed out. Lucas would have liked to have taken Ethan and Ben—they were his favorites—but they were both having some well-deserved downtime.

"Hey, hey, man. Congratulations," Max called to him. "You were awesome last night...stellar speech."

"Thanks, Max. Not too mushy?"

"Na. You kidding? You would have made a billion hearts swoon with that shit."

"You made me swoon, Lucas, and I'm straight as an arrow, buddy," Harry added with a smirk.

"Thanks. Paulina and Gavin sleeping off their late night, I'm guessing?"

"Yeah." Max looked thoroughly dejected. "Not before the fuckers gave us a blow-by-blow of the entire night and all of the stars and hotties they came across." Harry reached a consoling hand out and patted Max's shoulder.

Lucas laughed and offered to order a big breakfast for them both as a tiny step to making up for it. But just as Lucas reached for his phone, it started ringing. Unknown caller flashed on his screen, so Lucas considered not answering it. He had an unlisted number so no one should be able to call who hadn't been given his number. He slid the accept button across and put the phone to his ear.

"Hello. Lucas Evers."

For a moment there was silence and then a voice began talking and Lucas knew right away they were in serious trouble. The voice was clearly electronically distorted, and as soon as it began, the talker flew into a vicious rant decrying Lucas and his charmed life.

Lucas clicked his fingers to draw the attention of Harry and Max. They were beside him in seconds. Lucas put the phone on speaker and the three of them stood around listening. "Fucking undeserved success that needs to be taken away from you. How dare you think you are better than everyone, when you're just a fag who cares nothing for decent people. Your life is coming to an end and not before time..."

Max had his own phone in his hand and was probably recording the call. Lucas felt wobbly at the pure venom the caller was spitting all over him and had to clutch at the chair in front of him. He wanted to hang up but hoped if the call continued, with Max recording, it might somehow help the police to track this nut.

"If Leighton had done it the way I asked, you'd already be gone from our lives, but it won't be long now, Lucas Evers, and then you and that boy of yours will be in the fucking ground where your kind of filth belong." Thank god, the call ended then because Lucas wasn't sure how much longer he could listen to it. Who the hell hated him that much? The electronic distortion of the voice was chilling—the speaker could have been talking about how fucking cute kittens were and it still would have sounded evil.

Harry was already on another call by the time the caller hung up, and within moments, Paulina and Gavin had joined them in the room. Lucas could see they both had their weapons in their holsters. Usually they were not visible as they always had a jacket over them but time seemed to have been more important than discretion on this occasion.

Lucas crept back to the bedroom and pushed the door open as silently as possible—he just needed to check with his own eyes that Ryan was still safely where he'd left him. He watched the ball that was Ryan curled up under the blankets rise up and down with each breath. Satisfied, he inched back out of the room, closing the door softly behind him.

The living room was a flurry of activity when he walked back in. Gavin stood at the door to the suite, an extra barrier, in case the locked and chained door failed to keep someone out. Paulina, Harry, and Max were all on their phones. Lucas couldn't distinguish between the voices well enough to work out who was saying what to whom. All he could do was stand like a fucking scarecrow in the middle of the room, his insides in absolute tumult as the gravity of his situation dawned. He'd known, of course, after the car crash, but time had gone by with nothing, so Lucas had lost the fear; he'd thought the police may have been worrying for nothing. Fuck.

"Lucas. You with me?" Max cautiously approached as he spoke, probably frightened of spooking him even more.

"Yeah."

"Billy's gonna contact the studio and organize a private jet back to SFO. The teams are all going to meet us at the airport and we'll head back to your place together. Harry's on the phone to Detective Holland. He'll be able to get a warrant to find out the private number the call came from, and they can track it from there. Paulina's on the phone to Patricia to organize some extra measures. We've got this, Lucas. Okay? We've got this. No one's gonna get past any of us and get to you or Ryan."

"What? What do you mean get to us?"

Lucas closed his eyes at the sound of Ryan's voice coming from behind him. He'd do anything to spare him from this shit storm. Fame was already kicking the hell out of Ryan; he didn't need this on top of it. Lucas turned and walked straight to his man, pulling him into his arms and dropping a kiss to the top of his head. He held him tightly as he spoke into his hair. "There was a call. A nasty one. We're just being cautious, but we think...we think it was whoever set up Leighton. The guys have everything under control, though, so we're just gonna let them do what they have to and we'll head home. Okay?"

"How nasty?" came the muffled reply.

"Bad. I've gotta die type stuff." He'd spare Ryan from hearing that he'd been included in the death threat for as long as he could.

"Fuck. Oh Jesus, Luke. It's my fault. It's—"

"Stop it. Right now. This is not your fault, Ryan. I know you believe that it's because of Leighton and that they wanted me dead so they could have you, but I don't buy it. This person wants to hurt me... You don't need to take on the guilt." Lucas kissed him then. He kissed him because he had to, because he needed to. Ryan was his comfort, his home. Ryan was the world to him and he needed to connect with him so desperately.

THE TRIP BACK to San Francisco was uneventful. *Thank god.* Lucas had a new appreciation for their team of bodyguards. He'd never seen people so focused, move better than a well-oiled machine, and appear so fucking lethal. If he hadn't been so blindingly in love with Ryan, it would have been a huge fucking turn-on to watch these men and women do their thing.

As much as he'd wanted to switch his phone off, the police had asked for it to be left on in case another call came through. The more calls, the more evidence, and the more chance of catching this person. It was hard though. Every time it rang, and it rang a lot with the studio, friends, and family all trying to contact him after his win, Lucas felt sick to his stomach. He dreaded having to listen to that warped voice again.

Ethan and Billy were on the tarmac at San Francisco airport to greet them when their plane landed. The eight bodyguards walked him and Lucas to a large black SUV that was waiting just beyond the runway. Lucas and Ryan climbed in the back. Ethan and Billy hopped in the front, and Ben squeezed in the back with them. The other guards followed in two similar vehicles. Lucas felt like the fucking Queen of England in a motorcade.

Ten minutes into the forty-minute trip back to his place, his phone rang again, showing private number. "Shit. It's a private number," he announced for all of the car's occupants.

"Hang on," Ben said while reaching into his jacket and pulling out his phone. He fiddled around with it and then held it close to Lucas, signaling for him to answer the call.

"Hello."

Again the altered voice came over the line, spewing more vile words. "And it will not be fast, Lucas. Those mired in filth and evil do not deserve a clean death. Punishment is needed to cleanse your soul in order to rid the world of your wickedness."

On and on it went. Lucas did his best to tune it out by turning his full focus on Ryan, who was sitting so quietly and deathly pale in the face of such horror. Their eyes met and Lucas never looked away; he held Ryan transfixed in his gaze. It wasn't until Ben called his name that he realized the call had ended.

"Jesus Christ," Ryan breathed out. Lucas nodded and drew him into his arms. He could hear Billy up front talking on the phone again and gathered he was calling the police to notify them of the call. Ben sat on the other side of Ryan, bolt upright like a statue. He wondered if their bodyguards were worried. Did they think they'd bitten off more than they could chew? They seemed comfortable; they didn't appear to be freaking out at all. Maybe they'd seen plenty of shit the same as this before.

Once they were back at his apartment, Lucas wasted no time in getting both him and Ryan into the shower. Despite being naked together, there was nothing sexual about the shower this time. Lucas lovingly washed Ryan's body with a soapy cloth, not neglecting so much as an inch of that smooth, porcelain skin. Every ridge and crevice of Ryan's body was tenderly wiped clean as though it might also wash the taint of the phone calls from him. When he was done, Ryan took a cloth and cleaned him just as lovingly. Neither of them got hard. This was them connecting, being there for and soothing each other.

"We'll be okay, Luke. I know we will," Ryan whispered to him as they held onto one another under the flow of hot water.

"Damn right we will, Ry." He wanted to say more, be more convincing, but the words stuck in his throat. The truth was he was terrified. He couldn't remember where he'd heard it, but he knew there was some theory that anyone could be gotten to, even the president, as long as you were willing to die too. What if this person was willing to die to get to him or Ryan? How do you fight that kind of crazy?

When they had dried and dressed, they made their way into the dining room, where both teams of guards sat, enough food for a small army spread out on the table. All eight gazes turned to them. It was Ethan who stood and addressed them.

"Ryan, Lucas, come sit, and we'll update you." Max and Harry stood to give up their seats at the table and moved to stand against the wall behind them. Ethan continued on before they'd even sat. "Given this escalation, we've re-evaluated our practices. For the time being, there will be two of us on each of you whenever you are outside of these doors. Ben and I will be moving in here as extra backup as needed. Patricia and Roger have also suggested putting some bodyguards with your families. There's been no threat, but with people like this, you can't be too careful."

Lucas's gut flipped and ached at the mention of his family. He'd never, for a moment, supposed they were in danger, but Ethan was right. Who knew what this person might do? He hadn't seen his parents or brothers in person since shortly after his attack, but they'd called or Skyped frequently, and Lucas hoped their relationship was slowly stitching back together. He hadn't seen his sister for months, and as far as he knew, she was still in

Europe with the guy she'd met over there. Antonia Curzon had her own guards, and he'd be very surprised if she hadn't hired extra bodyguards for Anna. She certainly would after hearing about the latest.

"It's wrong and it's unfair, but until they catch this person, neither of you can be alone. You need to trust that we know what we're doing—because we do. I promise both of you that." Ethan finished.

Lucas nodded, but it was Ryan who answered. "We trust you guys. Whatever you say, we'll do."

"Perfect. Now, plenty of food here, tuck in and let's try to enjoy the meal."

Lucas's phone rang several more times that evening, twice from Philip Moyers, and once from Anna, who was in a flap over what was happening. She spoke to both him and Ryan and assured them both she had plenty of security around her. In fact, Antonia was whisking her away to Europe for a break. The fourth call was from Detective Holland.

"Mr. Evers, I wanted to touch base. We've spoken at length to your security team. They've sent us the recordings of the calls and a warrant is imminent which will allow us to access phone records to get the details of the caller. With any luck, that will lead us right to them." Detective Holland's gruff voice boomed over the phone, and if possible, sounded even more intimidating than in person.

"What will happen if you catch them? I mean what will they be charged with?"

"It will depend on what the DA thinks they can do with the evidence we get. What we'll try to focus on is getting evidence on the connection to Leighton White. That'll give us, hopefully, the option of conspiracy to murder. Frankly, from the tone of the calls, this could even be a hate crime."

"Well, if there's anything..." Lucas trailed off halfheartedly, wanting to help but wishing he'd never been in this position in the first place.

"You just worry about your safety and Mr. Lowe's. We'll deal with the rest."

Lucas wanted nothing more after that call than to fall into bed. Ryan was watching some kind of sci-fi movie with Ben, but he didn't hesitate to follow Lucas when he announced he was going to bed.

They made love that night, slowly and tenderly. Much like in the shower earlier, it was the need for connection and peace that drove them, rather than the usual blazing lust that consumed them and made them burn. When they'd eventually found their release, they remained tangled together, gazing into each other's eyes and pressing gentle kisses to their skin, wherever they could reach. Who knew how long they'd have this? Life changed in an instant. They finally drifted off in the early morning hours.

LUCAS AND RYAN had just gotten out of the shower and sat down for breakfast when his phone started trilling. Lucas huffed and put it on speaker phone, recognizing Detective Holland's number. At least he wouldn't have to repeat to the group whatever the detective had to tell them.

"'Lo," he answered.

"Mr. Evers, it's Detective Holland. Detective Bourke and I are on our way over. I'm afraid we've got some news—"

"What is it?" Lucas broke in.

"Mr. Evers, is your security team present?"

"Yeah." Lucas was starting to get a bad feeling snaking its way up his spine.

"We know where the calls originated."

Lucas felt his heart thrumming a million miles an hour in his chest. His breathing deepened and sweat broke out in glistening drops on his forehead. Beside him, Ryan reached out and grabbed his hand.

"Mr. Evers, the private number was yours. The calls came from the landline inside your home."

Chapter Twenty-Eight

Lovers *in hiding. What does this mean for* Samdom?

RYAN

"Jesus fucking Christ," Lucas spluttered.

"Move people," Ethan boomed. "Lucas, Ryan get a bag packed."

All hell broke loose the second the words fell out of Detective Holland's mouth. The room erupted into a flurry of activity. Ethan and Ben effectively glued themselves to his and Lucas's sides as they hurriedly packed a bag. Their other guards fanned out in the large apartment, inspecting every nook and cranny in case the horrifying idea that the person they were after was somehow still inside the apartment turned out to be true.

Ryan and Lucas were rushed back into one of those enormous SUV's before the detectives even arrived. Billy informed the staff at Lucas's apartment complex about what was going on and asked them to give access to the detectives as soon as they arrived with their crime techs. As far as Ryan knew or cared, the apartment would be gone over with a fine-tooth comb looking for evidence.

"Where are we going?" Ryan asked Ben once they were on their way.

"The Krispins have a place. It's tighter than Fort Knox. We'll head there until other arrangements can be made."

Ryan watched Ben's face as he spoke, and he could see his gaze darting around, ever vigilant. It suddenly occurred to him that this man, who he had come to really like and care about, might be hurt—for him. Any one of their bodyguards might. Each of them would put themselves in harm's way for him or Lucas. What did that say about them? In this increasingly self-absorbed world, how were there still people ready to sacrifice everything for others?

Lucas held his hand in such a vicelike grip that Ryan knew he'd have to shake the blood back into it once it was released. He knew Lucas was as frightened as he was, and yet the guards seemed to be perfectly calm. Ryan knew he'd sacrifice himself for Lucas, but for virtual strangers? He wasn't so sure he was that good of a person.

The place the Krispins had *was* a fucking fortress. It was something between a house and a mansion but was completely surrounded by nine-foot walls with cameras peppered all around, covering every inch of the grounds. The interior of the house was also covered by cameras, with the exception of the bathrooms and bedrooms.

"Ryan, you and Lucas are in here." Ethan led them to a large master suite. Everything was expensive and comfortable, yet tasteful. Ryan placed his bag on the bed and Lucas quickly dropped his beside it.

When Ryan turned to look at Lucas, he could see by the pasty pallor and his enormous eyes that Lucas was struggling to keep it together. He took him into his arms immediately, rocking him gently and whispering to him, "It's okay, Luke. It's going to be okay. They've got us." How desperately he hoped he was right.

"They were in my home...my fucking home."

Ryan had no idea how long they stood there wrapped up in each other, until a knock on their door pulled them apart.

"Sorry to interrupt." Ben popped his head in when Lucas called out for him to enter. "I wanted to make sure everything was okay and see if you had any questions. I know that all happened pretty fast, and you're probably both a little shocked by what's happening."

"I'd like to know the plan. What's going to happen now? How long will we be here?" Ryan recognized how strong and *together* he sounded, and he wondered why finding himself and Lucas in this dangerous situation hadn't left him cowering on the floor as he had been at Oracle arena a few weeks ago. He was scared—yes, but his anxiety wasn't spiking.

"You got it, Ryan. You and Lucas settle in, and when you're ready, come on through to the lounge. I'll get Ethan and Billy together so we can have a meeting." Ben nodded as he left the room. Confidence and calm exuded from the bodyguard and Ryan wondered if it was real or if Ben was a better actor than any of them.

"I'm gonna look for a place. Actually, no. I want us to look for a place. Somewhere secure that can be ours. For now, while this...this shit gets sorted, I need..." Lucas faltered, but Ryan knew what he needed because he needed the same thing.

"You need us to be together and away from your old place?"

Lucas nodded. "I do."

"I need the same. Even the thought of you not being in my sight at the moment is... It's hard."

"Agreed. So let's look for somewhere. I can't go back to that place, not knowing that person was in there. I'd never feel safe there again. And when this is all over, we can sit down and talk over what we want to do. But you have to know this, Ryan Lowe: the one thing that won't ever change is that I want you. I will always fucking want you." Lucas's mouth covered his and Ryan could feel the familiar heat start to burn its way through his body. How could he burn so much for this man and not be harmed by it? If he lost Lucas, though, he'd be hurt—beyond saving. He knew that for certain.

By the time they made it to the living room, Detectives Holland and Bourke were sitting with Ethan and Billy. Ben was ambling around the room, not really participating in the conversation between the detectives and the bodyguards, but Ryan knew he'd be absorbing every word that was spoken.

"Detectives," Ryan greeted them. "Any news?" Ryan and Lucas moved to the vacant seats on the long leather sofa. The detectives had an armchair each and Billy sat at one end of the sofa while Ethan was perched on the arm of it.

"We've got people going through footage from the security cameras now. Hopefully, we'll get something from that. We spoke to the doorman who was on duty yesterday...um, Edgar. Actually, we had some officers take him down to the station. He was less than forthcoming about his movements yesterday. Have you had any problems with him before? Noticed anything...unusual about him?"

"Edgar? No... I mean, he's always been polite, professional. He's a passing acquaintance, you know. Nothing more or less," Lucas replied, sounding perplexed by the turn the questions were taking.

"And you, Ryan?" Detective Bourke turned his quick, dark eyes on Ryan.

"Same. I rarely saw him. I tend to go out through the underground parking, but he was always nice."

A round of nods went through the men in the room as though both he and Lucas had given the expected answers. "You're thinking he's covering his ass?" Ben looked at the two detectives while he spoke.

"Exactly. We're kind of thinking he may have taken an unscheduled break, which gave our perp their way in. He'd want to try to hide that fact so he doesn't lose his job. He'll crack. I give it another twenty minutes and someone from the station will be calling to tell us just that, but of course, we have to chase every lead."

"What happens now?" Ryan asked.

Detective Bourke gave a little shrug of his shoulders before replying. "We follow the evidence. Your place is being dusted for prints. We've got uniforms talking to everyone in the building, and we've got the people looking through security camera footage. If we get lucky, this person is sloppy and we'll get a good look at them. We've got a trace on your phone, so if they call again, let them talk for as long as possible. With luck, this'll be wrapped up quickly. In the meantime, listen to your security team."

"We will be," Lucas promised.

The detectives left shortly afterward, leaving Billy to give Ryan and Lucas a rundown of what to expect from them.

"We're essentially prisoners," Ryan observed when he'd finished.

"No. You can go any place you want... You just can't do it alone," Ethan replied.

"I wanna look for a new place. I don't want to go back to the old place knowing... And I want it to be secure. Any suggestions?"

"Sure, we can give you some pointers; check it out for you once you've found something."

Lucas's phone rang, interrupting the conversation. Billy and Ethan jumped up immediately, and Ben moved closer to them. "Relax. It's my dad." Lucas told them. "Hey, Dad."

Ryan wished he could hear both sides of the call but had to content himself with working out the crux of the conversation from Lucas's side alone.

"I can't give out where we are, Dad. I'm sorry, but that's the rules."

The rest of the conversation was a lot of uh-huhs and umm yeahs from Lucas. They'd been told they weren't allowed to give out the address of the safe house to anybody. Not even the studio knew where they were, and he hoped Lucas's family would understand that. It wasn't a long call, but it had clearly frustrated Lucas by the time he hung up.

"Dad's pissed I wouldn't tell him where we are. He and Mom are still in LA, but Dad said he's sending Craig up to see me. He'll ring when he gets here to organize something. Apparently, he's been nominated family liaison. Dad also said the media's camped outside their place asking about our *sudden disappearance.*"

"If you need us to talk to them, Lucas, hand over the phone. I'm a pretty persuasive guy..."

"Ben," Ethan snapped. These two did that a lot. Ethan seemed to have a line, and whenever Ben stepped a toe over it, he snapped at his younger colleague, who instantly stiffened and usually quieted. Ryan wouldn't say they disliked each other; he'd caught Ethan smiling at some of Ben's antics, but there was some kind of tension between them. They were so different: Ethan was a model of stoic rigidity and Ben was more of an excitable puppy. He only hoped it never got in the way of them doing their jobs.

"ANY LUCK, RY?" Lucas's voice pulled him from his lewd thoughts. His lips were soft and he smelled vaguely of pineapple when he leaned in and kissed Ryan soundly on the lips.

"A few. Only one of them passes the Ben test though." They'd been scouting for a new place to live for the last week. It had been agreed Ryan's place would be no safer than Lucas's, so they'd stuck with Lucas's plan to buy something new. Their bodyguard, Ben Cronin, had very definite specifications for what would pass his security test, and so far he'd pooh-poohed each house they'd gone to view for one reason or another. Ryan had great hopes for the one he'd found today. It was a fortress, from what he could tell, but what had sold him was the giant fireplace in the master bedroom. The only thing his mind could concentrate on after reading about that was the image of him and Lucas fucking in front of a roaring fire.

"Craig called again, and he wants to see me. I've spoken to Billy, and he said Ethan and Ben will take us to the house where Craig is staying later this afternoon. Mum and Dad are still freaking out, and they want someone from the family to confirm with their own eyes that I'm still alive and well." Lucas smiled, but it didn't reach his eyes. They tried to make light of the nightmare they were in for their sanity, but they both knew it for the act it was.

The security cameras at Lucas's building hadn't revealed much, only a figure which could have been male or female, black, white, or purple and any age between twelve and a hundred and twelve, entering Lucas's apartment on the day the calls had been made. The figure wore gloves and a hat covering their face. Essentially, the image had yielded them nothing. A week had gone by and nobody was any closer to tracking down whoever was hunting them.

"Maybe we can pop in to see this place on the way back? Have a look at it. It's got a fireplace in the master bedroom, and I thought—"

"Fireplace fucking?"

Ryan laughed. "Yep, exactly. There are other pluses, but I'm kinda stuck on the fireplace."

"You've got a one-track mind, Ry, and I love it. Show me this place of yours then." Lucas leaned over Ryan's back as he scrolled through the images of the house on his laptop. It was such a domestic thing to do and was something Ryan never thought he'd have. Ryan loved every second he spent with Lucas, but these quiet times, when they did something any other couple on earth would do, were his favorites. He honestly didn't know how far his career would go, given his anxiety issues and his nasty introduction to fame, but it had led him to Lucas so he could never regret that.

"It looks perfect. Let me call the agent and see if we can sneak in a visit this afternoon."

Lucas stepped away from him to make the call and Ryan busied himself with another browse through the images. He'd gotten so used to only being alone in the bathroom and bedroom that he hardly noticed Ben and Ethan replace Christina and Harry. They'd hardly left the house in the last week and Ryan wondered if the bodyguards ever allowed their minds to wander while they sat around *minding* them in the safety of this fortress.

Both of their roles had been cut until the danger passed so they only had to film a few days a week, and it was all done in the studio—no more location shoots. For Ryan, though, the joy had been sucked out of his success.

Their fandom had exploded after the news of them actually being a couple had come out and now, with all of this mess going on, the fandom was hysterical. Ryan and Lucas had spent hours watching fan-made videos of them together. It had helped keep their minds off the danger lurking around them. The press was beside themselves with glee, once it inevitably leaked about the phone calls and threats, but they stayed away from any reports about that. Ryan snickered when he thought what their unbridled joy would be like if one or both of them happened to be killed by this nutcase. It was a tragically funny idea.

Chapter Twenty-Nine

Oh fuck! Lovers...

LUCAS

"So this is the brother you like?" Ben asked from the front seat of the dark SUV that Ethan was currently driving. They were on their way to meet with his brother Craig, and despite the small rift that had grown between him and his family, Lucas was looking forward to seeing him. Craig had rented a house on the outskirts of Oakland because his family had wanted a place closer to Lucas where they could stay when they came to visit. Once this whole mess was finished, he wanted to sit down with his family and work out an arrangement everyone could be happy with and put this money crap to bed.

"Yeah. Craig and I always got on well. Matthew and I were too alike, too close in age. We ticked each other off." There were five years between him and Craig, enough that Craig looked up to his big brother, and the gap meant he didn't have Craig tagging along with him in his teen years as he'd had with Matthew. "You got brothers or sisters, Ben?"

"Twin brother. Fraternal, in case you're hoping there's another hottie that looks the same as me walking around in this world. He's about five inches taller, muscles on his muscles, and guess what he does for a living?"

"Um, cop?" Ryan tried.

"Nope. He flies fucking choppers man...rescue choppers. Fucking hero." Ben smiled fondly.

"Wow, that's pretty impressive. How about you, Ethan?"

"We're pretty sure Ethan was hatched. I've never heard anything about his family." Ben laughed, and Ethan gave him a quick sidelong look before turning his gaze back to the road.

"I wasn't *hatched*, but no, I have no brothers or sisters anymore." There was an awkward silence after Ethan's revelation and Lucas suspected, from the grimace on his face and the tightening of his fists on the wheel, that he hadn't meant for the *anymore* to slip out.

Ben hadn't taken his eyes off Ethan and Lucas heard a barely whispered, "Sorry, man. I didn't know," slip from his mouth before he turned his head back to look straight out the front window of the car.

Paulina and Harry were in the car following behind them, and Lucas wished with all his might he was in that car right then. The uncomfortable silence remained for most of the journey, broken sporadically by a phone call to Ben, which was hushed and brief, and a comment from Ethan about the traffic flowing better than usual.

The rental Craig had found was a typical suburban house for the area though it was set on a larger block than most. It was a two-story with enough bedrooms and bathrooms for his entire family to stay there, if needed. Lucas was picking up the tab for it, but he had no objections to that. While it certainly didn't have the security he was looking for in a place, it had more than enough to ease his mind for his family's safety.

Craig met them at the front door, smiling widely and looking better than the last time Lucas had seen him at the hospital. There was a wide staircase directly opposite the front door that led to the second floor and Craig motioned for the group to enter, directing them to a large sitting room off to the left. Lucas and Ryan took a seat on the sofa while their bodyguards fanned out to reconnoiter or whatever they did once they arrived safely with their charges at a new location.

"Great place, Craig," Lucas said to his brother as Craig came into the room with some cold beers, passing one to Lucas and one to Ryan.

"Yeah, not bad. It'll do for what we need it for. Can I offer you and your guys a drink?" he asked Ethan, who was standing off to the side with his back to a wall and an unfettered view of the room.

"Thank you, but no. We're good."

"Ah can't drink on the job, right. I've got tea, coffee, water, juice?" Craig persisted.

"No. Thank you," Ethan answered. Lucas still couldn't see the other guards but knew they would be close by.

"Suit yourselves. Let me know if you change your mind." Ethan simply nodded in response and Craig turned his attention back to Lucas. "So, big brother, how are you both coping? All right?"

Lucas coming out to his brothers had been done over Skype before the press release and had been relatively painless. Matthew had only nodded and Craig had laughed, telling Lucas he'd just cost him a twenty-dollar bet with someone, which fortunately, he'd never have to pay. Lucas wasn't quite sure what that had meant, but he was relieved his brothers had been fine with it.

"We're doing all right. I'll be fucking relieved when they get this guy. It's frustrating not being able to live our lives."

"How about you, Ryan? Are you sick of this big douchebag yet?"

Ryan laughed and flicked a glance to Lucas before answering. "Not yet. Though I could do without the crumbs in the bed."

"Still eating in bed, man? Fuck, I remember Mom screaming at you about that when we were growing up. She swears she found a half-eaten pizza slice all mangled up in the sheets one morning. Most people count sheep to help them fall asleep, but doofus here has to eat to fall asleep." There was such fondness in Craig's voice that Lucas experienced the guilt again for the whole money mess he'd created with his family.

"What gets me, though, is where does he put it? I mean, if I ate as much and as badly as he does, I'd be packing on the pounds," Ryan questioned.

"Right. I know. Fucking lucky bastard—"

"If you two are gonna sit around and bitch about me, I'm going to take myself on a tour of the house." Lucas pouted.

"Sorry, Luke. But I do think it's only fair that somebody warns Ryan here just what he's getting into. Tell you what... I was gonna ask a favor. I had an audition a couple of weeks ago, and I got to the final round but lost out. I wanted you to have a look at my audition tape, maybe give me some pointers. You can do that while Ryan and I have our little chat. What do ya say?"

"Sure, Craig. Of course, I'll take a look."

"Thanks, man. Upstairs. I've got it set up in the study up there. I'll take you up."

Lucas stood and went to follow Craig up the stairs. Ben stood at the bottom of the staircase and raised his eyebrows in question, but Lucas declined his offer to escort them up.

"That must be annoying." Craig flicked his head back in the direction of Ben and Lucas knew exactly what he was referring to.

"Frustrating, yeah. But they're doing their job and they're all really nice. Hopefully, it'll be over soon, and we can go back to only needing security for events and whatnot."

"I bet you anything it's gonna be over really soon." Craig turned with a little smile and clapped Lucas on the shoulder. "Through here. Sound is real shitty on the tape, but it's better with the headphones on. Sorry it's such a mess in here. I've just kinda dumped my paperwork and stuff."

"Jesus, what is all this paperwork? You writing a screenplay or something?"

"Nah. I'm not that talented, bro. Lot of rejection letters in there, though."

It was a moderate-sized study. The house came fully furnished and whoever had decorated it had a fondness for giant glass-top desks and chrome bookshelves. A monitor and laptop were set up at the desk, so Lucas took a seat in the large office chair facing the barred window behind the desk. Lucas admired the grounds he could see from his position in the chair. A giant in-ground pool took up considerable space, surrounded by beautiful landscaping with a cabana, an outdoor kitchen, and dining area under a large gazebo. It would be perfect in the summer for a family get-together.

"Here, Luke." Craig handed him the headphones. "I really appreciate this."

"No worries. Just go easy on the tales to Ryan. I'd like to keep him." Lucas smiled.

"You got it. I'm happy for you, bro."

Lucas pressed play and began watching Craig's audition. He heard the door bang shut as Craig left and turned his concentration to watching his brother on the small screen in front of him. He stood in a bare room with sheets of paper in his hands and looked directly at the camera. "Craig Evers, and I'm here today to do a monologue reading for the part of Cain."

Lucas listened to his brother as he began his audition but what really struck him was the expression on his brother's face when he shifted into character as Cain. Lucas had no idea what the part was but could only assume from Craig's expression that Cain was evil. "And your punishment for your wickedness will not be swift, brother. You have taken too much and left so little for the rest of us. You and any memory of you must be cleansed from this earth along with your fag lover."

Jesus Christ, what kind of part was this, and why did it seem so eerily familiar? Lucas could feel his breath catching in his throat and he tried desperately to cough it out. Once he started, though, the hacking wouldn't stop. There was something there, something irritating him, making his breathing speed up as he fought to get more air into his lungs, but the air *tasted* off. Something was dreadfully wrong.

Lucas ripped the headphones off and spun in his chair. The bookshelves beside the entry to the room were ablaze and Lucas watched in horror as the flames licked up the door of the room, cutting off his escape.

Smoke was thick toward the ceiling and was falling quickly. Lucas hadn't been able to smell it because of his previous injury.

His coughing was getting worse, and it was getting harder and harder to get enough air into his lungs. He knew he only had minutes to save himself. He went to the window. It was locked and barred, but he desperately needed to get some clean air. His head throbbed and his eyes stung from the ever-increasing layer of smoke. There was no way he could fit through the bars on the window, anyway, and he turned to reconsider attempting an escape out the door.

Get down low blared in his memory, so he dropped to the floor, cowering under the glass desk to protect himself from the flames that were spitting out in his direction. From under the glass top he watched with morbid fascination as the flames flickered to life on the bookshelf closest to him. All of this paper was kindling to the building fire. His eyes watered and burned, and the hacking cough was now constant. His head thundered and he couldn't focus on anything, couldn't remember where he was, or if Ryan was with him. Ryan. No, fuck, please let him be okay.

Strange how he'd always thought his desire for Ryan burned him and now he really was going to burn. At least, with all of this smoke, he'd be gone before the flames began to char his body.

His vision was dimming and he didn't know if it was from the smoke or if he was losing consciousness. He thought he saw the door to the room fly open, but impossibly, a man stood there just beyond the flames before charging into the room, so he knew he had to be hallucinating. One last fantasy of rescue before the smoke took him.

The vision reached him and pulled at his arms with a strength Lucas knew had to be imaginary. He was unceremoniously flung over a broad shoulder and was being carried out of the room. He had no strength to keep his head from bouncing off the back of this imaginary creature his mind had created to comfort itself in the hope it and his body would be saved. He felt as if every ounce of strength he possessed went into stopping his insides from flinging out of his throat with each torturous cough. Someone, somewhere, was screaming "No" over and over—it may have been him, though his throat was so fucking raw it was unlikely he could get any sound out. It hurt to be alive now so Lucas thought the end must be coming. His eyes were so watery and sore he could no longer keep them open. He had no idea where he was when he felt the giant mythical creature who'd been shouldering him tilt and fall, sending both of them hurtling toward the ground. He never felt the impact.

Chapter Thirty

I can't stop crying! My heart is broken.

RYAN

Ben had raised the alarm. Ben, whose blood was now seeping through Ryan's fingers as he pressed down as hard as he could to try to keep it all from flowing out of his body, when all Ryan wanted to do was run up those fucking stairs and be with Lucas—even if it was the end.

Moments after Lucas and Craig had gone upstairs, Ben had come into the room talking quietly to Ethan. Ryan could tell immediately there was a problem. If Ryan had thought he'd seen the bodyguards vigilant before, it was nothing compared to what he witnessed now as Ben approached him.

"You need to come with me now." Ben had said. Ryan stood without hesitation.

"Get him out, Ben. I'm going after Lucas. I'll get Harry to get the car running. Don't wait for us." Ethan called across the room. Ryan could see Ethan already had his gun drawn and when he turned to look more closely, he could see that Ben did too. Ethan put his phone to his ear as soon as Ben got him walking toward the front door.

Ben and Ryan were closer to the exit than Ethan was, and he didn't miss how Ben put Ryan behind him as they made their way out. All Ryan wanted to do was run up those fucking stairs, grab Lucas, and get the hell out of there. He had no idea what was going down, but he trusted these two men, and if they needed him to get out, then he'd damn well get out.

Ben had the front door open and briefly stopped to scan the outside. He pushed Ryan in front of him, but before Ryan had made it a step outside, he heard a loud bang and felt the disruption of air close to the side of his head before he heard a *thunk*. Particles from the wall near his head blew out and nicked at his skin. He started to turn back into the house when he heard the second bang and felt his body being pushed down and to the side, covered all the way down by Ben's. Several more bangs sounded, and Ryan watched from under Ben as Craig's body punched backward and collapsed on the stairs, puffs of red exploding from his chest.

"Ben!" Ethan roared as Ryan watched him run toward them as they lay sprawled on the floor. Ben was lying on top of him, but Ryan could see one of his arms was outstretched with a proverbial smoking gun held firmly in his hand.

It had taken seconds for the world around Ryan to be blown to hell. It was Craig? Oh fuck, did that mean...? Lucas had willingly gone upstairs with Craig. Was he already dead? He needed Ben to get the fuck off him.

Suddenly Ryan's view was taken up by the kneeling figure of Ethan as he reached their side. Ethan stayed out of Ben's line of sight, allowing Ben to keep his bead on Craig.

"Ben, Jesus Christ, you're hit?" Ethan had more emotion in that one sentence than Ryan had ever heard him use, confirming the direness of the situation. Where the fuck was Lucas? They had to get to Lucas.

"I'm good, Ethan. You need to get to Lucas. Can't you smell it?"

Smell what? What the fuck was Ben talking about?

"Fuck...fuck."

"Ethan, look at me." Whereas Ethan's voice was strained, Ben's was absolute calm. "I'm good. Go get Lucas. Ryan, wiggle out but stay behind me."

Ryan felt Ben's body lift slightly, so he took the opportunity to slide out from under him. Ethan helped Ben sit, his aim never wavering. "Take his weight," Ethan instructed and then gently eased Ben back onto Ryan so that he was leaning against Ryan's body. "Press here." Ethan moved Ryan's hands so that they were wrapped around Ben's torso, pressed against his right pectoral. Ethan's hands came away bloody. Ben had indeed been shot. "Harry's got the car running and Paulina's coming around from the back."

Ethan stood and turned to run toward the stairs where Craig was lying, sobbing, and writhing in pain. Ryan watched as Ethan picked up the gun that was lying just out of Craig's reach and put it in his pocket. He turned back to Ryan and Ben. "You got him?" he asked.

"Yeah. I got him," Ben replied, not moving an inch, and then Ethan turned and ran up the stairs.

Ryan could now smell what Ben had been referring to seconds ago. Smoke. Fuck. Was Lucas...? No, he couldn't even think about that, not even for a second. Ryan could see the smallest of tremors starting in Ben's arm and wondered how much longer he could remain like this, especially with his wound.

"You fucking assholes!" Craig roared at them. "I'm gonna fucking kill you all."

"Not today, buddy," Ben calmly answered.

"Craig... Craig, where's Lucas?" Ryan tried.

"Dead. Your little fag lover is dead. I burned him. He fucking deserved to die, and if that stupid cow had done her job right the first time, I wouldn't have had to get my fucking hands dirty."

Jesus. *He* was the one working with Leighton. He had to be lying. Lucas couldn't be dead—he'd have felt it. He knew he'd have felt it the moment Lucas's heart stopped beating because his would have too. "You're lying. He's not dead. He's not." Ryan felt himself getting worked up. He wanted to go over there, put his hands around that fucking neck and squeeze until his windpipe snapped. He wanted to charge up those fucking stairs and get Lucas the hell out of here.

"Easy, Ryan," Ben whispered.

Craig didn't deserve easy. Not after this, not now. "Why? Because he cut back your fucking money?"

"Money. It should have been mine...all of it. He got every fucking thing, everything. I tried...I tried to do it myself, but I couldn't, and he wouldn't help. He had everything. Money, fame, a beautiful wife." Craig was really losing it now, and though Ryan thought he'd been shot at least once already, he could clearly see him attempting to get to his feet.

Ryan watched as Ben kept his gun trained on Craig as he stood. Once he was up, he took a faltering step forward, reached into the pocket of his jacket, and pulled out another smaller gun. Ben didn't hesitate. He pulled the trigger and Ryan's ears rang as two shots echoed in the entryway. Craig fell immediately, not even twitching as he hit the ground, Ben's gun arm following him all the way down, never wavering.

Ben eased back on Ryan some more, but still never lowered his arm. From above them, Ryan could hear banging, coughing, and movement, and it gave him hope that maybe he hadn't lost Lucas.

"Ben! Shit, the cavalry's on the way. Hang in there." Paulina appeared, seemingly from nowhere, and squatted down beside them. When she reached to take the gun from Ben's hand, he let her, his arm dropping to his side as soon as he released the weapon. She turned to Ryan then and said, "We've got to get out of here. Second floor's on fire."

The stench of the fire was getting stronger and wisps of smoke were visible on the second-floor landing. The pounding of feet was the only warning he got before he could make out an oddly shaped apparition running down the stairs. It was Ethan, huge coughs racking his big body, with Lucas draped over his shoulder, equally violent coughs tearing through him.

"No. No...oh god," Ryan screamed out. Lucas's body suddenly ceased its ferocious movements and was hanging limply over Ethan's shoulder as Ethan began staggering toward where they were near the front door. Ryan watched as Ethan fell to his knees, his watery eyes closing just as he pitched forward, both he and Lucas landing in an unmoving heap on the tiled floor.

Ryan could hear the sirens and knew help wasn't far away, but still it wasn't close enough for him. He shifted Ben, who'd begun screaming for Ethan as soon as the big man had fallen, over to Paulina's hold. He motioned for her to press against Ben's seeping wound exactly as Ethan had instructed him only minutes ago. How did something like this happen so quickly and yet feel as though it was a lifetime?

Lucas was only a few feet from him, but Ryan felt the distance keenly. He crawled to their side and did his best to untangle the fallen bodies. Once he had Lucas on his back, he frantically searched for signs of life: breath, pulse, movement. He put a hand to Lucas's chest and felt the gratifying, but shallow, rise and fall. The pulse of Lucas's continued existence was weak and Ryan could barely distinguish if it was real or the echo of his own throbbing body. The sirens were blaring in his ear now, so he knew help had arrived.

Ryan pressed a gentle kiss to Lucas's unyielding lips, unsure of when he'd next get the chance to taste their warmth and sweetness. Smoke was tickling at his own throat now, so he moved to action. He squatted behind Lucas, grabbing him under his arms, and dragging him closer to the open door. He'd hardly crossed the threshold when he looked up to see a handful of firemen sprinting toward them. Others were at the truck preparing to battle the now-raging fire. He couldn't have given less of a fuck about the house—the ravenous fire could have it, but it couldn't have Lucas.

In a frenzy of activity, masks were placed over both his and Lucas's faces, even as Ryan tried to tell them about the other people still inside. Two of the firemen lifted Lucas and ran him toward a waiting ambulance. Ryan stood and followed on their heels, terrified of being separated again.

"There's more people inside. Three alive and I think... I think one dead," Ryan screamed at the firemen as they turned to run back into the inferno. One nodded and Ryan was satisfied that his bodyguards would be saved.

In the ambulance, two men worked over Lucas, calling out words Ryan barely understood. Ryan had to turn away when one of them began inserting a tube down Lucas's throat. He wished so hard that he'd wake up from this fucking nightmare.

From where he was standing, he could see Ben being wheeled on a stretcher toward another ambulance. He was doing his best to sit up and he was screaming at someone. Ryan couldn't hear what he was saying over the roar of the burning house, the sirens, and the pounding in his ears, but he could see the near hysteria on his face.

He followed Ben's line of sight and saw Paulina standing over Ethan who was on his own stretcher, eyes closed and unmoving. Paulina was flicking her gaze between Ben and Ethan and eventually nodded to Ben and called something out. Whatever she said calmed Ben and he stopped thrashing on his stretcher, though he never lay down, only kept his gaze on Ethan as he was loaded into the back of another ambulance.

"In or out, sir?"

Ryan turned toward the voice and came face-to-face with one of the paramedics who'd been working on Lucas.

"We're ready to transport him. In or out?"

"In." Ryan jumped up into the back of the ambulance, joining the second paramedic before they changed their mind about taking him. Lucas was deathly still on the gurney, his dark skin covered in soot, and a tube down his throat. Ryan couldn't see any burns on him though. Ethan must have gotten to him just in time. He sat quietly in his seat for the duration of the trip, holding onto Lucas's hand and doing his best not to distract the paramedic's focus from saving Lucas.

When the vehicle came to a halt and the back doors were flung open, Ryan leaped out and was greeted with a barrage of flashes and calls for his attention. How had the media found out? Did they hang out in hospital receiving bays hoping for someone famous to be brought in? He did his best to ignore them and followed Lucas's gurney through the sliding doors and into the safety of the emergency department.

It was crystal clear to Ryan that a life of fame was not for him, but Lucas *was* his life; he was everything Ryan wanted and all that he needed. Somehow he'd have to make it work—if Lucas survived.

Chapter Thirty-One

Lovers *lives*.

LUCAS

His throat had been raw when he'd woken up three days ago. It was still raspy, but it didn't feel as though he was eating razor blades every time he swallowed now. He was sleepy most of the time, and he still needed oxygen sporadically, but he was going to be okay. All the damage had been done within his body with the exception of his eyes. His eyeballs were a brilliant red that made him appear evil when he'd first woken, but that too was fading to a lighter shade of pink.

He could see Ryan sleeping in the large chair beside his bed. Lucas knew he hadn't left the hospital since they'd been brought here from the fire. He must be fucking sick of sleeping in hospitals, watching over Lucas.

"I can feel you watching me, Luke." Ryan smiled and slowly opened his eyes. He sat up in his chair and stretched his long limbs while stifling a yawn.

"Why don't you go home, Ry, and get some real sleep?"

"I'll leave when you leave. Besides, someone has to keep every man and his fucking dog out." Ryan had vigilantly refused to allow anybody in, aside from family, and even then, he did it hesitantly. Lucas's family had been informed about what had transpired at the house with Craig, and Ryan had admitted to Lucas that he was afraid Lucas's family either wouldn't believe it or would somehow blame Lucas for Craig's actions.

Understandably, his family was still in shock about what had happened. They'd had trouble even mentioning Craig when they'd come to visit him. There'd be time to talk it through once he was out of the hospital, but Lucas knew it would take a long time before any of them would be able to wrap their heads around what had happened.

Everybody else could wait to get their piece of him as far as Lucas was concerned. The studio, the cops, the press...the public. They'd all get their needs met eventually.

"Are they all still out there?" Lucas asked, despite full well knowing the answer.

"As far as I know. The hospital's had the police in several times to try to get rid of the vultures, but they're hanging around. Anna said she heard the first photo of you post-attempted fratricide is worth a fortune, and if they manage to get just a recognizable fraction of me in the shot, then the price doubles."

"Jesus. That's...fucking crazy."

"Yep. You know what else Anna told me? Apparently my dear old dad gave an interview—such as it was, coming from his drunken lips. Told some trashy rag from Australia how good a job he'd done raising me despite all the obstacles he had to deal with...you know, the disappointment of having a fag son and all." Ryan laughed and Lucas hoped it was a genuine laugh and not one to cover his horror. But then Ryan's expression morphed into one of such seriousness that Lucas was almost more terrified than he'd been in that fucking room with the flames licking all around him.

"Luke, I um...I can't do this anymore. I'm in so far over my head. With the fame, I mean. It's nothing like what I expected. The drinking, the anxiety...this"—Ryan swept his hand around to encompass Lucas injured in his hospital bed—"is too much. All I wanted to do was act, but I don't want the rest. The price is too high. I'm going to quit the show, Lucas. I need to quit it, and I hope you understand."

If he were honest with himself, Lucas would admit he had kind of been expecting this, but it still came as a blow. What did this mean for them? Would Ryan leave him if he was unwilling to give up his own career? How the hell would this work?

"What, um...what does this mean for us?" God, he hated how fucking pathetic he sounded, but Lucas knew there was one thing in this world that had the power to ruin him and that was Ryan. How paradoxical that Ryan was also the one thing that had helped him attain absolute bliss.

"We'll work it out. I don't expect or want you to give the show up, but I need to stay in the background, maybe behind the cameras or out of the industry altogether. I don't know what, yet, but we'll figure it out. I can't be *Lovers* or *Sandom* anymore. You know?"

Lucas did know. Fame wasn't for everyone, despite so many seeming to want it and be willing to do anything to get it. The reality wasn't as picture-perfect as people imagined. It's not easy to have a camera shoved in your face every time you walked out the door or have a crowd of people hem you in, making you feel as though you can't breathe. Lucas understood that...understood Ryan wanting out. Aspects of fame had terrified Ryan.

"Ryan, I don't care if you're the biggest fucking star in the world or if you're the person bringing the biggest star their coffee. It was never Sam or *Lovers* or *Samdom* I fell for. It was always just you, Ryan Lowe—man who falls overboard when he meets his hero, snorts a little when he truly laughs, and still won't pee in front of me, even though I've been inside your fucking gorgeous body. That's who I fell for. Whatever you want to do...I'm beside you every step of the way. I love you, Ry, and I'll always fucking love you."

"Fuck, do you steal this romantic shit from the screenwriters?" Ryan laughed and leaned down to kiss Lucas firmly on the lips. "Thank you for understanding, Lucas. I fucking love you too."

"Hey...um, how's Ben?" Lucas had vague memories of seeing Ethan at some stage after he woke up. He'd been affected by smoke inhalation too as a result of pulling Lucas out of the fire but had fared better than Lucas. Ryan had told Lucas about the shooting and the way Ben had stayed conscious, probably on pure adrenaline, until everyone was safe and on their way to the hospital. As far as Lucas was aware, Ben hadn't opened his eyes since.

"They're gonna try to bring him out of the coma later today. Ethan was with him this morning. Oh and I met his brother Cameron too. Ben was right, though, you'd never pick them for brothers, let alone twins."

Lucas tried to keep the swell of guilt at bay, knowing that it was his own brother who had almost killed Ben. His brother who had tried to kill him. As long as he lived, Lucas would never be able to repay Ben for what he'd done for him and Ryan. According to Ryan, Ethan had told him that Ben had had a niggling feeling about Craig since they'd walked into the house that day, and he'd been the one who'd smelled the accelerant Craig had used and raised the alarm.

"Hey, it's not your fault, Lucas. It's not my fault, or your parents, or anybody else apart from Craig. I can't pretend to understand why he did what he did, but he's the only one at fault here." Ryan took his hand and kissed his knuckles. He had no idea what he'd done in this life or any other to deserve Ryan Lowe, but he was damn grateful.

"I know. I do. It's just fucking hard. My brother did all that. He tried to kill me...tried to kill you. I can't wrap my head around it. I grew up with him, we knew each other as well as any brothers, and I never, ever would have thought he could do something like this." Lucas knew no matter how many days passed, no matter how many hours he spent in therapy, he would never get over the shock of his baby brother not just wanting, but actually trying, to kill him. *Kill him.* How did this happen? How did he get over this?

"Hey, you up for a walk? We could go get a coffee. Maybe check in on Ben on our way through."

"Yeah. Let's do that." The more Lucas moved around, the sooner he'd get out of here, and he did want to check in on Ben. He slid out of bed and wrapped the cotton robe Anna had brought him around his body. He was still achy all over, but he could be achy at home just as easily as here in the hospital. He wanted out. He wanted to go home.

Ryan led them through the maze of hospital corridors and elevators until they came to the Intensive Care Unit. Only two visitors at a time were permitted. The man they approached for entry informed them Ben already had his quota of visitors, but he'd go and let them know Lucas and Ryan were here. Only minutes later, he returned with Ethan and another man, who Lucas could only assume was Ben's brother, following him. Lucas marveled at the brother's size. He thought Ryan was a big man but he'd been eclipsed by Ethan and now this man overshadowed even Ethan's bulk. He was huge.

"Hey, Lucas, good to see you up and about." Ethan offered his hand, which Lucas gladly shook.

"Thanks. You're looking good. How's Ben doing?"

"Good...yeah, go in and see. They're bringing him out of the coma soon, so this'll be your last chance to see him when he's quiet." Lucas appreciated Ethan's humor for what it was—a cover to mask his fear, but his worry for his colleague was evident on Ethan's face. "Shit, sorry. Lucas, this is Cameron Cronin. Ben's brother. Cameron, this is Lucas Evers, and of course, you've met Ryan."

They exchanged pleasantries before Ryan and Lucas were hustled in to see Ben before the doctors came to wake him. Ben had always been the smallest of the group of guards, and he looked even smaller—more fragile—as he lay there with drips and drains and monitors surrounding him, effectively caging him to the bed.

Did he speak to him? Hold his hand? Tell him how he would be forever in his debt for saving Ryan? No, that had to wait until he was awake and Lucas could be certain Ben understood the importance of what he'd done. It was awkward being there with the nurse constantly present. Lucas had no idea what to say or do.

In the end, he settled for a quick grip of Ben's hand and an almost whispered, "Thank you. Now hurry up and get better."

Cameron and Ethan were still in the waiting room when they returned, but Cameron quickly returned to his brother's side, while Ethan opted to go for coffee with Lucas and Ryan.

After walking for a while, it was Ryan who finally broke the silence. "Cameron seems nice, Ethan."

Ethan nodded and Lucas wondered if that was all they'd get out of the big reserved man. "Yeah. He's a good brother. Won't leave until Ben's...until Ben's Ben again. Not all brothers would do that."

Lucas felt a shiver up his spine at Ethan's words. He had to be taking a stab at Craig, but he'd never thought Ethan would be cruel like that. Perhaps it was just a thoughtless comment. Whatever motivated it, he seemed to realize what he'd said and stopped walking. He turned his pale, drawn face to Lucas. "I'm so sorry, Lucas. That was thoughtless of me. I wasn't thinking of Craig at all. Sorry."

Lucas didn't get a chance to accept his apology, before he'd turned and strode away, his long legs carrying him out of their reach. Ryan and Lucas shared a glance before racing to catch up.

As soon as they entered the cafeteria, they realized their error, but even Ethan's big body, stopped in the entryway as he endeavored to shield them, could do nothing to prevent the dozen or so members of the media from rising from the table where they'd been sharing a meal and approaching them. Or was it more stalking them, pursuing them like the big cats of the Serengeti, he and Ryan being the hapless gazelles with nowhere left to run.

"Lucas, how're you feeling?"

"Lucas, how do you feel about your brother Craig?"

"Lucas, did you have any idea that your brother was behind the attempt on your life?"

The mob hadn't even reached them before the questions started. All of them calling out at once, with raised voices to ensure their question would be heard over the others. After the first few, they all seemed to be garbled into one long question.

"Is your bodyguard still in a coma? Where are your parents? How is the family coping? How has this affected your relationship? Is it true that it was Ryan who actually shot your brother? Ryan, how do you feel about what happened?"

On and on it went. How the reporters expected them to answer a single question was beyond him, as they never stopped shouting out the questions long enough for them to get a word in. Ethan stretched his arms out in an effort to herd them back the way they'd come before they were completely surrounded by their predators. They'd started backing up when a single voice called out several questions over the top of all others and silenced the little group.

"Ethan, was it because of your own brother that you suspected Craig? Did Lucas know about your brother, Ethan? Lucas, did you know Ethan's brother is Stewart Lockard?"

Even though they had turned and now had their backs to Ethan, Lucas could sense him stiffen behind them. When he turned, he could see the color had drained from Ethan's face until he was as white as the stone statues his unmoving body now resembled.

"Ethan?" Ryan asked. "Ethan, are you all right?"

Lucas watched, fascinated, as a blank canvas shuttered down over Ethan's features before movement returned to his body. "I'm fine. Sorry. Let's go." And they were once again being ushered away from the pack of media, safe under Ethan's protective wings.

Security had been alerted by some unknown savior and the press was held back from venturing far enough into the corridors of the hospital to follow them to Lucas's room. Once inside, Lucas watched the blankness slip briefly from Ethan's face as Ryan approached him.

"Ethan, are you sure you're okay?"

"Yeah. Sorry. I didn't know... I didn't think they'd dig that deep into my background. I should have told you."

"Told us what?" Ryan continued.

"My name is—was—Ethan Lockard. My brother is Stewart Lockard. You may remember him as the St. Ann Street strangler."

Lucas wasn't sure about Ryan, but he was drawing a blank, though somewhere in the memories of his brain something was tapping away, warning him that he did know about the Lockard family. Obviously Ethan's brother was a killer and given that he had a moniker, he was probably a serial killer. He must have been the brother Ethan had been thinking of earlier when he'd been talking about Cameron Cronin.

"Jesus, Ethan. I'm so sorry. You clearly didn't want anyone knowing that, and they're gonna splash it all over the news. I'm sorry."

"Don't, Lucas. This is not your fault either," Ryan quietly told him. Fame did exact a high toll, but surely Lucas was paid up now.

"It would've come out at some point. Obviously, I don't advertise the connection, but my grandma always said the truth will out. I'm sorry, both of you, if this adds to the craziness you'll be getting from the media. I better call Patricia and Roger and hand in my resignation before they fire my ass."

Despite their protests, Ethan left the room. It was probably for the best and would give him some time to process what had happened. As soon as he left, Ryan had his phone in hand and Lucas knew he'd be googling Stewart Lockard.

"Fuck...he killed nine women—girls really—in New Orleans eight years ago." Lucas watched as Ryan skimmed through the information about Ethan's brother, shock and horror clouding his features as he read on. "Raped and strangled them. Left them naked and bound in public areas, to be found. Oh, Jesus, it was Ethan who handed him in."

"Shit. Poor Ethan. No wonder he doesn't want anyone to know who he is." How did you live with something like that? Lucas was struggling with his own brother and what he'd done, but it was different to what Ethan had been dealing with for at least the last eight years. And to be the one to find out and have to report him... Lucas couldn't imagine.

"He's right, though. This is just gonna add to the drama for the media. I'm thinking there's three weeks left of filming... What do you say if we take off as soon as we're done? We'll hide away from the mess, somewhere it can be just us and a king-size bed that we can fuck each other into whenever the hell we want. Whataya say?"

"I love the sound of that. You know, Australia is a mighty big country to get lost in..." Ryan moved closer to him and Lucas could feel that familiar heat begin to burn inside—the flames of his desire for Ryan roaring to life. He welcomed *these* flames...fanned them by pulling Ryan closer and slamming their lips together. Would this heat between them ever wane? Fuck, he hoped not.

"Well I do have a thing for Australian men so I wouldn't object to going down there and checking out the scenery." He smirked and then flinched as Ryan bit at his lip.

"There's only one Australian man you'll be looking at."

Lucas laughed at the touch of jealousy in Ryan's tone. "Why would I need to look anywhere else, Ry? It's like staring into the fucking sun with you; I can't see anything or anyone else."

"Flatterer." Ryan took another kiss before placing his hands on Lucas's cheeks and staring into his eyes. "I love you...so fucking much."

"I love you too, baby."

Epilogue

"I'VE NEVER SEEN sand like it. It's so white and fine." Lucas said as he sifted the fine grains through his fingers.

"Beautiful, isn't it?"

While Lucas had never been a money person, he had to admit there were some definite perks to having it. The chartered yacht was anchored a little off shore with the small crew and Ethan still aboard. He and Ryan had swum the short distance to the beach and they had about an hour of privacy before the crew brought their lunch ashore.

It was so beautiful here in the Whitsunday Islands—unfortunately, though, they'd come in stinger season and they'd had to wear stinger suits whenever they went in the ocean. Once they'd made it to the beach they quickly disrobed from the thick suits and Lucas was grateful to finally have a bare-chested Ryan beside him.

"Do you wanna go for a walk along the beach before lunch?"

Lucas hesitated before answering, and it was a long enough pause for Ryan to work out what he was worried about.

"I promise I'll protect you from any spiders, Luke."

"No mocking me. That fucking monster was in the shower with me...in the fucking shower!" Lucas shuddered as he remembered the giant huntsman spider that had crept into the shower with him two nights ago. The fact it had been stowed away on the boat with them for almost a week had terrified Lucas. How many others were there lying in wait?

"I guess that's your punishment for showering without me. Come on." Ryan grabbed his hand and set off, pulling Lucas along with him.

They walked along the shoreline for a short time before Ryan drifted toward the greenery that edged the beach and the walking trails that were clearly marked with signs there. They chose one of the midlength trails and set off, walking hand in hand whenever they could.

Lucas suspected what was coming and it didn't take long for Ryan to prove him right. "Luke, you wanna talk about it?"

He could try to dodge it, try to brush it off, and Ryan would let him, but in the end, it would be better out than in, so Lucas talked.

"It was for money, Ry. My brother almost killed me and you and Ethan and Ben for money. He did kill Leighton. He may not have been driving the car, but he talked her into doing what she did. He manipulated her when she was vulnerable, and she's dead because of him." Fuck, it was hard to get those words out. It would never get any easier to say the words "my brother killed someone and tried to kill me"—never.

"When I spoke to Detective Holland this morning, he told me they found gambling debts for tens of thousands of dollars. They don't think it had anything to do with me being gay or jealousy. It was plain old money. Why didn't he just ask me? I'd have given him anything if he'd have asked."

They'd reached a small lookout area, and Ryan drew him into his arms. "I know you would have, Luke. This is not your fault. Craig had a problem and he chose the worst possible way to deal with it."

"If I hadn't cut back; if I hadn't put them on a budget—"

"Don't do what-ifs; it'll just do your head in. I can't imagine what it must be like for you, but I do know that none of it's your fault."

Lucas wanted to believe that right down in his guts, but he wasn't there yet; he hadn't yet managed to shuck the guilt. Every day, he told himself it wasn't his fault, and his logical brain agreed with him, but in the core of him—right down in that fundamental place of who he was—he didn't believe it. "I'm trying. I'm really trying to believe it."

Ryan kissed him sweetly before placing both hands on the side of his face and commanding his attention. "I know you are. You're doing so well. Maybe you could talk to Ethan some more. If anyone knows what you're going through..."

Lucas and Ethan had spoken several times since they'd fled the US. Ethan did understand what Lucas was going through and then some. He'd lost his entire family when he'd reported his brother to the police. Lucas couldn't understand that; at least his family had stood by him. They still loved Craig, of course, but they were horrified by what he had done and they had never blamed Lucas for it.

"Yeah, yeah, maybe I will. Let's head back. I don't know about you, but a swim before lunch sounds great, even if we have to put those stinger suits back on."

"Oh I don't mind those stinger suits...they make your ass look fucking awesome." Ryan winked and turned to head back down the trail.

By the time they got back to the beach, they could see the launch being loaded up from the yacht. They had maybe half an hour before lunch would be here and wasted no time pouring themselves back into the wetsuit-like stinger suits.

Ryan was in the water first and delighted in splashing Lucas as he made his way back into the crystal-blue waters. The water was so warm that it was barely refreshing, but Lucas loved it. He swam to Ryan who was bobbing on the waves a little way from shore.

"It's so fucking gorgeous here that I can't even believe it," Ryan said as he approached.

"Maybe we could retire here one day? Right here on this little island. We'll build a little cottage with a giant fireplace and we'll spend our days naked and swimming and fucking."

"What about the spiders?" Ryan laughed.

"Fuck, I forgot those little monsters. Maybe we'll retire to Antarctica. I'm pretty sure there are no spiders there."

They played and floated in the water, completely wrapped up in each other despite the beauty of their surroundings. Occasionally one would drop a kiss on the other's lips, constant little affirmations of their desire for each other. Lucas planted his feet in the sand and pulled Ryan into his arms, reveling in the feel of Ryan wrapping his limbs around him, how perfect he felt pressed against Lucas—how right. Lucas knew what they'd be going back to; they'd had a hint of it before they'd escaped. The media circus, the constant intrusiveness into their lives—and worst of all for Ryan, the crowds. As hard as he knew it was going to be for Ryan, though, he was so damn glad he was willing to try.

"What're you thinking about, Luke?" Ryan's nose scraped along the side of his face, curling its way around behind his ear. Lucas knew he was inhaling him, and he felt the familiar pang of his lost sense. He knew Ryan would smell so fucking good with his usual scent mixing in with the aroma of the salt water.

"Thinking about you: how fucking gorgeous you are, how delicious you taste, how much I fucking love you." Lucas pressed his lips to Ryan's, more demanding than before. His tongue played along the seam of Ryan's lips before he was finally allowed entry. The familiar feel of Ryan's tongue dancing with his own, the easiness of the kiss—the sheer luxury of being able to kiss the person he loved above all others so openly never failed to turn him on. He pulled away while he was still able and nipped at Ryan's earlobe before whispering to him, though there was no one around to hear. "I was also thinking about how I can have you on the beach as soon as lunch is done. How fucking gorgeous you're gonna look splayed out in the sand, begging me to let you come."

"Jesus, Luke. Do we have to wait for lunch?" Lucas loved how his dirty talk got Ryan every time. He was so responsive to it that Lucas decided one day he was going to do nothing but talk dirty to Ryan to see if he could make him come without his touch.

"Well, the launch has arrived, so I'm gonna go with no...we have to at least wait till they're heading back to the yacht. Come on."

They lazily made their way back to the beach and walked hand in hand toward the rug that was being spread out on the fine sand. Unusually, Ethan was with Keith as he prepared the picnic for them. Lucas's gut pinched, hoping to hell nothing had happened.

"Hey, Ethan, come for a swim?"

"No. I'm sorry, Lucas, Ryan. I came to tell you that I'll need to organize to get back to the mainland ASAP and head back to the US."

"Is something wrong?"

"I...ah, I've just had a call from my sister. She's in trouble. She's in bad trouble and she's asked for my help."

Coming Soon from Karrie Roman

Sentinel

Until You, Book Two

Excerpt

PROLOGUE

"Last question."

"What now for you, Ryan?"

"Um...the short answer is I really don't know. I'm going to take some time with Lucas while the show is on hiatus and think about what's next for me. I hope people will understand why I've chosen to step out of the spotlight and will be gracious enough to give me the space I need to work out where to go from here. But for right this minute, Lucas and I are getting on a plane to locations unknown and we're just going to enjoy being us."

The press conference was a compromise between the very intrusive media and Lucas and Ryan. They wanted some peace, some space to recover from the events of the last couple of months and now that their show, Witches' Hammer, had wrapped up for a break, and Lucas had been given a clean bill of health, they were taking some time for themselves. Nobody deserved it more after what they'd been through.

Ethan watched, ever vigilant, as they stepped down from the podium and walked hand in hand toward the waiting car. His gaze rested on their joined hands for a second or two too long, but it was hard to look away from something that he desired for himself so very much. Not that he wanted either Lucas or Ryan. They were both great men and smoking fucking hot, but they weren't for him. He wanted what they had, though—the intimacy.

After years of self-imposed isolation from anything resembling a close relationship, Ethan wanted more.

Once his two charges were settled in the car, Ethan climbed into the passenger seat and gave the nod to Max. The big car roared to life and Max deftly drove them toward the airport and their waiting plane.

Patricia and Roger Krispin had to let Ethan go from their security agency when he called to resign, as he'd breached their no-skeletons-in-the-closet rule, but Lucas and Ryan had hired him as their personal bodyguard and had kept on the professional teams as backup whenever needed. Ethan would be traveling to Australia with them and Harry and Christina would meet them there for extra security, if needed.

"Looking forward to the Aussie girls in their bikinis, Ethan?" Ryan asked from the back seat.

"I'm more of a man in...what do you Aussies call them...boardies type of guy."

"Oh shit...sorry. Well there's plenty of them too. Maybe we can find a hot lifeguard for you while we're there." He didn't need to turn to know Lucas and Ryan would be giggling to themselves, no doubt planning some kind of setup for him. He loved working for these two men and often wondered at his good fortune, especially after the shit had hit the fan following the revelation of who he was.

For almost four weeks, Ryan and Lucas had dominated the front pages and headlined the news. When the media had discovered that Ethan Lockard had come out of the woodwork and was somehow embroiled in the *Lovers* saga, the scrutiny had begun to border on the ridiculous. Ethan had offered to resign and had given serious thought to running again. It would be harder to pick a new identity and hide this time, but he could do it. He was just so tired of running and so fucking tired of being lonely.

Eight years ago he'd lost his entire family, and though he hadn't allowed any of them to get too close, the men and women he'd worked with over the last few years had become a family of sorts. He wasn't going to let his brother take another family away from him.

"Okay, jet's fueled and ready. Wheels up as soon as you arrive." Paulina's voice sounded in his ear.

"Copy. We're about ten minutes out. All clear," he replied. Despite the press coverage and the revelations that had been made about him, nobody from Krispin's had seemed to care. They'd all accepted his apology for lying to them and admitted they'd have probably done the same if they were in his shoes.

The only person he hadn't seen or spoken to since his true identity had been discovered was Ben. He hadn't been back to see Ben since that day at the hospital when he'd been exposed. Cameron had called to let him know the doctors had successfully woken him and called a few more times with updates, but Ethan had refused when Cameron had told him Ben had been asking for him to visit. He was such a fucking coward, but he knew he couldn't bear to see disappointment in Ben's eyes. What if Ben hated him for the lies and keeping his past quiet? Ethan could stand anybody else's hatred—but not Ben's.

The private jet was waiting on the tarmac as promised and Max drove them virtually to the opened door. Ethan scanned the area as the car pulled up. He expected no trouble and, thankfully, he found none. Once satisfied, he stepped out and moved around the front of the car so he could open the back door nearest to the plane. Lucas stepped out, closely followed by Ryan, their hands immediately re-entwined as soon as they were both clear of the car. Ethan felt that pang of envy bite into him again at the intimacy the two men shared. God, he wanted it.

It wasn't the first private jet he'd been on, but it was one of the nicest. Lucas and Ryan were already seated on the sofa that ran along one side of the plane. Ethan took the single seat across from them. He'd seen the bedroom toward the back of the plane as he'd boarded and wondered, with a sly grin on his face, how long it'd take before Lucas and Ryan made use of that.

"How are you with flying, Ethan?" Lucas asked as he continued to settle himself in and clip his seat belt.

"No problem with it. I can't say I've done a huge amount, but I don't mind it. Once we're up at thirty-seven thousand feet, I'll pop this chair back, shut my eyes and they won't open again until we touch down." Ethan didn't miss the look the two men opposite him shared, no doubt delighted they would, more or less, have the jet to themselves.

The engines had been idling since they'd boarded and Ethan both felt and heard them roar to life now.

"All passengers, please ensure your seat belts are engaged and prepare for takeoff" came a disembodied voice over the public-address system. Ethan felt the jet push forward, slowly rolling toward the runway. It turned easily, nothing like the clunky turns of much larger passenger planes, before coming to a brief stop.

As the engines rumbled louder and louder and he felt that first pushback as the jet surged forward, increasing its speed to get it off the ground, Ethan felt a sudden, inexplicable urge to run to the door and jump from the moving craft. He knew deep in his guts he was leaving something—or someone—behind.

Ethan tried to escape that feeling of loss, after all, he was sure he had everything he needed and anything he'd forgotten he could buy in Australia. But as he looked over the lights of the city below he couldn't help thinking about vivid blue eyes that were usually dancing with laughter or mischief but had instead been filled with pain and determination the last time he'd seen them open. He knew in his heart then what he'd left behind— or rather who.

About the Author

Karrie lives in Australia's sunshine state with her husband and two sons, though she hates the sun with a passion. She dreams of one day living in the wettest and coldest habitable place she can find. She has been writing stories in her head for years but has finally managed to pull the words out of her head and share them with others. She spends her days trying to type her stories on the computer without disturbing her beloved cat Lu curled up on the keyboard. She probably reads far too much.

Website: www.karrieroman.com

Twitter: @karrie_roman

Other books by this author

Saved